DEATH IN THE COUNTRYSIDE

DEATH IN THE COUNTRYSIDE

A NOVEL

Maria Malone

NEW YORK

Books should be disposed of and recycled according to local requirements. All paper materials used are FSC compliant.

This is a work of fiction. All of the names, characters, organizations, places and events portrayed in this novel are either products of the author's imagination or are used fictitiously. Any resemblance to real or actual events, locales, or persons, living or dead, is entirely coincidental.

Copyright © 2025 by Maria Malone

All rights reserved.

Published in the United States by Crooked Lane Books, an imprint of The Quick Brown Fox & Company LLC.

Crooked Lane Books and its logo are trademarks of The Quick Brown Fox & Company LLC.

Library of Congress Catalog-in-Publication data available upon request.

ISBN (hardcover): 979-8-89242-159-1
ISBN (paperback): 979-8-89242-269-7
ISBN (ebook): 979-8-89242-160-7

Cover design by TK

Printed in the United States.

www.crookedlanebooks.com

Crooked Lane Books
34 West 27th St., 10th Floor
New York, NY 10001

First Edition: August 2025

The authorized representative in the EU for product safety and compliance is eucomply OÜPärnu mnt 139b-14, 11317 Tallinn, Estonia, hello@eucompliancepartner.com, +33757690241

10 9 8 7 6 5 4 3 2 1

For Mick

1

One of life's little tricks, Ali suspected. You got the thing you wanted only to find it wasn't quite what you were expecting.

For as long as she could remember, she had dreamed of becoming a police officer, one day returning home to Heft to pound her local beat. Now here she was. Sergeant Ali Wren and her springer spaniel, PD Wilson, getting to grips with their new patch—and finding Heft busier than Harrogate, where they had come from. A good deal busier, in fact. Remarkable that a remote town in rural North Yorkshire (population 1,923) could be so demanding of its local constabulary. Not that she had any regrets. Heft, home, was where she wanted to be. It was just taking some getting used to.

She woke early. Sunday, and the promise of that rarest of things, a day off, as evidenced by the single blank square amid a sea of scribblings and crossings-out on her calendar. Calls were on divert to the station at Skipden and she was free to go where she pleased—do anything, do nothing. In theory. Since Ali and Wilson were Heft's sole police presence, a day off—a *real* day off, one that elicited no appeals for assistance, no complaints, not a single report of a crime being committed—could not be taken for granted. Ever. Which was why she and Wilson were heading out of town before Heft was awake, intent on a good long tramp in the May sunshine.

Maria Malone

No interruptions. "We're unavailable," she told Wilson. "They'll have to manage without us." Wilson, ever the optimist, looked up from his breakfast and wagged his tail.

She made a sandwich, cutting thick slices from a seeded sourdough loaf, feeling a stab of disloyalty as she did so. Usually, Ali bought her bread from Hooley's, but there was a rival over the road now, Rise, a so-called "cakery-bakery," fast getting a name for its artisan loaves and fancy pastries. The menu changed weekly: choux buns oozing apple crumble and custard, lemon meringue confections, croissant cubes, dainty tarts filled with chocolate and pistachio. Ali had succumbed to wafer-thin slices of pastry layered with almond, topped with crisp meringues, sticky raspberry jam. Too good to eat. Almost.

For Evelyn Hooley, proprietor of Heft's long-established, family-run bakery, the arrival of the newcomers had caused consternation, Rise regarded as an intruder, unwelcome. Of late, barely a day went by without Evelyn complaining of some new baking-related outrage. As if by virtue of existing, the rival bakers were somehow breaking the law.

Now tables and chairs had appeared on the pavement in front of the new shop, prompting Evelyn to protest: "Is that allowed? Is it even legal?" Ali had promised to look into it. It was, it turned out, news Evelyn didn't take well. "What are they, a bakery, a café?" Both, it seemed.

Evelyn was in her sixties and well thought of in Heft. Strong and lean from years of heaving sacks of flour about, she cut a dash in her shop uniform of tailored boiler suit, *Hooley's* embroidered on the breast pocket, her blonde hair styled in a flattering pixie cut. Ali thought back to the day before, Evelyn's latest call. "Have you *seen* what they've done? Only copied our pies!"

For almost a century, the supremacy of the famous Hooley Heft—tender beef from an award-winning local herd, heritage potatoes, rich gravy, encased in buttery shortcrust pastry—had

2

Death in the Countryside

gone unchallenged. And Hooley's boast to bake "the best bread in Ravensdale" had long been accepted as fact. Now, Rise had produced a pie they were calling a "Hefty," one which to the untrained eye bore a striking resemblance to Hooley's well-known bake and, if that weren't enough, a sign had appeared in the window of the newcomer, promising "the *finest* bread in Ravensdale." *Finest* in an eye-catching, cursive script.

Evelyn was livid. She complained, citing theft of copyright, fraud, provocation. "If that's not a shot across the bows, I don't know what is."

Ali endeavored to tread carefully. In the interests of maintaining good community relations, she took seriously every grievance laid at her door, even those that weren't strictly police matters, listening, remaining impartial, doing all she could to calm frayed tempers. Usually it was enough and had worked well in a dispute between neighbors threatening legal action over the hedge that ran along their shared boundary. Ali's softly, softly approach had taken the heat out of things. Evelyn, though, would not be placated. And now, unfolding at an alarming rate on Heft's main street was what Ali had begun to think of as the Battle of the Bakers. A flour-power struggle, her husband Nick called it.

She wiped down the kitchen bench, popped a capsule in the espresso machine and put the sourdough back in the bread bin next to a crust from one of Hooley's farmhouse loaves. Nothing could compete with Evelyn's white bread. It made the best toast. Ali sighed. The friction between Hooley's and Rise was not really her concern. It wasn't an offense to open a bread shop. And yet. What if things escalated, threatened the harmony of the high street? Wasn't it her duty to do what she could to keep the peace?

"The best thing about Sunday is that the bakers are shut," she told Wilson. He thumped his tail on the floor in agreement.

She spread mayonnaise thickly onto the bread, cut slices of cheese, a tomato, wondering what Evelyn might say about the local law enforcement patronizing the enemy. It didn't bear thinking about. Hooley's didn't sell sourdough, though, and Ali still shopped with Evelyn, the custard tart on the kitchen counter proof, if needed, of her continuing loyalty.

She glanced at the clock. Early, not yet seven. Not too early for a work call, though, a knock at the door. It wouldn't be the first time.

This is what happens when you live on the patch, she told herself. Once you make yourself accessible, approachable, your mobile number displayed in the window of the Post Office, on the noticeboard outside the church hall next to signs for Italian conversation and Tai Chi classes. Day, or night, on duty or not, she and Wilson could be called upon, summoned from their beds even in the small hours.

Nick had sensed her desire to be so accessible might make privacy hard to come by, but when he said so Ali simply shrugged. She *wanted* to know the people she was serving, she said, wanted them to know her—to feel she was a presence, there for them. He raised an eyebrow at that. There's *knowing*, he said, and then there's a bit *too* knowing.

"In *The Beat*," Nick told her, "the local bobby never gets a minute's peace." Nick was Location Manager on a long-running police drama series set in the Dales in a different time, silly and nostalgic.

"It's made up, *The Beat*," Ali had countered. "Not real life."

Nick simply said, "If you ask me, real life can be a whole lot weirder."

He had a point.

Ali's predecessor, Barry East, a cynical PC who'd done his thirty years and couldn't wait to retire, was not exactly complimentary about the people of Heft. "A bolshy lot, never backward in coming forward." Complaints (whether or not they fell within the remit of the police, he said, mildly outraged) came in thick and

Death in the Countryside

fast. The best thing she could do was find somewhere to live out of town to avoid being bothered at all hours. Ali had told him she really didn't mind. It was why she was there, why she had chosen to relocate from Harrogate to Ravensdale, return to the town she knew, one that knew her. She had found space for an office at home, just big enough for a desk and a filing cabinet. Skipden, the nearest station, located twelve miles away, could be reached in under half an hour, and once a week she reported in person to the Chief Superintendent there. Otherwise, her base was Heft, an arrangement that suited her perfectly. She *wanted* to be visible. At the heart of things. She wanted—and her predecessor had laughed when she said this—to make a difference, however much of a cliché that might seem.

From the kitchen window she could see the bird feeders, a pair of bullfinches on the sunflower seeds, a blackbird underneath, and, beyond, the crag. She thought back to house-hunting with Nick, finding it disheartening initially, thinking they'd never find anywhere as nice as their place in Harrogate. He was confident, his work in TV, scouting for locations, giving him access to a useful network of contacts, including local estate agents, which was how he'd heard about Larkspur. The name alone was almost enough for Ali. A stone-built cottage, on the edge of Heft. Fruit trees at the back, a rose-strewn archway leading to a hidden nook, a summer house. Cold Beck at the end of the garden. It was perfect.

As Nick (and, in fairness, PC East) had warned, the downside of returning to live and work in Heft was quite how readily the locals called on their new sergeant and her dog for assistance. Even off duty and out of uniform—whether attempting a swift drink in the Fox & Newt with Nick (almost unheard of), a hurried dip in the River Lune (ditto) or walking Wilson—she had learned to be braced for a tap on the shoulder.

All manner of incidents came her way, many of which would not have got a look-in at her old station: vehicles minus the required

Blue Badge occupying the disabled bay at St. Michael's, a wing mirror damaged in the awkward little car park behind the hair and beauty salon, Nu-U. Reports of parcels flung carelessly over hedges and walls by under-pressure delivery drivers. All made their way to Ali. And more besides. Much more.

Often, she fielded complaints that fell more within the category of nuisance than actual crime. Always, she did her best. Showed patience, kept her good humor, turned incidents that weren't incidents at all but an unequivocal waste of her time, into stories she and Wilson could chuckle over together afterward. "Just as well I've got you," she'd tell the spaniel. "This lot would do my head in otherwise."

He sat now in his bed in the kitchen worrying away at his favorite squeaky toy, a ball with spikes, bright pink. Over time, he had amassed a collection in different colors and sizes, most of which he pierced within seconds, depriving them of their squeak. Somehow, the pink one must have been made of stern stuff because it was hanging on.

"So, here's the plan," Ali now told him. "Drive to Simonthwaite, picnic on the summit, a long walk along the crag, and back through the forest. How does that sound?"

Wilson looked up, squeaked a reply.

"Fresh air, clear our heads, ready for whatever madness comes our way next week. Because this is our *day off* and we're not doing *any* work."

Wilson gave her a look, trotted over, and deposited the toy at her feet. She sent it skittering across the kitchen floor and he shot off, pouncing on it. It made a gasping sound, as if winded, the squeak reduced to a dying wheeze. Ali flinched. Another one on its way out.

She wrapped her sandwich, put a slice of Evelyn's custard tart into a plastic box, and poured tea into a flask. Bonio biscuits and water for Wilson, sunglasses tucked into the front of her tie-dye

Death in the Countryside

vest, a hoodie in her rucksack. A waterproof, just in case. Even in May, the weather on top of the fell could be poor. If there was time, on the way back from Simonthwaite she'd call in on her parents. A week had gone by, and she had not managed to see them.

"Tonight, I'll cook," she told Wilson. Nick, away all week, would be back. "Roast chicken, the cakes I got from Rise." She shot the spaniel a conspiratorial look. "Not a word to Evelyn on that subject, understood?" Wilson wagged his tail. "Then a night in front of the telly, the three of us." Bliss. *Ghosts, Still Game.* "Nothing work-related. That's a promise."

2

Shortly after seven, she set off, Wilson at her side, rucksack on the backseat of the Hilux. The quickest way to Simonthwaite was through town but on that road, even on a Sunday, they might be seen, flagged down. The bright blue of the Hilux made it instantly recognizable (Nick had been right there too, white would have been a safer choice). She went the long way round on roads that were narrow and twisty, seldom used, Wilson leaning into the corners as she navigated dry stone walls that bulged ominously, threatening the pick-up's gleaming paintwork.

Until recently, she'd driven a Beetle, in the family for many years, her dad's pride and joy. Decades old, it was basic, lacking in frills, and temperamental when it came to starting in the cold weather. Ali loved it, its throaty chugging sound, the way it slogged up hills. It was dogged, a bruiser. A classic, she told Nick, who'd pulled a face and said she was stretching a point there. A car didn't become a classic by virtue of being old with dodgy suspension and a heater that didn't work, he said.

Ali smiled, slowing at a junction on the other side of Heft. Nick was biased, he'd never forgiven the Beetle for conking out on him on the Empress roundabout in Harrogate, the petrol gauge showing the tank half full when it was, in fact, empty. He'd not had his

Death in the Countryside

phone on him and had to push the car to the side of the road and walk home. For weeks he suggested she get something up to date, reliable—a Fiesta, a Clio, a Panda. She could not be persuaded. Now she hàd the Hilux, ideally suited to the Dales, and the Beetle was back with her dad who for years had been promising to do what he called a full restoration job.

The roads were clear. She rolled the windows down, letting in a rush of air that was fresh and cool on her bare arms. Wilson's ears lifted in the breeze. On they went, passing verges thick with bluebells, ox eye daisies, red campion. The sky was cloudless, a soft powder blue. The road dipped and they took a sharp bend, crossed the bridge over the Skir and, suddenly, there was Simonthwaite in front of them.

Ali felt her shoulders relax. She parked at the side of the river, Wilson on his feet, tail wagging, eager to be out. "Good lad, you know where you're going, don't you?" She put on boots, picked up her rucksack, let Wilson out. He ran to the waymarked path that led through a forest of pine and yew and together they climbed the stony trail up the hillside, Wilson delving into clumps of bracken, disappearing from sight, bouncing into view again somewhere else. Every so often Ali stopped to take in the view: a landscape swathed in green, sheep grazing, buildings in ruins, a herd of what looked like Belted Galloways on the hilltop opposite, a perilous crag. A long way off she could just about make out a shape, a point higher than its surroundings. Worcop Pike. Little wonder Nick was spoiled for choice when it came to finding locations.

The last time she had beèn up Simonthwaite was in March when it was cooler, rain in the air. It hadn't been bad going up, warm enough to take off her fleece and fasten it round her middle, but the walkers on their way down warned of challenging conditions on top and when she got there, she found herself alone, the wind raging. Sudden gusts blew in from every direction, tugging at her, lashing the enormous Black Stone that squatted on the summit. Boulders formed a protective circle around it, some jutting out over dizzying drops. The stones of Simonthwaite, how they came to be there, what they signified, were a source of wonder, sparking superstitions, tales of spirits who sought out the unwary and steered them dangerously close to the edge. In the Bull, the local pub, walkers told of feeling a hand on their back, something tugging at them, almost pulling them off their feet. Seasoned hikers left shaken, vowing never to return. Rumor had it that those who spent the night on Simonthwaite wouldn't see the dawn. The stories were what drew some to the hill—and made others stay away.

On that last walk, Ali and Wilson had taken shelter on the top, pressed into a narrow crevice at the side of the Black Stone. It provided a little refuge, still the wind found them. She had not dared take the flask from her rucksack for fear it would be snatched from her hand. Feeling she was in the grip of something wild, a storm that could lift her off her feet, she was afraid. No phone signal, no means of summoning help. Carefully, she began the descent, hair whipping about her face, in her eyes, the wind gusting, making her stumble. Wilson went ahead, low to the ground, ears flattened, sensing danger. Then, miraculously, everything changed. The wind dropped, all was calm.

Today the May breeze was light, the sun warm, the rocks seeming benign, welcoming. Ali looked about her. Wilson scampered off, careering in and out of the stone circle while she went toward a stack known locally as the Hawk. The rocks looked unstable, precarious, as if they might fall at any moment, and yet, having been there for at least three hundred million years, it was unlikely they would shift anytime soon.

She circled the Black Stone. Someone had placed flowers there, white chrysanthemums, their stems tucked into a crack at its base. The blooms looked fresh, as if they'd been left recently. She crouched down. In among the flowers was a card. She had a sudden

Death in the Countryside

sense the message might be private, that she shouldn't read it. Then again, it had been left in a public place, there for whoever happened by to find. She plucked the card free and turned it over: *Just so you know, you're not forgotten. Love you always xx.* Ali tried to recall if someone had died at this spot. Despite the lurid stories associated with Simonthwaite, there were few accidents, no deaths she could think of, not in recent years.

Below, was the expanse of water known as Dark Pool. As a child, she had thought it was bottomless, home to monster leeches. Some people swam there but she had never much liked the idea of wading through the reeds and slime at its edge, sinking into the still black depths. She couldn't help wondering what else might be in there: the odd stray sheep, birds, rotting away. A woman had gone missing, she remembered, five or six years back. Walking alone, failing to return to her B & B. Divers searched the pool but found nothing, which wasn't to say she hadn't ended up there. It didn't take much to drown. A moment of panic, one or two breaths, water gulped down. And Dark Pool was vast, deep. Was it her the flowers were for? Ali wondered, putting the card back where she'd found it.

She sat on a large flat stone, one of the few where there was a ledge below rather than a sheer drop, Ravensdale spread out in front of her. "Hey Wils," she called, and he trotted over to sit beside her. She put her arms round his neck and hugged him, pressing her face against his soft fur. Heft, a few miles down the road, seemed a world away, Evelyn Hooley and the Battle of the Bakers, no longer so serious. A misunderstanding was all it was, one that Ali would, in time, find a way to resolve. Common sense, she told herself, that's what was called for. "Anyway," she told Wilson, inhaling his familiar scent, "we're not thinking about you-know-what today, are we? W-O-R-K." He looked up, licked the side of her face in confirmation.

She gave him a handful of biscuits, took out the flask and

Maria Malone

poured tea, and they sat quietly. A bee worked its way through a patch of bright pink flowers; Wilson crunched on a Bonio. On the fell opposite a lone figure in a red top made its way along a steep narrow path. Beyond, on the other side of the ridge, were, Ali knew, the crumbling remains of long disused farm buildings. High Top Farm. It had featured on the last series of *The Beat*, the perfect hideout for a man on the run. An ideal location, high up, inhospitable, out of sight until you were almost on top of it, with only a single dirt track providing access from the valley below.

Getting everything up there in the crew Land Rovers was tricky but worth it. Later, Nick took her to see it, and they crept inside the gloomy wreck of a farmhouse, the stone outbuildings and byre, Nick showing her where they'd filmed. Ali was struck by how out of the way it was, what it must have been like to live there, farm the land, far from other people, from anything approaching civilization. Not that Snape, the nearest village, in the valley below, would have amounted to much a century or more earlier, which was probably the last time anyone had lived at High Top. A single pub would have been about all there was, a farrier. But there would have been people, whereas the farm was utterly isolated. It gave her the shivers thinking about being there in the depths of winter: an open fire for warmth, water fetched from the beck in all weathers. "Maybe that's how they liked it," Nick had said. "They'd have been hardy, self-reliant." Lonely, Ali thought, cut-off. No medical assistance. Had children been born there? she wondered. Not that it was unheard of for women in remote farms to give birth at home even now, no one in attendance, not even waking their husband to say the baby was coming. She could think of someone who'd done exactly that.

Snape was a tourist draw now with its thriving pubs and B & Bs, its well-stocked shop and deli. It boasted an award-winning cheese maker, a ceramicist who'd been on TV and in magazine spreads and could barely keep up with demand. These days, Snape

Death in the Countryside

had a teahouse where, alongside its standard Yorkshire brew, the menu offered lapsang souchong and rooibos, something called Dragon Well, and various other green teas. On the edge of the village was a timber and glass Scandi-style building, home to a coffee roastery and café. A bakery. Ali and Nick had bought sandwiches there, sourdough, the fillings an inch thick, she remembered.

She thought of Rise in Heft. Prior to opening, when work was being done on the new premises, the windows were kept covered and for a long while no one was sure what it was going to be. A butcher, Ali thought, with its own charcuterie. Local produce, thick slices of bacon, the rind left on. There was nothing like that in town. Nick had speculated on a coffee shop, another one, while Ali's mother, Violet, hoped for a bookshop. No one imagined a bread shop. Not when there was already one over the road.

Initially, Evelyn Hooley attempted to be gracious about the new arrival, even though it was obvious she was puzzled, concerned. Ali, sensing the stirrings of disquiet, had called with Wilson at the new shop ahead of its opening, hoping to meet the owners. Lights on, the sound of hammering, something heavy being dragged across the floor, a sign on the door that gave the opening date as less than a week away. Ali knocked and waited. No answer. More hammering. She went round the back where a gate led into a yard and stepped inside into a scene of clutter: offcuts of wood, tins of paint, ladders, a sanding machine, a glass-fronted cabinet, an old metal sign for Fry's chocolate. Making her way to the back door of the building she knocked loudly, and a woman appeared. Small and pretty, dark curls, dark eyes, cheeks flushed. T-shirt splashed with paint, leggings, work boots with steel toe caps. Ali, out of uniform and technically off duty, introduced herself and Wilson. She was passing, she said, saw lights on, thought she would say hello. The woman was Ruth Carlisle, Rise her business. She led the way into the shop where a blonde woman, hair in a cartoonish topknot, was putting up a painting of a grayhound in a pinstripe suit and monocle, trying to get it to hang straight. Ruth's partner, Terri Roberts. Both women in their early thirties, Ali guessed.

"Ignore the mess," Ruth said, finding Ali a stool, fussing over Wilson. "We're almost done, it's going to be great."

Ali didn't doubt it. The walls were painted soft yellow, the counter tops zinc. There were weathered terracotta tiles on the floor, a decorative mosaic centerpiece that looked expensive, ancient, the kind of thing you'd see in an Italian church. On a shelf in an alcove stood a gleaming espresso machine.

"It's just finishing touches now," Ruth said. "A cabinet to go over there"—she indicated the wall underneath the painting of the dog—"and some old bits and pieces we've found, scales and what not, and that's about it."

"The chandelier," Terri chipped in.

"The chandelier," Ruth confirmed, glancing up. "Let's just hope the ceiling can take the weight."

Ali wondered how best to broach the subject of Hooley's opposite. "You're not concerned there's a bakery across the street?" she asked carefully. "I mean, you don't think you'll be . . . in each other's way?"

Ruth laughed. "Oh, we'll be nothing like *them*. We specialize in sourdough, out-there patisserie, you know?" Ali wasn't sure she did. "You'd go to a bread shop for a standard loaf, a vanilla slice or whatever, but you'd come to an artisan baker for . . ." She frowned, thinking.

"A croissant cube," Terri chipped in. "A mango and lime bauble, maybe, funky cheesecake."

"Right." Ruth laughed. "I mean, that's it, exactly. There's literally *no* crossover, you know."

Both women spoke as if there were a question mark on the end of everything they said. Ali was trying to picture a "funky" cheesecake, a "bauble." She hadn't known lime and mango went well

Death in the Countryside

together. Ruth was saying something about classic old-fashioned sweets—sherbet lemons, acid drops, sugar-coated almonds—inspiring their pastries. Ali was lost. "Out -there" patisserie was a new one on her. Still, the women seemed friendly, enthusiastic, and what they were describing did sound a million miles from Hooley's, where baubles (whatever they were) were definitely not on the menu.

"It's a totally different market," Ruth was saying. "We won't be treading on any toes."

Now, drinking tea on Simonthwaite, Ali wondered about that. Had they told her what they thought she wanted to hear? Had they fobbed her off? An unpleasant thought came to her, an expression she disliked: had they *played* her? Because, since opening, it looked very much as if they *were* competing with Evelyn—making what was unmistakably their own version of the Hooley Heft, claiming *their* bread was Ravensdale's finest when for longer than most people could remember that was precisely what Hooley's was known for. Ali wanted to give them the benefit of the doubt, wanted to think they were simply insensitive rather than out to ruin Evelyn, but something felt . . . off.

That first evening in the shop, she had gone away feeling reassured, pleased with herself for doing her community policing bit. The next day she spoke to Evelyn Hooley and told her what the women had said, but Evelyn's reaction, a snorting sound, seemed to suggest she didn't think much of it. "Well," she replied, unconvinced. "It *sounds* all very nice, different markets, blah, blah, but I'm telling you, people won't be buying half their shopping there and coming to us for the rest. Who wants to walk into a bread shop when they've already bought cakes at the bakery over the road? No one. Trust me, folk will go to one or the other."

Privately, Ali thought Hooley's would have the edge, what with their reputation stretching back generations, their award-winning

15

Maria Malone

pies. Surely, no newcomer selling cheesecake, no matter how "funky" or "out there" it might be, could steal the thunder of the famous Hooley Heft.

Ali gazed out across the valley, where the lone walker in red was striding along the ridge. She bit into her sandwich. The crust, studded with seeds, took some getting through. She liked sourdough but it was tricky to eat. Perhaps that was the point. The chewing involved, the fact you could only manage so much, a slice or two at the most before feeling full, meant it was almost impossible to overindulge. She had read about a backlash, an actor complaining it was all you could get now in the cafés he went to in London, how it made awful toast—sharp-edged, hard enough to break your teeth, full of holes, butter dripping onto the plate. Ali smiled. Her mother wasn't a fan either for much the same reasons. In contrast, Evelyn's white bread was soft, nutty, delicious. It took almost no eating. Sometimes, when Nick was away, and Ali was making do with sandwiches for tea, cheese on toast instead of cooking, she managed to get through an entire loaf in record time.

Wilson's shoulder was pressed lightly into her side. She scratched under his chin. They had been together since he was a puppy, a scrap. Chestnut and white coat, knowing hazel eyes, impressive pedigree. Even more impressive, his kennel name, Gallus Valentino Luca Yin. The breeder, Glaswegian, exuberant, auburn curls and twinkly brown eyes (the same coloring as her dogs, Ali noted) was in the habit of calling her irrepressible puppy "son." *Come on, son. Here, son! There you go, son.* So much so, that Ali felt the little dog should have a name with *son* in it. Along the lines of . . . Hud*son*? Not quite right. Car*son*? Ma*son*, Rob*son*, Samp*son*. Dob*son*, Gib*son*? Something authoritative and at the same time unstuffy. The breeder, catching on, and of the firm opinion that when it came to doggy names longer was better, threw in Macpher*son*. When Ali finally landed on Wil*son* it sounded right, and the puppy agreed, bounding over when she tried it out on him. *Wilson.* Perfect. She

Death in the Countryside

had trained him, seen him become an outstanding police dog, scoop a prestigious Rising Star Award ahead of his second birthday, in recognition for solving a crime no one had even suspected. On a house call, Ali investigating a complaint of fly tipping, a skinny shirtless man had invited them in. It was his son they wanted, he said, sounding weary. Wilson had gone to a corner of the living room and scratched at the floor, tail thumping, a sure sign he had detected something of interest. Cash, it turned out, thousands of pounds, hidden under the carpet. The skinny man shrugged. He knew nothing about any money, Ali needed to speak to his lad about that. When she asked could she take a look around while she waited, he shrugged again, said to go ahead. In the airing cupboard on the landing, Wilson detected a stash of weed. The son was dealing. That boy, the skinny man said, with a look that suggested nothing about his wayward son surprised him. "Will he go to jail?" he'd asked, brightening. "Will I get my house back?"

Ali and Wilson made a good team. He was her best friend, a force for good. She confided in him, told him things no one else knew. When it was just the two of them—at home, in the car, out walking in the Dales, no one within earshot, the conversation flowed in a one-sided way, Ali talking through cases, venting her frustrations, Wilson attentive, a good listener, never interrupting, Ali in no doubt he took it all in, understood every word. What she said, how she felt. She could tell by the way he looked at her, the habit he had of putting a paw on her knee and resting it there, or leaning into her when she asked his opinion. Only rarely, and only when they weren't working—a long car journey, typically—would he curl up and go to sleep as she was midway through sharing something heartfelt. Which was more to do with the motion of the car, she decided, than Wilson's way of saying he'd had enough. Mostly, he paid keen attention, whether she was sounding off about dog owners who failed to keep their animals under control around livestock, or motorists who parked on double yellow lines, assuming it didn't matter in an out of the way place like Heft, then complained when they got a ticket. Or littering, a personal pet hate of hers. On these and other matters, she and Wilson were of one mind, she felt sure. She loved him, would be lost without him.

Other walkers were on the top of Simonthwaite now, exploring the stones, taking selfies, looking for a spot to sit and take a breath. Somewhere close by a bee hummed. The sun felt warm, and she pulled her cap low, shading her face. Could she have done more to stop things turning sour between Evelyn and the Rise women? Had she missed an opportunity? Perhaps she had been wrong to think two bread shops—even one that called itself a cakery-bakery—could be easy neighbors. Ruth had said they wouldn't be treading on anyone's toes but that was exactly what they were doing. And Ali, Ali had no choice but to be involved.

In a town the size of Heft there was no turning a blind eye, no trotting out something glib about it not being a police matter, since, inevitably, anything that upset the equilibrium would at some point find its way to her. Might as well do what she could to keep the peace now, before things got properly out of hand.

3

Her mum had been baking. Cheese scones cooled on a rack and beside them sat a sponge cake. The oven was still on, the scent of something sweet, chocolatey in the air. A practice run for the church fete, Ali guessed, even though it was months off.

Violet Wren's apron was dusted with flour and what might have been cocoa powder. Her fringe was pinned off her face, copper strands sprouting from a scrunchie at the back of her neck. She had been donating to the cake stall for many years, and yet, despite the compliments she drew, she was not a confident cook. Baking could always go wrong, she said. A cake might look all right on the outside but be disappointing once you cut into it. You only had to watch *Bake Off* to know that. Having had a run of poor Madeira cakes—an unexplained, dark seam running through the middle despite a scrupulous adherence to the recipe, she was determined that everything submitted to the fete would be perfect.

Ali peered at a chopping board where dozens of lemon segments lay. "Crystalized lemon," her mother said. "I'm trying something."

"And you need all these?"

"I need three."

Ali counted the segments, at least three *dozen*, and raised an eyebrow.

"It's the recipe," Violet explained. "You end up with some left over but it's fine, I can freeze them, use them next time I make a Madeira."

"I thought you were off the Madeira."

"I am. Was. I've found a different recipe. Ground almonds and crystalized lemon."

"It seems a lot of effort," Ali said dubiously.

"Well, that's what the recipe says." Violet gave Ali a look as if to say *don't ask me*. "Anyway, I want you to try one of these." She placed a warm buttered scone in front of her. "Tell me what you think. It's a new recipe, Gorgonzola."

"Where's Dad?" Ali asked. He would be the one—not a fan of blue cheese at the best of times—tasked with having to eat most of them.

"In the garden. Moving the rose bush from the front, the yellow one."

"Moving it where? Why?"

Violet looked up from filling the kettle and frowned. "He did say . . ." She pulled a face. "Ask him yourself when he comes in."

Ali opened the back door to let Wilson out. "Go find Gordon," she said, and he took off.

Her mother took a tray of something from the oven and inserted a skewer into its center. "Brownies," she said, "not quite ready. The timing takes a bit of getting right. You want them cooked but still with a hint of gooiness in the middle."

The kettle shrieked on the hob and Violet made tea, dusted down her apron, and came to sit opposite Ali at the breakfast bar.

"Are these stools uncomfortable?" she asked. "Your father's complaining of stomach pains, only at breakfast when we eat in here. I think it's sitting at a height, it's bad for your back as well as your insides. We should use the table in the garden room."

Death in the Countryside

Ali said, "I don't mind them."

"Maybe it's an age thing, advancing years."

Ali didn't think of her parents as old, even though they were in their seventies. It was easy to forget, given how active they were—all the walking they did, choosing difficult routes, steep climbs.

"We've been up Simonthwaite," she said.

"No crime-fighting to be done today?"

"Day off."

Violet's eyes narrowed. Ali had her mother's coloring, the red hair, green eyes. Her sister, Iris, older by three years, was also a redhead, more marmalade than copper, and with her dad's bluey-gray eyes, the color of a stormy sea. Of the two of them, Iris was the more striking, Ali thought. Predictably, Iris considered Ali to have come off best.

"A whole day?" Violet was saying, amused. "I wonder, how many strings were pulled to make *that* happen? Did you have to bribe someone to cover for you? Get Barry out of retirement?" No amount of money would be enough to get Ali's predecessor back on duty in Heft, not even for a day.

"I'll probably find all hell let loose in my absence." Although Sunday tended to be quiet, as if some unwritten rule had been agreed whereby minor misdemeanors were permitted to go unchecked. Which suited her. If there was anything, it would be parking-related: visitors pulling up on grass verges and double yellow lines, across driveways. For once, it wasn't her concern. Let Skipden deal with the worst Heft had to offer. "The scone is fine, by the way," she said.

"Just fine? That doesn't sound . . . wonderful."

"Lovely, then. Light, really cheesy. In a good way."

"Sure? Your father doesn't think there's a place for blue cheese in a scone. Not that he's actually tried one yet." She put a paper bag on the counter. "I've put a couple in there for Nick."

Ali nodded. "Someone had left flowers on Simonthwaite," she said. "At the Black Stone. And a card. Was there an accident there?"

Violet thought for a moment. "That young boy, but I'm going back years."

"I don't remember—what happened?"

"You were away, I think. Training"—Violet closed her eyes, thinking back—"yes, you were in London. A lad went missing. His car was found but there was no sign of him if I remember rightly. It was a long time ago."

"Did they find him?"

"I don't think they did."

Ali finished her tea and went into the garden where her dad worked a spade into the earth. Gordon Wren was in old jeans, a baggy T-shirt, a straw trilby. Turning over soil ready for the yellow rose he'd taken from the front, Wilson sitting nearby, observing, Gordon talking to the dog, explaining about the rose, how it hadn't liked its old spot in the border at the front. "If you ask me, there was a disagreement with the geranium, even though the grower seems to think those two are ideal bedfellows. I don't suppose we'll ever know what really went on. This one"—he indicated the rose—"haughty little madam, she's saying nothing." He looked up and saw Ali. "All right, love? I was just telling Wilson about the falling out at the front." He nodded again at the rose. "The Poet's Wife here, you'd think butter wouldn't melt, giving Rozanne what-for." He aimed another reproachful look at the rose. "The geranium, supposed to be a bit of company."

I dig gardens, it said on the front of his T-shirt. A present from her mum, Ali guessed. "Right," she said, "I didn't know plants fell out."

Gordon looked aghast. "All the time. As I was telling young Wilson here, a rose like this has to be center stage. It's no good if it feels overwhelmed. *Overshadowed* if you like." He aimed a tender look at the Poet's Wife, all curling leaves and drooping blooms. Ali had to admit it did appear a touch sorry for itself. "So, I'm putting her here where she can enjoy her own company. I'll give her a good

Death in the Countryside

drink, a bite to eat, and she'll be back on top form. Won't you, love?" He put the spade aside, nodded at Ali's tie-dye top and sporty joggers. "Not working?"

She shook her head. "Day off." Casual, as if it was normal, which was far from the truth. When last had she had a proper day off? She couldn't remember. "We went up Simonthwaite. Where no one could get hold of us."

Gordon seemed surprised. "Right," he said. "So you won't have heard about what's been going on here . . ." Fixing her with a steely look, sending a jolt of unease through Ali. Letting her know something had happened while she was away. Something untoward. Just like that, she was thinking, *Evelyn Hooley*.

"What?" she said, panic rising. "What won't I have heard about?"

Her father grinned. "Love, I'm only having you on!"

"Dad! You had me going there."

"Don't you know when I'm pulling your leg? I thought they drummed it into you about being suspicious—take nothing at face value, trust no one. Not even your old dad." He chuckled. "*Especially* not your dad."

"I'll get you back," she said, knowing she wouldn't.

He was quiet for a moment. "We did hear sirens, mind, when we were having our lunch . . ."

"*Sirens?*"

"Your face!"

She watched him put the rose in, taking his time, offering a few soothing words as he positioned it. "Some people don't like moving them, think they can't take the trauma," he said, talking to Wilson rather than Ali. "But there's no need to fret. I mean, right enough, a rose can be a sensitive soul, but it'll soon come round if you treat it well. Got that, lad?"

Wilson wagged his tail. Message understood.

Ali waited a moment then said, "You've heard about the bother on the high street? That new bakery, Rise, and Hooley's."

"Can't say I'm surprised. I don't suppose I'd be chuffed to have a rival open up on the doorstep either."

"It's a different kind of bakery," she said. "Fancy cakes, sourdough. A cakery-bakery, they're calling it."

Her dad gave her one of his *pull the other one* looks. "They're selling pies exactly the same as the Hooley Heft! Asking for trouble if you ask me. Not that it's any concern of yours. I mean, it's hardly one for the police." He frowned. "Is it?"

Ali resisted the urge to point out just how many of the queries and complaints that came her way would never have got past the front desk in Harrogate.

"I'm keeping an eye, that's all, so things don't escalate."

"Remember Ernie," her dad was saying. "A cautionary tale if ever there was one. Found himself at odds with a baker, both of them after the same woman." He caught Ali's look. "Awful, came to blows in the street. Tragic. Poor Ernie didn't stand a chance."

Ali shook her head. "I don't remember that."

"Ernie, you know," Gordon said. "Drove the fastest milk cart in the west." Ali looked blank. "And Two Ton Ted from Teddington, he drove the baker's van."

"Is this one of your jokes?"

"Poor Ernie caught a pork pie slap in the eye, knocked him flat," Gordon waited for her to catch up. "Surely you remember—it was top of the hit parade."

Ali rolled her eyes. Only her dad still referred to music charts as the hit parade. "I'd say Evelyn can handle herself."

He nodded. "I don't doubt it. One of those Hooley Hefts could do some serious damage."

Ali had an image of Evelyn in her boiler suit, armed with a pie. Stale, rock hard. If one of those hit you, you'd know all about it. When did a pie become an offensive weapon? Ali wondered. Once

Death in the Countryside

it was no longer fresh? She pictured a face-off in the street, Ruth, and Terri, their weapon of choice something artisan and inadequate. An out-there bauble. Pie or bauble? Ali knew who she would put her money on. She had an urge to laugh.

"Looks like something's tickled you," her dad said.

"That silly song of yours."

"Don't let the *you-know-whats* grind you down," he advised. "You're too soft, letting folk drag you into stuff they should be sorting out themselves. Tell them they're wasting police time. Book them! I would."

Ali wasn't fooled. Gordon might talk tough but he was a big softy. When she was little and had an irrational fear of moths, her dad would capture them, even those that were delicate and papery, almost impossible to handle, and carefully put them outside. In summer, he could be found in the garden reviving a bee with a saucer of sugar water. More than once he had taken in an ailing hedgehog and stayed up with it all night, filling hot water bottles until he could get it to a rescue center, expressing delight once it recovered sufficiently to attempt to bite him. Kind-hearted, patient, ready with a helping hand. That was Gordon.

Evelyn's husband, Alan, a bowls buddy of Gordon's, had passed away suddenly, unexpectedly, way too young. She was someone he'd do anything for. It occurred to Ali that Evelyn might not be as fiery or self-possessed as she made out. Running a business on her own couldn't be easy. Who, other than Ali, could she turn to? Even a woman as impressive as Evelyn Hooley could be vulnerable. Ali had seen it first-hand, older women poorly treated, often because there was no man in the picture. It was infuriating, unjust. Ageist, sexist. She had dealt with a dispute in Harrogate, a young family moving in next to an elderly woman and making her life intolerable—parking their car across her drive, hacking down the beech hedge it had taken years to grow. Dismissing her (polite) objections. When Ali went to investigate, the younger woman

25

acted as if the neighbor was of no consequence, as if her life was over. A batty old bag, she called her, when Beatrice Devlin, at ninety-two, was bright, sharp, an interpreter at the UN for most of her career. What Ali wanted to know was, had the next-door neighbor been a man, the type who wasn't about to put up with unauthorized hedge cutting or inconsiderate parking, would the younger woman's attitude be different? Of course, she already knew the answer.

Had the arrival of Rise posed more of a threat to Evelyn's wellbeing than Ali had realized? Was *she* feeling bullied, intimidated by the young women opposite? Perhaps the Battle of the Bakers wouldn't simply settle down, as Ali hoped.

It might become an awful lot worse.

4

On the way home, she took a detour along the high street, slowing to a crawl as she went past Hooley's and Rise. All quiet, as far as she could tell. She drove on, passing Blackett's Executive Coaches, turning into the narrow lane that led to the cottage. Nick was back, his Discovery parked on the road. An old E-Type Jag had pulled in behind, making it tricky for Ali to get into her usual spot. Before she reached the front door, her hands full with the rucksack and her mother's baking, Nick appeared. Looking awkward. Wilson bounded up to him and Nick bent to run a hand over his back.

Usually, when he returned after a shoot, there were hugs. He might even scoop her up and carry her inside. Nick was six-four, strong. Lifting Ali, who weighed less than nine stone and was a good eight inches shorter than her husband, presented little in the way of a challenge. Ali gave him a curious look. "What's up?" she said.

He tilted his head in the direction of the kitchen. "You've got a visitor." Giving her a meaningful look. "*Work.*"

"I'm not on duty today." She suppressed a ripple of irritation. The effort she had made to have a day off. Just the one. It didn't seem too much to ask. Couldn't he have sent whoever it was away? *Who is it?* she mouthed. He shook his head and stepped aside to let

27

her go in front. In the kitchen was a man she knew by sight: short wavy hair, pewter-colored, glasses, his blue shirt perfectly pressed, sharp creases on the sleeves. The teapot was on the table, two mugs. She wondered how long he'd been sitting there. This had better be good.

"Hello," she said, "I'm Sergeant Ali Wren."

He got to his feet. "Brian Bright," he said. "I live out on Snipe Road, Glebe Farm."

Ali knew it. A big place, outbuildings, no longer a farm.

"I'm sorry to bother you on a Sunday, I just didn't know what to do."

Ali nodded, although what he might have done was made a call which Skipden would have had to deal with. "I did try phoning," he said, as if he knew what she was thinking, "but it went through to Skipden and, well, they didn't seem all that helpful. They couldn't send anyone out they said, not today. Something about being short of people. Sunday's a bad day, or so the woman I spoke to seemed to think." Jean, Ali thought. "She suggested I might be better off speaking direct to the officer in Heft . . ." Ali nodded again. *Give me strength*. What was the point of them taking her calls if all they did was bounce them right back? She intended to have words.

Brian Bright peered at her. "I hope you don't mind."

She sighed inwardly. "Of course not. Please, sit down. What can I help you with?" Something straightforward, she hoped. Non-urgent. She sat facing Brian Bright, a man she knew nothing about, even though he lived only a mile or so away, she realized. One of those people she rarely saw in town. Wilson had positioned himself close to Brian, the dog almost sitting on the man's foot. It was a sign of intimacy, something he tended to do in times of distress, although Brian Bright seemed calm. On the surface, at least. Not everyone appreciated Wilson getting quite so close, but Brian Bright was stroking the dog, ruffling the curls on his ears.

"Lovely dog," he said. "We had a collie cross. Going back a bit,

Death in the Countryside

in Bradford, when I was growing up. Intelligent, quick to catch on. Good company." He turned to Wilson. "You're a handsome fella, aren't you? Good lad."

"What did you want to see me about?" Ali prompted.

"I'm seventy," he said. He looked younger. "There's nothing I don't know about cars, old ones. Classics, vintage models." He smiled. "MGs, they're my passion, if you like. I'm working on a Roadster I practically dug out from under a pile of rubbish in a garage, bringing it back to how it's meant to be."

Ali thought about her dad's Beetle now in the garage, unused, and wondered if Gordon knew about Brian Bright, on the doorstep practically, an expert in restoration. "Is this to do with your car?" she asked.

"You'd think someone technical minded, you know, a person with the know-how to strip down an engine and rebuild it," Brian said, ignoring her question, "would find a washing machine easy enough to operate."

Was this about his *washing* machine?

His shoulders slumped. "Truth is, I haven't a clue and there's no manual. They don't give you a handbook now, it's all online."

"Right," Ali said, thrown. Was he unwell?

"That's how I know something's happened."

Ali was lost. "I'm not sure I follow," she said.

"My wife does all that stuff. Washing machine, cooker, microwave. Domestic appliances, I haven't a clue. Cars, that's my thing."

Ali, unable to think of anything to say, waited for him to go on. "I mean," he said, "I wouldn't ask her to fit a set of brake pads and, likewise, she wouldn't expect me to manage an economy wash. Never."

He might as well have been talking in riddles. Ali sent a pleading look at Wilson under the table.

"No, of course," she said at last. "My husband puts the bins out and I load the dishwasher." Brian gave her a peculiar look, as if Ali was the one making no sense. Perhaps he was suffering from some kind of memory loss, dementia, she thought. An episode of some kind. At this rate she would end up accompanying him to A & E and having to sit with him until he was seen. How long would that be? Four hours, five, more. Then again, he'd managed to drive so he wasn't exactly incapable. Still, she decided to tread warily. "What about your wife?" she asked. "Can't you ask her?"

"Haven't you heard what I've been saying?" Agitated suddenly, as if she hadn't been paying attention.

"Mr Bright . . ." Ali began. "Brian."

"I *would* ask her, that's the first thing I'd do. Only I can't." A shake of the head. "Take the chicken thighs in the fridge; she roasts them, lovely they are the way she does them." Ali thought of the chicken in her own fridge, the one *she* was planning to roast. Nick's welcome home dinner. She should have the oven on by now.

"I wouldn't know where to start," Brian went on. "I opened a tin of corned beef instead." He thought for a moment. "Even that wasn't without its challenges, believe you me."

Ali sympathized. She hated the fiddly key on the tin, its tendency to snap in two at just the wrong moment. Corned beef wasn't something they had very often but when they did, Nick was the one who dealt with the tin.

"Have you and your wife had a disagreement?" Ali asked.

Brian looked puzzled. "No, nothing like that. We don't argue. We know who does what. The cooking, she always takes care of it, and if that makes us old-fashioned so be it. I know that's not the modern way, but it suits us." Talking as if he was ninety, not seventy, Ali couldn't help thinking.

"I'm sure you do your share of the washing up," she said.

Brian gave her a withering look. "Not if the dishwasher's involved."

They seemed to be going round in circles, Ali beginning to

Death in the Countryside

think there was no good reason for him being there, intruding on her time off. On a Sunday too. He seemed perfectly lucid, if a little . . . peculiar. She glanced at the clock. Gone five. Nothing suggested Brian intended to leave any time soon. She wondered if indeed there was a wife or if she was a figment of his imagination. As for the stuff about restoring cars, was it even true? Perhaps he was a fantasist, lonely.

"Maybe I could take a look at the oven for you," she said, thinking that might be enough to persuade him to go home.

"*You*?" Taken aback.

"Or the washing machine if you'd like me too. I'm not bad with appliances." Couldn't open a tin of corned beef to save her life but she'd worked out how to set the timer on the oven, which had been needlessly complicated. Wishing now she had thought to set it earlier.

"You're a police officer," Brian said. Stating the obvious.

"I am, yes," Ali confirmed.

"So, isn't your job more about crime, not"—he frowned, searching for the right words—"domestic troubleshooting?"

"Ideally," she said, "but people come to me for all sorts of reasons, not always police matters. If I can help, I do."

He seemed confused. "Wait, you think I'm here about my *oven*?"

Her head was starting to spin. Was she being dense? "Sorry, I'm still not entirely sure why you're here."

"My *wife*," he said, in a tone that suggested Ali hadn't been listening. "Melody. *That's* what I've been telling you—she's missing!"

5

"**S**he couldn't be visiting someone?" Ali asked.

"Without a word?" Another withering look.

"Might she have left a note you've not seen?"

Brian Bright's brows knitted together in annoyance. "We've a pad on the shelf in the porch. You can't miss it. For messages. It was the first place I looked."

Ali made a note of everything he'd told her. Took a description of Melody: blonde hair, wavy, not quite shoulder length. Brown eyes. Slim. Tall. "About your height," Brian said. Ali wrote down 5ft 8ins. Sixty-six years old. A little younger than her husband, then. There at breakfast the day before and nowhere to be seen when Brian got home in the evening later than expected after dropping off a car, an Austin A40.

It didn't look to him as if she'd taken anything, although her car, a yellow Mini Cooper, was gone. Ali called Melody's mobile number. Voicemail. She asked for a photo. He'd have to get one from home, he said. As tactfully as she could, Ali asked if Melody was depressed, worried about anything. Was it possible—Ali braced herself—that she might be . . . seeing someone?

"Someone? What sort of someone?" Brian said, baffled. "A friend, you mean?"

32

Death in the Countryside

"A friend. Or . . ." Ali hesitated, not sure there was a tactful way of asking if Melody Bright might be having an affair, not willing to incur another of those withering looks. "A male friend, perhaps."

It took a moment for him to catch on. "On the *side*, you mean?" Brian looked appalled, indignant.

"I'm sorry, I have to ask, it's just routine." The words came out in a rush.

"You think she's run off with a fancy man?" he snorted. "Melody? You're way off the mark. Never, not in a million years."

"I'm not suggesting that's what's happened, it's just something to consider. I didn't mean to cause offense."

At this point Brian was meant to say he understood, she was just doing her job. Instead, he stayed silent, his face red, Wilson still parked on his foot. The atmosphere in the kitchen felt over-heated. Ali wanted to open a window, the door into the garden, let some air in.

The business of missing persons could be murky. Some chose to leave. Others disappeared in a way that was immediately concerning. Often, it wasn't apparent who fell into which category and it was a balancing act, a delicate one, gauging whether or not a disappearance should be treated as urgent. In Harrogate, Ali had dealt with various missing persons incidents and got her fingers burned once or twice. She was thinking of the woman reported missing, her husband insistent she'd been abducted, who was actually living on the outskirts of Leeds in a big house—electric gates, SUV on the drive—with her new romantic interest (an estate agent) memories of her old life fading fast. She had not thanked Ali for "intruding," for "dredging up the past." She wasn't *missing*, she pointed out, she had *left*. Upped and gone because her marriage was over. Not that her husband could see it. And he had no right getting the police on her. Ali suggested she at least let her husband know she was okay, put his mind at rest, but she said no—although if Ali wanted to tell him, that was up to her, as long as she didn't say where she was or lead him to think she might one day be back because that was *never* going to happen. "Tell him he's welcome to keep the prints we brought back from Madrid, the ones in the hall, even though it was me that paid to have them framed." Right. "And if he wonders how I am, say I drive a BMW X5 these days."

Another case from her time in Harrogate came to mind, one that until recently had resurfaced every year or so. A man whose wife had vanished almost thirty years earlier. He claimed to have no idea what had become of her but there were those (her sister, one or two friends) who suspected he'd done away with her, and on countless occasions he was brought in for questioning, his garden dug up, an area of bleak moorland near Thorcross Reservoir, (once a favorite spot of the couple) subjected to a further intense search, as well as the cottage near Flamborough where the pair were in the habit of spending their summer holiday. Another lovely garden excavated, flower beds trampled over, ruined. Half his life, the poor bloke was under suspicion, whispered about, branded a killer. All this until a woman who'd worked with his wife happened to run into her by chance in Bakewell, finally putting an end to decades of gossip and rumors. Working as a school dinner lady, it turned out. She had simply left without a word.

The point was, Ali knew that things weren't always what they seemed, that sometimes reports of missing persons had, if not a happy ending, an innocent one. Not that there was any point saying this to Brian Bright, who was adamant his wife was missing— in the sense of properly gone—and in a manner that was both suspicious and alarming.

She suggested Brian go home, that there might have been a mix-up, his wife could well come back. Might even be there.

"Where will you start looking?" he asked, showing no sign of wanting to leave.

"From what you've said, I don't think there's enough to warrant a search, not just yet."

Death in the Countryside

Ali saw his face fall. Melody Bright had been gone little more than a day. And from what Ali had been told, there was nothing to indicate anything sinister. Not yet.

"I promise I'm taking what you've told me seriously. I'd just say, well, she's not been gone long."

He opened his mouth to object and Ali pressed on. "Go home now, sleep on it."

Was it an urgent matter, one she should look into further tonight? On balance, she didn't think so. "See what the morning brings, and I'll come over first thing."

6

The only way to get him to leave, Ali realized, was to go with him. She ran upstairs and changed into her uniform of black combats and matching T-shirt, swept her red hair into a tidy ponytail. Downstairs she laced up her work boots and clipped Wilson into his harness.

She poked her head round the door to the living room where Nick was on the sofa, TV on, the screen filled with birds soaring above a bare rocky mound jutting from an expanse of choppy sea.

"These birds," Nick said, "they're amazing. They dive from, like, thirty meters, hit the water at something like sixty miles an hour."

"Incredible," Ali said.

"The Bass Rock. We should go, you can do a boat trip. It's the biggest colony of northern gannets in the world. I mean, the *world*. That's got to be worth seeing."

"Definitely."

Nick paused the TV. "Off out, then?"

"Sorry, won't be long."

He smiled. "It's your day off, remember?"

Ali grimaced.

Death in the Countryside

Outside, Brian Bright was in the E-Type. Waiting. Ali and Wilson got into the Hilux and followed him back to Glebe Farm.

The farmhouse, stone-built, austere, was set back from the road and screened by trees. Honeysuckle wound its way up a trellis next to the front door. The sound of persistent hammering, a woodpecker driving its beak into the trunk of a tree nearby, greeted Ali as she got out of the pick-up. Brian opened up and Ali heard voices.

"The radio," he said, catching her look. "We leave it on when we're out."

He showed her along a flagged passage and into a roomy kitchen at the back where she asked him to wait while she and Wilson took a look around.

Together, they checked the other rooms downstairs: a sitting room painted pale green, leather sofas, television in the corner, remote on the glass-topped occasional table alongside a neat stack of magazines at one end—*Good Housekeeping, Homes & Gardens, Tatler.* On bookshelves in an alcove were collections of classics with matching spines: Dickens, the Brontë sisters, George Elliot, Daniel Defoe. There were paintings, abstract works, a gloomy palette of black and gray, crimson; on the mantelpiece a clock flanked by beeswax candles in intricate metal holders. A photo in a silver embellished frame. Ali picked it up. A studio portrait, posed, its subject looking off to one side. Blonde, slender, white shirt, a dark stone on a short chain just visible at the neck. Melody Bright, she guessed. Ali put it back, took one last look around. No cupboards, no hiding places. Wilson had been all over the room, sniffing, showing no sign of having found anything of particular interest. They moved on to the dining room. Sash windows on two sides, the walls painted blackish blue, a mirrored sideboard and, beneath a heavy metal light fitting, a table and eight wishbone chairs. It felt chilly, forgotten. Ali guessed the room wasn't much used.

Maria Malone

A third door off the hallway was locked. Ali returned to the kitchen. "The room that's locked?" she asked. Brian produced a key. "My office," he said. Inside a painting hung above a desk and computer. A woman, rough brushstrokes, more an impression of a face than a true likeness. There were filing cabinets, a radio on the windowsill playing to itself, built in storage units along one wall. Ali slid open the doors and checked inside each one. Looking for what? Melody crouching out of sight? Her body, stuffed inside?

Upstairs, she checked the main bedroom, inside a wardrobe where one half held men's trousers and shirts, jackets, suits, the other dresses, blouses, skirts and trousers, knitwear. There was a shelf with handbags, a rack with a neat arrangement of women's shoes, one or two designer pairs among them. No obvious gaps anywhere, nothing to say items had been removed. In a chest of drawers were scarves, only scarves: Hermes, YSL, Liberty. Some in boxes, encased in monogrammed tissue paper. Wilson searched under the bed and popped out. Nothing to report. The other three bedrooms felt unused. Ali opened doors, looked inside wardrobes, all of which were full, spare capacity for Melody's clothes, it appeared. In one, stood a set of matching suitcases. Again, it didn't seem as if anything had been removed. Wilson padded about with her, peered under beds, poked his head among coats and dresses. In the airing cupboard on the landing, Ali found the hook for the hatch into the loft. She lowered the steps and went up. You never knew what to expect with a loft. Some she'd searched were so full it was almost impossible to get in and take a proper look—boxes stacked up, storage bags, bits of furniture everywhere. Others held nothing but a layer of insulation. This was one of the neat ones. From her position on the top step, she shone the beam of her torch all around, into the furthest corners and up into the eaves, unable to spot anything unusual. Finally, she got right inside and walked the length of the roof. All clear.

Downstairs, she remembered what Brian had said about the message pad in the porch and went to see if Melody had left a

Death in the Countryside

note, something to say where she might be, what was going on, but there was nothing.

In the kitchen, she found Brian standing in front of a vast larder fridge, both doors wide open, staring at the contents. It looked to be well-stocked. At least he wasn't about to go hungry, even if he couldn't work out how to use the oven or microwave.

He turned. "What were you expecting to find in the loft?" he asked.

Ali gave a small shake of the head. "Just being thorough," she told him.

She asked for the key to his workshop, his car keys, and went outside, opened the boot of the E-Type. He watched from the front door, arms folded, shaking his head in disapproval.

"Really?" he said. "Is this necessary?"

Ali didn't answer. He was the one who'd insisted she come and now she intended to do her job properly.

The workshop was big enough for more than one car. The Roadster undergoing restoration was parked over a pit. She crouched and looked underneath, checked the boot. Everything in order. She returned to the house.

"Is the photo on the mantelpiece in the sitting room relatively recent?" she asked.

Brian went with her to take a closer look. He shifted uncomfortably. "That's not Melody," he said. "It's Dolores. My first wife." Not looking Ali in the eye. "My late wife."

7

"So," Ali told Nick over dinner, "it turns out, Melody is wife Number Two."

While she was with Brian, Nick had put the chicken in the oven, roasted the potatoes. There was broccoli, broad beans, Yorkshire puddings, gravy. Ali had showered and they were on their second glass of Marlborough, her hair still wet, wound into a copper braid, a damp patch on the back of her T-shirt. Wilson was in his bed in the corner, flat out. It had been a long day.

"Two wives. Not that unusual."

"But the photo in pride of place on the mantelpiece is of his *late* wife rather than the woman he's now married to. *That's* unusual, don't you think?"

Nick helped himself to another Yorkshire pudding. "Hmmm."

"I went into every room and there are no pictures of Melody, not one. There's a wedding photo on the windowsill in the bedroom, but—guess what?—*that's* his first wife too. I mean, the *bed*room."

"Brutal. I'm starting to see why she might have left."

On the noticeboard in the kitchen, half obscured by shopping receipts, was a recent snapshot of Melody, which Ali had borrowed. "She's not unlike his first wife. Same build, blonde. He definitely

40

Death in the Countryside

has a type." Ali thought she might have seen Melody Bright around town but couldn't think where.

"Actually, I know him," Nick said. "Well, not *know*, exactly. Let's say our paths have crossed."

"Really? How come?"

"His company supplies cars to the film and TV industry. Classics. We're using one at the minute on *The Beat*, a 1973 Alfasud." Nick cut into a potato. "I've seen him once or twice on location, dropping cars off, although it's usually one of his workers brings them over. When he turned up here earlier, I recognized him straight away, but it was obvious he had no idea who I was, so I didn't bother saying anything. Didn't seem much point. He was preoccupied, anyway, not in the mood to chat—not to me anyway."

"Where's his business?"

"Bradford. Brian Bright Classics. We call him the man from the BBC." Nick looked thoughtful. "I couldn't tell you anything about him, other than he's reliable to deal with, his cars show up on time, they're always in good nick. Aside from that, what kind of person he is, I haven't a clue. As I say, he doesn't often show up on location."

Brian Bright. The man from the BBC. A man with traditional views of married life, one who considered the kitchen the sole domain of his wife, hence his woeful lack of knowledge regarding domestic appliances, his inability to cook a meal. (Then again, Ali thought, her dad might not fare much better if Violet suddenly became unavailable. When had Gordon last cooked or done the laundry?) Clearly, Brian was stubborn, he knew how to get his own way—look how he'd sought out Ali on a Sunday (her day off!) waited in her kitchen for her to get home, then twisted her arm to go to Glebe Farm. A man careless of the feelings of others, she suspected. Why else would he have photos of his late wife in the home

41

he now shared with Melody? Ali thought about how she would feel if Nick did that to her. Not that Nick had a late wife.

Brian had struck her as clumsy, thoughtless. Perhaps his second wife felt undermined, humiliated. Imagine having to live with wife Number One on the mantelpiece. If that didn't make you feel second best, Ali didn't know what would. Under the circumstances, perhaps it was almost inevitable Melody would eventually leave. *If* that was what had happened.

Perhaps Brian had done away with her. But if he had, would he have been so keen to get the police involved quite so fast? Maybe he was clever. Smarter than he might appear. Not being able to work a fan oven didn't mean he wasn't cunning. He was a businessman, after all. Successful. Shrewd, no doubt.

"He and Melody have been married almost ten years. His first wife died in a car crash thirty years ago," Ali said.

Dolores. On a pedestal on the mantelpiece, in the bedroom too, in the painting on the wall of his office. Ali had picked up on Brian's wistful expression when he explained about Dolores, the tenderness in his voice when he spoke about her. A woman who was no doubt less than perfect but now remembered with something approaching reverence. It was what happened when someone died too soon, too young.

When she said all this to Nick, he said, "I guess that kind of explains the photos."

"Does it?"

"A sudden loss, unexpected. The shock of it, the unfairness. He probably never got over it."

"So why marry again?"

"Maybe because he doesn't much like being on his own. He meets someone, falls in love, knows in his heart she'll never be a match for the late Mrs. Bright—which isn't something you'd admit, even to yourself, never mind your new love interest, not wanting to scare them off. And Melody probably thought she understood.

Death in the Countryside

Hoped to be the one to bring some happiness back into his life, heal him, or whatever." Nick frowned. "And maybe she does, except it turns out that living in the shadow of another woman, one who's practically a saint in the eyes of her husband, is a burden. One she *thought* she'd be able to bear but, in the end, can't."

Ali looked impressed. "You should be a therapist. Or a script writer." It was the kind of story she could see playing out on *The Beat*.

"Imagine having to dust those photos. Put them back in pride of place. Wouldn't that tip you over the edge eventually?"

"What makes you think Brian doesn't do the dusting?"

Nick gave her a look. "The guy was here for nearly an hour before you got back and just looking at him I could tell he wasn't the type to dust. Or cook or clean. Or iron that shirt he had on, which *someone* had done a great job of pressing. Don't ask me how I knew, he just didn't strike me as . . . domesticated."

He was right about that.

She helped herself to more gravy. Nick's Yorkshire puddings were perfect: well-risen, light, crisp. Superior to the ones she made.

"What's the secret to the Yorkshires?" she asked.

"Make the batter early, let it sit," he said.

She looked surprised. "Is that all it is, really?"

He smiled. "I haven't a clue. Add a spoonful of water to the mix, a drop of olive oil . . . everyone's got their own thing."

Ali wondered about that. Her mother had always had a difficult relationship with Yorkshire puddings which had a habit of collapsing the moment they came out of the oven. Ali's weren't much better. Of late, Violet had taken to adding chopped spinach to the batter, which was surprisingly tasty and helped make up for the poor rise. Ali touched Nick on the wrist. "From now on, you are the Yorkshire pudding king."

"Ah. Shot myself in the foot there."

Ali glanced at him. Luckily, they both enjoyed cooking,

although Nick was the more accomplished of the two, the more adventurous, willing to source new recipes—attempt a soufflé, a pannacotta, make his own pasta. She tried, and failed, to picture Brian Bright presenting his wife with a homecooked meal.

From what she'd seen, Melody Bright appeared to have a decent life—successful husband, nice house, car. When Ali had asked if she worked, Brian looked surprised. Never stops, he said—keeping on top of the house, all the cooking and cleaning, the garden. So, not a job in the sense of earning, but productive. Clothes from Phase Eight, Hobbs, Jaeger. A Mulberry tote, LK Bennett espadrilles still in their box. If Brian was the sole breadwinner nothing hinted at him being mean with his money where Melody was concerned.

"So," Nick said, breaking into her thoughts. "Are you concerned? For her wellbeing, I mean."

"Not yet. I mean, she's taken the car." That was the clincher. She hesitated. "And . . . it's not the first time she's taken off." She thought back to the moment she'd asked Brian if it was out of character for Melody to leave without a word. They were in the kitchen, Ali getting ready to go.

"Absolutely, she would never leave me high and dry. It's just not in her nature."

"Right, so she's never done anything like this before?"

Brian had looked awkward then, his gaze suddenly on the wall behind Ali, as if he'd spotted something interesting there. There was a pause before he spoke. His face was flushed.

"Not *exactly*," he said. "Not in the sense of *leaving*."

8

Ali was awake the following morning before it was light. In the alder, what felt like inches from the open bedroom window, a blackbird was in fine voice. She lay for a moment listening to its song, then glanced at Nick, who seemed to be in a state of deep sleep. He was on a late start, having scheduled a day to recce locations for a forthcoming episode of *The Beat*. First on the list was the church of St. Michael and All Angels in Hubberholme, then what he called a dry pub crawl, in the hope of finding somewhere with bags of character. He was after a hall or stately home too. In the end, it would come down to whichever had the best driveway and entrance, where much of the action would take place.

She got out of bed, trying not to disturb him, pulled on jogging pants and an Alice Cooper T-shirt, and went downstairs where Wilson was already up, bright-eyed. As soon as she began moving about, he was alert. No matter how little noise she made, even creeping down the stairs practically on tiptoe, he would hear her.

"Good boy," she said, ruffling his fur. "Quick walk before breakfast?"

The sun was coming up over The Horse's Head, pale golden light spilling into the sky. She went briskly up the lane to a nearby

45

Maria Malone

wooded area, Wilson at her side. No one else about, only pheasants and squirrels, the sound of sheep bleating at each other on a fell somewhere.

Ali ran through in her head what she needed to do. Evelyn Hooley, a welfare check, just to make sure she wasn't more overwhelmed by the rivals over the road than she was letting on. First, though, she intended to call in on Brian Bright at Glebe Farm. She had passed details to Skipden about Melody, the car she was driving. Brian insisted she wasn't depressed or in any way vulnerable, which meant she was deemed low risk—especially given that it was not the first time she had left her husband.

Brian disagreed. This was different, he told Ali, explaining the lengths Melody had gone to before to make sure he would cope without her—leaving meals for him, detailed instructions on how to work the oven, the washing machine. A note that said why she was going and where she would be (a hotel an hour's drive away in Grassington). Not abandoning him. She wouldn't, he said. Ali had listened, thinking those instructions of Melody's would come in handy now, asking had he kept them. Brian surprised, shaking his head. No need, he'd gone after her and a day later she was back, things returning to normal. Ali asked what had made her leave. Nothing terrible, Brian said. A blip. He'd been taking her for granted, his business occupying too much of his time. She felt neglected, frustrated. He had put things right since, taken her to the coast for a long weekend, where they'd talked. Fixed things, he said.

Perhaps Melody hadn't thought so.

Wilson snuffled at the base of a towering fir tree. A squirrel somewhere overhead, Ali guessed. She tried to picture Melody Bright, a woman who seemed the type to consider her actions, their consequences. Not one to do a flit. She must have thought long and hard before leaving that first time, must really have meant it, and yet she had come back. Almost at once. Brian had to have done

Death in the Countryside

some groveling, Ali guessed, a good deal of apologizing, promising things would be different in future. And perhaps he'd kept his word, for a while at least, before slipping back into his old ways, prompting Melody to leave a second time. Only, maybe, this time she didn't want Brian talking her into coming home, giving things another go. Perhaps this time she was off for good, which was why she had left no instructions, no note, no forwarding address. Not wanting Brian to find her.

Not that she knew any of this, she reminded herself. What would make someone leave without a word, shrug off their old life? Something seismic, surely. Or, perhaps, nothing more than a growing sense of dissatisfaction. Wilson splashed in the beck and, up ahead, a squirrel scampered away along a path. Shafts of sunlight poked through the trees, dappling the ground.

When she returned home Nick was in the kitchen, coffee brewing on the stove. Ali could smell toast. It was still early, just after six. On the radio someone was talking about a murder trial, a man who'd slit the throat of his sister's boyfriend on New Year's Eve the year before. He had pleaded not guilty but the evidence, courtesy of his home CCTV system, appeared damning. Ali knew the officers who'd been first on the scene. Bloodbath, one called it.

She slid her arms round Nick's waist. "I thought you'd want a lie in."

"That was the plan but the blackbird outside the bedroom window singing his heart out had different ideas." He poured coffee while Ali gave Wilson his breakfast.

"I was thinking about my missing woman," she said. "And how if you're planning to leave and don't want to be found you'd go without a word. Phone switched off, no goodbye note on the kitchen table, just get in the car one day and drive away. I mean, it's possible to disappear, even now when people put so much of themselves on social media. If you're determined to drop out of view, you can."

"Did you look, is Melody on social media?"

47

"Brian said she didn't bother. I did a quick trawl, couldn't find anything."

Nick was quiet, thinking. "Say she has left him, isn't it a bit odd she'd go in that manner? It's what you'd do if you were trying to escape a threat or . . ." He looked at Ali. "An abusive partner. Anything make you think that's what's going on?"

"Nothing on record, no complaints," she said. "But then, why take off like that?"

"Not that you know for sure that's what's happened." Nick pointed out. "Memory loss, an accident, could be anything."

"Right, but just say she did." She sipped at her coffee. Nick put toast on the table. Evelyn Hooley's famed white loaf, sliced thick, the best bread in Ravensdale. Ali took a piece, slathering it in butter, marmalade. "Maybe it's not that Brian's a bad husband in the sense of, you know, knocking her about. I mean, abuse can cover all sorts. Maybe she'd had enough for whatever reason, but things weren't *so* bad, and she didn't trust herself not to cave in and go back if he came running after her. I've seen it before, women unhappy in their marriage—I mean, had it up to here, a husband that drives them to distraction—then they say they're leaving and, whoosh, suddenly he's on his best behavior. Promises the earth: it's all going to be different from now on. And she thinks, okay, why not? So they stay, then they find—surprise, surprise—it's all exactly the same." She bit into her toast and tasted bitter orange. "I sense Brian can be persuasive."

Nick dug a spoon into a jar of peanut butter. "Could be right. What happens next?"

"See if the car shows up, have another chat with Brian, find out if there's anything he's not telling me."

"Like what?"

"Honestly, I don't know." She ate the last of her toast, finished her coffee. Nick gestured at the pot for a top up and she nodded. "Maybe she's been unhappy for ages," she said, "and Brian knows

Death in the Countryside

but doesn't want to say. Too proud or whatever. Or they argued, she took off and now he's worried something might have happened." She gave a shrug. "All that's hypothetical, of course. My fertile imagination. The only thing I know for definite is she's gone."

9

Just as the pips were sounding for the 8 o'clock news, Ali's phone started ringing. Evelyn Hooley.

"Someone's been in the shop." Evelyn sounded slightly breathless.

"A break-in?"

"As I let myself in I knew something was . . . off. I could *feel* it in the air. Before I even had a proper look around." She sounded agitated. "You'll need to come and take a look yourself. Now, if you can, before I open."

Ali had been about to head up to Brian Bright's, see if he'd had any news, but Evelyn's need seemed suddenly more pressing.

"There's no one there?" Ali said. "You're not in danger?"

"No, I don't think so."

"Okay, give me five minutes, I'll make a call and come straight over."

Brian answered on the first ring. "Anything from Melody overnight?" Ali asked, hoping for good news.

"Nothing." His voice was flat. "What about the investigation, have you made progress?"

Ali winced. It wasn't yet an "investigation" in the sense Brian might think. Melody's details were being circulated, the registration

50

Death in the Countryside

of her yellow Mini flagged, that was all for now. Ali promised to brief him properly in person in an hour or so, not sure she would have anything more to add. She was going to have to manage his expectations.

She called upstairs to say she was going. Nick appeared on the landing, barefoot, rubbing at his wet hair with a towel, the faded denim shirt he wore to death not yet buttoned up. Sometimes, without warning, seeing him took her straight back to the night they'd met. An end of series party for *The Beat*, which Ali was at only because her old boss, Billy Leonard, now retired and advising the series on police matters, couldn't make it, and asked her to go in his place. "For me," he said. "They're a nice bunch." She looked at Nick now, remembering how reluctant she'd been to drive thirty miles to Nether Rigg, the village on the edge of the moors where the series had its base, and spend an evening in the company of strangers. The production people were staying over, something she wasn't keen on, but an email had come from the location manager, Nick Pope, to say he'd booked her a room.

It was quite a do. Champagne, stalls serving burgers, Goan street food. A traveling funfair that featured in the season finale had been drafted in—dodgems, a big wheel, a waltzer that looked ancient, its livery red, blue and gold, *Charlton*, the name of the operator, emblazoned in flamboyant italics on the back of each car. She'd felt out of things and wished she'd been able to think of someone to take but on a Thursday night everyone she knew was working the next day. She stood watching as the waltzer clattered past, a man in drainpipe jeans, waistcoat open over his bare chest, roaming among the cars, spinning each one, a chorus of screams as the ride got faster, Desmond Dekker's "Israelites" belting from the sound system. A stranger at her side. Dark hair, messy, eyes that were . . . blue? Green? She couldn't decide. White shirt loose over jeans, work boots. Not dressed up, not needing to. Nick saying hello, asking was she having a good time. She didn't need to

51

question why she'd caught his eye since she guessed she was one of the few outsiders there. When the waltzer stopped they got on, and minutes later stumbled off exhilarated, the night changed, charged, alive. Nick like one of the fairground people, Ali remembered thinking—unconventional, untamed, a kind of wild energy.

She smiled up at him now. "You know I love you. Even without your socks on."

He laughed. "And I love you, even in your work clothes. Especially in your work clothes." She was in sturdy combat trousers, a T-shirt in the kind of Aertex fabric that reminded Ali of school PE lessons. A stab vest handy for its pockets, one of which held a stash of treats for Wilson. Black wasn't her favorite color, she found it drab, but it was practical, much like her unfussy ponytail from which several copper strands were already escaping. Nick came down the stairs and kissed her. Wilson, the soul of discretion, took himself off to wait at the front door, politely looking the other way.

"I was just thinking about the night we met," she said, "the waltzer." Her green eyes sparkled.

"You mean when I swept you off your feet." He tucked the loose hair behind her ears. "Made your head spin so you couldn't think straight."

"Sly," Ali said, stroking his face. "It worked, anyway." The Kinks blasting from the speakers as the ride came to a halt. She kissed him. "I've got to run. Evelyn Hooley phoned. She's had a break-in."

Evelyn ushered her into the shop, made a fuss of Wilson. "That sign there, *No Dogs Allowed*," she told him. "That's not for you to worry about. You're welcome any time, son, whether you're working or off-duty."

Ali scanned the premises, not finding anything obvious to indicate a burglary. "I'll have a look at where they came in first, then."

Death in the Countryside

"Well, that's the thing," Evelyn said. "I don't actually know."

"I thought there'd been a break-in?"

"That's what *you* said," Evelyn told her. "What *I* said was there'd been someone in the shop."

Ali was confused. "So you've not been burgled?"

"Not *as such*." Evelyn pursed her lips. "*But*. I've had an intruder. More than one, for all I know." She aimed a meaningful look in the direction of Rise. "On Saturday, when I locked up, I left the place the way I always do, everything in order. Floor swept, counters wiped down, till empty." She had removed the glass shelving from the display cabinet and cleaned it, left it out to dry. "Only this morning, the shelves had *moved*." She indicated the cabinet. "*Someone* put them back." Before Ali could speak, Evelyn went on. "And, no, before you ask, it wasn't me. I'm not going doolally, I'm meticulous. Somebody, person, or persons unknown"—another glance in the direction of the rival bakery opposite—"came in and moved them."

Ali was quiet, thinking. It seemed improbable, unlikely. Why would anyone do such a thing? "You're certain?" she said at last.

"Absolutely. I may be approaching pension age but I'm all there."

Ali didn't doubt it. Evelyn certainly came across as sharp, switched on, in her stylish boiler suit and Converse boots, but what if underneath it all she was less self-assured than she seemed?

"There's more," Evelyn was saying, leading Ali and Wilson into the back of the shop, all stainless steel surfaces, the industrial ovens on, the day's bread, the Hooley Hefts, baking inside.

"What time did you arrive?" Ali asked, looking around.

"The usual, just before five," Evelyn said airily.

"You didn't think to call me straight away?"

"At that time of day? A bit too early, I'd have thought. And I had to get on, otherwise I'd have had nothing to sell today."

She indicated a spillage, a neat mound of flour in the middle of

53

the floor. "That wasn't me," she said. "I'd never leave the place like that." She looked affronted. "And that, that's not my flour either."

"Are you sure?" Ali asked. The flour looked ordinary, no distinguishing features, as far as she could tell.

Evelyn gave her a cool look. "I've been baking all my life. If there's one thing I know, it's my own flour."

Ali glanced at the back door, which led into a courtyard. The lock seemed intact. "No sign of anyone forcing their way in?"

"If I had to guess, I'd say they got in through the cloakroom over there." Evelyn gestured at a door at the far end of the room. "That window doesn't lock." Ali frowned. "Which, I might add, has never been a problem. Until now."

Ali took a look. Behind the door was a small lobby with coat pegs, a locker, and, beyond, another door that led into a cloakroom with a window, its catch mostly for show. Ali gave a gentle push and the window opened. She closed it again, aimed a disapproving look at Evelyn, not that she noticed, too busy stroking Wilson, asking how he got his hair so shiny. Ali studied the window. Anyone getting in that way would find the toilet cistern a handy step down. Ali shone her torch, checking for shoe prints, dirt dragged in from outside—it had rained through the night—but found nothing. She and Wilson went out into the courtyard, Evelyn trailing after them. "One of my tea towels is missing," she said. "White linen, *Hooley's* embroidered in gold. Very distinctive. Find that, you've got your man. Or *woman*." Another meaningful look, a note of triumph in her voice.

"Was that the only thing taken?" Ali asked, studying the window from the outside now, opening it with little effort, the catch performing no useful function.

"There's nothing much else to take." Evelyn looked thoughtful. "The soap, I suppose. Penhaligon's. Costs a fortune, and you have to go to Harrogate for it, but it lasts and, personally, I think it's worth the money." She was quiet for a while. "What's worrying is

Death in the Countryside

that someone was tramping about inside the shop, *fiddling* with things—bringing in flour, contaminating the premises—*that's* what's bothering me."

Ali walked around the courtyard, Wilson at her side. They reached the wall at the back where a gate led into Evelyn's garden, her house a short distance away through an orchard. It wouldn't be difficult to come through the garden and into the shop premises under cover of darkness. She unclipped Wilson's lead. "Go on boy," she said, "have a look, see what you can find."

Wilson trotted off, nose to the ground. "I'm a bit stumped, if I'm honest," Ali said, returning to where Evelyn waited. "It's not your typical breaking and entering. A prank, perhaps, kids mucking about?"

Evelyn snorted. "Kids would make a mess, empty a bag of flour. *My* flour. They'd hardly think to bring their own just so they could arrange it into a neat pile in the storeroom."

"No, I . . ."

"I'll tell you what I think," Evelyn said. "*I* think someone's playing games." She gazed at Ali, letting this sink in. "A way of saying I'm not safe, the shop's not safe. Who's brazen enough to come in when I'm at home, not even a two-minute walk away? Knowing I might hear something and come over to see what's going on? Catch them in the act." She gazed at Ali. "Then what?"

10

Ali spent longer with Evelyn than she'd intended, going back to the house with her, wanting to be sure she had better security at home than she did at the shop. She followed Evelyn, Wilson at her heel, in through a side door—one that opened with a turn of the handle, no key required—and along a cool, tiled hall into the kitchen. It was a big house, too big for one person. Perhaps all the years spent there with her late husband, and the fact the house was next door to the business, made the idea of living somewhere else unthinkable.

The kitchen was bright, the walls painted gray-green, copper pans on hooks along one wall, a dresser, mismatched crockery on every shelf. A baker's block. Evelyn caught Ali looking and said yes, she baked at home too: scones, carrot cake, brownies, lemon drizzle cupcakes. Things you wouldn't get in the shop. "It's what I love," she said, "the thing that gets me up in the morning." Ali thought about her mother's baking, the kitchen filled with too many scones, her father's valiant efforts to eat everything that came out of the oven, and wondered who Evelyn baked for.

Evelyn filled the kettle, fetched a cafetière from a cupboard, a canister of coffee. Cups and saucers, a milk jug from the dresser. A

Death in the Countryside

cake appeared on the table. "Orange and almond. You'll have to help me out, I'll never eat it."

Ali was conscious of Brian Bright waiting, time ticking on, but it seemed impossible to leave with Evelyn making coffee and warming cups, heating milk on the stove. Perhaps she *was* lonely. Running a business, managing a house this size, must take a toll. Every decision resting on the shoulders of a single individual, no one to share the load. It would be a lot for anyone. Clearly, Evelyn was capable, but even so. Might the arrival of Rise have prompted her to consider a different life, an easier life, one with fewer challenges? Ali didn't think so. Evelyn struck her as someone destined to pop up on the local news still running Hooley's as she celebrated her hundredth birthday.

"Don't you lock your doors?" she asked.

"Not the side one," Evelyn said. "I've been known to forget my keys, lock myself out, so I leave that one on the latch, just in case."

"It might be an idea to keep it locked, given you've had an intruder in the shop."

She shrugged. "I suppose if someone wants to get in, they'll find a way."

She didn't have to make it easy for them, Ali thought. "The business at the shop, you really think it was about making you feel threatened? Who'd want to do such a thing?"

Evelyn poured coffee and cut thick slices of cake. "I don't want to accuse anyone."

"No, course not."

She sighed. "Only I've never had trouble before. I'm *from* here, people know me, they've always shopped at Hooley's. And then, along comes another bakery. On the doorstep. And I get my first break-in. Interesting timing, don't you think? Coincidence?" She shook her head. "I know what those girls are saying about catering to a different crowd, not being in competition with me et cetera . . ."

57

she tailed off. Ali waited for her to continue. "I wonder, though, what sort of people would set up shop right opposite the local baker, the one that's been here for generations? *I* wouldn't. Never. Maybe they see an old woman, nearing the end of her shelf life, beyond caring"—she caught Ali's look—"and assume it's only a matter of time before I'm gone, Hooley's a thing of the past." Evelyn straightened her shoulders, gave Ali a defiant look. "Maybe they're thinking they'll give me a nudge, speed up the process. Well, if that's the plan, I'd say they don't know me very well."

Ali was going to have to speak to the women at Rise. Without accusing them. "We don't know this is anything to do with them," she pointed out.

"That's true," Evelyn said, in a manner that indicated she was in no doubt.

Ali found herself thinking of Harrogate and Beatrice Devlin, the interpreter. Witty, good company. Unjustly written off by her new neighbors on the grounds of age, of being alone. Was something similar in motion now with Evelyn? Was a sense of being sidelined, overtaken, something only too familiar to many older people, now coming Evelyn's way? Despite her show of confidence, the arrival of the cakery-bakery was bound to have had an impact. Hooley's, the business she cared about so passionately, under threat by a showy newcomer with its on-trend sourdough, its extravagant pastries. It must feel like a personal attack.

"What you said before about why someone would come into the shop like that," Ali said, trying to find a sensitive way of asking Evelyn if she felt unnerved. "Does it make you feel . . . vulnerable?"

Evelyn laughed, a hollow sound, unconvincing. "You're thinking I'm an old woman, it might be time to shut up shop?"

Ali protested. "That's not what I was getting at."

"Good. Because I'm going nowhere."

11

By the time Ali got to Brian Bright, he'd had time to do some research, which had led him to a recent high-profile missing person case where details had been posted in the online version of the local newspaper, police making appeals to the public for information, all within hours of a man being reported missing.

"Melody's been gone two nights now," he said, once they were in the sitting room, facing one another across the coffee table, "and nothing's being done, no sense of urgency." He looked exasperated, bemused. "You'd think she'd nipped out to the supermarket and taken a bit long getting back."

Ali looked at the story he'd printed out from the *News*. A man of fifty-two who'd vanished after a hospital appointment. He'd been given bad news (which wasn't made public) and had a history of depression. The family had good reason to think he might harm himself, hence the urgency attached to the case, the decision to publicize it without delay. Police officers found him that night, cold and disorientated, sitting on a bench next to the river where he liked to fish.

"Of course, that was *Harrogate*," Brian said, as if such matters were somehow elevated there, given special status, which Ali knew was not the case.

"It depends on the circumstances, what we know about the individual's state of mind, for instance," she said. She glanced at the mantelpiece where the photo of Brian's late wife gazed down at her.

"It's a postcode lottery, you mean," he said.

"I assure you it's not. I'm taking Melody's disappearance seriously." Two nights, time for almost anything to have happened. Ali had checked with the station. No reports of accidents locally, no hospital admissions. Still. "It's just that . . ." she hesitated.

Brian kept his eyes on her, waiting for her to explain. "We don't have anything to say she was in a distressed state or in any way . . . vulnerable." That word again. She held Brian's gaze. If there was something he had failed to mention, now was the time. He stayed silent. She went on, "It's possible she simply left. For reasons we don't yet understand."

Brian looked aghast. "*Left*?" He shook his head, the look he gave Ali letting her know he considered this impossible. "Forgive me, Sergeant Wren, but if your husband vanished and you couldn't contact him—had no idea where he'd gone—would you not be concerned?"

"Yes, of course."

He crossed his arms tightly across his chest. "And rightly so. I don't think I'm being unreasonable to ask for a press conference."

Ali knew that wasn't an option, not yet. There were other avenues to explore first. She had already spoken to her boss at Skipden about what to do next. Given what they knew so far, Chief Superintendent Jacob Freeman had decided there was no immediate cause for alarm, suggesting Ali dig deeper into Brian, find out what she could about the circumstances of the death of the first Mrs. Bright. Look at where Melody might have gone. Friends, family. "There must be names, favorite places—something he can give you," Freeman said. Was Brian Bright a man who'd be aware if his wife was dissatisfied, planning to go? the Chief Super asked. Ali had her doubts.

Death in the Countryside

Brian was on his feet, pacing up and down between the sofa and the coffee table, muttering about a two-tier system of policing, everything geared to what he called the townies.

"Have you eaten?" Ali asked, stopping him in his tracks.

"What? No. I don't have much of an appetite."

"Would you like me to make you something?"

He looked puzzled. "I'm not hungry. And shouldn't you be looking for my wife?"

"I still need to ask you some questions. We can chat while you eat." She gave him an appraising look. The day before, she had thought he looked younger than his years. Now he looked older. "You won't be much good to anyone if you don't keep your strength up."

Brian sat at the kitchen table while she looked in cupboards, finding a dozen eggs, ripe tomatoes in a bowl. There was strong cheddar in the fridge, one of Evelyn's crusty white loaves in the bread bin. She grated cheese and chopped a tomato, beat three eggs, pouring them into a pan of foaming butter. Nick was the one who made omelettes at home, she tended to overcook them and burn the bottom, something that only became apparent when she folded them in half. She took more care with Brian's and when she put it in front of him, he seemed surprised, as if he hadn't noticed what she was doing.

"Start," she said, "I'll make some coffee."

By the time she sat down, he was pushing a piece of buttered bread around the plate, mopping up the last of the omelette. "Thank you, that was very good," he said awkwardly.

"I wonder, now you've had some time to think, is there anyone Melody might get in touch with? Close friend, someone she might not see much of? Family?"

He sat thinking. Glanced at Ali over the rim of his coffee cup. "A sister, Lillian, but I wouldn't say they're close. Lives in Newcastle. Melody goes up to see her, spends the day. I've not met her,

61

couldn't tell you much about her. Dealing with Lillian was like walking on eggshells, Melody always said. For years they had nothing to do with each other." A shrug. He went and found an address book with Lillian's number. Ali made a note.

"What about friends in Heft?"

"No one she's close to"—he stopped abruptly, as if he'd just remembered something significant and was working out whether to mention it—"just people she passes the time of day with. When she's out shopping, that kind of thing."

Ali gave him a sharp look. "You seemed about to say something."

He shook his head, pushed his plate to one side.

She pressed on. "Church, the WI?"

"Didn't bother with any of that."

Ali was getting desperate. Was Melody a walker, might she have gone into the Dales on her own? No, Brian said. "Hobbies?"

"Pottery," he said eventually. "She started going a few months back, a place in Skipden."

At last.

12

The pottery studio was on the outskirts of town in what looked like an old livestock shed at the side of a farmhouse, its windows dark and blank. It was hard to tell if anyone actually lived there. Other than a sign that read Forbes-Cliff, the surname of the potter, there were no obvious indications the place was in use. The barn door, wooden, dilapidated, was open a crack and Ali, Wilson at her heel, gave a knock before heaving at it and squeezing inside. It was chilly, colder than outside, the place littered with pots of different shapes and sizes—on worktops, the floor, industrial-style racks along the walls—a few brightly painted and glossy, most bare, awaiting their finishing touches. Ali gazed about her. As a workplace, it felt chaotic, disordered. And yet Carla Forbes-Cliff was successful, her work in demand, the large pieces selling for hundreds of pounds. Ali had seen Carla on TV, a local news item about an exhibition of her work that was being staged in a smart gallery in York. Clearly, she had no need of a fancy studio to create fine art.

Ali called out, "Hello." No answer. She unclipped Wilson, signaled for him to go ahead, and followed as he picked his way among the clutter that took up much of the floor. There was a color theme, Ali realized, each decorated pot bearing Forbes-Cliff's signature wildflower design, hand-painted a vibrant grassy green with splashes of yellow and white, vermilion.

At the back of the workshop, a woman in an oversized jumper, corduroy trousers with holes in the knees, was working a piece of clay, deep in concentration. Wilson stopped, glanced at Ali.

"Hello?" Ali tried again. "Excuse me."

Carla Forbes-Cliff looked up, surprised. Serious brown eyes, paint on her chin. "Sorry, I was miles away. Give me a minute, would you?" The clay, almost magically it seemed to Ali, transformed into a shallow bowl. Carla sat back, satisfied. "What can I do for you, Officer?"

Ali explained about Melody Bright and asked when she had last seen her.

"She was here on Saturday morning." The day she went missing. "Called in to collect a pot I'd fired for her. It was a bowl, rather lovely, actually."

"Did she say where she was going?"

"Home, at least I assumed so."

"Was there anything you noticed that seemed out of the ordinary?" Ali asked. Was she agitated, anxious? In a hurry?

"Well, I wouldn't usually see her outside of classes, so that was unusual, but she'd phoned and asked to swing by for the pot." Carla was quiet, thinking back. "She did say she couldn't make the next few classes, something about a prior commitment."

That was all she knew. She was easygoing when it came to her weekly classes. If a student had to miss a few for one reason or another, it was fine with her. "Sorry if that's not very helpful," she said. "I didn't know her that well."

It was something, anyway.

Ali headed into Skipden to update the Chief Superintendent. Jacob Freeman had a shaved head, a steady gaze. Ex-military, a keen marathon runner, the walls of his office decorated with photos from

Death in the Countryside

races he'd run, raising money for a charity that worked with ex-soldiers left damaged by their experience of fighting in Iraq, Afghanistan. His efforts had earned him an OBE.

Freeman happened to love dogs and occasionally sounded off on the various and numerous qualities that made them superior to most people ("Loyalty, integrity. Train them and you can trust them to follow commands without question, without messing things up. Unlike some I could mention.") He had a border collie called Doris who went with him on his morning runs and would have come to work with him if he could have wangled it. All this meant Wilson's presence guaranteed Ali an enthusiastic welcome at Skipden. She unclipped his lead so he could charge into Freeman's office, tail wagging, and the boss crouched and fussed over the dog. "What's that? You've missed me? I've missed you, boy. Here, see what I've got for you." Magically, a small yellow tin appeared, and Wilson, knowing the drill, sat nicely, carefully taking the treats Freeman fed him, ensuring not a single crumb went on the carpet, all the while the Chief Super chatting away, shaking the dog's paw, calling him a clever lad, smart, keen. "You could teach some of my lot downstairs a thing or two about bucking up their attitude, I'll get you in for the next training day."

How different things would be, Ali mused, watching Freeman give Wilson another treat—"that's your last"—if the boss wasn't a dog lover.

Once the Chief Super was back in his seat, Wilson settled at his side, Ali briefed him on Melody Bright.

"Gut feeling?" Freeman asked once she'd finished.

"She might have walked out on her husband, simple as that."

He considered this. "Why not just tell him, then—leave a note, avoid all the drama?"

"Maybe she thought he'd stop her. I don't mean physically restrain her, just beg her to stay, say he's lost without her, he wouldn't cope." Which was true. He certainly couldn't find his way round the kitchen. Ali was already forming an impression of Brian, she realized. Yet when it came to Melody, the kind of woman she was, she had little so far to go on. "It can be hard to walk out on someone who's determined to cling on," she said.

Freeman nodded, patted the spaniel's head. "She's right there, isn't she?" Talking to Wilson, not Ali. "I lost count of the number of times my little sister, Precious, left her husband only to go back. *That's it*, she'd say, *I've had enough*, and we'd all get behind her. Then back she'd go—*after* we'd all agreed he was a right so and so, of course." He rolled his eyes at Ali. "*But this time it's different*, she'd say, *he's promised to change*. Et cetera. Never did."

Ali was intrigued. Freeman rarely shared anything personal. A sister, Precious. Well, well. Not that he was confiding in Ali but Wilson, who was so often the one people entrusted with their secrets. "Believe me, the definition of madness," Freeman said, stroking Wilson's ear, "is doing the same thing over and over, thinking you'll get a different outcome."

Ali's gaze strayed to the wall, to the pictures of Freeman in running gear, slender, long-limbed, tackling marathons in New York, Boston, Sydney. Alongside, a formal portrait from his time at Sandhurst prior to joining the Force showed a different Freeman—distinguished in his uniform, all braid and ribbons, medals on his dress jacket. She knew nothing about his Sandhurst era and hoped that one day he might spill the beans on that chapter to Wilson while she eavesdropped. Going back twenty or so years, more, he would have been one of very few Black recruits at the elite military academy. "Madness," he said again. Wilson gazed up at him, rapt, although whether that was more to do with the yellow treat tin, still in view on the edge of the desk, was debatable. Ali chanced an interruption. "And are they still together? Precious . . . and her other half."

Freeman turned to look at her. "They are not, no. She finally saw the light. Took her about twenty years, mind." He pulled a face. "Never get involved in other people's marriages, Wren," he said.

"And if you're asked for an opinion don't give it. Never ends well, take it from me."

Neither spoke for a moment. "Brian mentioned Melody has a sister. Not exactly best of friends, he says, but I'll speak to her." She had already left messages for Lillian who, so far, had not called back. Ali wondered if she was away. Freeman nodded. "Anything fishy on the late Mrs. Bright?"

"Not as far as I can tell."

"A man who manages to lose two wives ... you wonder if there's something going on." Addressing this to Wilson, who sat up, eyes on Freeman, paying close attention.

Ali's conversation with Brian about his first wife had been uncomfortable. It was clear he hadn't wanted to go there and only when she pressed did a stilted account emerge of the day Dolores died. They'd been out for Sunday lunch, he said, and were coming home across the moors. February, the forecast poor, the road not one you'd use if you were expecting snow. Dolores liked it, though. Wild, she said, bleak. The weather had turned and caught them out, snow, pelting down. Brian was driving, taking his time, hardly able to see the road, the wipers not doing much. The car was old but sound; how it ended up wrecked, he didn't know. He considered himself a good driver, safe, and yet it had to have been him, he must have lost control, misjudged the bend, because afterward when the car was checked over, it was deemed in good order. A Hillman Imp, he said, one of the first ones made. No seatbelts. He hit his head—on the steering wheel, the windscreen, he wasn't sure—Dolores didn't survive. The inquest recorded a verdict of accidental death, the coroner making a point of saying Brian was not responsible.

Not that it changed how he felt. One way or another, he was to blame.

His wife was remarkable, he said. Exceptional. They'd met at a dance, Brian twenty-one, Dolores just nineteen and full of life, spirited. The DJ played "Mony Mony," and he asked her to dance.

"Everlasting Love," "Build Me Up Buttercup." Singles he'd bought in his teens, still had. Dolores could dance, he wasn't bad. "You're thinking what she was doing marrying me?" Ali wasn't. She was picturing the younger Brian, his life in front of him, a man who loved pop music and went dancing and was confident. A man who had little in common with the dejected soul facing her now.

Life took it out of you. Death, loss, certainly did.

"I was her anchor, her touchstone," he told Ali. "That was what she always said." They were married almost twenty years.

Ali was beginning to grasp why Dolores's picture was on the mantelpiece, why Brian felt the need to keep her center stage. Guilt. Grief. Regret. A life ended too soon. "What did she do?" she asked.

"She painted. She was at college when we met. Francis Bacon, he was her inspiration, if that means anything." Her pictures—figures, abstracts, largely monochrome—now hung in the sitting room, on the staircase, the landing. The one in Brian's office a self-portrait. He was right, she was talented.

Poor Dolores, Ali thought. Poor Melody, having to live with her ghost. And Brian, who still called Dolores his wife. As if Melody was a stand-in, not the real thing. Maybe she had realized things would never change, and that was why she had gone.

"Dolores Bright died in a car crash," Ali said to Freeman. "Brian driving. The weather turned foul and they came off the road on the moors. No suspicious circumstances, an accidental death verdict."

"Nothing more to it than that?"

"I've asked for the coroner's report, and I'll see what there is in the newspaper cuttings from the time. It was 1994, there's nothing online."

"What do you make of him? Genuine? Something to hide?"

"Ordinary, hardworking. His business provides the cars they use on *The Beat*." The day Melody left, Brian was on set dropping off a car. Waiting around to collect another. "From what I saw in

Death in the Countryside

the house, the clothes hanging in Melody's wardrobe, they're comfortably off. Very, I'd say." She hesitated. "He's not a man who copes well on his own." And yet, somehow, he had when Dolores died. "Baked beans, soup," he said, with a shrug when she asked. "Hasn't a clue when it comes to household appliances, can't even work the oven." She caught Freeman's look. "Melody took care of that side of things."

Freeman nodded. "Course, we've seen this before, bloke frantic about their 'missing' wife and it turns out it's all an act—they've done her in, then do what they can to throw us off the scent."

"I don't think that's him, sir."

"No, well, I hope you're right."

"He was asking . . ." she hesitated. "About doing a press conference, getting the word out."

"I'm not inclined to go down that road, not so soon."

Ali suggested putting up posters appealing for information. If Brian Bright had harmed his wife, he might just crack under the strain of seeing Melody smiling back at him from shop windows and lampposts every time he went into town. Freeman agreed.

He thought for a moment. "I had a case, a chap whose wife died. He meets someone at a bereavement group. Lovely guy, you'd think. Kind, thoughtful, understanding." He gave Wilson a knowing look. "Perfect, you might think. Then the second wife goes missing and he's in a dreadful state, puts on a convincing show of being beside himself. We put him in front of the cameras, got him to do an appeal—which he sailed through." Ali knew what was coming. "He'd killed both of them. The new wife was wealthy, generous with it as well—he didn't even have to work—but it wasn't enough. Greedy so-and-so wanted to get his hands on the lot." He gave Ali a sharp look. "This isn't going to turn out to be one of those, is it?"

"No, sir."

She hoped not.

69

13

On the Tuesday, two days after Brian had reported his wife missing, a piece went up on the website of the *News*. A few lines. Flimsy on detail. Ali hadn't been able to establish what Melody was wearing when she was last seen. Brian didn't know, Carla Forbes-Cliff wasn't sure. It might have been a white shirt and what Brian called floaty trousers. Or stretchy ones with a stripe down the leg, the kind of thing you'd think were for the gym but seemed as much for going out in nowadays. The last time Ali had heard anyone say nowadays was on Radio 2, a discussion on Jeremy Vine's show. Melody was fond of jackets that didn't have sleeves, Brian said. A gilet? Ali asked. He looked blank. Moments later his face lit up. He had remembered something. A scarf, he said, definitely. It was the one thing he was sure of. She always had one with her, ever since she'd found a hedgehog curled up in the road one day, wrapped it in her scarf, something so delicate the animal's prickles put holes in the fabric, then took the little chap to a sanctuary where they identified him as a girl and named her Liberty after the turquoise print draped about her when she arrived. Once in an incubator with food and water, Liberty had perked right up. Melody talked about it for ages and from then on never left the house without taking a scarf. In case she had to conduct another rescue of some kind.

Death in the Countryside

Ali had looked again in Melody's wardrobe, hoping to jog Brian's memory. White shirts, Ali counted seven; wide-legged trousers; capri pants, the stretchy gym-style Brian had mentioned. Gilets, one dressy with sheer panels, another in utilitarian khaki, one fashioned from faux fur. Nothing as obvious as empty hangers to indicate where items had been removed. Brian went through the clothes with Ali but couldn't be sure what, if anything, was missing. They looked through the drawers containing her scarves, some still with their tags on. Ali loosened the ribbon on an orange box, lifting the lid to reveal an exquisite silk square, the designer's certificate of authentication, Brian, watching, saying, "I got her that one. I don't think she ever wore it."

Ali wasn't expecting much from the appeal in the *News*, which said little other than that Melody had gone somewhere in her car and not come home. Nothing traumatic hinted at, no mention of mental health worries. Not enough to make readers concerned for her. Not yet. And, of course, there was the question of her age. Ali knew that a woman of sixty-six was unlikely to generate the same level of interest as, say, an attractive twenty-something. Frustratingly, it was also to Melody's disadvantage that she wasn't a mother, a grandmother, since in the context of a missing person, as far as the media were concerned, such things mattered. *Loving mother. Much-loved grandmother.* Ideally, this was how the *News* would have wanted to describe Melody for their readers. Instead they had to settle for *wife*, which carried considerably less emotional weight. There was the photo, too, which really needed to be Instagram perfect, taken with the aid of a filter, to be awarded maximum and repeated exposure. Melody's snapshot, sadly, was just not sufficiently eye-catching.

Ali warned Brian not to get his hopes up. Privately, she hoped Melody would see the piece in the *News* and get in touch, confirm she was alive and well, not missing at all—although it would be crushing for Brian if she had indeed left of her own accord. Only

Maria Malone

three calls came in, the first from an elderly man who thought Melody might have stopped for him at a pedestrian crossing. The car was green, or black (or dark gray?) if that was of any help, the driver a lady, wavy hair, blonde (or light gray?) and sunglasses. She had smiled at him. Lovely smile, genuine. Could she be the missing woman? he wondered. The operator who logged the call said she got the impression he simply wanted to talk since, entirely unprompted, as soon as she attempted to wind up the conversation, he swerved smartly off the subject of Melody and on to the volunteering work he'd done since retiring—some sort of literacy program, working with young offenders—seeming to forget all about his original reason for getting in touch. The others who rang in were even less promising. People keen to help but when pressed unable to offer anything useful.

Later that day, Ali sat at a desk in the archive library of the evening newspaper in Bradford, a folder with a pile of cuttings from 1994 in front of her, Wilson under the desk, his chin resting on her foot. The inquest into the accident in which Dolores Bright had died had been reported in detail. As Brian had told her, the change in weather was sudden, the conditions abysmal. No witnesses. All the coroner had to go on was what Brian could tell him and since he remembered little, it was sketchy. The car was discovered maybe an hour or so after it came off the road by a farmer checking his livestock, its front end rammed into a rock, Brian slumped on the steering wheel, the windscreen shattered, Dolores on her back in the snow, her head resting on a boulder. As if she were simply lying down. Her neck broken.

Brian's explanation for choosing to drive over the moors, recklessly some might have said, given you only had to look at the sky that day to know snow was coming, was accepted. Dolores was an artist, Scar Moor a place she loved for what she called its savage

Death in the Countryside

landscape. The fact the weather was about to change only made her more insistent on going that way.

Brian hadn't been drinking. The car, a 1963 model, one of the first Imps made, was mechanically sound. No seatbelts, which weren't required in a car that age. A tragedy, but one that was deemed to be no one's fault.

There were photos of the mangled car, of Dolores in a studio studying a canvas almost as tall as her, paint on the floor, on her overalls. With Brian on their wedding day in 1975, her long dress flaring out at the hem. Brian in a suit with wide lapels over a waist-coat, shirt open at the neck. No tie. It was the photo of Brian that stopped Ali in her tracks. Beaming at his bride, a shock of dark hair that grazed his shoulders. Good looking, striking even. Jim Morrison, a young George Harrison.

She found a profile piece on Dolores, whose work had been exhibited at galleries in Bradford and Leeds. *Artist killed in horror smash*. A feature on Brian, an entrepreneur who'd turned his passion for old cars into a business. The picture (one that was taken before the accident, Ali guessed) showed him next to an elegant saloon car which, according to the caption, had recently featured in a medical drama.

Dolores's funeral was there too, the hearse in front of St. Oswald's Church, Brian, head bowed. A headline that spoke of a gifted artist, a life cut short.

Ali made notes, all the while thinking about Melody. How much about his past had she known, wanted to know? When she married Brian, did she truly understand the depth of the tragedy he had suffered and how it had left him? Stuck in another time, forever blaming himself for his wife's death. Did he tell Melody? Did she ask? Perhaps she hadn't wanted to go there, hadn't wanted to lift the lid on Pandora's Box. She couldn't have seen the press cuttings, not without making an appointment to come into the newspaper archives library, and, according to the librarian, prior to Ali, the last time they were requested was in 1995 when Brett McSweeney, one of the reporters, did a "one year on" piece. Ali had it in front of her, a bringing together of everything known about the couple with the addition of a single previously unseen photograph that showed the terraced house in Wibsey once shared by Dolores and Brian.

Ali had found nothing suspicious, nothing to make her think Brian hadn't been honest with her about his past. She read through the account of the inquest again. Nobody objecting to the accidental verdict, nobody saying anything critical.

Nothing to ring any alarm bells.

14

Ali checked her messages before leaving Bradford. Still nothing from Melody's sister, Lillian. A WhatsApp from Nick with a photo of the inside of a church: gleaming mahogany pews, stained glass above an altar perched high above the nave. Ali had never seen anything like it. *Found my church*, he wrote. *Wow, where?* Ali replied. St. *Maurice's, a place called Burdon.* She couldn't think where that was. *Looks amazing*, she wrote. A heart emoji came back. *Off to the pub now . . . work!* She sent him a thumbs up, two hearts.

There were voicemails, left when she was in the newspaper library, her phone on silent, one from Nick gushing about the church, hidden at the end of a road he'd almost missed. "There's a sign but you'd never see it, it's covered in ivy." The next message was from Roger Felton, who lived in the old vicarage in Heft next to St. Michael's and was in the habit of making a note of the registration plates of anyone parked in the disabled bay without displaying a Blue Badge. Roger, a surveyor, almost but not quite retired, was still prepared to do the odd bit of freelancing if the property in question proved sufficiently interesting. In the course of a fifty-year career he had seen inside most of the houses in Heft at some point. When Ali asked if he'd do the survey on Larkspur, he told her there was no need, he'd done one before (twice, in fact) and knew the place inside out. It was solid, she and Nick could take his word for it.

In his job, Roger had become used to writing lengthy and detailed reports, a task he enjoyed. Simply because he was no longer working full-time, he saw no reason to stop and, at least once a month, would submit a document—beautifully written, forensic in its detail—to Ali, mainly regarding parking misdemeanors at St. Michael's. While she sympathized with his complaints, she found his methods questionable. Over time, however, Roger—and his reports—grew on her. He took to providing illustrations—photos of cars shoddily parked, closeups of dashboards missing a Blue Badge. Sometimes, if he happened to see the perpetrators in the act, he would add a description, a few lines that painted a picture: "Male, forties, T-shirt, illegible message scrawled on the back (looked to have been done with a paintbrush and very little care), shorts that would have benefited from having an iron run over them." Female accomplice, similar age, multicolored trainers. Against Ali's advice, Roger had printed up an official-looking notice outlining parking restrictions and warning of possible prosecution, which he left on offenders' windscreens. From his vantage point in his own front garden, he logged the reactions of car owners, which ranged from confused to apoplectic, on returning to find what looked like a fixed penalty notice on their vehicle.

She listened to his message now, not entirely sure where he was going with it. "We were due a parcel today," he began, "something Phoebe ordered. I suppose I ought to say what it was, since that's relevant"—a pause, and the sound of him asking his wife something—"that's right, a commemorative plate to do with a coal mine in"—another pause, a further muffled exchange—"a place called . . . Rigsby? *Rigby.* You'd have to get Phoebe to tell you why it's of particular interest, I'm sure she has her reasons. Anyway, it came today. We knew what time it was expected, and we were here. I'd been at the bowls club but made sure to be back. Practice

Death in the Countryside

session, we've a match against Litton at the weekend . . ." Ali listened, wondering if he was ever going to get to the point. Before he did, he was out of time. A second message followed. "I don't know what happened there, Sergeant Wren," Roger began. "I was cut off. I don't *think* it was my end, although sometimes the signal drops out, nothing to say why." A pause. "Where were we? That's right, *Rigby*. The plate we were expecting was due between 13.22 and 14.22—no idea why they have to be quite so precise about the times, as if two minutes here or there is going to matter . . ."

Ali wasn't sure she could bear any more. She dialed Roger's number. "It's Ali Wren."

"Ah, Sergeant Wren, thank you for getting back to me. Did you get my message?"

"Something about a parcel?"

"Which we made a *point* of being here for. Not that I mind especially, I mean if you order something online, whatever it is, it does mean you ought to be at home when the items you've requested arrive. Don't you agree? Otherwise, well let's just say problems can arise. While the cat's away, if you follow. We learned that the hard way with the rose bushes we ordered—from a reputable supplier, I might add—"

Ali stopped him. "Roger, I'm on my way back to Heft. Shall I call in? It might be easier, to be honest, I'm struggling to hear you." She could make out perfectly well what he was saying, but at this rate wasn't convinced he'd ever get round to telling her whatever it was that had prompted him to get in touch in the first place.

She ended the call and turned to Wilson. "We're going to see Roger," she said. "You like him, don't you?" Wilson looked keen.

Roger and Phoebe Felton were dog lovers who talked a great deal about their late standard poodle, Rory. Although Rory had died a good many years before, his memory was very much alive, his picture all over the house—on the sideboard, the mantelpiece, almost every windowsill, even above the washbasin in the downstairs loo. Roger frequently brought Rory into the conversation, recounting his various exploits, how as a puppy he had chewed his owners' shoes—"one shoe from each pair we'd left in the hallway," he'd say, chuckling. "Every pair ruined!"

She parked (legally) at the side of the church, Wilson, trotting on ahead to the front door of the old rectory.

Roger, tall, broad-shouldered, short graying hair, was in smart twill trousers, a check shirt, polka dot tie. He ushered them in, fussing over Wilson, promising him a treat. She was going to have to put her foot down regarding treats.

The house was quiet, Phoebe at one of her committee meetings, Roger said, which was "just as well" since he was "in the bad books." He showed them into the sitting room. Ali perched on the sofa, not wanting to get comfortable, hoping whatever it was wouldn't take long. Wilson, whose ears had pricked up at the mention of "treat" stuck close to Roger, who sank into an armchair. "What have we got here then?" Roger asked Wilson, producing a handful of dried snacks from his pocket, holding one up so the dog could see it. Wilson sat, one paw resting on the man's foot. "Good boy," Roger told him, holding his hand flat so Wilson could help himself. Ali watched for crumbs landing on what looked to be an expensive carpet square, possibly an antique. Remarkably, there were none. Wilson really was a dainty eater.

"Seeing you sitting there," Roger said, turning to her, "reminds me of how Rory used to sit on the settee with us watching TV. He'd have his bottom *on* the seat, front paws on the carpet! Sitting up, eyes glued to the box—just like us!"

She smiled. "He sounds quite a character."

"Oh, he was," Roger agreed, lost for a moment in his thoughts.

"The delivery you wanted to tell me about," Ali prompted.

"Of course. We were in, although really and truly I don't know why they bother giving you a time because no one came to the

Death in the Countryside

door. Didn't knock, didn't ring the bell—which is working, by the way, I checked—nothing. They expect you to be mind readers."

"So they didn't leave the parcel?" Ali said.

"Oh, they *left* it—flung it over the hedge onto the drive. Just sitting there, it was." He looked at her, perplexed. "Why would you do that with something that's clearly marked 'fragile' on the box? I mean to say, a *plate*."

Ali was thinking that maybe the driver was running late, that his schedule didn't allow time for parking and unlatching a gate, walking up what was a fairly long drive, then ringing a bell and waiting for someone to answer the door. Ever since seeing *Sorry We Missed You* she had felt sympathy for delivery drivers, often under pressure, not always well paid. All the same, she took Roger's point.

"So, when you found the parcel—the plate—was it damaged?"

"I couldn't say." Roger absent-mindedly stroked Wilson, who still had an eye on the pocket the treats had come from. Ali quietly clicked her fingers, causing him to glance across and send a sheepish look her way. He knew he wasn't allowed to beg for food.

"So the plate *wasn't* broken?" she asked.

"Yes! In pieces! Once the delivery slot had been and gone, I went out, thought I might as well do another hour at the bowls club, I mean, you don't want to be shown up, do you? Most of the Litton team are a bit younger than our chaps, think they've got the edge."

Ali gazed at him, no further forward.

"So, I said to Phoebe I'd be an hour or so and she stayed in—in case the parcel arrived, you know?" Ali nodded. "I got the car out of the garage and"—he pulled a face—"*felt* something as I was going down the drive, a sort of extra *crunch* on the gravel, if you like. The plate, of course, which in my defense I didn't know was there. I drove right over it! Now *I'm* in trouble"—a glance at Wilson—"the doghouse, if you like, for breaking the thing. *If* I did.

For all anyone knows, it was in bits before I went over it." He turned to Wilson. "Life's not fair, is it boy?"

Ali said, "Right, I see."

"I can show you, if you like," Roger said, getting his phone out. "We've got one of those cameras on the doorbell, it's all there." Ali went over. "Here we are."

The footage showed a van pull up in front of the house and double park. In fairness, it was murder to get parked anywhere near Roger and Phoebe during the day. A chap got out, approached the gate, and hurled the parcel over it. It all took just a few seconds.

"See what's going on here, fella?" Roger asked Wilson. "See what we have to put up with? I reckon that plate was shattered long before I went anywhere near it."

Ali was used to hearing grievances aired directly to Wilson while she looked on. As if he was the one who would put things right. Simply having him there seemed to make most people feel better straight away. "That's what goes on in this day and age," Roger continued. "Progress, so I'm told." Rolling his eyes, scratching the dog's ear. "Between you and me, and I wouldn't like this to find its way back to Phoebe, I wasn't all that struck on the plate anyway. I don't even know where we'd have put it. Somewhere you wouldn't have to look at it, hopefully." He chuckled, gave the dog a knowing look. "What's that? Drive over it deliberately? Never! It was an accident, M'lud!"

Ali helped him upload a copy of the damning footage to the retailer in question and arrange for the ruined package to be collected.

"They won't send another one, will they?" he asked hopefully.

"Not if you request a refund," Ali advised.

"Thank you," Roger said, ticking the relevant box. "And Sergeant Wren, if Mrs. Felton should ask why I didn't arrange a

Death in the Countryside

replacement, can we say I meant to, I must have got mixed up. A small fib."

Ali gave him a stern look. "You're on a slippery slope there."

His eyes pleaded with her. "Just trying to do what's best. Imagine if we had another performance like today, more upset, another damaged item quite possibly. It's not good for the stress levels and we're both getting on . . ."

She raised her hands in a gesture of defeat. "You win, Roger, I won't say a word."

15

Brian Bright was at a loss. Usually, when he got back from work, Melody was in the kitchen cooking, the radio on, *Just a Minute, I'm Sorry I Haven't A Clue*, something light, silly, the kind of thing they both enjoyed. He'd smell onions, garlic, something in the oven. She was a good cook, constantly tearing recipes out of the color supplements, a magazine, poring over her considerable collection of cookery books, keen to try something new. Sometimes, when she said what she was cooking, he had no idea what to expect until it was put in front of him and, occasionally, turned out to be something familiar. Cassoulet, for instance, what he'd have called sausage casserole, albeit a fancy one. French, Melody said, when he expressed an interest. They'd had it recently and it was lovely, one of his favorites, the sauce rich and spicy, the sausages dense and herby.

He stood now at the fridge, doors open, scanning the shelves. What he'd give now for one of Melody's meals. It didn't have to be the sausage casserole, the *cassoulet*, anything would do. Even the mixed bean affair, which, being honest, he wasn't keen on, but professed to like because Melody had once said it was a devil to make.

He selected a large piece of fruit and examined it, not sure what it was. A small melon? He put on his specs and studied the label.

Death in the Countryside

Mango. What did you do with a mango? Did it have to be peeled? Perhaps the skin was edible? He felt ignorant, unsophisticated. A man of his age defeated by a humble melon. *Mango.*

He didn't have much of an appetite and the contents of the fridge failed to tempt him. Cheese. He could have cheese and biscuits. An apple. As Sergeant Wren had pointed out, he needed to eat. He had a business to run, even if his wife was missing.

He continued to gaze at the fridge. Was cheese what he really wanted—again? He should have paid more attention to how Sergeant Wren had made that omelette. It seemed to take mere moments. He still had half a dozen eggs. How hard could an omelette be? He put the mango back, his thoughts returning to Melody, sensing he had let her down, not been the man she was hoping for. He had never pretended to be anything other than who he was: reliable, straightforward. Not terribly interesting, perhaps, but he did his best. And he was generous. He tried. Even took her with him once or twice to some of the TV shows he supplied cars to, not that she seemed at all impressed.

The kettle was boiling. He poured water onto a teabag using a mug from breakfast, one he'd only rinsed rather than washed properly. Melody wouldn't have stood for that. But Melody wasn't here, was she? And he was having to make do. He stirred the tea, added milk, left the spoon in the cup. She had pulled him up over that before, drinking tea and coffee with the spoon still in the cup, but where was the harm? It was something he'd done since he was a boy, something he could never imagine undoing, not now, not at his time of life. Some things were too ingrained. Plus, not everyone found it annoying, a harmless habit to take him to task over. Dolores had never minded.

He reached for the block of cheddar. There was pickle somewhere, but he hadn't the energy to look for it. Cheese would do. And bread, even though it was a few days old. If he remembered, he'd call in at Hooley's, get a fresh loaf. He ended up with a cheese sandwich for the second night in a row, letting the tea go cold, pouring a glass of red wine instead, emptying crisps into a bowl, which made it seem more of a meal.

He found a certain pleasure in sitting at the table, no one watching, able to do as he pleased. His manners were far from perfect—he still had trouble if there was too much cutlery in front of him. His mother had paid little attention to such things. She was not the kind to berate a small boy for using the wrong knife or dunking bread and butter in his tea, making a sandwich out of whatever she put on his plate. They'd always had bread and butter on the table. Not anymore, not with dinner, unless it was garlic bread or focaccia, sometimes ciabatta served with olive oil and balsamic vinegar. Yet some of the sauces Melody made cried out for bread to mop them up. He peeled open the sandwich on his plate and inserted a few of the crisps, their salty crunch a perfect companion for the strong cheddar. Suddenly, he had a hankering for a plate of chips, the way his mother made them. Chips with soft white bread, lots of butter, salt, brown sauce. Memories flooded back. Thinking about it, that was the kind of simple food he loved. He looked about him. Did they even have a chip pan? The blocks of lard needed to make proper chips? When he was growing up the chip pan lived on the stove top. Such things probably no longer existed. If Melody came back—*when*—he would talk to her about getting one.

Dolores had not been much of a cook. She had neither the time nor the patience. When she was in her studio painting, she'd lose track of everything. Often, he came home from work to an empty house. While he waited for her, he would put something on the record player, turn it up loud: The Beach Boys, Dusty Springfield, the Beatles. *Rubber Soul* played to death.

When Ali Wren asked about the crash he'd felt his heart rate shoot up. Talking about it wasn't something he wanted to do, especially as he couldn't see how something from so long ago could

Death in the Countryside

have any bearing on what was happening now, but she was insistent, saying things like, *you never know*, and *it might be helpful*. He couldn't see how. Perhaps she wondered if there'd been more to it than a tragic accident. If she did, she didn't say. The strange thing was that, in the event, talking about Dolores, having someone listen, felt comforting. Sitting in the kitchen, drinking tea Ali Wren had made, that dog of hers resting its chin on his foot, he had described the snow, not being able to see the road, how the sky, the moorland changed in an instant, everything white, no longer a road he knew well, one he had driven on countless times, but a featureless expanse, a wasteland. Pressing on anyway because going on rather than turning back seemed the right thing to do, the only thing, the Imp's wipers making frantic, hopeless efforts to keep the windscreen clear. And then, a collision—a mound, its snowy blanket concealing a boulder. He had left the road and hit it, how he didn't know.

Now and then she had nodded, jotted something in her notebook. Mostly, she simply listened, while under the table Wilson shifted position and sighed, as if in sympathy, as if he understood, the presence of the dog soothing, Brian realized.

He finished his sandwich, tipped more crisps into the bowl, and poured another glass of wine.

The appeal in the *News* had made no difference. No calls worthy of following up, Ali Wren said. Didn't people care? His wife had not been seen since Saturday—four long days—and the police, it seemed, were more interested in him, his past, his first marriage. None of which, in his view, bore any relevance to what was happening now. He thought back to the night before Melody left. Not *left*, he corrected, *went missing*, since he was still unable to accept that she might have chosen to go. Had there been clues something was wrong? Something he had failed to notice? He closed his eyes for a moment, concentrating hard, struggling to recall what they'd talked about over dinner that night. They always

85

had fish on a Friday. Not the battered kind he'd grown up with, never the chips he craved. Pan-fried salmon, cod with capers and brown butter, sea bass. He wasn't complaining, it always tasted good. He'd arrived home excited about an old Rover he'd been to look at. Chap in Bradford who'd inherited it from his grandfather, had it hidden away in the garage for years. No one even knew it was there. Eight thousand miles on the clock! One of those rare finds, the kind you dreamed of, the moment when the garage door opened to reveal a gem—gleaming, preserved, immaculate. He had brought home a bottle of prosecco, the good stuff, to celebrate. Come to think of it, he might have gone on a bit much about the Rover, but old classics were his passion. He lived for those moments. And it was thanks to the cars they were comfortably off. The cars paid for all those designer scarves, some (many) still in their wrapping, never worn. A couple of glasses of prosecco inside him, he'd said he had to work the next day, take a car up to Nether Rigg for *The Beat*, but that once he was back, they could go somewhere, have a run out. Harrogate, or Ilkley if she liked, afternoon tea at Bettys. On a high from the Rover, the prosecco, feeling expansive. And Melody had said yes, that would be nice. Not nice, *lovely*. She seemed happy, he remembered. Perhaps he should have arranged more outings, made a bigger effort to keep things special. Sometimes (often) at the weekend they saw hardly anything of each other, him in the workshop doing up a car, Melody in the house, the garden. Assuming she didn't mind but now, thinking about the months he had spent on the E-Type, the talk of a radiator he'd had to have specially made, the chap restoring the leather seats, sparing her none of the details, he wondered. Had she felt bored, lonely? Was that why she'd gone?

No.

She hadn't gone.

She was missing.

16

Ali was at the stove stirring a pan of pasta. Nick had got home first and made a sauce with ricotta, broccoli, walnuts. The table was set, a bottle of Chianti open. He chopped lettuce and tomatoes, cucumber, spring onions, and tossed them in balsamic vinegar while she described her visit to Roger Felton.

"Hang on," Nick said. "He got you round there because a *parcel* was left on the drive?"

She smiled. "That's what he said but I think it was an excuse. What he really wanted was some Wilson time."

Wilson, who'd already had his dinner, and was in his bed gnawing at a toy in the shape of an ice cream cornet—a gift from Ali's mother—heard his name and looked up.

"Everywhere you look," she said, "there's a picture of Rory. And he always has treats for Wilson." The spaniel wagged his tail at the mention of *treats*, another word he knew well.

Nick frowned. "Remind me how long it is since he lost his dog."

"A while," Ali said.

They sat down to eat.

"Wouldn't it be easier to get another dog," Nick said, "instead of you having to go round there on false pretenses? Why don't you try telling him, any more calls like that and you'll have to charge

87

him with wasting police time? Actually, that wouldn't be a bad idea when it comes to most of the calls you have to deal with. The time-wasters. Lay it on the line. Cut your workload at a stroke." He looked pleased with himself. "I reckon I've just come up with a genius plan here."

Ali laughed. "It would never work. And I don't mind the time-wasters, as you call them. I prefer to think of them as"—she searched for the right word—"*eccentric*. Like Roger. They make life interesting."

"By interesting, you mean they keep you run off your feet. Imagine how much more laid back life would be if you filtered out the stuff that shouldn't even come your way in the first place."

"Where's the fun in that?"

"Tell Freeman there's too much work for one person, given that Heft is clearly in the grip of its own peculiar non-crime wave."

Ali twirled linguine round her fork. "You're probably right," she said. "About Roger. He should get another dog. I'll have a word."

Nick shook his head. "You're a lost cause."

"Anyway, tell me about this church you found?"

"I got lucky there."

He was looking round St. Mary's in Forde, thinking it might be suitable when one of the wardens showed up, bringing flowers for the altar. They got chatting and she told him about St. Maurice's, said it was worth a visit. For the frescoes, dating back to the fifteenth century, and the staircase hewed from stone leading to a high altar, its backdrop a medieval stained-glass window depicting the Crucifixion and Resurrection. The staircase was the thing, she said. As far as she knew there was nothing else like it locally.

Nick drove straight to Burdon. "Went through the village, couldn't see the church. Doubled back, still couldn't find it. No one about to ask, of course. I stopped and got out of the car, found a signpost, which you could hardly see for the hedge it was buried in,

Death in the Countryside

ivy all over it. St. Maurice's was at the end of a lane I hadn't even noticed, almost a mile outside the village. Completely hidden away."

"I've not heard of it. It's still in use?"

"They have a service every Sunday. The porch is full of notices, the cemetery buzzing with bees, bird life. I counted eight goldfinches in a tree."

"Wow. So that's the one?"

"I think so."

They were quiet for a moment, then Nick said, "Everyone's talking about Brian Bright." One of the runners on *The Beat* had spotted the appeal in the *News* and made the connection with the man from the BBC who supplied the show with its classic cars. Word soon went round.

"Good," Ali said. "That's the point of an appeal, to get people talking. With a bit of luck, we might find out what's going on, where she is."

"They all think he's done her in," Nick said.

Ali was taken aback. "Why?"

"Because they work on a crime drama, and we've just had an episode where the butcher also reported his wife missing." He waited a moment. "He killed her, of course, drove her to the woods and concealed the body, although not particularly well. A hiker's about to find her."

Ali gazed at him. "The butcher? Bert Fairmont?"

"That's right."

"*Bert Fairmont* killed his wife? *Bert*, who slips an extra link of sausage, a slice of black pudding, to his hard-up customers?" Nick nodded. "Bert who dresses up as Father Christmas every year and gives presents to the kids?" Nick gave a shrug in confirmation. "I don't believe it, he's lovely. And so is his wife. What's her name again?"

"Angela."

"They've been together forever. Didn't they just celebrate a big wedding anniversary?"

"Fifty years; they renewed their vows in the last series."

"And now he's *murdered* her?" Ali was appalled. "Who thought that was a good idea?"

"It's not real, you know, it's only telly."

"Try telling that to the viewers."

"Not a word, by the way. We're only just shooting those scenes, they won't go out for a while. If it gets leaked—before the press office officially lets slip, anyway—there'll be uproar." They were silent for a moment.

"I don't think Brian Bright murdered his wife," Ali said, eventually. For one thing, he had spent most of Saturday on the set of *The Beat*, as witnessed by the very people now gossiping about him.

"No." Nick dug his fork into his pasta, speared a piece of broccoli. "Just . . . have you looked inside the boot of his car? His many cars?" Ali frowned. "That's how Bert Fairmount got Angela to the woods." Nick raised an eyebrow and helped himself to more salad.

"Is that really what people think?" Ali said, putting her fork down. "That Brian's a killer?"

"Probably not. It's just gossip, you know how much TV people love a lurid story."

"Isn't there enough of that already with *The Beat*?"

Nick made a face. "You'd think so. And that's just what goes on *off* camera."

Ali let it go, took another helping of pasta. "This is lovely, you're very clever."

"It's the only pasta I ever make."

"It's still delicious."

"It doesn't mean anything," he said, back on the subject of Brian and what was being said about him on set. "Idle chitchat, that's all. They'll soon tire of it when something else comes along." He grinned. "Once Jay Flynn's fling with one of the runners comes

Death in the Countryside

out, no one's going to be talking about Brian." Jay Flynn played PC Alex Ford and was one of the stars of the show.

"Isn't he married?" Ali asked. "In real life?"

Nick nodded. "Trust me, when that particular bombshell gets dropped, Brian Bright and his missing wife will be old news."

Ali stayed up late going through her notes, everything she knew about Melody, which wasn't a great deal, she realized. Who was she? A woman who gardened and was learning to make pots, a collector of expensive scarves, most of which she never wore. Ali felt she was scratching the surface, struggling to see her, *really* see her. She sat for a moment thinking. The most likely explanation for Melody's disappearance still seemed to be that she had simply taken herself off. A tiff, perhaps, one Brian didn't want to own up to. Her car was missing, she had gone to Skipden and called at Carla's workshop, collected her finished pot.

Then what? Where did she go?

At last, after several attempts, Ali had managed to speak to Melody's sister. The conversation was brief, on a mobile with poor reception, Lillian vague about when she and Melody had last spoken. In the messages Ali had left, she had chosen her words with care, not wishing to sound alarming. She had been clear, however, about needing to establish Melody's whereabouts. Hoping Lillian would say that Melody was staying with her, or that the two of them had been away together. Something innocent. Lillian had not seen her sister, though. "She's definitely not with you?" Ali persisted, to be met by silence, the line breaking up, Lillian saying no, certainly not. Nowhere near as concerned as she might be, Ali felt, not very interested. Was she covering for Melody? Ali wondered. Unconcerned because she knew she was safe? Whatever Melody was up to, wherever she was, Lillian claimed to be very much in the dark.

Without knowing more about Melody, what made her tick, it

was impossible to know what she was capable of. Was she kind? Cruel? Impulsive or cautious? Had she just woken up one morning, looked at Brian and decided she was unhappy, that she would never be happy? Was the realization she had married a man who would never do his own laundry, never even master the basics of the washing machine, more than she could stand? Had Brian and his talk of classic cars become all too much? Or had his habit of wandering off the point (something Ali was already familiar with) driven her half mad? And those looks of his that came out of nowhere and somehow conveyed disapproval, incredulity, irritation, all rolled into one—had they become too much to bear? Then there was Dolores, the first Mrs. Bright. Dolores on the wall in Brian's office, on the mantelpiece, Melody living in her shadow. Enough, Ali suspected, to wear anyone down. Then again, it was unfair to focus solely on the negatives. On the plus side, Brian seemed decent, loyal, generous. It was clear he cared about his wife. What he'd gone through, losing Dolores, would inevitably leave a wound. Perhaps, Ali thought, before the crash there was another Brian, a Brian who was more fun, less car obsessed. Then after the crash, all that went, and he became serious and cautious, no longer his old self.

It occurred to Ali that Melody wasn't the only one living in the shadow of Dolores. Brian was too.

17

Roger Felton had sent one of his lengthy reports. For once, its main concern was not parking misdemeanors but "worrying developments" at Heft Hall. He attached a message from Pam Shaw, one of Ali's old teachers, now a parish councillor, regarding planning and access matters. Ali remembered Miss Shaw well. In the habit of slipping into French and doling out lengthy detentions for minor indiscretions. Not a woman to cross.

Heft Hall had been sold recently to an American billionaire, Troy Conrado, who'd made a fortune in the beauty industry, and his wife, Delice, a former glamor model who favored clingy jumpsuits and overwhelmingly big hair. On the rare occasions Delice ventured into town she literally stopped the traffic. It wasn't yet clear what the Conrados intended to do with the Hall and surrounding land, although their reputation as go-getters, ambitious, always an eye on the next opportunity, made it hard to imagine them living out a quiet retirement in rural North Yorkshire.

Within weeks of them moving in, local residents staged a protest in front of the gates after the lawn at the front of the house was dug up and replaced with artificial grass. Placards were wielded: *Fake grass, no class*! Ali had gone up there after a call from the protesters, led by Miss Shaw, who felt certain the installation of plastic

93

Maria Malone

turf within sight of a historic building was in some way against the law. Troy Conrado's secretary had also alerted Ali, demanding on his behalf that the protesters be moved on. *Tout de suite*, as Miss Shaw might have said.

Ali had spoken to the protesters first. Miss Shaw, still an intimidating figure despite being at least eighty by Ali's reckoning, insisted she was familiar with the law. "You might want to take a moment to check, Alison," she said in her authoritative schoolteacher way. Ali had and, as far as she knew, artificial grass (which, granted, was a crime against nature) wasn't actually against the law. When she said as much she was greeted with boos and cries of *shame*. The closest thing to a mob Ali had yet seen in Heft—elderly women, churchgoers, most of them, WI members, volunteer litter pickers—each one a pillar of the community. She appealed for calm. "I take it we are being refused any support," Miss Shaw said. "We're on our own, ladies. Abandoned by our local police service. Well. *C'est la vie.*"

As long as they kept their protest peaceful, Ali said, and stayed off estate land, they could stay. Which went some way to mollifying tempers.

At the hall, the door was answered by a cool young woman with jet black hair almost to her waist. Conrado's secretary. "I'm not sure the dog can come in," she said, looking dubiously at Wilson.

"He's here in an official capacity," Ali pointed out.

The secretary shrugged, muttered what sounded to Ali like, "Your funeral," and left them in the cavernous hallway while she went to find her boss. Ali took in her surroundings, the flagged floor and sweeping marble staircase. On the landing, an enormous stained-glass window. Above her, a domed ceiling decorated with elaborate gilded plasterwork. At her side, Wilson stood alert, his flank touching her leg, the tension in his bearing palpable. From outside, came the chants of the protesters. *Turf out the fakes*! *Turf*

Death in the Countryside

out the fakes! Inside, another raised voice. Conrado, Ali assumed, letting rip. *Goddamn . . . peasants . . . can't hear myself think*!

A door was flung open and through it rushed a figure in a billowing white kaftan. Ali recognized Troy Conrado from his photo, which featured frequently in the gossip columns. He almost ran at her and Wilson, who remained utterly still.

He pointed at the spaniel. "No dogs! Get that goddamn dog out of my house!"

Ali coolly introduced herself and explained that Wilson was on duty. Up close, Troy Conrado's face was smooth, from using his own products, he claimed, his famous 10-step regime, although over the years photos had surfaced of him leaving the clinic of a renowned plastic surgeon in Los Angeles, his features concealed by dark glasses and a bulky scarf, leading to speculation he'd been under the knife. Repeatedly. "They send a *woman* with a *dog*!" he bellowed, the fury in his voice at odds with his expression, which, courtesy of his surgeon, remained fixed and utterly benign.

Ali gave a tug on Wilson's lead, a signal they were leaving. "I can see you're upset," she said. Conrado's face was really something. Immobile, impassive, unnaturally shiny. As if he'd been too close to a blazing fire. She had a sudden urge to laugh. "Let me know when you're in a better frame of mind, feeling calmer, and we can talk then." She heaved the door open wide. The protesters, who'd fallen silent, began their chanting again. *Fake grass, no class*! "And since you have a 'no dogs' policy," Ali added, "it might be best if you come to the station at Skipden."

Now, according to Roger Felton, Pam Shaw—Miss Shaw—claimed to have got wind of what Troy Conrado intended to do with the hall and surrounding estate. Plans were being drawn up for a health-based members only "restoration club" for the super-rich. The grounds, where an informal right to roam had existed for generations, would in future be off-limits to locals. There was talk of some sort of medical facility offering high-tech beauty and cosmetic procedures. Again, aimed exclusively at the wealthy. As Miss Shaw put it, Conrado was determined to ruin the character of the place, turn a historic pile into a tawdry money-spinner. And in the process shut out the local community. *Une catastrophe*, she said.

Bound to set the tabby among the pigeons, Roger wrote. *Thought you should know.* Ali read the email again. It could just be talk. Still, she was grateful to Roger. If trouble was brewing, she wanted to know. She made tea and took it to the end of the garden, sat on the bench overlooking the beck. Wilson went with her. The sun sparkled on the water. In the distance, just visible, stood Worcop Pike, its peak smothered in cloud. Out toward Simonthwaite, it looked to be raining. Even when it was glorious elsewhere, it could be cold and wet there, whipping up a gale around the Black Stone. Little wonder tales of dark forces lurking on the summit persisted.

"So," she said, wanting to fill Wilson in on latest developments, "it's all kicking off at Heft Hall again. Remember that man we saw? Troy Conrado." She looked at Wilson who put a paw on her foot, letting her know he most certainly did. "That's right," she said, stroking his head. "The rude one with the funny face." Ali enjoyed these conversations, where she could be unguarded, come out with things she wouldn't dream of saying in the presence of, say, Chief Superintendent Freeman. She chuckled. "A *woman!*" Mimicking Conrado's accent (he was originally from Queens, in New York, according to the papers). "A *woman* with a *darg!*" Wilson, who appreciated these moments as much as Ali, wagged his tail. "That's you," she told him, ruffling one of his ears. "You're the *darg!*" Wilson pushed his nose against her knee. She put her tea down, bent and cradled his head in her hands. "Silly man, isn't he? Miss Shaw thinks he's going to turn the Hall into some sort of hideaway for rich people like him. *Quelle horreur!*" A discreet plastic surgery facility in the plans, perhaps. "I always thought rich people loved their dogs. Took them everywhere on their private

Death in the Countryside

jets. Wasn't that what landed Johnny Depp in bother with the Australians? Anyway, I'd like to see him try and tell his rich chums they can't bring *their* dogs. What do you think?"

A voice interrupted. "Who are you talking to?"

Ali turned to see Nick coming toward her.

"Wilson," she said. "We're discussing goings on at Heft Hall."

Nick looked amused. "You know you're in trouble once you start having serious chinwags with the dog. Isn't that right, boy?" Patting Wilson on the head, who grinned.

"You're doing it now," Ali said.

"I am, aren't I? Are all these chats one-sided or does he sometimes surprise you and answer back?"

"I can tell by looking at him what he thinks." Wilson sat up straight, gazing at her intently. "Smart lad, you know what's what, don't you?"

Nick sat down next to her, planted a kiss on the top of her head. "This is unexpected, finding you at home relaxing—sorry, *debriefing*—instead of running round Heft chasing down rogue delivery drivers."

She smiled. "You're back early too."

"I've been on a recce, took the director to see that church I told you about yesterday. Which he loved. We called in for a drink on the way back, a pub I thought might work for another episode."

"Any good?"

"The bar's great, ancient looking, tons of atmosphere, but the guy serving kind of spoiled it. Made us take our drinks outside because we hadn't booked a table. I mean, this was three o'clock, and the place was empty. Talk about awkward."

"Where was this?"

"Speight. The pub's The Speight." He raised an eyebrow. "Imaginative, I know. A bit out of the way, I've driven past before, but it's always been shut. Today the door was open, so we thought we'd drop in, on the off chance."

97

"You'd think they'd be glad of the business."

"Damian, the director, was unimpressed. We won't be shooting there."

They were silent a moment. "I'll make some tea," Nick said, leaving her to her thoughts.

Word had come back from Melody's bank regarding her finances and Ali had asked the new tech guy at Skipden, Spence, to cast an eye over them, a task he had completed with impressive speed. No activity on her account since paying for groceries in Heft a few days before she disappeared. Interestingly, in the last six months or so, she had got into the habit of making regular cash withdrawals, £200 here and there, amounting to almost £7,000 in total.

"What was she spending it on?" Ali now asked Wilson.

Or had she been tucking it away, ready for the moment she would take off? Ali knew it was possible to vanish, leave no trace, that some people went to great lengths to disappear, plotted their going with meticulous care. Usually, they had a good reason. In the case of Melody Bright, what might it be? As Freeman had said, why not just say you're leaving and save everyone—Brian especially—a lot of grief. Perhaps she simply couldn't face it.

The news that Melody had been raiding the ATM led the Chief Superintendent to suspect she had been planning her escape for some time. "All that money," he said, "and no evidence of her spending any of it." Still using her debit card to pay for groceries, petrol, visits to the hairdresser. "People generally don't bother as much with cash these days, so what was she doing? I mean, seven thousand—it's a significant sum." Ali, thinking the same, could offer no explanation. Still, she wondered if the case merited additional resources. "I can't justify the officers," was Freeman's response, "not when it has all the hallmarks of a wife leaving of her own accord."

In the back of Ali's mind lurked the nagging doubt that she

Death in the Countryside

was missing something. What if someone knew Melody was carrying all that cash and had robbed her? Or she had run off the road somewhere remote? Unlikely, she knew, since every police officer was aware of the missing woman and keeping a lookout for her car. If there'd been an accident surely someone would know. Even in remote spots, farmers were out on their land every day. A bright yellow Mini wouldn't be difficult to spot. Unless of course it was in a ravine. Or hidden.

"Someone would have seen the car, don't you think?" she asked Wilson, who sighed and rested his chin heavily on her knee.

18

Melody's sister, Lillian Firth, lived in a 1930s semi a mile or so from the center of Newcastle. On Thursday, a few days into the investigation, Ali was on her way to see her. She drove along a high street that was busy, past a discount store with a chaotic window display, a Wetherspoons, nail bars, Savers, a library, coffee shops, an Italian deli. Sandwiched between charity shops, was a Greggs, where there was a queue. She turned off and moments later was driving past another parade of shops and restaurants: a wholefood store, bakery, tapas bar, a café.

Following her initial highly unsatisfactory conversation with Lillian, the mobile signal cutting in and out at exactly the wrong moment, Ali had finally managed to speak to her again. It had taken several attempts to get through because, it turned out, Lillian made a point of ignoring calls from numbers that were unfamiliar to her. Perhaps, Ali thought, wanting to give her the benefit of the doubt, she had not properly understood the situation regarding Melody. Which would certainly explain why she had appeared so unmoved by the news she was missing.

In her follow-up call, Ali was at pains to stress that Melody was officially a missing person, her disappearance cause for concern.

Death in the Countryside

Already the posters Freeman had agreed to, appealing for information, were up in Heft.

"Right," Lillian said. "I see." Had she heard from Melody? Briefly, the line seemed to go dead and in the background a man asked if he should pause *Escape to the Country*. Lillian said yes, and could he go back to the bit where the people arrived at the mystery house?

"Mrs Firth?" Ali prompted, still not convinced the woman had grasped the severity of what she'd just been told.

"Sorry," she said, "we were in the middle of something." Her tone cool, bordering on offhand. "No, she's not been in touch. And until you popped up, I had no idea my sister was missing, none at all." Managing to make *missing* sound as if there were inverted commas around the word. When Ali asked if it would be all right if she came to see her, Lillian Firth said yes, only to immediately cast doubt on how helpful she could be. "We're not exactly close," she said, in a way that let Ali know she had no wish to be.

Once the call ended, Ali turned to Wilson. "Well. That was weird." He gazed up at her and she scratched his ear. "Between you and me, it sounds like there's not much love lost there." Perhaps Lillian was in shock, she reasoned, which could do odd things to people. She would soon find out.

She parked at the end of Laidlaw Avenue and walked with Wilson past a row of well-kept properties opposite a park. Number 39 was two-thirds of the way along, hidden behind a tall, expertly-clipped privet hedge. She unlatched the gate. Scented roses surrounded a mimosa, clumps of heather sprung from a rockery.

"Right," she told Wilson, pressing the doorbell, "let's see what we can find out."

Lillian Firth had white-blonde hair in a neat bob. Her eyes were the color of slate. She wore a billowing shirt in a zebra print,

Maria Malone

leggings, boots with a blocky heel. Red lipstick. Musky perfume, a little overpowering. Ali wondered how closely she and Melody resembled one another. It was hard to tell from the photos she'd seen. She followed Lillian into the front room where a man in a hooped rugby shirt and denims, thinning gray hair and glasses, waited.

"This is my husband, Des," Lillian said.

Ali nodded. "Thanks for seeing me."

They stood for a moment, an awkward little group, Wilson straining to sniff at Des's foot, which was almost within reach. Trekking sandals, Ali noticed. Socks. Lillian indicated a leather armchair next to the fireplace and Ali sat, Wilson at her side. She glanced about her: navy walls, shelves with books and knick-knacks, a cabinet filled with colored glassware, a painting of the Swing Bridge over the Tyne, roses in a vase. Photos of Lillian and Des. Lillian settled into the armchair facing Ali, Des went to make tea.

"I'm sorry to be in touch with such difficult news," Ali began. "I mean, a call out of the blue to say your sister's missing, it must have been quite a shock."

Lillian laughed, a sound that was harsh, mirthless. "I'm past being surprised by anything Melody does. I mean, she's missing—*missing*—what does that mean, exactly?" She gave Ali a hard look. "She's gone off again, I suppose. Is that what's happened?"

"You're saying this isn't the first time?"

Lillian gave a shrug. "It's what she does. Once she tires of something"—she hesitated, frowned—"some*one*, usually, she does off. Never satisfied, always searching for a better ... *whatever*." Another shrug.

Does off.

Des popped his head round the door. "Sugar?" he asked Ali.

"No, thanks," she said.

102

Death in the Countryside

He returned with mugs, a plate of chocolate digestives, then retreated to stand behind the sofa. Wilson gave him a curious look. Lillian took a biscuit and bit into it.

"It doesn't worry you at all, Melody disappearing?" Ali asked.

Lillian didn't answer immediately. Ali glanced at Des, who was frowning at the wall, as if surprised to see the painting of the Swing Bridge hanging there.

Ali persisted. "You're saying it's normal for her to up and go without a word."

Lillian swept crumbs off the front of her shirt. "I'll tell you about my sister," she said. "The first time she went missing we were frantic. Worried sick. I can't remember how old she was, nineteen, maybe. She'd been out with the lad she was seeing, some pub in town, and he'd gone to the bar to get drinks. When he came back, no sign of her. He thought she'd gone to the loo. He waited, and waited, but she never came back. So he went looking for her, checked outside, asked people drinking on the pavement if anyone had seen her, no one had. He wandered all over, searched high and low—pubs they'd been to in the past, everywhere he could think of—couldn't find her." She paused, sighed. "Melody's two years younger than me but I was still living at home, we both were, so finally he showed up there. I was having a quiet night in, me and my mam watching telly, face masks on"—she rolled her eyes at Ali—"you can imagine how happy we were when *he* turned up in the middle of *Tales of the Unexpected*, or whatever it was. We'd not seen her, so now we're all fretting. Dad got back from the Fat Ox, the police were called, asked all sorts of questions, took away a photo, practically turned the place upside down"—her brow creased, thinking back—"in case she was in the house, I suppose. Like we might have her stuffed in a cupboard, or something." Another roll of the eyes. "They looked under the beds, in the airing cupboard . . . the fitted wardrobes in Mam and Dad's bedroom.

103

Which was funny, really, because when we were kids that was where I used to put her when she was being annoying."

Ali had a vision of a small child imprisoned inside a dark wardrobe and a shudder went through her. Lillian added, "They even checked the loft, although all we had up there were the Christmas decorations. Very thorough, they were."

Ali took a drink of tea. So sugary it almost made her gag. She glanced at Des, statue-like behind the settee, his face giving nothing away. Lillian waved her mug at him, and he went off to make a second cup, then returned to his spot. Ali sent a bemused look at Wilson whose gaze slid to Des and back again. *No, me neither*, the spaniel seemed to say.

"Would you like to sit down?" Ali asked Des.

"He's fine," Lillian answered.

No one spoke for a moment. Lillian fiddled with a button on her shirt.

"The police found her, though?" Ali asked, returning to the subject of Melody.

"She was never *lost*, Sergeant. She'd been with another lad and when she was ready—two days later, this was—she came home. Just like that. Wondered what the fuss was about."

"So . . . what, she met someone else while her boyfriend was getting drinks?"

Lillian shook her head. "She had two on the go at once. Was going to finish with the lad she was out with, so she said, but the bar was noisy, you couldn't hear yourself speak . . ." She cradled her mug. "So she did a runner. Never expected him to make a big deal of it, get the police on her." She looked suddenly gleeful. "She was *livid*."

Ali digested this.

"She's led a charmed life, my sister," Lillian was saying. "Flitted from one bloke to the next, I couldn't even tell you their names, she's had that many." She gave Ali a hard look. "Don't look so

Death in the Countryside

shocked, Sergeant, she's no angel, I can assure you. Course, I blame the parents—*our* parents. She was the favorite, you see, absolutely ruined. Singing lessons, ballet, posh school. Life revolved around her. It was all *Melody this, Melody that.* No wonder she ended up an absolute nightmare." She held Ali's gaze. "You're thinking that's my sister I'm talking about, and, yes, it is. It took me long enough to see through her. For years I put up with her, bent over backward, and it got me precisely nowhere. If you want the truth about Melody, she's selfish and scheming and manipulative. A taker. The only person she cares about is herself. Which is why the last time she was here I sent her packing and made it clear she wouldn't be welcome back. Ever."

Ali tried to imagine what Melody could have done that her own sister would banish her for good. Something beyond the pale—stealing from her, doing drugs, setting fire to the house, making a pass at her husband. Ali's gaze tilted toward the settee and Des, silent, still, half obscured by upholstery, not entirely present. The idea of Melody (or anyone) seducing Des seemed unlikely. Something else then. Reversing her car over the cat (if there was a cat). She pictured a blazing row, accusations hurled, words that could not be unsaid. Ali ran an appraising eye over Lillian, cool, unruffled, now on her second digestive. Not the sort to put up with any nonsense. Hadn't she just admitted to locking her little sister in a wardrobe? Ali's thoughts abruptly turned to Iris, the times they'd argued, usually over Ali "borrowing" clothes without asking. Iris had been blazing mad when she saw the mark on her favorite dress, which Ali had no business taking, but they had never, not ever, come remotely close to a rupture that was beyond being healed.

"Do you mind telling me what happened?" Ali asked. "In the end, I mean, when you . . . sent her packing."

Lillian didn't answer right away. "She *attacked* me," she said at last.

105

"Oh." Ali was taken aback. An image came to her, Lillian and Melody slugging it out in the front room, Des behind the settee, politely looking the other way. "Did she hurt you?"

For the first time, Lillian looked uncomfortable. Again, it was a while before she spoke. "It was a *verbal* assault but, yes, actually, she *did* hurt me. What she said, the way she spoke to me, here, in my own home . . ." She tailed off, indignant.

Was that it? They'd had *words*. Ali was staggered. "And this was recently?" she asked.

Lillian gazed past her, shrugged.

Was this the reason for Melody going missing? "When exactly?"

"2012. I remember the Olympics were on in London."

Ali felt her jaw drop. 2012! "Hasn't she been visiting these last few months? Coming to Newcastle. Meeting up with you?"

Lillian gave her a hard look. "Believe me, I've no wish to see her."

Ali pressed her. Was she sure? Lillian was affronted. Of course she was. In which case, where had Melody been going? Who had she been seeing? Had she even been coming to Newcastle? Ali persisted, not quite able to believe what Lillian had told her. "All because you . . . argued?"

"As I said."

So that was it. Two sisters estranged, permanently by the sound of things, because one had spoken out of turn. There had to be more to it, surely.

"Did you know she was married?"

Lillian gave another of her shrugs. "Pulled the wool over some poor bloke's eyes, then."

"From what I've seen, he loves her," Ali said. "He's extremely concerned about her."

Lillian stayed silent.

"His name's Brian, he runs a car business, classic models," Ali went on. "You don't know him?"

Death in the Countryside

"Never heard of him," Lillian said, "and I doubt he knows her, not really. Secretive, our Melody is." Her gaze slid to the TV listings magazine lying open on the table at the side of her chair. She looked up, focused briefly on the mantelpiece. "That fuchsia needs water," she said, turning to Des. He shuffled off into the kitchen.

"Is there anything else you want to tell me?" Ali asked. "About your . . . falling out."

Lillian gave her a stony look. "You think it sounds petty, trivial, don't you? A bit of name calling. Nothing we couldn't have resolved."

"I mean," Ali said, "she's your sister. All that history. I just thought you'd both want to put things right."

Lillian leaned forward in her chair. Tears in her eyes. Ali sensed she had touched a nerve, that Lillian was more affected than she made out about the rift with Melody. "Smooth things over, pretend it never happened, invite her back for more of the same?"

"All I meant—"

"You know," she snapped, "you sound just like her." She thumped her mug down, annoyed.

"I didn't mean to offend you," Ali said, suddenly aware she had upset Lillian without meaning to. Perhaps Melody had done the same.

"Is that everything?" Lillian asked. Composure firmly back in place.

"Yes, thank you for your time."

"Sure you don't want to take a look around?" Sarcastic. "In case she's in the house somewhere."

Ali got to her feet. Wilson jumped up. "Thanks, that would be great, save us having to come back."

Lillian's expression darkened. "Is that really necessary? I told you we've not seen her."

"It'll only take a minute."

107

Maria Malone

Lillian shadowed them as they checked the bedrooms, Ali peering under the beds, sliding back the doors on the fitted wardrobes in the main bedroom, sending Wilson inside to ferret among shoes and handbags. She opened the airing cupboard, the loft, Lillian protesting the whole time.

"Don't you need permission to search a house?"

"That's right," Ali said, "I'm grateful to you for offering."

Lillian glared at her.

"I'll just check outside at the back," Ali said cheerfully, "then we'll be on our way."

Wilson zigzagged across the lawn, nose to the ground. In the corner furthest from the house, he relieved himself against an apple tree. Ali heard Lillian make a loud tutting sound. The door to the shed was open and Ali went inside. Tidy, ordered, nowhere to hide a body. Not that she was looking for one. She was making a point, putting Lillian in her place. Letting her know the police were taking Melody's disappearance seriously even if her sister wasn't. If Lillian had been a bit kinder, shown just the teeniest bit of concern, Ali would probably be on her way back to Heft by now, via Greggs on the high street.

She went along the path at the side of the house. "Could you open the garage?" she said. As if by magic, the door began to roll up, revealing Des on the other side, a remote in his hand, behind him a white Skoda Fabia.

"Thanks," Ali said, whistling to Wilson, busy snuffling in a bed of geraniums, enjoying being out in the air. He charged over and Ali signaled for him to check the garage as Des pressed another remote and the doors to the Fabia unlocked. He gave Ali a shy smile.

"I assume you'll want to look the car over."

"Thanks," she said. "Here, Wils."

Wilson jumped into the footwell at the front, sniffed about, hopped out and into the back. Des opened the boot. Lillian looked

108

Death in the Countryside

ready to kill him. Wilson pushed his snout into the corners, found nothing of interest. Scrambling out, he returned to sit at Ali's heel.

"If that's everything, Des will see you out," Lillian said.

"All done, thanks, you've been very helpful."

Lillian turned and stomped back into the house, banging shut the door behind her. Des walked Ali and Wilson to the garden gate.

"We had a dog, a mongrel. Bobby. Lost him a few years back, broke our hearts."

Ali had a sudden sense of Bobby in the drive, Melody reversing without looking where she was going, running over the poor dog. Lillian in floods of tears. *Get out! Just go!*

"What happened?"

"Old age," Des said. "He was seventeen."

They were beyond the gate now, Des still walking with her. Neither spoke for a moment.

"It must have been quite some falling out," Ali said. "I mean, Lillian and Melody. A few cross words and they never speak again? Is there really no way back?"

"It wasn't just that day," he said. "Something about Melody, the way she carried on—sailing through life, Lillian said, going on trips to places you'd read about in the travel section of the Sunday papers but never dream of seeing: Hawaii, Kampala, Petra. It got to Lillian. The golden child, she called her. That day, you know"—he sent a furtive glance back at the house—"I was in the kitchen when it all kicked off. Ructions. Lillian was"—he frowned, searching for the right word—"fizzing. Ready to blow a fuse. I kept out of it. Lillian phoned her a few weeks later, just to deliver another ear bashing, really. According to Lillian, Melody was a disgrace—despicable, vile, self-obsessed. Never did a single nice thing for anyone." Glancing again at the house, lowering his voice. "I never thought she was that bad, I mean she was good to us, she wasn't *evil*. But . . ." he sighed, gave a Lillian-style shrug.

"Right," Ali said, still no clearer about what lay at the heart of the rupture. "Where do *you* think she might have been going? I mean lately, when she was supposed to be coming here?"

Des shook his head. "Not a clue," he said.

"And you'd no idea she'd got married?"

"I thought if she ever did it would be to Jimmy." He was quiet, thinking. "JC. Her soulmate, she called him. He was the one she was with when, you know, she went missing. Then they split, she went off with someone else, so did he. I never met him, before my time, but she still used to talk about him as if he was the one. I remember her saying they were meant to be, as if they'd end up back together one day." He gave Ali a wry smile. "But if she married this Brian, I'm guessing she gave up on that idea."

"Where is he now, Jimmy?" JC.

Des shrugged. "No idea, sorry."

19

In recent months, Melody Bright had told her husband she was driving to Newcastle for the day to see her sister. The sister from whom she was estranged. Mending fences, she told Brian, putting things right. And yet, according to Lillian, who'd sent her packing more than a decade earlier—a *decade!*—she'd not had so much as a phone call in years, a card, let alone set eyes on her.

So, where had she been going? And if she wasn't seeing Lillian, then who?

Could Lillian be lying? She seemed to detest Melody. Still, it would have taken an Oscar-winning performance to fake the look on her face when Ali persisted in asking about Melody's "recent visits." Incredulity. Fury. Offended, almost. For a minute, longer, she had been silent, digesting what Ali had said. When she finally managed to speak, her rage was clear to see. "That's utter rubbish. Bullshit. She's lying." Then, moments later, "Or *he* is. The husband."

Was Brian telling lies, sending Ali on a wild goose chase, wasting her time? Why? What was in it for him? Distraction, Freeman might say, an attempt to throw her off the scent. Not that she was *on* the scent, she couldn't help thinking. It was like doing a jigsaw, a thousand pieces, something tricky, where the picture on the box

111

didn't seem to match what was in front of you. It may well turn out that Brian was a good deal cleverer than she gave him credit for. Ali tried to picture Brian, appearing to ramble, taking an age to get to the point, deliberately misleading her, but all she saw was a man adrift, puzzling over how to work the oven. She just could not bring herself to regard Brian as a suspect. But what if she was wrong? *It's always the husband.* Not this time. She reminded herself that on the day Melody Bright had driven out of Heft and swung by the potter's, Brian had been elsewhere. Hard at work, delivering a car to *The Beat* at the same time as Melody was at Carla's studio. Brian, toiling to keep his wife in her beloved designer scarves.

Another reason Brian was off the hook was that Wilson had taken a shine to him. Which told Ali everything she needed to know.

On the drive back to Heft, she weighed up the events of the past hour. What Des had said about Melody's supposed soulmate, Jimmy, was interesting. Or possibly a red herring. He knew nothing useful about the elusive JC. Not his last name or where he lived, what he did for a living. "We need her phone records," she told Wilson, secure in his doggy seatbelt on the passenger seat, attentive, his furrowed brow seeming to say that was just what he was thinking too. It was always reassuring to run things past Wilson. "I'll get on to the mobile provider, give them a nudge." Wilson gave her one of his smiles. They were beyond Richmond, bulky dark shapes in the sky, military helicopters, she guessed, the big ones that couldn't decide whether they were a chopper or a plane, coming their way, heading toward Catterick.

Wilson's eyes were on the road ahead, alert for the turn off to Ripley, where she had promised to stop and give him a run. Ali was convinced he could read road signs. Not "read," exactly, but understand when they were nearing a place of interest. The whiny sounds he made, the way he quivered, eager, full of anticipation, were a giveaway. If he was sleeping, he'd wake at just the right moment.

Death in the Countryside

Ready for the off, for work, for play. Uncanny. He had even seemed to recognize Lillian's street, which was not possible as it was his first visit, and yet as they'd rounded the corner into Laidlaw Avenue, suddenly he was up, raring to go.

"Clever lad," Ali told him. His tail thumped against the seat.

Nick had rolled his eyes when she told him about Wilson's ability to understand road signs, his knack of knowing when they'd arrived at a place of some importance.

"You know he's a dog, right?" Nick said. "A smart one, admittedly, but still."

Ali had tried to explain about what she called the spaniel's intuitive know-how. "It's like he's got a sixth sense," she said.

"Or," Nick countered, "he's caught on that when you slow down it means you're arriving at your destination."

Ali had tried to say it was more than that, that even on a motorway when there was no slowing down involved, Wilson reacted at the sight of a relevant signpost. "In that case," Nick had said, "better get him on *Britain's Got Talent*." She didn't mind, Nick could make all the digs he wanted, Wilson operated on a level that was impossible to explain in simple, logical terms. Tintin's Snowy with special powers.

"What about those two today, what did you make of them?" she now asked.

Wilson, not wanting to miss the Ripley turn off, kept his eyes firmly fixed on the road ahead.

Neither Lillian nor Des had paid him any attention, which was unusual in Ali's experience, since even the iciest of souls showed signs of thawing when they spent any amount of time in his company. With obvious exceptions. Troy Conrado, for instance. Some people had a pathological dislike of dogs. They were the ones, in Ali's wholly unbiased view, you had to watch out for.

20

"That can't be right," Brian said, when Ali broke the news about Melody's non-visits to her sister in Newcastle. She had gone straight to Glebe Farm on her return from Lillian's. "Why would she say she was going there if she wasn't?"

Because she was meeting someone else. Up to no good. Because she had a life Brian knew nothing about. Ali followed him into the kitchen, which seemed to be where he spent most of his time these days. Newspaper spread out on the table, butter dish, salt and pepper, a plate speckled with crumbs. The ironing board was up, a shirt that was creased to ribbons, awaiting pressing. Fancy iron, Ali noticed, one of those bulky steam generators. Another appliance for Brian to get to grips with. Had he any idea how to iron a shirt? Without asking if she wanted a drink, he went to fill the kettle. On the radio a discussion was underway about a spate of dog attacks. "I wouldn't destroy the dogs," a caller was saying, "but I *would* put the owners down, castrate them or whatever."

Brian faced her, ashen, looking as if his legs might go from under him.

"Here," Ali said, steering him to a chair and sitting him down. "It's a lot to take in, I know." Did she, though? How would she feel

114

Death in the Countryside

if someone broke the news that Nick had been lying to her for months? Destroyed, probably, as if her world was at an end.

"There has to be an innocent explanation," Brian said, attempting to rally. "Must be. Unless, of course, the sister's lying."

Lillian had said the same. *She's lying. Or he is.* Someone was.

"I don't think so," Ali said as gently as she could. "I can't see what she has to gain."

Brian was silent. The kettle boiled, Ali took over making tea, knowing where to find what she needed, Brian's kitchen almost as familiar as her own now.

"It doesn't make sense," he was saying. "She would come home from those trips full of it, where they'd been, what they'd done."

Ali poured the tea. Wilson had made himself comfortable under the table, his chin on Brian's foot. Making his presence felt, literally, letting Brian know he was there for him.

"Here, drink some," Ali said, putting a mug in front of Brian. "I've put sugar in." He gave her a questioning look. "For the shock."

Brian shook his head as if to say there was no need for that. His face told a different story. "They went shopping," he said, taking a drink, the unfamiliar sweet taste causing him to pull a face. "Fenwick's," he added, "the department store. It's famous, apparently. That was where Melody went with her sister." Abruptly, he got up and left the room, returning a minute or two later with a scarf. Scarlet and teal, some sort of abstract design. A wrap more than a scarf. It looked expensive, a work of art, lovely enough to be on the wall. He handed it to Ali. Fine wool with a silky feel, a label she'd not heard of, Pazuki. "She got this on one of her trips," Brian said, as if the wrap was proof, irrefutable evidence that what he was saying was right. "From Fenwick's. Wrapped beautifully, tissue paper, ribbon. Pleased as punch she was. Next time she went to see her sister"—he stopped himself and frowned at the table, before plowing on, undeterred by what Ali had told him—"a week or two later, the next time she went to see Lillian, she wore it."

Ali wasn't sure what to say.

"They'd get a bite to eat in town," he went on, "sometimes in the food hall at Fenwick's, or a Spanish place up from the Quayside. Best tapas she'd had, she said." He gave Ali a defiant look. "You're not telling me she made it all up, that none of it happened."

Ali sighed inwardly. It wasn't that she didn't believe him. Perhaps Melody *had* done those things—shopped in Fenwick, eaten out—just not with Lillian.

"She was estranged from her sister for years," Ali said. "How did Melody explain them being back in touch?"

"She was poorly last year. Melody, I mean. Pneumonia. Nasty. It laid her low for weeks. Once she was on the mend, out of the blue, she said she felt bad about Lillian. Maybe they could put things right." He was quiet, thinking. "She never told me why they fell out; something trivial she said, cross words, a misunderstanding. Easy to offend Lillian without meaning to, she said." Ali could vouch for that. "I wasn't sure about her getting back in touch, but I told her to do what she thought best. Suddenly she was up and down to Newcastle every other week."

"She never suggested you go with her?"

"I wasn't sure I wanted to, not that I said so, I just know it's not always a good idea letting tricky people into your life. Family, especially. Always the risk they'll turn on you. I couldn't see why Melody bothered. The last few times she went up she said she was always putting her foot in it, apologizing for saying the wrong thing. It didn't sound much fun to me." Brian looked at Ali perplexed as if to say it all seemed too fraught, a pointless exercise. He went on, "We'd go together once things were on an even keel, she said. If they ever were." Under the table Wilson shifted position. Brian reached down and ran a hand over the dog's head.

They sat in silence, Ali thinking hard. Clearly, Melody had

Death in the Countryside

been up to something, but what, exactly? Lying about where she was going, what she was doing, who she was seeing. Up and down to Newcastle. Why so many cash withdrawals? Were they intended to fund her other, secret life? Was she spending the money (and if so, on what?), or giving it to someone (who?) Putting it aside for reasons that were as yet a mystery? A thought came to her. "Does Melody have a passport?" she asked.

"Yes, of course," Brian said.

"Do you know where she keeps it?"

Ali followed him to the room that served as his office where he took a key from an ornamental box, unlocked a drawer in his desk and removed a large white envelope. Folded, an elastic band securing the contents. The holiday envelope, Brian said. He peered inside, frowning, eventually taking out a passport. A piece of paper was tucked inside. He removed it and studied it for a moment before turning to Ali. "We keep the passports together," he told her. "I look after them. Travel insurance documents, any currency we have left over, it's all in here." Reaching again into the envelope and extracting a modest bundle of foreign notes—euros, US dollars. "We don't bother hanging on to coins, just leave whatever small change there is with the airline."

Ali waited. Other than the envelope, the drawer held only a few items—pencils, an old pocket diary, a small spiral bound notepad with an embossed cover, strong mints in a tin.

"This one's mine," Brian said, handing the passport he was holding to Ali. Still frowning, raking through the bits and pieces in the drawer, picking up the diary, the mints, the notepad. Not looking at her. Pulling the drawer out, searching again. Hoping to find what was evidently missing from the holiday envelope. The other passport, the one belonging to his lost wife.

"It was here," he said. "They both were. I'm particular about keeping them together."

"When did you last see Melody's passport?"

Brian looked bewildered. Still holding the slip of paper found inside his own passport.

"Well, not since we came back from Fuerteventura. End of October."

Ali double-checked the envelope, the contents of the drawer. "Could I see that?" She nodded at the piece of paper in his hand. The color had drained from his face. *I'm sorry, I've done something. I didn't plan it, it wasn't intended. I just wasn't thinking. I got carried away. I'm so sorry about it all.*

"It's Melody's writing," he said, "but my name's not there, we can't assume that was meant for me." He sent Ali a desperate look. "See, she's not even signed it. She might have been . . . doodling, anything. And we don't know when it was written, what it's supposed to mean."

Ali was in little doubt as to the significance of those few lines. A note left inside Brian's passport in a drawer that was kept locked, home of the precious holiday envelope. It seemed safe to assume Melody had known where to find the key. Now her passport was gone and, in its place, a few inconclusive lines which Brian was bound to find at some point.

"We write messages on the pad in the hall," he said stubbornly.

Not when you want to delay the finding of the message, Ali thought. Allowing Melody time to leave before anyone began to seriously search for her. Ali was more convinced than ever that Melody had gone of her own accord. She just hadn't had it in her to tell Brian what she was doing. That was how it looked anyway. She gazed at Brian, head bowed, studying the carpet, and Freeman's words about it always being the husband came back to her. Was the missing passport, the note, a ploy to make it *look* as if Melody had left of her own accord? If she had simply walked out, where was she now? Was she safe? Ali felt a sudden twist of anxiety in the pit of her stomach.

Death in the Countryside

"Did she have other friends in Newcastle?" she asked. "Anyone from her past she might have caught up with?"

Brian frowned. "No. I don't think so. No one she told me about."

"What about . . . Jimmy?"

Brian looked blank. "Who's Jimmy?"

21

Brian was in the kitchen making his tea. Despite appearances to the contrary, he wasn't entirely useless, he could rustle up something simple when required, just about. He'd had to before. After Dolores. Baked beans, toast, tins of soup. That's what he told Ali when she asked, although it wasn't the whole story. His mother was alive then and most nights he was there for his tea. Then she died and his Aunt Mona stepped in. No one was called Mona anymore, or Dolores, come to think of it. A neighbor, Gloria Harold, had started doing his cleaning, taking care of the laundry. Didn't even want paying but he insisted, of course. Thinking back, he hadn't had to fend for himself at all. No wonder he was finding it such hard going now.

The radio was on, Ruth in *The Archers* trying none too subtly to find out who Pip's new love interest was, getting nowhere. He could have told her, of course, having caught the episodes that were on earlier in the week. "It's Stella," he said, wanting to put Ruth out of her misery. "Your daughter's fallen for your best friend." As if these outlandish things happened in real life, Brian thought, seeking to use the goings-on in Ambridge as a distraction from his own situation. One which, frankly, was far-fetched enough to find a home in any drama series: his wife missing, vanished without a trace,

Death in the Countryside

and now the suggestion she was leading what some might call a double life. Just the sort of thing you got on TV. What he was going through wasn't some story, though, it was his *life*, his *wife*. And Melody was simply not capable of such deceit, such . . . appallingness (if that was a word). There had to be an explanation, one he could live with. A bump on the head, a loss of memory. Something. Because the idea she was sneaking off to Newcastle on the pretext of seeing her sister when she was, in fact, meeting a man possibly called Jimmy—which seemed to be where Ali Wren was going with the investigation—was not something he could get to grips with. She had never mentioned any Jimmy to him. Then again, she wouldn't, would she?

Brian was old-fashioned enough to believe in the idea of innocent until proven guilty. He would not leap to wild conclusions until faced with hard evidence. There was the missing passport, of course, and the note that made no sense. She was sorry—sorry for what? And if it were intended for him, why leave it hidden away in a drawer that was kept locked? (Because she didn't want him to see it straight away, Ali Wren had hinted, an idea he found, frankly, absurd. Melody wasn't like that. Was she? The possibility that he didn't know his wife was too much to bear.) The note, he couldn't fathom it. As for the passport . . . perhaps she had needed photo ID for . . . He thought long and hard, unable to come up with a reason, still clinging to the hope an innocent explanation would at some point emerge. For now, he intended to file what Ali Wren had told him under "miscellaneous-likely-erroneous" and in the meantime keep calm and carry on.

On his way back from work, he had stopped in Heft and called in at the Epicurean, bought eggs and tomatoes, a small piece of Wensleydale from the deli counter, milk. On impulse, he bought a packet of the granola Melody liked, the one that came from a farm in the Dales somewhere. Five items in his basket. Shopping for one. When he went to pay, he thought there'd been a mistake. It couldn't

Maria Malone

be so much for so little. "That can't be right," he said. It was, though. The thick end of twenty pounds. He even had to pay for a bag. Hessian, "Epicurean" in elegant lettering on the side. Three pounds fifty for the bag! He didn't dare ask if they had cheap plastic ones. Perhaps there was no such thing now, how would he know, being horribly out of touch? Still, he had the granola. For Melody, for when she came back. Once she regained her memory. He continued up the main street where his wife's picture was in the window of the Post Office, on the noticeboard next to the bus shelter, a lamppost. Ali Wren had moved fast there. He wondered if people knew him, realized he was the husband of the missing woman. Unlikely, since he rarely came into Heft. When he got to Hooley's, Melody's face was there again, smiling at him from the shop window and he felt suddenly ashamed, as if he had no right to be out in the late afternoon sun when his wife was missing, as if people would wonder what on earth he was thinking strolling along with his hessian bag from Epicurean, when he should be out searching for her. *Doing* something. What, though? And he had to eat, as Ali Wren constantly reminded him. Starving himself wouldn't help anyone.

All Hooley's had left were two farmhouse loaves and a bag of bread buns. He took the lot. Again, he queried the price, this time because it seemed not nearly enough for what he had. The woman serving, short blonde hair, red lipstick, a look about her of the actress who caused such a fuss crossing her legs in a film some years back, said, "It's the end of the day, my love, they'll be no good to me tomorrow, might as well sell them cheap if I can and get off home." Following him to the door, ready to lock up.

"Are you Evelyn?" Brian blurted out before he could stop himself.

She flipped the sign to closed. "That's right, I am." On her guard all of a sudden, as if Brian was about to give her trouble. He knew about the bother with the bakery over the road, the

Death in the Countryside

newcomers treading on her toes. Melody had put him in the picture, not that he'd paid much attention, he remembered, feeling guilty.

"My wife always shopped here." He corrected himself. "*Shops*, I mean."

Evelyn Hooley gave him an appraising look. "Oh, who's your wife, then?"

Brian flushed. Wished he'd kept his mouth shut. "It's Melody," he said, attempting to get out of the door.

Evelyn put a hand on his arm. "It's *your* wife that's missing?"

Brian dropped his gaze to the floor. Black and white tiles in a diamond pattern, similar to the ones they'd had in the house he'd spent his childhood in. "Anyway," he said, "we always have your bread. Best in the Dales, Melody always said. *Says*." Speaking too fast.

Evelyn gripped his elbow. "You must be frantic," she said. "Are you managing? Is there anything you need?"

To his horror, he thought he might cry. A single stranger showing kindness and he was ready to fall apart! He focused on the floor, the pleasingly worn look of the tiles. Tiles that might have gone down when the shop first opened, which was, what, a hundred years ago, something like that, so many pairs of feet walking on them since then, thousands and thousands, and still they were doing their job. This was the kind of establishment Brian appreciated— family-run, an emphasis on quality, a reputation for baking excellence that was hard-won over years, decades, a century. What he wanted for his own business. He knew some people found him stuffy, his attitude out of step with the modern world, but he was also known for being reliable and fair, for having high standards, being a man of his word. Brian Bright Classics and Hooley's, two of a kind.

"Wait," Evelyn was saying, interrupting his wandering thoughts. She went to the counter and reached underneath for something. "Take these," she said, giving him a brown paper bag.

"A couple of Hooley Hefts. You can always freeze them. I was going to drop them in for the Feltons, but they don't know I'm coming, so you have them."

Brian glanced up. The look on Evelyn Hooley's face, such concern, such kindness, made him feel suddenly overwhelmed. "What do I owe you?"

"Nothing," she said. "Just you take them, love. Take them and enjoy them."

For the next few minutes, Evelyn talked warmly about Melody, even though it was apparent they weren't friends, that she hardly knew her. A regular, she said, partial to an iced bun, a custard tart. Really? Brian hadn't known that. Always a smile, Evelyn said, some lovely scarf on. That scent of hers, what was it? Brian had no idea. Still trying to pay for the Hooley Hefts, which seemed only fair, but Evelyn wouldn't hear of it. Was he an object of pity? A charity case? Was that how people like Evelyn Hooley saw him? Or was she simply a decent woman who wanted to do something nice for someone going through a hard time? The latter, he decided. When he got back to the car he had a good cry.

Now, he set out his shopping from earlier and did what he could to make it look appetizing, a meal rather than a series of random bits and pieces. He put it on a wooden board: the cheese, the bread, a Hooley Heft, which, after a minor skirmish with the oven, he had warmed up and sliced into four. Tomatoes in a separate dish, cut in half, salted, a splash of olive oil. Where he'd come up with that, he wasn't sure. Anyway, it all looked very good. He ate at the table in the kitchen, the radio on for company.

The bread was the best part of the meal. On its own with a bit of butter it would almost have been enough. He cut a piece of crumbly Wensleydale. Utterly delicious. Good food, simple. Why hadn't he and Melody ever eaten like that? Bread and cheese, a glass of red wine. Had she felt obliged to cook every night, to put what she considered to be a proper meal on the table? Had he ever

Death in the Countryside

suggested she take a night off, that the kind of picnic tea he was enjoying now would be perfect? No. Every few weeks he took her out for dinner, somewhere expensive, the food rarely as good (in his view) as what they had at home. It had become what they did, how they lived, elaborate food every night of the week. He sighed and cut more bread, helped himself to a slice of the Hooley Heft, the pastry melting in his mouth. Tender steak, gravy, potato cooked just right. It came back to him, Melody saying that Evelyn was on her own, how hard it must be in the big house she'd shared with her husband, keeping the business going alone. Maybe that was why those young women had moved in over the road with their cakery-bakery (fakery, Melody hinted), positioning themselves for the day when Hooley's was no more, ready to take over. Not that Evelyn had any intention of going anywhere any time soon. She was a tough nut, Melody said, a grafter. Devoted to a business that had been in her husband's family for generations, determined to keep it alive for as long as she could. And then what? Leave it to the cat, Melody had said, smiling. There weren't any children. Was there a cat? Brian wondered.

Evelyn Hooley had felt sorry for him, he had seen it in her eyes. That was what made him cry. He welled up again, remembering. So far, he had held things together by keeping busy. Fixing brake pipes, welding the underside of an old MG. Putting a bit of T-Cut on a Triumph Stag, making the paintwork gleam. He was happy taking cars out to *The Beat*, which took up at least half his day. Occasionally he'd see Ali Wren's husband on set and, now he knew who he was, they'd exchange a few words, always car-related, never anything personal, certainly nothing about Melody, for which he was grateful. Nick, who called himself Pope, not Wren, which Brian couldn't fathom—didn't people have the same surname once they married these days?—had invited him to stay for lunch and they sat together at the back of the catering bus discussing the ins and outs of what made old cars so appealing and, sometimes, so

Maria Malone

infuriating. The choke, Nick said. Fan belts, according to Brian. The food on set was unbelievable, three different main courses to choose from (Brian had sea bass, Nick chose moussaka). Steamed pudding for afters: apple crumble, custard; cheese and biscuits, fruit, yoghurt, coffee, a selection of teas, most of which Brian had never heard of. Some of the production people looked a bit, well, dumpy, and no wonder if that was how they ate most days.

After lunch, Nick walked him back to the Rover, now finished with, ready for Brian to take back to Bradford. Told him to take care. Not some throwaway remark, seeming genuinely concerned for his safety. Did Nick feel sorry for him too? Perhaps. Then again, his wife was missing, there was every reason to.

22

"I've remembered something," Brian told Ali.

She was back in his kitchen, Brian watching closely as she made coffee, noting which spoon she used, the amount of ground coffee that went in. Water up to the bottom of the handle. He opened a packet of shortbread biscuits and snapped one in half, offered a piece to Wilson, who glanced at Ali, tempted, but unsure something that smelled delicious and sugary and was clearly unrelated to the usual dried liver snacks he was given as treats was allowed.

"Sorry, can he have one?" Brian asked.

"Just this once," she said. Wilson happily crunched the biscuit down. Brian gave him the other half. Ali winced. "No more," she told Wilson.

They sat at the table, in the same seats as before. She pushed down the plunger on the coffee and poured them each a cup. Waited for Brian to tell her what was on his mind.

"What you said about Melody being close to anyone in Heft," he began. Ali nodded. "Well, she's not, not really, but when I got thinking she occasionally mentioned someone she speaks to. Not so much a friend . . ." He tailed off, frowning. "Probably not worth bringing up."

127

"Who are we talking about?"

"You see—and this doesn't put me in a good light, I realize that—it's Melody who does all the gardening. She's good at it, you should see how much she's done since we moved in. That lavender at the front, she planted all that, the plants were only a few inches tall, a bit sorry looking, I didn't think they'd survive. Not that I said anything. But she got them all into that border and, well, you can see for yourself, they're thriving now. Covered in bees, and the scent is something else."

Ali was getting used to Brian's meandering. She decided to be patient, see where he was going with this. "They're lovely, they look really well established."

"And they've only been there a couple of years," he said. "Hard to believe, isn't it?"

Ali agreed it was. Opposite her, he sipped his coffee, deep in thought. "I've never made a decent pot of coffee," he said. "I don't do the gardening. You must be wondering what exactly I *do* contribute."

"Honestly, it hasn't crossed my mind."

"To be honest, a good deal of my time revolves around the business, the cars"—he gave her a pleading look—"too much, you might think. Cars take up almost all my free time too. There's always a wreck in the workshop, some big restoration or other. The E-Type out there took four years to put right and back on the road."

Ali nodded. A picture was emerging of Brian and Melody each engaged in their separate interests. Ships that too often passed in the night. She picked up on what she guessed was his sense of guilt for not doing enough, not spending as much time with her as he could. Now she was gone and, understandably, he was fretting over how he might have done things differently. Ali suspected that what he'd said was probably true of many relationships. Sometimes, a week would go by, more, when she and Nick hardly saw one another, both of them in jobs that meant unsociable hours, unexpected call-outs for Ali, early starts for Nick, night shoots when he had to stay

Death in the Countryside

in Nether Rigg. Even when they were both at home, it wasn't as if they did everything together. Often, Nick would be working in the garden while she was inside. Hadn't she painted the bathroom while he constructed a pergola? Being close, having a harmonious relationship, didn't necessarily mean being joined at the hip.

"It's Melody who deals with the garden waste," Brian was saying. "And a place this size generates plenty. It means she's at the tip a lot. Every week, probably. Not that I'm here, so I can't be certain. She'll sometimes say she made two trips, eight bags of rubbish, ten!"

He went quiet, thinking. "It takes some carrying all that. Have you felt the weight of grass cuttings?"

Ali pictured the lawn getting long, Brian leaving it because he wasn't sure how to work the mower, Melody's lovely garden gradually becoming overgrown without her there to tend to it. The garden, the house, all the things he wasn't used to doing, now preying on his mind.

"How are you coping?" she asked.

He seemed surprised. "Not bad, I'm managing, anyway." He looked to have lost some weight, his face was drawn.

"What about food—are you eating?"

"I just have what I fancy. There's plenty in the fridge."

He wouldn't be cooking, Ali sensed, since he didn't know how. "Have you thought about ready meals?" she asked. "Just for now. You can get all sorts and they're not bad."

Brian stared into his coffee. "I'm not much of a cook."

"That's the thing, all you have to do is warm them up. In the oven, the microwave."

She saw his face. "While I'm here, I'll show you how the oven works." It was a newish one with symbols that didn't correspond with those of Ali's oven at home. She'd Googled the instructions to find out which was the fan setting. Even for a novice like Brian, selecting the temperature was straightforward enough, although the dial made it tricky to read. She wrote it down for him.

129

"Brian," she began. He looked up. "If you're feeling bad, as if leaving the gardening to Melody is the reason she's not here, then don't. From what you've told me, she loved gardening, creating something special." Ali was thinking about Glebe Farm as she remembered it going back a few years when there was no garden as such. A rhubarb patch at the front, a scrubby square of grass. Washing lines, laundry flapping in the wind. Now lavender flanked both sides of the footpath leading to the front door and the borders were bright with asters, geranium, crocosmia. Melody had taken charge, made the garden her own. Her choice, it seemed. Had she not wanted to be so hands-on, she could have suggested they employ a gardener. Brian surely could afford it.

"I could have done more to help," he said, "and you're right, I do feel guilty for leaving her to it." He took a breath. "But that's not why I think she's not here. I think someone . . . took her." Still refusing to acknowledge what the missing passport, the "so sorry" message might mean. "And I've an idea who it might be."

23

Ali knew what could happen when emotions were running high, that even the calmest individuals could behave in ways that were entirely out of character, do things you'd never have thought them capable of. (Nick's story about Bert Fairmont in *The Beat* killing his beloved Angela came to mind). Brian had finally got to the point and managed to say what was on his mind, the "thing" he'd remembered, the reason for asking Ali to come round.

Melody had got friendly with a man in Heft, Brian said. "So-and-so said this, so-and-so said that." Brian looked perplexed. "As if this . . . *fella* was the be-all and end-all."

"Are you saying they were involved?" Ali asked.

"Oh, I'm sure he'd like to have been," Brian told her.

"But you don't know for sure?"

"It makes me wonder, how well does anyone know another person? I mean, who they are when they shut their front door at night. It's one thing coming over all friendly and helpful to the outside world but in private you just never really know, do you?"

Ali wasn't sure whether it was Melody he was getting at or *the fella*, as yet, unnamed.

"What makes you say that?" she asked carefully.

"There was a woman at a nursery. Did you read about her?"

Ali was afraid he was about to go off on one of his tangents again. "Brian, I . . ."

"Upstanding citizen, so-called. Wonderful, the children loved her. Rated outstanding, the nursery, in one of those reports they do. And then, no warning, she was arrested." He let this sink in. "For abusing children."

"Was this somewhere round here?"

"Down south," he said. "Not that it matters. The point is, she wasn't who everyone thought she was. What I'm saying is, how do you know? How can you know? There are people living ordinary lives—good home, shopping at the local supermarket, everyone thinks what a nice person they are, pleasant, polite, when the truth is . . ." he seemed to run out of steam. "The truth is something different."

"This man," Ali said, treading carefully. "This . . . *fella*. Can you tell me anything about him?"

"Mr Helpful. Always there at just the right moment to lend a hand. Know-it-all, keen gardener. She'd come home with cuttings, ideas about plants she wanted to buy. So-and-so says there's a geranium that's wonderful for ground cover, flowers all summer, comes back year after year. He knew what he was doing, all right. There's me, out of the picture, head under a bonnet, trying to shift a nut that seized up decades ago, leaving the way clear for him to act like he's Charlie Dimmock"—he stopped, reconsidered—"Wait, is that a woman?" Ali nodded. "The other one then, with the dogs. Filling my wife's head with ideas."

"And you think this man might have something to do with Melody going missing?"

"I do, yes, I do. Worth looking into, don't you think?"

"I can certainly try to find out who he is," Ali said, wishing he'd said something before now.

Death in the Countryside

"I *know* who he is," Brian said giving her one of his withering looks, as if to say she hadn't been paying attention, which was unfair, Ali felt, since she had hung on his every word. "Leslie Masters. Lives on Hagg Bank on his own, house with the blue door."

24

It went through Ali's mind that Melody may have been getting more than gardening tips from Leslie Masters. Having an affair, perhaps. Then again, would she have been quite so open about how helpful he was being if she had something to hide? It seemed unlikely. Unless, of course, all the talk of Leslie and his gardening expertise was a ploy, a neat way of throwing Brian off the scent. Go on so much about someone they almost become part of the furniture.

When she asked how Melody had met Leslie (thinking he might work at a garden center, the nursery out at Mirlaw, perhaps, which her parents said was the best, the staff really knew their stuff) Brian gave her another of his looks. As if he'd already gone into the ins and outs of it all. Which he hadn't. "At the tip," he said. "That's where he works."

Ali could see how that would work. All those trips Melody made with garden waste, Leslie heroically on hand to lift the heavy bags from the boot of the car and empty their contents into the skips.

She wanted to know why Brian hadn't said anything about any of this before. A man who was friendly with Melody—didn't he think that was important? It hadn't occurred to him, he said, although Ali found that unlikely, remembering one of their earlier conversations when she had sensed he wasn't telling her everything.

"It's not helpful if you're going to withhold information," she told him.

"No, well, I didn't want to mention any of this. Didn't see the need. I was sure Melody would be back by now," he said.

After a damp start, the sun was shining, the day warming up. It was Friday, almost a week since Melody had gone. Ali drove with the windows down, Wilson sniffing the air. Heft's main street was busy, shoppers dawdling outside the old-fashioned sweet shop, its window display evocative of an earlier time. As they went past St. Michael's Ali saw the disabled bay was occupied by an SUV. She hoped it had a Blue Badge correctly displayed or woe betide the driver. Further on, on the pavement outside Rise, there were tables and chairs, people having coffee and pastries. The smell of baking drifted into the Hilux. Wilson craned his neck. "I know," Ali said, "smells good, doesn't it? Makes you want to call in and pick up a treat." He gave her a hopeful look. "Not today, and don't look at me like that." Despite Evelyn's objections, it was clear the cakery-bakery had injected energy into the high street. It was a definite improvement on what had been there before, an empty shop with whitewash on the windows and peeling paintwork. Ali hoped that over time things might settle down between Evelyn and the newcomers.

She parked at the bottom of Hagg Bank. Identifying what she felt sure was the home of green-fingered Leslie Masters wasn't too difficult. Toward the end of the row of cottages, the garden of number three stood out. Dazzling, full of color. Purple aubretia tumbled over the front wall, scented pink roses hung from an arch

Maria Malone

above the gate. No lawn as such, more a meadow with yellow rag-wort and cornflowers, a sprawling buddleia that was host to bees and butterflies. The borders that edged the path to the front door were crowded with grasses and daisy-like blooms in yellow and burned orange, spiky crimson salvia, tall poppies. In their midst, gerbera in shades of red and pink, gold, brilliant yellow, like the ones Ali's father grew. Unruly white roses clambered up the wall at the side of the front door. It looked natural, as if it had happened by chance, although Ali doubted it. Something so lovely had to be the creation of someone who knew what they were doing. She rang the bell, noting that the door was teal, more green than blue. Around her, the air seemed to vibrate with the sound of bees making their way from one plant to another.

Ali wasn't sure she would find Leslie Masters at home. There was a chance he'd be working. When a man of about sixty came to the door, white shirt, sleeves rolled up to the elbow, smart navy trousers, tan brogues, she thought for a moment she was at the wrong house.

"Leslie Masters?" she asked.

The man nodded. "That's me."

Ali tried not to appear surprised. From what Brian had said, she assumed Leslie Masters spent every bit of his free time working outside—digging over a border, doing a spot of hedge-trimming, checking the roses for greenfly—and had therefore imagined a slightly disheveled figure, possibly wearing wellies caked in mud, old trousers tucked in, a jumper full of holes. In short, much like her dad when he was gardening.

"I'm Sergeant Ali Wren, based in Heft. Is it all right to come in for a moment?"

Leslie Masters nodded. "By all means." He turned to Wilson. "And who's this handsome chap?" Wilson wagged his tail, acknowledging another fan.

"This is Wilson," Ali said.

Death in the Countryside

"Wilson. Sounds . . . solid, official. Like you mean business, boy." He gave Ali a smile. Piercing blue eyes, fresh, soapy smell. "Wouldn't have quite the same gravitas if he was called, I don't know, Pongo. Or Peanut." Another smile. "Very nice to meet you, Officer Wilson." He held out a hand to the spaniel who offered a paw. They shook, all very formal.

Leslie Masters showed them into the sitting room at the front of the house. It was small, just able to accommodate the leather settee, the single armchair at the side of the tiled fireplace, the mahogany writing bureau facing the window. The desk was open, a pen and a pad left out. Either side of the chimney breast were shelves crammed with books and what looked like family photos in frames. Ali glimpsed the titles of one or two of the books: *Wolf Hall, The Singapore Grip*. Above the fireplace was a painting, a seascape in black streaked with gray. No television that she could see. Whatever Ali had expected of a man who lived alone and worked at the tip—clutter, disorder, mess, perhaps (she felt a stab of shame for making such an assumption)—this wasn't it. She sat on the settee, Wilson at her feet. Leslie took the armchair. At its side on the floor a book lay open.

"What can I help you with, Sergeant?" If Leslie Masters felt anxious about a visit from the police, it didn't show.

Ali came straight to the point. "I wanted to ask you about Melody Bright. She's a friend of yours?"

"That might be overstating things," Leslie said, "although I do know Melody a little—from work, mainly."

"You work at the tip?" Ali was keen to clarify this. She was starting to think Brian Bright had got the wrong end of the stick. It was difficult to picture the man now facing her in a hi-vis vest and work boots, dealing with other people's rubbish.

"That's right," he said. "Melody's a regular. Garden waste, mostly. That's how we got talking."

So Brian was right. "You gave her advice on gardening."

He rubbed his chin. "I did, yes." Wedding ring, Ali saw. Perhaps he didn't live alone, as Brian had said. She glanced again at the bookshelves.

"How well do you know her?" Ali asked.

He sat thinking. Ali craned her neck to read the title of the book he was reading. *Middle Age.*

"Not all that well," he said. "She's a gardener, like me. When she said she was starting from scratch at Glebe Farm I offered what advice I could, gave her one or two cuttings, that sort of thing."

"Have you been there?" Ali asked. "Glebe Farm?"

"No, she didn't ask me to go and, well, I'm quite busy with my own garden and work and"—he shrugged—"so on, you know."

"Did she ever visit you here?"

"No. We saw each other at the tip. If I had cuttings to give her, I took them to work with me, handed them over when she came in. Which she did, almost every week."

"Have you worked at the tip long?" Ali still couldn't quite picture Leslie emptying Melody's sacks of grass cuttings, dragging old appliances into skips. He seemed too . . . elegant, too cultured. Another wave of shame hit her. Was she being a snob? Why shouldn't a man appreciate the finer things at the same time as tackling menial work?

He smiled. "I moved to Heft almost twenty years ago and landed my dream job shortly after." Another smile. Those eyes. Ali could see why Melody might have been taken with him. "In case you're wondering, working at the tip is truly my dream job. Out in the open, decent colleagues, people coming and going. All manner of fascinating items, all with their own history, dropped off." Making it sound like an auction house, a collection point for rare and valuable family heirlooms, rather than a repository of rubbish.

"Isn't most of it junk?" Ali asked before she could stop herself.

He laughed. "It rather depends on your point of view. I'll give

Death in the Countryside

you an example." He indicated the writing bureau. "A fine piece of furniture destined to be dumped. Nothing wrong with it. The chap who brought it in had got a new desk, something suitable for a computer and didn't have room for the bureau, so I asked if I could take it. It's walnut, eighteenth century. But I don't suppose you really came here because you're interested in the tip." He became serious. "Is Melody all right?"

"When did you last see her?"

Without having to think about it, Leslie said, "Last Saturday." The day she had gone missing. "Why? Has something happened."

"She didn't come home on that day. As far as we're aware, she's not been seen since."

Leslie seemed shocked. "She's missing?"

Ali watched him closely. "You've not seen the posters in town?"

He thought hard for a moment. "I'm not in town a great deal, I tend to do most of my food shopping online, but now you mention it, I do remember seeing something . . . A notice of some sort next to the bus shelter." He looked uncomfortable. "I'm afraid I didn't investigate."

"Can you just give me the details of that last encounter you had?" She had her notebook out.

"On the high street. I was coming out of the shoe repairer, and I saw her go past. Obviously, I know the car from when she comes to the tip."

"She didn't pull up—you didn't speak to her?"

"No, nothing like that."

"Do you remember what time it was? Which way she was going?"

"About ten, I think. I don't pay close attention to the time at the weekend, I'm afraid. She was heading in the direction of Skipden."

On her way to Carla's studio, then, Ali guessed. "This is a long shot, but you didn't happen to see what she was wearing—what kind of top she had on? A scarf, maybe?"

He shook his head. "Actually, to be accurate, it was the car I saw, and only from behind. I can't even be sure it was Melody driving."

25

"Did you search the house?" Brian wanted to know when he called Ali later. "Because I think you should."

"Melody didn't go to his house," Ali said.

Brian snorted. "Is that what he said? And you took his word for it?"

She didn't answer right away. She had seen no reason to disbelieve what Leslie Masters told her. Nothing about him, or the house, had been cause for concern. And Wilson had liked him on sight, which was the clincher. She was curious about the books, the photographs on the shelves. When she asked if he lived alone, he said yes but wore his wedding ring because he hoped one day he and his wife would work through their difficulties (without saying what they were) and start again. Ali was desperate to know more but had no good enough reason to probe further. Unless Melody was why Mrs. Masters was absent. Not that she detected any sense of impropriety there, nothing that hinted Leslie was lying about what he said was an entirely innocent relationship. Ali liked to think her intuition was good, that she was able to read people, and her reading of Leslie Masters was that he was straightforward, hardworking. She had met enough slippery types in her time, charmers with something to hide. The ones who gave her the creeps. She could spot them a mile off. And Wilson, well, she trusted his instincts even more than her own. He was discerning, not one to offer his paw to just anyone.

"I'm satisfied with what he told me, yes," Ali told Brian. "If there's reason to look at him again, I will, I promise."

Brian muttered something. "We might have a prime suspect on the doorstep and we're doing nothing."

Ali wasn't sure what Leslie was suspected of—abduction? Worse? Did Brian think Melody was having an affair, that while Ali was in the sitting room chatting to Leslie, she was upstairs keeping quiet? Hiding in plain sight? She had come across that before but, again, she trusted Wilson to alert her if something didn't feel right. Would he have sensed the presence of someone else? Would he have reacted? Yes, she was certain.

"What if her car's in the garage?" Brian wanted to know. "There's a shed at the back, did you look inside?"

Ali hadn't asked about a garage or checked the back garden. It hadn't seemed necessary when Leslie's only encounters with Melody were in public, at his place of work. Was he really the "prime suspect," as Brian put it, or was this more about blaming someone (anyone), a case of clutching at straws?

"Brian, let me do my job. Please." She waited a beat. "And I don't want you going round there. It wouldn't help."

She called Freeman and brought him up to date, feeling as if what she had to report didn't amount to much. He listened, occasionally saying *Right*, or *What's your gut feeling on that*? The Chief Superintendent was a great one for instinct, intuition. They were on the same page there. What his intuition was telling him now was that Melody Bright had left her husband almost a week earlier, having spent months planning her departure. Her passport was gone, money withdrawn from her bank account. On top of all that—and this spoke volumes, in Freeman's view—was the note she had left. He felt certain Melody was having an affair. *But*. They weren't there yet. Until she was located, they would, with a degree of caution, continue to treat her as a missing person. Privately, Ali wondered if enough was being done to find Melody yet; given what they now knew, it was impossible to disagree with her boss's assessment. When he asked what she'd made of Masters, she hesitated. Brian had sown a seed of doubt and Freeman picked up on it in her voice.

"Okay. What did Wilson make of him?"

"They got on, sir," she said.

Like her, Freeman put his faith in Wilson. "There you are, then," he said. "You can't pull the wool over a dog's eyes. They can sense good from bad, right from wrong. If something was up, he'd know. And he'd find a way of letting you know."

She wondered what Brian would have to say about the weight (disproportionate, he might feel) given to Wilson's opinion.

26

"Any progress on your missing woman?" Nick asked.

"Brian 'remembered' something," Ali said. She told Nick about Leslie—the books, the artwork in his cottage. She described the garden in Hagg Bank, glorious, she said, like something you might get at the Chelsea Flower Show, only less gimmicky, and how Leslie and Melody had clicked during her frequent jaunts to the tip.

"She kept arriving with sacks of garden waste and Leslie, being a gentleman, gave her a hand getting them into the skip."

"He works there?"

Ali nodded. "Not that you'd know to look at him. I mean if you're thinking wellies and a hi-vis jacket, forget it, he's seriously smart. Good-looking, as well."

"I'm jealous."

"Of Leslie?"

"Working at the tip. I've always thought it must be the best job."

"Seriously?"

"Seriously. Outside all day, endless comings and goings, all kinds of interesting things to rummage through."

"That's what he said."

"There you are then."

"Anyway," Ali said, "from what I can make out, he didn't know

Death in the Countryside

Melody particularly well, but now Brian's got it into his head he's somehow involved with her disappearance. The prime suspect, he called him."

Nick made a face. "What's he actually accusing him of?"

"Stealing her away, holding her captive in the garden shed." How did Brian even know about the shed, that there was a garage? Had he been spying? She would have to warn him to stay away.

"No chance he might be right?"

"I ran his details through the system. No convictions, law-abiding citizen. He seems . . . ordinary."

"Ordinary like Julian Stott?"

Ali looked blank. "The apprentice at the garage in *The Beat*," Nick said. "Lovely Julian, the type to help old ladies with their shopping." Ali vaguely remembered. She shook her head. "Before your time, maybe. We're talking early on, before you were a fan. Young girl went missing on her way home from school, Julian helped search for her. Couldn't have been more helpful."

"I can guess where this is going."

"He had her, tied up, a gag to stop her screaming"—he paused, letting this sink in—"and guess where she was?"

"Tell me."

"In the cellar of the house he shared with his mother. The police found her, thankfully. As for Julian . . . very disturbed. And no one had any idea."

"I bet his mum did."

Nick smiled. "She claimed to know nothing. But the girl *was* in her cellar . . ."

"What does your Julian have to do with anything?"

"Just being helpful. Did you check the shed?"

"Brian asked the same thing. No, I didn't."

Nick raised an eyebrow. "Okaaaay."

"Wilson liked him."

"That's all right then."

145

Maria Malone

They sat in silence, Ali thinking. "I'll go back tomorrow."

"Why not tonight? Why not now?"

Ali thought for a moment. He was right. She went upstairs and swapped her comfy drawstring pants and sweatshirt for the police T-shirt and combats she'd had on earlier. If she put off going, she'd be awake half the night worrying, imagining Melody locked in Leslie's shed. Tied up, face streaked with mascara, a strip of duct tape over her mouth.

He wasn't surprised to see her. "Come in, Sergeant," he said. "And officer Wilson." Wilson politely held up a paw, which Leslie took.

"Two visits in one day," he said, addressing the spaniel. "Aren't I fortunate?"

He turned to Ali. "Did you forget something?"

"I wondered . . . do you have a shed?"

"I do, yes."

"A garage?"

He nodded. "Indeed. I keep my car there." Ali wasn't sure if he was having a dig. He hesitated. "Would you like to take a look?"

"I'm sorry, I should have asked when I was here earlier."

They went through the hall and into the kitchen where there were signs of cooking—a pan on the stove, the smell of butter melting, a leek on the chopping board in the process of being shredded, mushrooms—and she started to apologize for interrupting, but he held up a hand in a way that said it didn't matter, then went to the cooker and turned the gas down.

He took keys from inside a cupboard, and they went out into the garden at the back, which was every bit as lovely as the one at the front. Tall grasses fringed a pond where lily pads floated, stalky yellow flowers in their midst. Leslie led the way to the shed in a corner at the back and undid the padlock.

"Help yourself," he said, standing aside.

She unclipped Wilson's lead and he went ahead, snuffling about

Death in the Countryside

among the tools lined up against the walls. On shelves were pots of different sizes, seed packets, books on British birds and butterflies, wildflower meadows. Under the work bench, a stack of plastic boxes containing bird food.

No Melody struggling to free herself from her restraints, no sign of her having been there.

Leslie unlocked the gate in the wall and crossed a cobbled lane to the garage opposite. He opened it up to reveal an old Morris Traveler. It occurred to Ali that Brian might be interested to see it. Might even want to buy it.

"This is your car?" she said unnecessarily.

Leslie smiled. Those eyes of his. "I only do a few miles and, even though it's getting on, it's reliable. A bit like its owner."

Ali felt a flush of guilt. The idea of Leslie Masters abducting Melody—killing her—seemed ludicrous. *Brian's prime suspect*. Still, it was important to be able to say she had taken his suspicions seriously. While Wilson looked over the garage, Ali, starting to feel conspicuous, checked the car, asked if she could open up the back. Leslie said to go ahead, it wasn't locked.

"Thank you," she said. "I know this must feel intrusive."

"Doing your job. I understand."

It came back to her what Nick had said about *The Beat* and lovely Julian Stott keeping a girl prisoner in the cellar of his mother's house. Gagged, bound. "Is there a cellar?" she asked.

Leslie seemed amused, as if he knew what was going through her mind. "No cellar, Sergeant Wren."

She called Wilson and they left by the back lane. She didn't much feel like going into the house and through the kitchen past the ruins of whatever it was Leslie had been cooking before she arrived.

"Nothing," she told Nick. "And I felt ridiculous searching the place, practically accusing him." Two visits in one day seemed to her to

147

smack of incompetence, as if she had needed a nudge in order to do her job properly. Not that anything in Leslie's manner suggested that was what he thought. He had been perfectly nice, courteous, uncomplaining. No hint that her arriving just as he was making dinner in any way put him out. Which only made her feel worse. *Did you forget something?* The man was no fool, putting his finger on why she was there the moment he set eyes on her. As if he knew she should have conducted a search earlier of places where a missing woman and her car might be hidden. Under Leslie's scrutiny, Ali, who was usually conscientious, meticulous, felt as if she had committed a basic error and been found out. It left her feeling foolish.

"You weren't accusing him," Nick pointed out. "Just following up on information, a possible lead."

"It wasn't information, though, was it?" Brian having a go at a man who happened to be friendly with his wife was what it was. "Brian's jealous, that's what's going on there."

"See, this is what happens when you let your wife go to the tip alone," Nick said. "Some good-looking bloke in a high-vis jacket catches her eye over the bottle bank and . . ." he made a face, drew a finger across his throat.

"Stop it."

For a moment they were quiet, Ali wondering if the move to Heft, where what passed for crime could be minor, trivial, sometimes, where on a day to day basis she was her own boss, left largely to her own devices, had somehow made her less sharp. Hadn't Freeman warned her to be on her guard about becoming too settled, too at home? Was that what was happening? It paid to remember that things aren't always what they seem, she thought. Brian, Leslie. What did she really know beyond what they'd told her? And Melody. A woman of mystery. Secretive, Lillian said. Ali was working on the assumption Melody had left Heft by choice, driven to the potter at Skipden, then on to who knows where. But what if she

Death in the Countryside

hadn't? What if she had returned home and her subsequent disappearance was linked to something that happened there, something involving Brian, who was just very clever at coming across as bumbling and innocent? Or was Melody involved with Leslie and things had turned sour between them? Then again, experience told her that women—and men—*did* sometimes choose to leave without a word. For all anyone knew, Melody could have been planning her departure for weeks, months. All those cash withdrawals. Why, though? Brian wasn't so terrible she couldn't have left a note he would find at once. Or was he? Perhaps there was a side to him Ali had not yet seen.

"At least now you know," Nick said, breaking into her thoughts.

Did she? All she knew for definite was that Leslie's shed was full of gardening tools and that he was among the minority of people who parked their car in the garage. Beyond that, she was as much in the dark as before.

149

27

Brian Bright had mixed feelings when it came to the police. In general, he tended to think they weren't always as helpful as they might be. Twice, in recent years, his premises in Bradford had been vandalised and no one from the local constabulary had come near. Not even one of those community support officers (in his eyes not even police officers in the proper sense of the term). In fairness, the damage to BBC was minor—a broken window, a poor attempt to jemmy a lock. All the same, that was hardly the point. A crime is a crime, surely. Zero tolerance et cetera. Yet all that happened was that Brian was allocated a reference number for insurance purposes and that was the end of the matter. He heard nothing more. Not so much as a visit from the crime prevention people. It had left him with little faith in the police. No wonder people took the law into their own hands.

Of course, he could see that Ali Wren was a good police officer, kind and dedicated. And that dog of hers, Wilson, had something about him. They made a good team. The sort to go out of their way to be helpful. The sight of Ali at the stove in his kitchen making him lunch, showing him how to rustle up an omelette, came back to him. If it wasn't for her, would he even have found the ground

Death in the Countryside

coffee yet? (Why did Melody keep it in that corner cupboard where the cups they never used were?). Without Ali, he'd never have worked out how to run the economy program on the washing machine. She was doing her best, he knew that, in ways that went above and beyond. He had no problem with her, none at all. *But.* It was unrealistic to expect that all her time, every bit of her energy, was going into finding Melody. There would be other cases to look into, other complaints. Brian was out of the loop, pretty much, with what was going on in Heft, but even he knew about the feud involving Hooley's and those cakery-bakery women.

A trivial matter in the great scheme of things, hardly enough to warrant police attention or distract from a missing persons case, but he felt sure Ali Wren would be embroiled all the same. In a place like Heft, people expected the local bobby to be available, to spin plates the whole time. And then there were the protesters waving placards about in front of Heft Hall. He had no idea what was going on there (some quarrel over the right to roam?) but again it was bound to be a drain on Ali's time. Time that would have been better spent on Melody. A week had passed. It seemed an eternity. He felt a sudden stab of guilt. Here he was, expecting so much of his local constabulary when he had been less than open with Ali, not entirely honest.

Not that he had lied. Not as such. It was more that he had kept certain things to himself. Things that might have been useful for her to know about. What his own informal investigations into Leslie Masters (still the prime suspect in his opinion) had thrown up, for instance.

The search of Masters' home might have led nowhere, but for several weeks, well before Melody went missing, Brian had been busy gathering evidence of his own. Prompted by how often Melody mentioned Leslie, Brian had been to the tip to observe him at work. Found a place to park at the bottom of Hagg Bank and

151

watched him arrive home on his bike, outside in the garden filling bird feeders, snipping dead flowers from the buddleia. And while it felt slightly shameful to be spying in this way, he felt justified, needing to know whether Leslie Masters posed a threat to his marriage. Now his wife was missing, and he was desperate. People would understand.

What he knew was that on Mondays when the tip was closed Leslie Masters was in the habit of getting into his Morris Traveler (a lovely car, in Brian's professional opinion, excellent condition) and driving to Simonthwaite, parking in the forestry car park, putting on a pair of walking boots, taking a rucksack from the back seat, and heading off up the green trail toward the summit and the Black Stone. What he did up there, what was in the rucksack, Brian had no idea. He could simply have been going for a walk, of course, entirely innocent, like everyone else visiting the Black Stone. Or there could be more to it. On one occasion, Brian thought he saw Leslie put a bunch of flowers wrapped in cellophane into his bag, although since he didn't have the best view from the other end of the car park where he was hunched low in his seat, he couldn't actually swear to it. Who took flowers with them on a walk? It got him thinking.

To his frustration, Brian knew little about Leslie Masters' past. He had noticed he wore a wedding ring (binoculars coming in handy there) but there was no Mrs. Masters. Why not? What had gone on there? Ignoring the most obvious answer, that the marriage had simply ended and they'd gone their separate ways, Brian allowed himself to speculate. Wildly, at times. Perhaps Leslie had done away with her. Pushed her off the Black Stone. And now, filled with remorse and regret, in a twisted act of remembrance, he took flowers to lay at the spot. The very spot where he had . . . killed her. This was where Brian's feverish imagination had led him.

On four occasions (all he was able to manage, given his own

Death in the Countryside

work commitments) over a period of six weeks Brian had witnessed Leslie's journey to the Black Stone, and the peculiar business with the flowers. In neat handwriting, he noted down every in detail—what he saw, what he thought he saw, the conclusions he came to—surprised how much he was able to glean simply by watching a man drive to a beauty spot and take a walk. In his notes were details of what Leslie wore on these occasions, a close-fitting jacket, the sort of modern, narrow-legged tracksuit bottoms Brian found unseemly, yet his rival—as he thought of him—seemed able to get away with. Watching Leslie, Brian felt a sense of inferiority, comparing his own chinos, his shirt with its button-down collar, with the youthful leisurewear and mirror sunglasses a man Leslie's age should never have been able to carry off and yet, frustratingly, managed to. He looked at home in the hills, as if he'd stepped from the pages of one of those outdoors catalogues that sometimes arrived unsolicited with their images of individuals, strong, rugged, staring into the distance, laughing for no apparent reason. It was plain annoying.

The eureka moment came on his third surveillance mission, a fortnight before Melody disappeared. On that occasion, Leslie descended from the Black Stone, and instead of heading back to Heft, drove in the opposite direction along the valley. Brian almost missed this important change of routine. Bored with sitting in the car park for almost three hours, he had been on the point of leaving. Instead, he followed the Morris along the valley and watched it pull up outside the Bull, where a woman—more a girl, really, long fair hair, baggy jeans, sweater slipping off one shoulder—rushed out, the two of them very familiar. *Very.* Leslie giving her hand a squeeze, sitting themselves at one of the picnic tables at the front of the pub. Brian would have loved to know what was going on there, although it was obvious really—to him, anyway—that Leslie Masters and the young woman, the *girl*, were involved.

153

Maria Malone

As he waited, someone else appeared with a tray of drinks. A young man in a T-shirt and shorts. He put the drinks down and shook hands with Leslie. Brian was thrown. Had he misread things? No, he didn't think so. His gut told him there was something between Leslie and the girl, something deep, significant. The man could be anyone. A friend, her brother. The more Brian watched, the more convinced he became that he was on to something.

He tried not to think about what Ali Wren might make of his behavior and focused instead on how grateful she would be when he pulled together what he thought of as the missing strands regarding his prime suspect and presented them to her. The encounter he had witnessed at the Bull between Leslie and the young woman, surely there was motive, right there, for getting rid of his wife. And if he was capable of killing once . . . He disregarded the voice inside his head that told him, in a faintly mocking tone, that he was getting carried away, concocting a fantastical story that was far-fetched, ridiculous, a means of making sense of what he already knew. Thought he knew. When there was no evidence for any of it.

He sighed and concentrated on the papers, his "findings," now littering the kitchen table where a mere seven days earlier he'd had breakfast with his wife, no hint of what was to come. So far, infuriatingly, his efforts to discover more about Leslie Masters' background had drawn a blank. Using the computer at his place of work, he had searched for murder + wife + council refuse worker + Leslie Masters. Nothing. In an age where everything was online, wasn't that odd? There was no one Brian knew well enough in Heft to ask what the gossip on Leslie might be. He remembered Melody encouraging him to get to know people, join the local bowls club, when they first moved there. He kicked himself now, wishing he had taken her advice, sensing his investigation had stalled, come to a dead end.

Death in the Countryside

His findings were incomplete, and he was reluctant to share them with Ali, but the time had surely come. She would be able to do more—access the police database or whatever—fill in those missing gaps.

Make sure Leslie Masters was stopped in his tracks.

28

Ali was due to spend the evening with her parents when a knock came at the door. Brian, clutching what appeared to be a folder of some kind. Keen to share something "significant," he told her.

Her heart sank. She had been about to leave. "I don't suppose it would wait until the morning?" she asked hopefully.

Brian seemed taken aback. "Not really," he said. "No, I wouldn't have thought so."

She didn't mind, not really. Unexpected knocks on the door were, she reminded herself, the nature of the job. It was Sunday, though, a special occasion, her parents' wedding anniversary. Forty-five years, which warranted a celebration. Her mother had been cooking, making a big effort, judging by the string of texts Ali had received from her since first thing: *Was four hours long enough to marinade the meat*? *Was Nick OK with lamb*? *It would be well done, not pink, because that's how her father liked it—was that all right*? Violet had planned on doing dauphinoise potatoes but—and again, this was Gordon—it would be roasties, which had thrown her timings. On and on. Ali replied each time to say it was fine, whatever she cooked would be lovely. Why her mother, who didn't

Death in the Countryside

much seem to enjoy cooking, insisted on putting herself through culinary hell like this, Ali couldn't fathom. Nick had phoned to say he'd been held up at work and would see her there. Now it looked as if she would be late.

Brian sat at the table in the kitchen, awkward, the folder in front of him, Wilson at his side, watching with interest. Brian reached out a hand and ruffled the dog's hair.

"Have you eaten?" Ali asked as the kettle boiled.

Brian shook his head. "I've not had time."

A man used to someone looking after him, little know-how when it came to taking care of himself. Looking slightly rumpled, even thinner in the face. She had quiche, chutney, a bag of salad leaves, and before he could object, she put it all out with a fresh loaf from Hooley's, told him to help himself, and got on with making a pot of tea.

"Sorry," Brian said, "are you going out?" Seeming suddenly to register that she was wearing a dress, something long and floaty, instead of her usual uniform of combats and T-shirt, and that her hair was loose, arranged in soft copper curls, rather than in its customary ponytail.

"Seeing my parents, but you're all right, I'm fine for time." A lie. "What's bothering you?" She carried the teapot to the table and sat facing him. "Has something happened?"

Brian waited a moment. "I know the police are stretched," he began. "I mean, it's obvious. We're always hearing we need more officers." He looked at her, frowning. "Police stations closing, some in places you wouldn't believe. Cleckheaton. I mean, who in their right mind would think a place that size can do without a station?" He shook his head in disbelief. "There was a time, if you called the police to report a crime, someone would come out." Ali opened her mouth to say something, but Brian hadn't finished. He fixed her with a penetrating look. "I'm not having a go at you. I know how much you do, what you're doing for Melody, and, believe me, I have no complaints, none. This isn't about you."

She glanced at the clock. Any minute now, her mother would be on the phone, asking where she was.

"I told you about what went on in Bradford with my business," Brian was now saying. Had he? "The break-in," he went on. "*Attempted* break-in, at any rate. It was only because I'd made the place secure, decent locks, bars on the windows, that kind of thing, they didn't get in, but they had a damn good go." He glanced at Ali. "Those cars of mine are worth a bit, unique some of them. I've a Rover, 1971, immaculate, they've used it on *The Beat*. Imagine if someone made off with it, we'd all be in the mire. So you see, I can't risk losing a car." He looked briefly outraged. "Half the time the ones trying to get into a place aren't even there to steal whatever's inside, they only want to cause mischief."

Ali thought about Evelyn Hooley's break-in. Flour on the floor, the glass shelves not where she had left them. No damage, as such, just a mess. *A message.* Things had gone quiet on that front. It struck her she had not given Evelyn much thought since the "break-in" almost a week earlier, her mind too full of Melody. Guilt washed over her, and she made a mental note to check all was well there. She was silent as Brian ate the quiche.

He swallowed, put his knife and fork down. "And I got no help from the police, no one even came out. A crime number, that was the extent of it. As if it was nothing, when it's my livelihood at stake here. Not that they cared about that. And I'm not the only one feels like that, practically everyone you talk to will tell you the same. The police aren't interested, not in what they consider the small stuff, the little people. Like me." He looked up. "As I say, none of this applies to you."

"Brian," Ali began, "does this have something to do with Melody?"

Death in the Countryside

He seemed surprised. "Not directly, no. It's just, I understand resources are limited, that there's only so much you can do."

The "Missing" posters around Heft, in Skipden and beyond, had brought some calls, members of the public who might have seen Melody. Nothing concrete.

"I wonder," she said carefully, "what you make of her withdrawing so much cash from her bank account, if that puts a different perspective on things, means it's more likely"—Ali hesitated, not sure how best to say that in her opinion Melody had simply left him—"well, I mean, there's no evidence she's come to any harm, is there?" All those trips to Newcastle.. *If* that was where she'd been going.

Brian didn't seem to be listening. He drank down his tea. "What do people really want when they come to the police? To be listened to, that's what. You want to feel they're *doing* something. You know? No stone left unturned if you like. Whether it's a stolen bicycle or a missing person. You need to know you're being taken seriously." He fixed her with a long look. "That's how I feel, at any rate, and I think I'm in tune with the general population."

Ali sneaked another look at the clock. She should have been at her parents' house twenty minutes ago. Instead, she was listening to another of Brian's ramblings, which, as far as she could tell, had no bearing on his wife's disappearance. Being patient, polite. And why? Because she felt for him. She tried to imagine what Freeman might say if he could see her now, pandering to a man some would consider a nuisance. *Feeding* him, for crying out loud. Talk about a soft touch. Her phone beeped. A text. Her dad: *Nick's here. Where are you?*

"I'm sorry, Brian, I'm going to have to get off," she said.

Brian nodded. He had eaten the quiche, most of the salad, some of Evelyn's bread. "Right, he said. "Well. I think I've made my point."

159

What point was that, then? Something vague about the shortage of police officers, the lack of urgency when it came to tackling all but the most serious of crimes? Or had she switched off at some stage, missed something important? Her head was spinning.

"Anyway, I'll leave you in peace." He placed the folder he had brought in front of her. "It's all in there."

29

She hadn't been going to look at it. It would be to do with falling police numbers, victims of crime complaining they'd been let down. Clippings from the papers to do with another missing person case that was, unfairly, getting a good deal more coverage than Melody. It wasn't fair, Ali knew that better than anyone. Life wasn't fair. And Brian was the type, she suspected, to pounce on newspaper stories that fed into his sense of injustice. Then again, why shouldn't he? She stared at the file. Wilson had retired to his bed and was chewing on a squeaky sausage roll, having decided they mustn't be going out after all. Ali called him and he was up at once, the toy abandoned. Another text arrived, this time from Nick: ?????? Brian's folder called to her. Whatever was in it would have to wait. She hesitated. It couldn't hurt to skim the first page or so, just to confirm it held nothing of importance, otherwise it would be on her mind all evening. Wilson stood at the door, tail wagging, eager to be off.

"Sorry, boy," she said. "Five minutes."

He slunk back to bed and resumed tearing into the sausage roll.

She was wrong to think that if she didn't peek at Brian's file it would prey on her mind and spoil her night, because her cursory

Maria Malone

examination of the contents managed to have precisely the same effect. All the time she was with her parents celebrating their anniversary, toasting them with champagne, the real stuff, looking through the wedding album, eating the feast her mother had prepared (the lamb, well done at her father's insistence, perfect, the roast potatoes he had requested, just right) all she could think about was Brian and the fact he'd been carrying out his own surveillance of Leslie Masters. Brian Bright's secret life. She'd not had time to read the entire file, but from what she'd seen so far Brian was obsessed. And, worryingly, had been for several weeks (long before Melody vanished) convinced that Leslie Masters was pursuing her. Had Melody known what Brian was doing? Had Brian's fixation with Leslie Masters prompted her to go? Brian said no, insisting she knew nothing about it. The file was disturbing in its detail. Dates, times, what Leslie had on, the steps Brian had taken to disguise his own appearance—hats and scarves, jackets with the collars turned up. Driving an anonymous Ford Fiesta rather than the E-Type. Clearly, Brian had been spending an unhealthy amount of his time monitoring Leslie and as a consequence knew far more about his life, his habits than Ali did. But then, unlike Brian, Ali hadn't deemed him worthy of investigation. As far as she was aware, his connection to Melody was tenuous. She pictured Brian skulking about, tailing Leslie, keeping far enough back so as not to arouse suspicion. He had thought of pretty much everything other than that his actions amounted to stalking, bordering on madness. She wasn't sure what to do about it, that was the problem. Brian, doing his best to be helpful, getting it so badly wrong.

"Calling planet earth," her father said, pulling her back to the present. "You look miles away."

"Working too hard," Nick said.

Ali looked round the table. Gordon frowning, Violet attempting a bright smile, Nick giving her a look that said he knew what was up, that she wasn't really there, her brain still engaged on work

Death in the Countryside

matters. She looked at Iris, who was facing her. Iris, who'd managed to have her hair done and arrive on time despite having to drive up from Harrogate.

"Sorry," Ali said, picking up her wine and taking a drink. "A bit preoccupied."

"She never stops," Nick said.

Ali caught the flicker of worry in Violet's eyes. Her mother, to Ali's surprise, had struck a note of caution when she said she was returning to Heft. "I mean, I want you home," she'd said. "It's just . . . careful what you wish for. I wonder if you'll get a minute to yourself." Echoing Ali's predecessor. "You know what people are like, they'll all want you involved."

"Trying your patience, are they, the locals?" Iris said, mischief in her voice. "I know what they're like—Dad wanting you to help out in the garden, Mum foisting all her surplus baking on you."

"We hardly see her," Violet protested.

"She has a very full caseload," Nick said.

"Sounds like you're overstretched," Gordon said. "Can't you get any help?"

"I'm fine," Ali told them. "It's all manageable. The hours are unpredictable, that's all."

"It's not nine to five, that's for sure," Nick said.

"Neither is television," Ali shot back, a little more sharply than she'd intended. "I'm just saying," she went on, catching Nick's look, softening her tone, "most jobs have their . . . moments. When you're required to put yourself out a bit, do some unpaid overtime. It goes with the territory."

"Tell me about it," Iris said, pulling a face. She taught eleven to sixteen year olds at a private school, part of the Institute group, where the approach was supposedly holistic, experimental, the emphasis on creativity and spiritual awareness, their mission to find a child's purpose, unlock their full potential. It sounded airy-fairy, cranky, her dad said, but the fact was they got excellent results. Like Ali, Iris worked long hours. At least she had the holidays, although even then she seemed to have something work-related on the go. If anything, Iris was even more conscientious when it came to her job than Ali.

"Is it all petty stuff you're dealing with?" Iris wanted to know. "Disputes about hedges, someone parking outside next door's house, that kind of thing."

"There's a woman gone missing," Violet said. "That's what Ali's busy with."

"That'll be the husband," Iris said. "It's always the husband."

Ali sighed, thinking of Brian arriving at the house with his folder just as she was about to leave, his "reports" peppered with words like "prime suspect" and "incriminating evidence." Brian Bright, P.I.

"Is that what people are saying?" She looked at Gordon, then Violet. "In town—do people think Brian might have done something to her?"

"Nobody I talk to," Violet said, getting to her feet. "There's pudding, you know. Pannacotta. Raspberries. Cream, if anyone wants it."

Gordon beamed at her.

Ali gave her mother a hand to clear the table.

"You're looking tired," Violet said once they were in the kitchen. "It's not too much, is it, being here? People expecting so much of you."

"It's fine," Ali said, "honestly." Was it, though? She had no clue to the whereabouts of Melody Bright, and Brian playing detective threatened to further complicate matters. The lack of meaningful progress felt frustrating. She was still waiting for Melody's phone records, which Freeman was now chasing up. Finding out who Melody had been in touch with prior to her disappearance was vital. With luck, the call log would provide essential clues about where she was going when she had driven away a week earlier. Ali

Death in the Countryside

had spoken again to Lillian (almost impossible, as usual, getting hold of her) in the hope that Melody had been in touch. "I've told you," Lillian had said, sounding put out, as if Ali had interrupted something crucial, some must-see afternoon TV, perhaps, "we don't speak." Ali had reminded her to get in touch immediately if she heard anything, to which Lillian replied, offhand, "I'm the last person she'd call."

"You don't think it was the wrong decision . . . to come back?" Violet said. "I worry there's not enough for you here, outside your work. The people you knew aren't here now."

Valerie Cartwright, Ali's best friend from junior school, still her closest chum, had recently moved away, her husband's job taking them to Penrith. Valerie had been in Heft forever. It was a blow, awful timing, Valerie leaving just as Ali got confirmation the Heft job was hers. A bad omen. Ali had been so looking forward to spending more time with her. Of course, she now realized, she was so busy they would hardly have seen one another.

"Really, Mum, don't worry."

"Everyone says such lovely things about you. Roger Felton's a big fan. I'm always hearing how you've done someone a good turn." She gave Ali a long look. "Although a lot of it doesn't sound like police work, to be honest, and I wonder . . . you don't think folk are taking advantage of your good nature?"

Not deliberately, perhaps. "It's the obvious thing to do, turn to the local bobby when you're not sure what else to do, isn't it?"

Violet nodded, tipping individual creamy puddings onto plates.

"They look good." Ali was impressed.

"I've been practicing. We've had a fair few of these in recent weeks, me and your dad."

"I don't suppose he was complaining."

"How he stays so slim with that sweet tooth of his I'll never know."

"It's the gardening."

They were quiet for a moment while Violet adjusted a raspberry here and there. "Iris looks well," Ali said.

"She does."

"Did we fight much when we were growing up? I mean, was there ever anything really bad?"

"You ended up with a fishhook in your hand one day. The two of you digging round in your father's fishing bag, which you'd been told not to touch."

Ali smiled, remembering. "You took me to hospital. I thought they were going to cut my hand off."

"You howled, didn't want the doctor anywhere near you."

"We never came to blows over anything, though?" Her thoughts on Lillian, her catastrophic breach with Melody. Lillian gleefully locking her little sister in the wardrobe in her mother's room.

Violet poured cream into a jug. "There was the business with the dress, the white one. She didn't know you had it, then you put it back covered in red wine."

"Not *covered* exactly," Ali said.

"A stain in the shape of . . ." she tailed off, trying to remember.

"Sicily," Ali said.

"That's right. Never did get it out. Iris was in floods over it."

Ali, remembering her sister's tears, her fury, couldn't recall how they'd got past it. She had no memory of them going longer than a day or so not speaking. Iris had not sought revenge or even demanded Ali pay for a new dress. Ali had groveled, apologized, arranged for a local florist to deliver flowers, an enormous bouquet of irises. Never again did she plunder her sister's wardrobe, not without her knowledge and permission.

Violet inspected the plates. "Nearly forgot the soil," she said.

The *soil*? Ali remembered when pudding meant stewed plums, ice cream, tinned mandarins. Strawberry jelly, often studded with peanuts, an invention of her mother's. When did Violet become so

Death in the Countryside

adventurous? Violet spooned what looked like some sort of chocolate crumb onto the plates and wiped the edge of each one with a tea towel. Like a professional.

"I was speaking to Evelyn Hooley," Violet said, something in her tone causing Ali, a pannacotta in each hand, about to head back to the dining toom, to pause. "Said she nearly burned the house down. Or at least someone did."

"When? What do you mean?"

"A few days ago," Violet said. "She left a pan on—or *someone* did—and, it caught, made quite a mess in the kitchen."

"Who's this 'someone'?"

"Well, that's the mystery. There's only Evelyn. And Trevor." Ali looked blank. "Her ginger tabby, very handsome. You must have seen Trevor?" Ali hadn't. She had sat in Evelyn's kitchen and somehow failed to spot anything to indicate the presence of a cat. Was there a cat flap? Not that she'd seen.

"Well, it wouldn't be Trevor," Violet was saying, "although he can open doors, turn the handle, apparently, so maybe he *could* switch the gas on, although I doubt even Trevor could manage the ignition. Anyway, Evelyn's very particular about checking she's switched everything off before she goes out, and yet . . ." Violet gave a shrug. "*Some*how the gas managed to turn itself back on and reignite. Which obviously isn't the kind of thing that would happen of its own accord."

"So she had an intruder." Ali was thinking about the bakery, the flour on the floor, the missing tea towel, the dodgy catch on the window at the back, Evelyn's habit of failing to lock up when she left the house. Too trusting, too casual when it came to security. "Mum, how come I'm only hearing about this now?"

"I got the impression she wasn't sure it could be classed as police business."

"If someone went in and put the gas on hoping to torch the place, it definitely *is*."

"*If* they did. She's a lot on her mind, what with those young women over the road putting a dent in her trade. She might have forgotten to switch the pan off."

Or someone was targeting her. First the bakery, now at home. Where she lived alone. Not counting Trevor, who apparently knew how to open doors, and to make himself scarce when Evelyn brought a stranger in. A stranger like Ali, with a dog. Clever Trevor. Ali sighed.

"I'll go and see her."

"You're already snowed under and here I am adding to your workload."

"Anything else I should know about?" Ali asked. "Any more tales of the unexpected taking place right under my nose without me noticing?"

Violet raised an eyebrow. "You can't know everything."

"I can. I should. That's why I'm here."

"Everyone has things they keep to themselves, every place as well. You might as well get used to the idea you'll never know everything, not about Heft, or the people who live here. Even the ones you might think you know inside out will have their secrets. The stuff they think paints them in a bad light, makes them thought less of. *Oh, not as decent as he looks, then*, or, *Losing her marbles by the look of things*."

Evelyn Hooley, not entirely sure if she was the one who'd left the pan on and almost set fire to the house herself.

"You think you've got the measure of someone then they surprise you," Violet said, looking at Ali as if to say *I should know*. Did she mean Gordon, who had, unexpectedly, over dinner, declared his intention to do the Great North Run "before it's too late"? "Come out with something . . . *bonkers*"—definitely her father, Ali decided—"utterly baffling, completely out of character." Gordon, running man. Brian, playing private eye.

"We can't know what we don't know," Violet told her.

30

Ali intended to call on Evelyn first thing Monday morning but before she'd even finished breakfast another matter came her way: Roger Felton on the phone to say an alarm was going off in a house at the back of the church. "Half the night the thing's been clanging away," he said sounding crabby. "Every so often it stops, and you think, thank heavens, peace! Then it's off again." He attempted to replicate the racket, managing to sound as if he were having some kind of seizure. "Imagine," he said. "We've barely slept. And this is not the first time. I'm not unreasonable, Sergeant, I appreciate that technology sometimes goes awry. *But.*" The culprit was a holiday home, which the owners, a family from somewhere near Hull, rarely visited. "There must be a law against it, surely," he was saying. Ali couldn't help smiling. A law against having a second home you left empty most of the time, did he mean? She'd be all in favor. "It's a damn nuisance, excuse my language," he said. "Noise pollution." She braced herself for more complaints. Roger's property wasn't the only one within earshot. Ali sympathized and said she would contact the people, although it turned out Roger didn't have a number for them. "They use a cleaning service, I've seen the van," he went on. "Presumably it's too much for them to have to tidy up after themselves on their rare visits." More sarcastic

169

Maria Malone

than she had ever heard him. The cleaning people could no doubt put her in touch. Ali made a note of the company's name. Maid in Yorkshire. Catchy.

From her office at home for the next hour she fielded more complaints about the alarm. Pam Shaw had kept a note of all the times it had gone off in the past month. She offered to drop it round. *"Un petit quelque chose."* Ali asked if she would email it to her. *"Mais non,"* she said, since it was handwritten, in a notebook, and you can't email a notebook. Ali sighed inwardly, offering to pick it up later. The Maid in Yorkshire people were on answerphone. She left a message, trawled through her emails.

A wall of the office was dedicated to Melody Bright's disappearance, every detail Ali had learned so far on a whiteboard. She studied Melody's photo, the yellow Mini Cooper she had driven off in, a car people might notice, you would think, yet it was now more than a week since anyone had seen it. Ali's gaze swept across the board, taking in the information it held: the cash withdrawals, the trips to Newcastle that weren't what they seemed, the missing passport, the note slipped inside Brian's passport. What Melody had said to Carla about skipping her classes for the next few weeks, mention of a prior engagement. It was all there. Enough to persuade most people that here was a straightforward case of a woman leaving her husband. No suggestion of foul play. And yet. It was what Ali *didn't* know that troubled her. The gaps seemed to jump out at her. Violet's words the night before came to her: *You can't know everything.* Intended to be reassuring yet having the opposite effect, making her feel there was something she *ought* to know but didn't. At the top of the board in red was Melody's mobile number. Ali dialed it and got the familiar message, the operator saying the person she was trying to contact was not available. Brian had been calling it repeatedly, "just in case," every day, at different times. "What were you up to?" Ali asked the image of Melody in front of her. "Why were you going to Newcastle? Who

Death in the Countryside

were you seeing?" Too many unanswered questions. "Where *are* you?"

Evelyn came to the door in a pinny, wiping floury hands on a tea towel. "Come in," she said, "although it's a bit of a mess, just getting straight after an . . . incident."

Ali followed her in, Wilson at her heels. No sign of the elusive Trevor. Not the slightest trace of cat smell, just fresh paint. In the kitchen, a tray of scones were about to go in the oven. And, sitting at the table, Brian.

Brian.

"Oh," Ali said. Brian, the last person she'd expect to find in Evelyn's kitchen. In anyone's kitchen, other than his own (and hers).

"Brian's been giving me a hand," Evelyn said, as if it was the most natural thing in the world. The oven pinged and she slid the scones onto the top shelf and set a timer. "He's painted the ceiling," she told Ali, sending a grateful glance his way. "Which I'd never have managed. I can't do ladders."

"Right." Ali looked from Evelyn to Brian and back to Evelyn. How come she hadn't known they knew one another, well enough for Brian to call round and do some decorating in her hour of need? *We can't know what we don't know.*

Brian nodded at Ali. "Sergeant Wren." Wilson, delighted to see Brian, who was now practically an old friend, padded over to say hello. Brian ruffled the silky fur on his ears. "Now, lad," he said, sounding broad Yorkshire, "what's up, eh?"

"You'll have coffee?" Evelyn said, already taking an ornate cup and saucer from the dresser. A cafetière was on the table. She poured a cup for Ali, topped up Brian's. Brian had a mug, Ali saw, solid, chunky, suitable for a worker. A tin was on the table, lid off, revealing shortbread biscuits. "Help yourself," Evelyn said. "I hope you'll be able to stay for a scone."

171

Ali felt as if she had stumbled in on an afternoon tea party. "So, Brian's been painting the ceiling." Repeating what Evelyn had said, trying to keep the disbelief out of her voice. Thinking, *Why? How? What's going on?* Again, Ali looked from Brian to Evelyn and back. *Brian.* A man she thought had no friends, no real connections in Heft. *Brian.* Of all people.

"I suppose you heard about my near miss," Evelyn said.

"I heard you thought you might have had an intruder," Ali said. No point beating round the bush.

"I'm not sure that would be my choice of words," Evelyn said, "although, yes, I did wonder if someone had been in." She had put a pan on and done a fry-up in the morning before leaving for the shop. Just fancied it, she said. Switched the gas off. She gave a nervous laugh. "I *think* I switched it off." She went to the stove and twiddled with a knob, as if to demonstrate. "I mean I always check. I've Trevor to think about."

Trevor. Ali wondered where Trevor was now and why there was nothing in the kitchen to indicate the presence of a cat. No food bowl, no water dish. Perhaps he had his own room, the house was big enough after all.

"So you turned the gas off," Ali prompted. "Then what happened?"

"I came back at lunchtime. The *smell* when I opened the door. Awful. Burning. I ran in and the gas was on, up high, mind you, the pan completely dry, blackened, almost burned right through." She shuddered. "I'd left a pair of oven gloves on the counter next to the cooker, which was careless of me, they were starting to smolder."

Ali was thinking. Had someone been snooping about outside and seen Evelyn leave? Breaking in was one thing, quite another to put a light under a pan and leave it to burn. Who would do such a thing? Would the women from Rise really be willing to risk torching the home of their rival? She glanced at Evelyn. It was easy enough to leave gas on under a pan. She'd done it before. Put eggs on to boil, wandered off and forgotten about them. Gone back hours later to find the pan dry, ruined, the eggs having exploded, bits of them attached to the ceiling. She was in her teens then, easily distracted. Her parents had to get a decorator in. So, accidents could happen, although if Evelyn had sat down to a fry-up for breakfast and failed to turn the heat off under the pan, wouldn't she have noticed it was starting to burn before she went out?

"You're sure you switched the gas off?" Ali asked.

"Well, yes," Evelyn said, not sounding sure at all.

"And the house was secure?"

The timer went off and Evelyn went to the oven to retrieve the scones, golden and perfectly risen, smelling utterly divine. Ali suddenly felt ravenous. "We can probably have one in about ten minutes," Evelyn said brightly.

"You locked up?" Ali persisted.

Evelyn filled the kettle. "I'll make some fresh coffee. Brian?"

"That would be grand, thanks."

Ali sighed. "Evelyn, the house."

"I'm not in the habit," Evelyn told her, looking uncomfortable. "We've never locked up, there's no need. People look out for each other in Heft." She aimed a grateful smile at Brian, who flushed with pride.

Was Ali missing something here? Instinctively, she had weighed up whether Melody's disappearance might have been to do with another man (Leslie, the "prime suspect," as identified by Brian) and yet it had not occurred to her that Brian might be the one having an affair. Had she failed to spot a vital clue, one that was right under her nose? Brian and Evelyn. No, not in a million years. Brian wasn't like that. And Evelyn, Evelyn certainly wasn't. *You think you've got the measure of someone then they surprise you.* Violet's words coming back to her.

She wanted to ask what was going on, when they'd become so

173

Maria Malone

pally, but what if she said the wrong thing and offended the pair of them? She would need to choose her words carefully. Evelyn produced a fresh pot of coffee. The scones appeared on a plate with a doily. A butter dish, a knife with a worn bone handle, were placed on the table. Evelyn distributed delicate side plates and napkins, invited them to help themselves. Ali took a scone and buttered it. Thinking. About Brian and Melody, Evelyn. Evelyn's almost fire which she may or may not have started herself. She bit into the scone. It was delicious. Occasionally she made scones, but they never rose so spectacularly, or tasted as good. Warm, melting butter, properly cheesy. Perfection. "These are fantastic," she said in between mouthfuls, Brian agreeing, saying, "Aye, a proper treat." Then silence until the last morsel was gone, the pair of them struck dumb by Evelyn's glorious baking. Ali wondered if Evelyn would give her the recipe, or if it was a Hooley family secret.

She said, "Has there been anything else? Other than the pan. Anything . . . untoward. At home, in the shop?"

Evelyn picked at a crumb on her plate. "Nothing particular," she said, as if she wasn't sure. "I'm probably just doing too much. Overstretched." Like Ali, then.

Brian cleared his throat. "If you don't mind my saying, Evelyn, you were a good deal more upset the other day, I mean straight after the *incident*. You were definite you'd not left that pan on."

Evelyn fiddled with her napkin, folding it into a triangle and setting it aside.

"That same day, I was in the shop," Brian went on. "I could see something had happened."

"Why were you in the shop?" Ali asked, as if such behavior was suspicious.

He looked surprised. "I was getting a crusty loaf."

"Brian asked how I was, and I told him about the fire. *Near* fire. He offered to give me a hand putting it right."

"Why didn't you call me?" Ali said.

Death in the Countryside

Evelyn trailed a finger around the edge of her gold-embossed plate. "I was going to and then . . ." she gave a shrug. "You start to doubt yourself. And"—she hesitated, thinking about what else she wanted to say—"you've got bigger fish to fry. I mean, finding Melody."

"Did you know her?"

"She came into the shop, we'd have a word, so I put a poster up. Didn't think too much about it if I'm honest." She shot Brian an apologetic look. "I had problems of my own, never really stopped to think about who was at home waiting for news. I mean, I knew nothing about Brian, I'd never even set eyes on him—"

"Melody did all the food shopping," Brian interjected.

"—then he came in, said that's my wife on the poster, and we got chatting. I'd been about to call you about the girls over the road. They've had tea towels done with the shop name on, put them in the window, and, well, they're *exactly* like mine. Same lettering, I mean, identical."

"Like the one that went missing when the bakery was broken into?" Ali said.

Evelyn gave a terse nod. "Then Brian showed up and it put my problems into perspective. Made them seem trivial."

"Evelyn's been very kind," Brian said.

"Going through something like this on his own, I can't imagine," she said.

"I was glad to lend a hand with the painting. Took my mind off things."

"Things" like tailing Leslie Masters, creating an incriminating dossier, no doubt. Ali looked from one to the other, searching for a sign that they were concealing some guilty secret. Nothing. A picture of innocence. Wouldn't they have looked mortified, caught out, when she arrived unannounced with Wilson if they had anything to hide? Evelyn and Brian, on their own, offering one another a helping hand. That was all it was. Where was the harm? She felt a ripple of shame for having entertained the idea they were carrying on.

"I don't suppose having tea towels made is against the law," Evelyn said.

No, but breaking in to steal one was, Ali thought.

"And the pan going up. It's nothing compared with trying to find someone who's missing." She gazed at Ali. "So, you see. I decided not to bother you."

"I'll do a report," Ali said. "About the fire." *Near* fire. "And I'll look into the tea towel, find out where it was made, see if yours was used as the template." It would be easy enough to check. "And please, *please* lock up in future."

Evelyn looked away.

"You could always get an alarm," Brian piped up.

"Oh, I don't think so," Evelyn said. "I'd forget to set it, or I wouldn't remember the code. They're such a nuisance as well, they go off for no reason. One of those holiday homes behind the church, their alarm goes off all the time when they're not there, it's enough to drive you mad." She looked at Ali. "I'm surprised you've not had complaints about *that*."

31

The next day the cakery-bakery was busy. A woman buying two dozen cakes. "I'll let you do a selection," she was saying, "whatever you think." Ali watched Ruth Carlisle slide slabs of something custardy into a box where croissant cubes and raspberry tarts waited. "We have nothing like this in Skipden," the woman told her. Who could be bothered to come all the way from Skipden for cakes? Ali wondered.

A pair of walkers—rucksacks and walking poles, jackets in high-vis orange, handy if you needed rescuing—ordered coffee and almond croissants. Wilson sniffed at the backs of their legs. Terri put the pastries on a tray and said they were welcome to sit at one of the tables, she'd bring the coffees out.

"Sergeant Wren," Ruth said, as the customer buying cakes departed. "Lovely to see you. Can I interest you in a raspberry slice? Better be quick, they're flying out of the door."

"Did you hear there was a fire at the home of Mrs. Hooley?"

Ruth made a horrified face. "I did hear about that, yes, how awful."

Terri had her back to Ali, grinding coffee beans, making the walkers' coffee. The shop smelt intoxicating—the coffee, the pastries, the racks of sourdough bread. No wonder the business had taken off.

"You didn't happen to see anyone hanging about?" Ali said. "Outside the bakery, perhaps."

Ruth frowned, thinking. "You know, I didn't," she said giving Ali a bright smile. "Then again, we're still newish here so we haven't really worked out what's normal and what's not." She reached for a glass jar labeled doggy delicacies and extracted a bone-shaped biscuit. "Here you go, Mister," she said, coming round the counter and offering it to Wilson. He looked away. "Come on, boy," she said wafting the treat in front of him. Wilson's attention was on the display cabinet, now housing cakery-bakery tea towels.

"Isn't he allowed?" Ruth asked, still waggling the treat at him. "Is it the doggy equivalent of drinking on the job or something?"

"He's allowed," Ali said. "It's just he's wary about taking food from strangers." Or people he doesn't like. Ali liked to think that Wilson understood the hurt the newcomers with their fancy patisserie and claims to make the best bread in Heft had caused Evelyn. Wilson, in Ali's considered and entirely biased opinion, had a way of instinctively sensing right from wrong. She picked up a tea towel. "These are nice," she said.

"Thanks, take one, a souvenir."

Ali examined it. "Identical to the Hooley's tea towel, did you know that?"

Ruth gave Ali an innocent look. "Really? Great minds and all that."

"Or ... you took a tea towel from the Hooley premises." Ali waited for her words to sink in. "And had it copied." No point pulling punches.

Terri's shoulders seemed to stiffen as she poured hot milk into the cups before taking them out to the walkers and staying to chat, in no hurry to come back inside and join in the awkward

Death in the Countryside

discussion about a tea towel being taken (stolen) from a competitor, their design ripped off.

"I've no idea what would make you think such a thing," Ruth said. Back behind the counter now, the doggy delicacies once more on the shelf.

"Actually, my reasons for thinking so are impeccable." Ali gave her a hard stare. She had spoken to the owner of Dale's Printing—a glaring error with an apostrophe, she assumed, until she discovered the owner was called Dale—who confirmed he had been asked to replicate the Hooley's design. "I thought it was strange," he said, "but I got the impression they were part of the same outfit." Ali had barely been able to contain her anger. Ruth picked up a pair of tongs and fiddled with a croissant cube. Her throat was pink.

"You'll remember the break-in at Hooley's. A tea towel was taken." She waited until Ruth looked up and met her gaze. "Stolen." Another long, hard stare until she once more looked away. A customer had come into the shop.

"Can I just serve this gentleman?" Ruth said.

"In a moment," Ali said. "The same tea towel *stolen* from Hooley's turned up at Dale's Printing, the people you asked to make these." She waved an offending cakery-bakery tea towel in the air. Wilson was suddenly on his feet, interested. He knew this game. Ali would wave a towel at him when she was drying him off, get him to grab the other end, and they'd have a bit of a tug of war, Wilson growling and snarling as if the rag was an enemy to be subdued. It was something they both enjoyed. She allowed the tea towel to drop and shook it in front of him. Wilson grabbed it and pulled. Ali pulled back. Wilson growled. Ali pulled harder. More growling, louder, threatening. The man who had come into the shop retreated.

"You realize, I could throw the book at you," Ali said. A phrase she tended to use when she had no idea whether she would be able to bring charges. "Breaking and entering, criminal damage"—thinking of the flour deposited on the floor of the bakery—"theft, intimidation"—always a good one to slip in, she had found—"breaches of copyright." Ruth had gone pale. "I could go on. And as for the fire at Mrs. Hooley's home, forensics are examining the scene"—a fib that was warranted, Ali felt—"and if there is anything to tie you to that, I mean *anything*, I will"—she hesitated, not wanting to repeat the threat of throwing the book at her again, since once was usually enough—"come down on you like a ton of bricks. Are we clear?"

She let go of the tea towel, a signal to Wilson that the tug of war was over. Usually, he was not permitted to keep whatever it was they'd been tussling over but on rare occasions, like now, Ali signaled to go to town, rip into it. There was a tearing sound which Ali ignored.

"I want all those tea towels gone," she told Ruth Carlisle.

"But we had five hundred made."

"You should have thought of that." She glanced at the window, where the tea towels were strung up like bunting, a slap in the face to Evelyn. "They need to come down. Now, please."

Ruth, now scarlet in the face, unhooked the string holding them up and whipped them from the window. Outside, Terri was stalling, running a cloth over the same table for about the hundredth time. The walkers had swiveled round in their seats to see what drama was unfolding inside.

Ali waited while Ruth emptied the cabinet of tea towels and took them into the back of the shop. "I'll be needing those," she said. "Evidence. Box them up, if you would, and I'll be back later for them." Ruth seemed about to say something then changed her mind. "I'll be in touch," Ali said. "Regarding charges."

Off she went, a spring in her step, Wilson at her side, what was left of the bedraggled tea towel trailing from his mouth. They crossed the road to Hooley's, where Evelyn was peering out from the doorway, the poster of Melody Bright beside her.

32

"So you think she was leading a double life?" Nick asked, incredulous.

Ali sighed. It seemed so. Wednesday. Another few days and Melody would have been gone two weeks. An email detailing her phone activity for the last twelve months had just arrived. Ali had so far only managed to skim the details. The last time Melody had used her phone was on the day she went missing. Since then, it had been switched off. The log mainly comprised calls to Brian, usually on his mobile, sometimes at his place of work. Calls to landlines, which Ali would need to check. One of the local numbers had stood out, all fives and zeros. It rang a bell with her. The Nu-U salon in Heft, it turned out, where a few weeks after moving back Ali had called in without an appointment to ask if they could trim her fringe. Since then there'd been no time for hair appointments and the fringe had grown out, which she found she didn't mind, it was easier to manage.

Sandra, whose salon it was—tawny-eyes, immaculate makeup, a uniform that resembled a glamorous version of hospital scrubs— had already let Ali know that Melody was a regular: highlights and a cut every six weeks, regular blow dries in between, a facial once a month, something involving what she called high frequency and

181

LED. "Fabulous for older skin," Sandra had said, giving Ali an appraising look. "Improves pigmentation, fine lines, poor texture." Before Ali could reply, she was on the receiving end of a shameless sales pitch about the benefits of red light for stimulating collagen and elastin production. "Six treatments at weekly intervals, then one a month for maintenance, if you want the best results," Sandra said, pressing a price list on her, Melody forgotten, Ali the focus of her interest.

Another number had jumped out, a mobile, one that appeared frequently. Over a period of months, calls coming in and going out, messages. Melody had received a call from the number in question on the day she was last seen. She had called it back. Twice in the morning, again at midday, then in the afternoon. The calls were mostly short, voicemail messages it seemed. She had sent WhatsApp messages to the same number—eight in total. Several more landline calls, one lasting eight minutes. Ali had considered ringing the mobile number and seeing who answered but she wanted to find out who it was registered to first and since her contact at the provider had gone for the night it would have to wait. She wondered if Spence, the tech guy at the station in Skipden, might be able to help but there was no reply on his office line.

"Earth to Ali," Nick said, interrupting her thoughts. "Your missing woman—you reckon she had a secret life?"

"Sorry, yes, it looks like it." They were at the pub. Ali hadn't felt much like going out, she'd have preferred to spend the evening poring over Melody's phone records, but staying in would have meant cooking, which she didn't feel like, and Nick, usually happy to rustle something up at short notice, wasn't in the mood either, suggesting they eat at the Fox & Newt. An evening in each other's company, no distractions. Ali had smiled at that. "A catch up," Nick said. "Remind you what you see in me." He had been away for two nights hunting for locations, then a read-through in Leeds ahead of the new block of filming and Ali had been too busy to miss him,

Death in the Countryside

had almost welcomed his absence which allowed her to focus purely on work. Not good, she told herself. He was right, a night together, no distractions, was just what they needed. It wouldn't hurt to put the phone records aside until the morning.

She was wearing ripped jeans, a crocheted top in loud lime green, sandals that revealed toenails painted silver. Her hair, released from its usual ponytail, sprayed with dry shampoo and blasted with a hairdryer, was wild-looking, a copper mane. All in all, her look screamed "not working." She hadn't thought she was hungry but the smell of food being cooked changed her mind. Suddenly, she was starving. She ordered steak pie, a side order of spring greens, hand-cut triple cooked chips, even though the pie came with mash. "To share," she said when the girl taking their order gave her a questioning look. Nick chose chicken with chorizo, a sauce of some kind, new potatoes. "We could forget the chips," he said but chips were what Ali wanted. She asked if she could have the chips before everything else.

"Like a starter?" the girl asked.

"Exactly," Ali said. Another look from Nick.

"Does Brian know Melody was up to no good?" he asked once they were alone.

"We don't yet know what she was up to."

"Fair enough but whatever it was she was lying about it, so it's unlikely to be entirely innocent."

Ali suspected Melody had another man, that her jaunts to Newcastle "to see Lillian" were convenient cover. The scarf Brian had produced as proof his wife had shopped at Fenwick, a gift from her lover, perhaps. Ali had checked and it was expensive. Not that Melody was short of cash. It was possible, of course, she had treated herself, Ali just didn't think so. She had asked Brian if she could take the scarf, she wasn't sure why. It was eye-catching, unusual, she doubted they sold them by the dozen. Perhaps someone in Fenwick would remember who bought it. The store would have CCTV. Not that Ali knew exactly when it was bought, which was a drawback. The fabric still carried a scent, something floral, a perfume she half recognized. Similar to Eau Dynamisante. She offered it to Wilson, who took his time examining the fabric, no doubt detecting far more than Ali was able to. It might prove useful, she told herself.

The chips arrived, crisp, a dusting of salt. Ali took one. The Fox & Newt made the best chips, not counting her mum's. She'd not really eaten since breakfast she realized. She looked up and saw Roger Felton leaning against the bar. *Please, Roger, leave us in peace.* When he spotted her, her appearance so at odds with the sober working version he was used to seeing, his expression was priceless. Ali gave a polite nod, and he took his drinks to a table hidden by a pillar.

"She had a soulmate," Ali said. "Melody. When she was in her teens, into her twenties, she was with someone called Jimmy."

"Jimmy. Not the most romantic of names," Nick said.

"Is there such a thing?"

"Some names have a certain something of the hero about them—William, Alexander, Hector—"

"*Hector*?" Ali interjected.

"*Hector*," Nick confirmed. "Trojan warrior, courageous, strong. Ralph, pronounced *Rafe*, has a definite whiff of the romantic about it too."

"JC, that was what Melody called him."

"That's more like it," Nick said approvingly.

"Well, *Jimmy*, JC, was the love of her life, according to her brother-in-law. It was Jimmy she was with the night she went 'missing' all those years ago, when the police searched the family home and her frantic mother wept, while Melody was shacked up in Byker with her soulmate."

"Course, you're talking, what, forty years ago?" Nick said. "Lot of water under the bridge since then."

Death in the Countryside

Ali was hoping the as yet unknown number Melody had been calling, the one calling her, was Jimmy's, and that, somehow, they'd found one another again, found their happy ever after at last. Devastating for Brian, of course, but in Ali's view not the worst possible outcome. That would be the one where something bad had happened to Melody, something bad and final.

"He was on set the other day," Nick said, "Brian."

"How did he seem to you?"

"A bit . . . lost, I thought. Still wearing perfectly pressed shirts, though."

Ali flushed. She had ironed three of Brian's shirts and left instructions (which he had asked her to write down) on how to do them himself next time. Passed on details of a firm in town that did laundry and ironing, Brian saying that wouldn't be necessary since he expected Melody to be back "before it came to that." Ali wasn't about to tell Nick she was doing someone else's ironing, a job she generally avoided at any cost.

"Poor Brian," she said.

"Poor Brian," Nick agreed.

Their food arrived. Ali tipped what was left of the chips onto the side of her plate.

"Mash and chips," Nick said smiling.

"You can never have too many potatoes," she said seriously. When she was about fourteen, potatoes were almost the only thing she wanted to eat: chips, mostly, creamy mash, her mother's floury potato cakes, oven baked King Edwards in crinkly jackets, roasted Maris Piper, tender new potatoes (Jersey Royals in season) steamed and drenched in butter and parsley. Violet had been endlessly creative, serving up whatever Ali fancied. Tempting her with crispy rosti, a bowl of creamy dauphinoise. Years later, when Ali asked how she had tolerated such whims, Violet simply said she didn't see the point of making a fuss, and that as long as Ali was eating, enjoying her food, even if it did revolve almost exclusively around

Maria Malone

the humble potato, that was okay. "I knew you'd grow out of it in your own time," she said, which was what had happened, although she might wonder if she could see Ali now, dipping a chip into her mash and gravy.

"So what happens next?" Nick asked.

"I need to speak to the mobile provider in the morning, identify some of these calls." The ones to and from Melody's phone on the day she was last seen. "Then we'll see who she was in touch with, who she was seeing on her awaydays."

33

Early the next morning, Ali was in Skipden updating her boss.

"Everything points to our missing woman leading a double life," Chief Superintendent Freeman said, echoing Nick. "Which raises all kinds of questions, don't you agree?"

"Yes, sir," Ali said.

Freeman clicked his fingers and Wilson went to him, tail wagging, anticipating his usual treat. The Chief Superintendent was nothing if not predictable. He put out a hand and the dog solemnly offered his paw. "Good lad," Freeman said, reaching inside his desk drawer for the tin of Beautiful Joe's and tipping out a small handful of treats.

"All those cash withdrawals amounting to thousands in recent months, then she gets into her car one day and drives off. It looks to me very much like Melody left home of her own accord. Not under duress of any kind. Is that your reading of things?"

Ali nodded. Less than an hour before, she had heard back from Spence on the phone records and now knew that the mobile number Melody was in touch with so frequently belonged to one James Champion. Jimmy, Ali supposed. JC. He owned a string of sofa shops and lived in Newcastle. Ali had yet to speak to him. She was about to go to Newcastle, see if Melody was with him,

187

enjoying a new life, perhaps driving a different, better car, the case Ali had dealt with in Harrogate, the woman who'd bagged an estate agent and a shiny new BMW, coming to mind. If Melody was shacked up with Jimmy Champion and Brian had been dropped without a word, then what? Ali would have to break the news, that was what.

If she wasn't there, if they'd had a falling out and Jimmy claimed to have no idea where she was, then what? Ali didn't want to think about that option, the one where something untoward might have occurred.

"I'll have a run up to Newcastle, sir," Ali said. "Get the measure of things, see if I can put the final pieces of the puzzle together."

"She'll be with our Mr. Champion, I'd put money on it," Freeman said. He frowned. "And if she is, I want to know why the hell she didn't just tell someone what she was doing, save us all lot of trouble."

Ali hadn't yet mentioned to Freeman about Melody going "missing" in her teens, "doing off," as Lillian would put it, to be with the lad she was then besotted with. The infamous JC. Melody had form for wasting police time. Ali had struck lucky with North of Tyne Police, getting hold of a helpful clerk who had trawled through the paper records from 1976 and managed to locate the report concerning Melody's prior disappearance, although there was little in the way of detail. Turned up unharmed, no further action, was the gist of it. Ali hoped for a similar outcome this time. It struck her that if Melody was with Jimmy now, it had a kind of symmetry to it. Not the kind Freeman would appreciate, however.

"Right," Freeman said, "keep me up to speed."

"Yes, sir."

"Before you go, shall we have a brief word about another friend of ours, Troy Conrado?"

Death in the Countryside

Ali sighed inwardly. "Of course," she said, bracing herself.

"Powerful man, used to getting his own way. Did you know he was a regular at White House dinners? On first name terms with our King too. Three state banquets at Buckingham Palace he's been on the guest list for. *Three*."

"Well connected, then," Ali said, her heart sinking.

"Extremely so. And now he wants to be Mr. Big in Heft." Freeman leaned forward, drummed his fingers on the desk. "And, believe me, he will get his wish the way he's throwing money about. St. Michael's have just received a sizeable donation for the organ restoration fund. The woman in Gorvale with the donkey sanctuary"—he hesitated, thinking—"what's it called?"

"Neddies."

Freeman rolled his eyes. "Neddies. A very generous donation there too."

Ali sensed Conrado buying his way into the community, that she would have to return to Heft Hall—without Wilson—and issue a groveling apology. Get him back on side. Before Conrado took his complaint up a notch, ran it past the Chief Constable during a round of golf, or at a police benevolent fund do, which, given his impeccable connections, seemed depressingly inevitable. She only hoped Miss Shaw never found out. *Quel dommage*, she might say disapprovingly.

"So," Freeman was saying, "what we don't want is for him to see us as the enemy." His gaze went to Wilson. "Do we lad?" Wilson sat up straight, offered his paw again, ever hopeful the treats would keep coming. "We need to find a way of rubbing along with him, don't we?" The spaniel's tail thumped on the floor. "Unfortunately, you two got off on the wrong foot." Looking at Ali now. "Which wouldn't take much doing judging from the poor punctuation in his letter of complaint." Another raised eyebrow. "Here's a man who has no idea what the apostrophe is for. Difficult to deal with someone like that in my experience, nigh on impossible. I don't care how much money he's throwing about."

Ali was with him on the apostrophe. Its incorrect use spoke volumes. She'd had a tricky conversation with Ronnie Cross, Heft's cobbler, after a sign appeared in his window offering a special deal on "ladies shoe's."

"However, we will have to find a way, because you can bet a bloke like Conrado will have friends in high places all over the county, and the last thing we want is him complaining that the policing in Heft is below par. Do we?" Gazing at Wilson, who put his head on one side, as if considering this. "You might have to take a backseat on this one, boy, owing to his *allergy* business. Anyway, I'm sure you get my drift." Back with Ali again. She nodded. "So let's tread carefully."

Neither one spoke for a moment.

"We're agreed we don't think there's anything sinister going on, then?" Freeman said at last. "With your missing woman, I mean."

It seemed not, but Ali wanted to tie up the last loose ends before she filed Melody away under missing, presumed having a lovely new life. "It looks that way," she said. Yet something, she wasn't sure what, was bothering her. Despite everything pointing to Melody "doing off" in typical fashion—the cash withdrawals, the phone calls, advising Carla she'd be missing pottery classes—Ali couldn't quite believe it. The night before, she had slept badly, her mind on Melody, on all the things that might have befallen her. She recalled how shortly before leaving Harrogate for Heft there was a baffling missing person case, a father of two in his fifties who'd disappeared without warning, his wife adamant he had no reason to go, insistent something must have happened to him. The police traced and retraced his last known route, a relatively short car journey undertaken late at night when the roads were quiet and

Death in the Countryside

found nothing. Eventually, his car was discovered in the middle of a roundabout, concealed by trees and vegetation. He had driven straight onto it. No skid marks on the road, nothing to indicate an accident of any kind. You had to look really closely, which someone eventually did. A cardiac arrest at the wheel, it turned out. Ali could not stop thinking about how long it took to find him, the best part of two weeks, when all the time he was there, a ten minute journey from home. Recalling his case, relating it to Melody, in the small hours her stomach had cramped up, the pain so severe she'd had to get out of bed and go downstairs, fill a hot water bottle, and curl up on the sofa for an hour. Nick hadn't stirred. For reasons she could not explain she felt suddenly anxious. What if Melody was in danger and the authorities (by which she meant herself) had failed to take her disappearance seriously? It made her determined to look at things in forensic detail.

"What more do we know about your man, James Champion?" Freeman said.

Wealthy. His business had been around decades. Married, children. No brushes with the law, not even a speeding fine. "Successful," she told Freeman. "Law-abiding. Something of a local hero in his hometown." Ali had looked at his house on Google Earth. A large property, detached, nice and private, at the far end of the back garden a wooded area. Ali imagined finding Melody, secateurs in hand, happily dead-heading roses. Or buried in a shallow grave in the woods. The thought of the shallow grave was what had kept her awake.

"What's on your mind, Wren?" Freeman asked. "Something bothering you?"

"Just that we don't yet have all the answers, sir." Whatever she discovered, good or bad, she was going to have to tell Brian and there now seemed little chance of bringing him good news: *Sorry, she's in Newcastle living with someone else.* How would Brian, so lost, so convinced Melody would never have walked out on him, take it? Poor Brian. Or *I'm so, so sorry, I have some very bad news, I think you should sit down*. Which was worse? The latter, undoubtedly, although for Brian either would be catastrophic. He would be distraught.

"I was just thinking, sir, if we find her in Newcastle and she doesn't want her husband to know where she is, I don't think he'll take it well." An understatement if ever there was one.

"I wouldn't worry about the husband just yet. We still don't know he's got nothing to do with any of this."

34

Should she contact Jimmy Champion—*JC*—let him know she was coming, or just arrive unannounced? "The element of surprise, Wils," she said. "Like the Spanish Inquisition." Wilson wagged his tail. Thanks to her dad, a fan of all things Monty Python, Ali had grown up with the phrase, "Nobody expects the Spanish Inquisition." It was up there among Gordon's favorite comedy moments, along with the chandelier crashing to the floor in *Only Fools and Horses*, Eric Morecambe playing "all the right notes but not necessarily in the right order," and The Germans episode of *Fawlty Towers*. All it took was a simple "Don't mention the war," for Gordon to crack up and dissolve into fits that teetered dangerously on the edge of hysteria.

"We'll go full Spanish Inquisition then, shall we?" she said. The risk, of course, was that they'd get to Newcastle and Jimmy wouldn't be there. In London on business, sunning himself in the Maldives. With Melody.

Ali made a call to what was described as the flagship store of Champion Sofas and asked if the boss was in. The voice on the other end of the line said, "I'll put you through." Before Ali knew it she was speaking to a woman who announced herself as Audrey Harris "on behalf of Mr. Champion" and asked how she could help. Ali asked to speak to Mr. Champion. A moment of silence followed, then Audrey Harris said, "Were you expecting him to be here? Because he's not due in today." Ali asked where she might find him, prompting Audrey to switch smoothly from solicitous to suspicious. "May I ask who's calling?" Ali said not to worry and hung up. Damn.

"We'll just go up," Ali told Wilson, busy tucking the cakery-bakery tea towel under his bedding. He looked up. "And hope we find him."

Ali packed biscuits, a flask of coffee, nibbles and a drink for Wilson. If it turned out to be a long day, she didn't want to get caught out again, calling at Greggs for emergency rations only to be told the last of the steak bakes had gone. She sent Nick a message to say she might be late back and left a pink Post-it note on the table, *I love ewe* scribbled under a drawing of something vaguely resembling a Swaledale sheep.

She made good time and by midday was at Jimmy Champion's house. Jesmond, an affluent part of Newcastle, just two cars parked on St. George's Avenue, a Porsche Spyder, and a BMW saloon built like a tank. Ali parked the Hilux between them. "Lowering the tone," she told Wilson, smiling. The houses were screened by trees, walls, gates. All seemed to have cameras and intercoms. A street where nobody wanted callers arriving at the front door unless by invitation. "Looks like sofas have been good to JC," she said to Wilson as she pressed the buzzer and a woman said Hello.

Ali said who she was, that she was looking for Mr. Champion. "Oh," the woman said, "About the fire?" Fire? A buzzer sounded and the gates swung open. Sweeping gravel drive, garden the size of a small park, grand-looking house, Art Deco style, painted white. As Ali and Wilson approached the front door it opened and a woman, slender, blonde, flawless glowy skin, hair in loose waves halfway down her back appeared. Jenny Champion, she said. Another JC, then, like her husband.

Death in the Countryside

She showed Ali and Wilson into what she called the reception room. Pristine, deep pile white carpet (Ali wishing she had removed her shoes) plush leather sofas, also white, no doubt from Jimmy's own range. An oversized glass coffee table bearing glossy magazines in an artful fan arrangement. Artificial flowers in the hearth. A sitting room that felt little used and was chilly. Ali had the feeling she and Wilson were the first ones to have set foot inside in a long while. On one side of the fireplace, an entire wall was made of up glass doors, revealing what appeared to be another living room, almost identical to the one they were in.

"I didn't know the police were looking into the fire," Jenny said. "The insurer's dealing with that."

Ali said, "That's not why I'm here. I just need a word with Mr. Champion. On another matter."

Jenny nodded, unconcerned, nothing in her manner suggesting marital disharmony.

"Busy running his business empire, I'm afraid."

"Do you know where I'll find him?"

Jenny gave this some thought. "I used to know off the top of my head at one time," she said. "It was always set days in different stores. If it was Wednesday, it was Westgate Road sort of thing, but he dropped all that, didn't want the staff knowing when to expect him." She beamed. Perfect teeth, even, white. "Keeps them on their toes, he says."

When Ali had Googled Jimmy Champion, she discovered he was famous locally for his no-frills TV ads. "Sofas—they're champion!" was his cheery (cheesy, some might say) catchphrase. He had quite a following on social media, thousands of likes. He knew his market all right. In the North-East, JC was as well-known as Alan Shearer, Sam Fender.

"Have you seen the ads?" Jenny asked, as if she knew what Ali was thinking. "'Me, I love sofas, and so will you,'" adopting an accent that was broad Geordie.

Ali nodded. "Catchy."

"Where did you say you're from?"

"Heft, the Yorkshire Dales."

"Everyone here knows Jimmy." Beaming proudly. "He's the go-to man for sofas, the furniture equivalent of a Greggs pasty, if you like. You know where you are with a Champion sofa he always says. He still goes on the shop floor, you know, does a bit of selling. The personal touch counts for a lot."

"Will he be on the shop floor today?" Ali asked.

"Give me a second, he might have put something on the calendar." She went to check.

Ali looked around. Above the mantelpiece was a framed photo, a formal studio portrait. She went over for a closer look, Wilson at her side. Jimmy and Jenny surrounded by what Ali assumed was their entire family. A good-looking bunch. Three couples, five children, dressed to the nines in suits and dresses, all except the smallest boy, about two by the look of him. Dungarees, a straw hat, the biggest, sweetest smile. Oor Wullie. What was Jimmy up to with Melody, putting his entire domestic setup at risk? *If* that was what was going on. Perhaps nothing was going on, just two old flames back in touch, all above board. Somehow, Ali didn't think so.

She went back to the sofa, so vast and soft she didn't dare sit back for fear of ending up flat out. Wilson settled down again into the hollow he'd left on the deep pile of the carpet. Other than the family photo, the room felt soulless. Two chandeliers hung from the ceiling and again Ali thought of the moment in *Only Fools* when the wrong one came crashing to the ground, a scene guaranteed to leave her father who'd seen it hundreds, maybe thousands of times, with tears of laughter streaming down his face.

Jenny was back. "I've had a look. He's at the Westgate Road branch today. The flagship store."

"I phoned there earlier," Ali said.

Death in the Countryside

"Oh, Audrey wouldn't tell you anything," Jenny said. "She's the gatekeeper, fiercely protective. Even *I* can't get past her."

"Okay," Ali said, getting up. "Thank you, that's very helpful."

"Sorry, I didn't even ask if you wanted a drink," Jenny said. "It's just it's Alma's day off and I've no idea where anything is." She gave a helpless shrug. "I usually go out if I want something."

As hopeless as Brian, Ali thought, although he was catching on fast. "No problem," she told Jenny.

"There's a café on the corner," she was saying, "The coffee from there is wonderful, the Ouseburn people. I could get them to deliver . . ."

"It's fine, really."

Jenny nodded. "Shall I let Jimmy know you're coming?"

"No need, I wouldn't want to worry him."

Jenny gave a knowing smile. "The element of surprise, eh?" The way she seemed able to read Ali was uncanny. Her eyes, the palest blue, were like lasers. "Catch him unawares, keep him on his toes, like. Jimmy would approve."

197

35

It wasn't hard to spot Jimmy Champion. He was on the shop floor with a couple looking at a leather Chesterfield with a price tag of almost four thousand pounds. "I love a classic design, me," he was saying, "and for that you need look no further than our friend here, the Chesterfield. Iconic." Was a sofa iconic? Ali wondered. The word seemed overused these days. She'd seen an item on the local news not long ago, a derelict building crumbling into the River Skir, a structure that should have been pulled down long ago, suddenly decreed "iconic" now it was collapsing. The Royal Pump Room Museum in Harrogate was iconic, Ali thought, the Ribblehead Viaduct, York Minster. Not some grotty tumbling down building once occupied by the local council then left to rot. "It's a four-seater, mind, generous proportions," Jimmy was saying, "and you'll be in very good company with one of these. Churchill had one, and you know that fancy new bar on Grey Street"—the couple nodded, impressed—"we supplied them." He tapped the side of his nose. "Rumor has it Amanda Staveley herself is a fan." Thanks to Nick, who read the sports pages, Ali knew about Amanda Staveley, her near cult status in Newcastle for having breathed new life into the city's football club, the crushing sense of disappointment that had accompanied her departure.

Death in the Countryside

Jimmy smiled. "Not that I can confirm or deny that, of course. Confidentiality and all that."

Ali watched, impressed. He was good, very good.

The couple looked keen. "Our hairdresser's got one in reception," the woman said. "You can sit four people on it, no bother, and you don't feel a bit squashed up."

"One of mine, I hope," Jimmy said, winking. He caught sight of Ali hovering with Wilson. "Tell you what, I'll leave you lovely folk to have a think. Back in a minute."

Jimmy was better looking in the flesh than he was in the photos Ali had Googled, or even his famous ads, where the makeup artist seemed to have slathered on a good deal more pancake than was strictly necessary. His eyes were friendly, a brilliant blue. Silver hair cropped short, white T-shirt under a navy suit. "You must be Sergeant Wren." Soft Geordie accent. Waiting for her. Alerted by Jenny that the police were on their way. So much for the element of surprise. He dropped to his haunches and spoke to Wilson. "And who's this canny lad?" Wilson wagged his tail and pushed his snout at Jimmy, who ruffled his fur. "What's your name, son?" Ali told him. "Wilson, that's a good name. We've a striker called Wilson." Before Ali knew what was happening, he was singing, what sounded very much like a football chant. The couple looking at the Chesterfield watched. "Howay the lads," the man chipped in.

"Aye," Jimmy said. "Howay, Newcastle!"

Not the moment, Ali decided, to say her husband shared his name with the Newcastle goalie (cruel irony, since Nick was a Leeds fan). She waited for Jimmy to straighten up. "Can we have a word in private?" she said.

"Is this about the fire?" he asked when they were in his office. "Because we know who started it and the lad's sorry. It was an accident, the insurance will cover the damage." He frowned. "I thought Audrey had called the police to say we didn't want to press charges."

199

"It's not about the fire," Ali said, still no idea what fire he and Jenny seemed so keen to discuss. "I'm here about Melody Bright."

Jimmy, who over the years must have picked up the rudiments of acting from starring in his own commercials (although little acting was required since he was playing himself, just a louder, brasher, more Geordie version) made a valiant effort to stop his face from giving him away. It was no good. The color drained from his honeyed skin in an instant.

Ali, seizing the advantage, pounced. "Have you seen her?"

The office door opened and gatekeeper Audrey, blonde bob neatly ironed, Chanel-style tweed suit, heels, swept in bringing coffee and miniature shortbread biscuits in the shape of Scottie dogs. "Anything else, JC?" she asked. So they really did call him that.

"The couple looking at the Chesterfields," he said, "can you get Paul to look after them?"

"No bother," she said.

The moment the door closed behind her, Ali said, "I take it you know why I'm asking about Melody."

Jimmy shook his head. He had recovered some of his composure. "Not really, no."

"When was the last time you saw her?"

He took out his phone and opened up his messages. "Week before last." He checked the date. The day Melody had disappeared. "We had coffee together."

"Where was that?"

"A pub, Piercebridge, just off the A1. The Fox Hole. Coffee and a catch-up, that's all."

Piercebridge had to be a good hour's drive from Newcastle, even further for Melody coming north. "Isn't that a bit of a trek for a coffee?"

"It was Melody's idea."

Ali wondered about that. The phone records showed that Jimmy had been the one to initiate contact that day. Only then had

Death in the Countryside

a flurry of calls from Melody ensued. She let it go for the time being.

"And was this meeting . . . planned?"

He looked uncomfortable. "More what you'd call spur of the moment really. Melody had something on her mind and we're old friends, we go way back, so . . . I said okay."

"Mind telling me what was bothering her?"

"It was a private conversation, I mean, I'm not sure she'd want me sharing it." Rallying now, aiming a steely look at Ali. "Last time I looked, it wasn't a crime to have coffee with a friend."

She matched his steely gaze. "Melody's missing," she said, going for the jugular, "and you may have been one of the last people to see her."

Jimmy, who had just started to get his color back, went pale again. "Missing?"

"That's right. You weren't aware?"

"I wasn't, no."

"You didn't find it strange when a friend, one you'd drop everything for and drive fifty miles to have coffee with, suddenly went silent?"

He didn't answer.

"I mean, I've seen Melody's phone records"—Jimmy looked gray—"so I appreciate the extent to which the two of you were in touch. A ton of calls and messages over the last few months. Then it all went quiet, not a peep. And it never crossed your mind to wonder why. Really?"

He shook his head. "Forty," he said after a long silence.

"Pardon?"

"It's more like forty miles to Piercebridge, not fifty."

Ali stared at him. "Oh, well, that makes all the difference in the world." She sighed, adopted a softer tone. "Look, Jimmy, normally I wouldn't be in the slightest bit interested in what you do with your time, whether you drive fifty miles, a hundred, whatever, for a cappuccino. That's your business. Under normal circumstances. *But.* Melody is missing and I need you to be straight with me."

"Right," he said. "Aye."

"So, *please* tell me what was so urgent she wanted to see you in *Piercebridge* of all places *on the spur of the moment.* Was it a regular haunt of yours?"

"No! I'd never been there." He was quiet, thinking. "Nice pub, though, the menu looked good. Not that we ate. We just had coffee."

"And?" Ali prompted.

"A croissant. Well, I did, Melody didn't bother, she had an Americano, hot milk on the side."

"I *meant* why were you meeting there that particular day?" Ali asked, exasperated.

"Ah. I might have to rewind a bit."

"Go on, I'm not in any rush."

"Nothing went on, you understand." He frowned. "I just wouldn't want Jenny getting the wrong end of the stick."

What end might that be, then, Ali couldn't help thinking.

36

Melody had tracked him down on social media, he was all over it these days: Twitter, X it calls itself now. Facebook. TikTok. Not that he had the foggiest how *that* worked. Someone else handled that side of things for him, a lad straight out of school. The one who'd started the fire at the Scotswood Road branch, Jimmy said, without elaborating, but they'd put all that behind them now. Clean slate. Jimmy was a firm believer in forgiveness, moving on. He gave Ali a meaningful look. Anyway, Melody had sent a friend request and he'd responded. Glad to hear from her, of course he was. Surprised, mind. They'd been close at one time, "in another life," but he'd heard nothing from her in years. Decades.

"We were an item," he said, "when we were kids. I only had the one shop then. In Gateshead." He raised an eyebrow. "If you can believe *that*." Ali wasn't sure why a shop in Gateshead might be considered unbelievable.

"Wrong side of the river for me," Jimmy explained, catching her baffled look. "So, we messaged, you know, then spoke on the phone." Embarrassed. "I always thought the world of her, thought we'd end up together." As Melody had, according to Des. "I don't even know why we split up, something stupid, probably. I wasn't reliable then. Not like I am now." He caught Ali's look. A forty-mile dash down the A1 at no notice to meet your ex while your wife was at home, hardly counting as reliable. "Well, you know."

Melody was coming up to Newcastle, she said, so they arranged to meet. All entirely innocent. They had a bite to eat in Fenwick, did a spot of browsing, walked along the Quayside, a drink at the Crown Posada. "One of our old haunts." It became a regular thing.

"All above board. Meals, the theater once or twice. I suppose we got a bit carried away, talking about old times, what might have been if we'd stayed together."

"You were having an affair?"

"No! Nothing like that. I tell you, nothing happened. We'd meet up and talk daft about running away together but that's all it was, talk." He was quiet for a moment. "Then it all turned a bit . . . dark. Melody on about what would happen when she died, where she'd end up. She was almost obsessed with what you might call final arrangements—the burial plot, that kind of thing." Brian would be laid to rest with the first Mrs. Bright, she said, but where did that leave her? Alone. Again. "She'd get quite upset about all that," Jimmy said, frowning. They were both silent, Ali digesting this. "I mean, we'd gone from sharing small plates at Kaltur to something you'd not exactly call . . . fun."

Poor Melody, Ali thought. Pouring her heart out to Jimmy, thinking he was going to rescue her. "You were leading her on," she said.

"I wasn't, I swear. It was a laugh, delving into the past, thinking about what might have been. We were both married, we'd put down roots with other people. Me and Jenny, we're in it for the long haul." He gave Ali a pleading look. "I mean, we've got a box at St. James' Park, for crying out loud. No one in their right mind's going to walk away from that, the season we're having."

"A box."

He gave her a pleading look. "If I give it up now, I'll never get it back."

Death in the Countryside

Ali stared at him. *Give me strength.* "Good to know romance isn't completely dead," she said dryly.

"I don't mean it like that," Jimmy said. "All the ties me and Jenny have, well, I wouldn't break those lightly. It's a big anniversary next year, forty years, we're planning a party."

He'd had an attack of conscience during a conversation with Jenny about where to have the anniversary do. She had her eye on the Copthorne, while he was leaning toward the football ground, Shearer's Bar. It suddenly struck him his encounters with Melody, even if "nothing was going on," amounted to an act of betrayal. But just as he was getting cold feet, Melody seemed to have got it into her head they had a future together.

"What about her husband, Brian?" Ali wanted to know. "Didn't he figure in any of this?"

"Aye, well, she felt bad there," Jimmy said. "Decent enough bloke from what she said. Never going to set the world on fire, like, but still. It was just . . . well, Melody felt like an imposter. The first wife was the one, the real one, she said, always would be, while she was second best. Like Rebecca, she said. Not that I've the faintest who she is when she's at home." He was quiet for a moment before he continued. "She said he had his wife's photos up in the house, his *first* wife. Paintings she'd done." His brow creased. "Sounds a bit *off*, if you ask me."

Ali had thought so too. It had struck her as thoughtless. Now, though, knowing Brian as she did, she couldn't imagine he was being deliberately hurtful. His love for Melody seemed genuine. He just had a funny way of showing it.

"She didn't blame him," Jimmy was saying. "It was up to her to say something, she just couldn't bring herself to. Didn't feel it was fair to complain about a woman who wasn't there. Poor Brian, she'd say, clueless kind of bloke, apparently."

She was right about that.

Another long silence ensued. Under the table, Wilson sighed.

205

"Weren't you worried Jenny would find out what you'd been up to?" Ali asked at last. "I mean, people know you. Weren't you seen?"

"Oh, I'm recognized wherever I go," Jimmy said, pleased. "No one thinks anything of it, though, when you're out in the open, no attempt to hide away. For all anyone knew I was in a business meeting, entertaining a client."

Brazen.

He could see where things were headed so on the day Melody disappeared he had called and told her he wouldn't be seeing her again. Which was when she insisted they meet, that he tell her to her face. He'd had to invent a sofa-related crisis to get away, go shooting off to Piercebridge. Otherwise, she would come to him, she threatened, turn up at the house. "Obviously, I couldn't risk that."

"She took it badly, then?" Ali said. "Getting the brush off." The love of her life, the man she thought she'd end up with, running for the hills.

He looked away. "Aye, she wasn't happy."

Ali had a vision of Melody with Jimmy in The Fox Hole, tearstained and pleading, her hopes of starting afresh with her perfect match dashed. Jimmy, JC, The One, her soulmate, no longer in the mood to linger over coffee, a croissant, flirting and reminiscing about old times. Instead, in a hurry all of a sudden to get back to his wife and the plans for their anniversary bash. Jimmy and his gorgeous family—children, grandchildren, the glossy, glowing heirs to the Champion empire—not about to throw it away for a bit of fun, a sideline, a distraction. Once things got heavy he wanted out. As for Melody, what was left for her now the dream of Jimmy was no more? Brian, that was what. And the ghost of his first wife, his "real" wife. Jimmy had hoped to get away with a single phone call ending things. Hoped that Melody would understand and accept that whatever was going on between them—"nothing happened!"—had run its course. Hoping she would leave him alone.

Death in the Countryside

It hadn't worked out like that.

Before he had done ten miles on the A1 North, heading home, Melody was calling, bombarding him, leaving messages begging him to reconsider. So he did what any self-respecting husband would do and switched off his mobile, hoping that was the end of it.

Ali showed him the call log from Melody's mobile, the rash of 0191 calls in and among the increasingly desperate ones she'd made to Jimmy's mobile number during the course of the day. He studied the numbers. "They're the shops," he said, running a finger down the list, reeling off locations: Westgate Road, the Fossway, Scotswood Road, Killingworth, Blyth. "She must have rung them all trying to get hold of me."

"And she's not been in touch since?"

"Nothing." He looked sheepish. "I was relieved if I'm honest. I thought that was the end of it, that she was getting on with her life."

Instead, she had disappeared.

"No one's seen her since," Ali said. "Any idea where she might have gone?"

Jimmy sighed. "A hotel?"

"She's not used her bank cards." She let this sink in. "No activity on her account. Not since she saw you nearly two weeks ago."

"God almighty."

"Didn't she say where she was going?"

"Home, I assumed."

Neither one spoke. The silence stretched between them. Under the desk Wilson yawned. Outside, traffic moved slowly up and down Westgate Road. The curry house opposite looked to be doing a good trade in takeaways.

Eventually, Jimmy cleared his throat and said, "You might try the beach house."

37

So Melody had a beach house, which was news to Ali. News to Brian too. When she phoned to ask what he knew about it he was completely thrown. "A holiday place, you mean?" he said. "Is that where she is?" Suddenly hopeful. Ali told him Melody owned it, as far as she could work out, but Brian said that wasn't possible, he'd have known if she had a property somewhere.

Ali wondered. Lillian had said she was secretive. So much so she had successfully concealed having a property. A secret it appeared she had shared only with Jimmy. Melody had sent him pictures of the house, modern, sleek, tucked away in the dunes. *Driftwood* it was called. She had been there in recent months, Jimmy confirmed. On a few occasions they'd been due to meet then something came up at short notice—family-related, usually— that meant he couldn't get away. Rather than cancel her trip North, Melody had instead gone to *Driftwood*. Their "love nest" Melody said, causing alarm bells to clang in Jimmy's head. Not far from Alnmouth, he told Ali, at the same time insisting he had never actually been there. "I keep telling you, *nothing happened*, nothing like *that*," he said for the umpteenth time. "A bite to eat, a bit of shopping, a stroll in town. North Shields once, aye, the fish quay.

Death in the Countryside

Public places, all above board." Despite herself, Ali was inclined to believe him.

The beach house had been left to her, according to Jimmy. For years, Melody had been the live-in companion of an elderly woman in the Scottish Borders. A woman who was loaded, no one to leave her money to. "Melody was the nearest she had to family." Jimmy's brow creased. "The cat got a tidy sum, apparently." Ali thought of Evelyn Hooley, the unseen Trevor. "She never said who the woman was, when she passed away, where she lived." He shrugged, awkward.

Ali was beginning to think that beyond the world of sofas and all things Newcastle United, Jimmy didn't know much about much. He was utterly exasperating. And yet. She could see why Melody had fallen for him all over again. He had something about him, an easy confidence, charisma. And those eyes. A bit like her father's only bluer, more intense. And Wilson, Wilson had taken to him. Padded round Jimmy's office, sniffing at carpet samples, examining a football—"signed by the entire first team, 1995"—before settling down under the desk (on what Ali guessed was a Persian rug, a real one) with a miniature Scottie biscuit courtesy of Jimmy, risking crumbs on the lovely rug, not that Jimmy seemed to mind, not a bit.

Wilson had definitely taken a shine to Jimmy.

Ali put Alnmouth into the satnav and drove north on the A1. An hour later she was pulling into what might have been a small town or a large village, it was hard to tell, following the one-way system past the golf course, parking on the main street. She couldn't see any evidence of beach houses. She checked her phone. A message from Spence to say that Melody's last call from her mobile had pinged off a mast near Alnwick. Ali sensed she was on the right track.

Maria Malone

She rolled down the passenger window and Wilson breathed in the sea air, keen to get out an explore. "Give me a minute to call Nick, then we'll have a walk, stretch our legs," she told him.

"You're where?" Nick said.

"Northumberland, a place called Alnmouth, up the coast from Newcastle."

"The one with the Tobermory houses?"

"Are there? I've not seen any."

"Just a second, I'm Googling it." There was a pause. "Yeah, that's it, there's a row of houses painted different colors overlooking the estuary. Looks nice, actually."

"I'll see if I can find them. I need to give Wilson a run, he's been cooped up all day. Then I'll have a look for the beach houses."

The tide was out, the beach quiet, a few dog walkers muffled up against the wind blowing in from the North Sea. Wilson tore off, aiming straight at a mound of glossy bladderwrack, burrowing into it before taking off again, coming to an abrupt halt, a comical emergency stop, to dig into the sand, clouds of it sprayed high into the air, before charging, full pelt, back at Ali. "Good lad," she said, throwing a ball for him. In the distance, at the shoreline, hundreds of birds had gathered, shuffling about as the sea caught at their feet.

She turned to look back at the little town (village?) and saw the houses Nick had mentioned, painted in bright colors, pink and blue, yellow. How did she not know about Alnmouth? How did she not know about Melody's beach house, her secret hideaway? How did Brian not know?

Back on the main street, she popped into the Schooner. "Any beach houses nearby?" she asked the barman.

"Further up the coast, past the golf club, Foxton Hall," he told her. "There's chalets there. Five minutes."

210

Death in the Countryside

"Would people class them as Alnmouth?"

He gave her a look. "If you weren't from here, aye, you might." He gave her directions and she set off again.

She missed the turn-off. Twice. No signpost. Finally, she saw a man with a small brown and white dog heading up a narrow track. She asked if he knew where the beach chalets were and he pointed back the way he'd come. Off she went again, bumping down a lane that took her through sand dunes. At the end was a caravan, an SUV parked at the side, surfboards propped up, wetsuits draped over a cylindrical washing line. No houses, as far as she could see. A sign, red lettering on a white board, read: Private: No Public Access. She had a choice, left or right. She chose right, heading south. "Right sounds right, doesn't it Wilson?" she said, crawling along an even narrower track, marram grass either side, taller than the roof of the vehicle. It was not yet four o'clock but already the light was changing, the sun hidden behind a bank of clouds, dark, dense. Another caravan, blinds drawn, no sign that anyone was staying there. The sea, on the other side of the towering dunes, was completely out of sight. The place had a wild feel, cut off, as if hundreds of miles from civilization, not just a few minutes' drive from the nearest town with pubs and cafés and galleries, houses that were probably in the million pound bracket.

"Should have gone left, then," she said, reaching a dead end, having to reverse all the way back to the caravan she'd seen before, pulling into the parking space there. She walked back and knocked at the caravan with the wetsuits. A man in a T-shirt, baggy shorts and flip flops appeared. The beach houses were a bit further north, he told her, well hidden by the dunes. He hadn't heard of *Driftwood* but there weren't many, eight or nine, he guessed, so it shouldn't be hard to find.

She carried on, driving at walking pace, keeping an eye out for Melody's car. The dunes, covered in bracken, ensured she went straight past the first couple of houses without even seeing them. When she spotted the edge of a roof poking above the vegetation, she stopped and got out, taking a narrow path, the beach and sea suddenly spread out in front of her and, in the distance, an island with a lighthouse. The tide looked to be coming in, waves breaking onto the shore with a gentle whooshing sound. The air felt fresh and cool. She had Wilson on the lead and almost immediately he was pulling on it, steering her past the first two properties, wooden, blending in with their surroundings. They came to an old railway carriage, green and cream livery, faded and weather-beaten, that looked to have been there for many years. No one home. On past a miniature house painted bright yellow: pitched corrugated roof, fussy lace curtains covering the windows. Further on lay a modern structure, oblong, flat roof, some sort of gray cladding. The path took them away from it, snaking along the back of the dunes. Briefly, Ali found herself back on the England Coast Path at another junction, one way pointing inland, the other becoming a sandy track that went straight on. Another sign warning there was no public access. The closer they drew to the property, the more it was obscured by its surroundings, seeming almost to disappear beneath bracken and the branches of a hawthorn tree. Wilson, alert, pulled her forward. "Okay," she told him, "good lad." They drew level with the house, which had no windows at the back, and then she saw it, the brilliant yellow of the Mini, Wilson straining now, keen to get to it. "Easy, boy," Ali said, checking the car's registration plate. Melody's. No wonder nobody had seen it, it was too well tucked away.

Nothing on the house to give away its name but as she approached the front, she saw the twisted piece of driftwood, as tall as she was. Clever, she thought. Her heart was beating hard, Wilson emitting a low whine. Ali went to the front where the blinds were down. She knocked. Wind chimes hanging from a hook made

Death in the Countryside

a soft musical sound. No answer. The decking was home to a host of plants in pots and she put on gloves, going from pot to pot, checking under each one for the key. Wilson's hackles were up. Something wasn't right. Maybe she should phone Nick, or the station at Skipden, tell someone where she was. She got out her mobile. No signal. Wilson growled. In her gut, she knew this exactly fitted the scenario they'd covered a hundred times in training where you didn't proceed if *anything whatsoever* indicated it was not safe to do so. She looked out to sea, the sky streaked with pewter, a threat of rain. Checked under the last of the pots. Nothing. Knocked again, her gaze sliding to the wind chimes where she saw the key hanging among them. For a minute or two she stood with the key in her hand, not sure what to do next. Do not proceed if there is *anything whatsoever* concerning you, her instructor had said all those years ago in the days when she was raw, ready to follow the rules. Now, though, she had the benefit of experience. Which didn't necessarily mean she knew better than the man who had stood in front of the class and hammered home the message about being safe and swerving unnecessary risks, more times than she could remember. The main difference now was that she had Wilson. Standing at her side, alert, his entire body quivering, making an awful mournful sound. She hesitated. The main road was only a few minutes back, she would surely get a signal there. *Do things by the book*, she told herself.

She slipped the key into the lock and attempted to turn it. Unlocked already. *Go back, tell someone where you are.* "Sit," she told Wilson. "Stay. Good boy. Stay." She opened the door and stepped inside into a tiny porch. Sour air filled her nostrils. Old smoke, something else. She put up a hand and covered her nose, her mouth.

"Hello, she called out." Silence. "Police, hello."

Moving through the porch in just a couple of strides, passing a row of hooks holding coats, waterproofs, boots and trainers, a pair of bright orange Crocs. Careful not to touch anything. Emerging into the living room.

Stark white walls, a wood burner.

A shape stretched out on the sofa.

Melody.

38

It seemed an age before officers from the North of Tyne Force were on the scene, although it was barely thirty minutes. Uniformed officers first to arrive. Next, what turned out to be a DI—"Steppenbeck, top dog," one of the uniforms informed her, impressed. While the DI was inside, a black van, windowless, rocked up. The body crew. Ali looked away. How long had Melody been lying there? If only she'd had the phone records earlier. If only she'd known about Jimmy Champion from the outset. *If only.* She waited with Wilson at the side of the Hilux, far enough away not to get in anyone's way, near enough to clock the various comings and goings. More uniforms arrived, a man in a silver Volvo SUV. The pathologist, Ali guessed.

The DI was coming her way. Fifty-something, black hair cut short. No-nonsense bearing about him. "Are you Wren?"

She nodded, "Yes, sir."

He looked at Wilson. "And who's this, then?"

"PD Wilson, sir."

Wilson sat up straight, alert. Adopting his professional pose. Recognizing a superior officer and keen to make a good impression.

"I hear you had the good sense not to contaminate the scene," the DI said to Wilson. "Good lad." He looked at Ali. "Terry Steppenbeck, North of Tyne. I'm in charge here. Not sure what we're dealing with yet. Suspicious death for now. Which of course might in the end turn out to be nothing out of the ordinary, given the age of the deceased. On the other hand . . ." His voice tailed off, leaving another possibility (foul play) hanging in the breeze coming off the sea. "Want to give me the story so far?"

She outlined the salient details surrounding Melody's disappearance, soon getting to the lead she had been handed earlier in the day by Jimmy Champion—

Steppenbeck cut in. "Jimmy Champion the *sofa* man?" She nodded.

"You mean 'Me, I love sofas' Jimmy?" That's the one, Ali confirmed.

"Well, I never," Steppenbeck said, laughing. "My first sofa came from him and it's still going strong." He gave a low whistle. "Jimmy Champion," as if he didn't quite believe it. "JC himself, one of the most notable figures in Newcastle. Well, well, well, that *is* a turnup."

Ali could only agree it was.

"And the deceased was involved with Jimmy how?"

"Old friends." Ali hesitated. "Although from what Jimmy told me, she wanted something more."

Steppenbeck smiled again. "Something more, eh? How thoroughly quaint you make it sound, Sergeant Wren. I take it what you mean is they were carrying on, she wanted him to leave Mrs. Champion, and he was having none of it."

"Well . . ." Wanting to protect Melody, Jimmy too (for reasons she didn't fully understand). She felt slightly foolish all of a sudden, the hick from the sticks, way too green to be anywhere near what might turn out to be a murder scene. Steppenbeck was right. They *were* carrying on. Carrying on was exactly what they were doing,

Death in the Countryside

in full view of anyone who cared to look. "I don't think you could call it an affair, sir," she offered.

"Not an affair," Steppenbeck echoed, amused. "What, then? Afternoon tea in Fenwick's, the occasional matinee at the Theater Royal?" Managing to capture the essence of what had been going on with uncanny accuracy.

"Pretty much, sir," Ali said.

"What do we think about that?" Turning to Wilson, who seemed to feel sufficiently at home with this new important person to thump his tail on the sandy track in reply. "Yeah, mate, I'm with you," he told the spaniel. "Stretching credulity to absolute breaking point."

He gave Ali a smile, one that seemed to say her revelation about Jimmy Champion had more than made up for having to come out into the wilds at short notice. "Jimmy Champion," he said again, suddenly serious. "Bloody legend in these parts, he is. A bit of a hero, actually, does a ton of stuff for charity. When word gets out, the press are going to be all over this."

Ali asked if it would be okay if she and Wilson took a walk along the beach in case there was anything of interest there. "I mean, unlikely, sir, I know," she said, "but worth a look, perhaps."

"Absolutely," Steppenbeck said. "You're not in a hurry to get back to"—he hesitated, frowned—"where is it you're from?" Heft, she told him. When he looked blank, she did her best to give him a sense of where the town lay in relation to Harrogate, Bradford, bigger places he may have been more familiar with. He shook his head. "In the middle of nowhere, basically," he said, nodding at the Hilux. "No wonder you need a beast like that to get around. Weather bad in the winter, is it?"

"Can be, sir."

He nodded. "The Hilux is popular up here too," he said. "In town, mostly, the school run." He grinned, bent down, and ruffled

217

the fur on Wilson's ears. "Right, lad, off you go, see what you can find."

Ali followed the path back to a set of stone steps that led to the bay. At the base, she walked toward the headland where *Driftwood* stood, almost on the point itself, the best position of all the beach properties. Even from below, it was well-screened. Wilson ran ahead, sniffing at the sand, the rocks that jutted up at the base of the dunes. Inside *Driftwood*, Ali had checked Melody's pulse, even though it seemed clear she had been dead for some time. On the low table in front of the sofa was a note, a few lines, which she read but was careful not to touch.

> *Brian, I'm sorry. I've done something stupid, caused a lot of bother. Forgive me if you can. I didn't mean to hurt you, that was the last thing I wanted.*
> *Melody*

As soon as Ali left the property and called in what she'd found, she scribbled down Melody's words, words that echoed the message found in Brian's desk drawer at home.

A suicide note? Or something else?

Jimmy was in big trouble now. In no time, Steppenbeck would be on the doorstep of the Champion home in Jesmond. Just as the family were enjoying a meal together, perhaps, police officers in sandy shoes trampling all over the white shag pile. What all this would do to the plans for the anniversary celebration was anyone's guess. Would the two JCs even make it to their forty-year landmark once it came out what Jimmy had been up to behind Jenny's back?

Wilson was scrambling up the steep side of the dunes, finding footholds in tufts of grass, poking his nose into what looked like rabbit holes. "Careful," she called, thinking of the sand martins

Death in the Countryside

that nested there too. Wilson stopped, tail wagging furiously, his eyes on a burrow, his body rigid. Barking to signal something of interest. "Good lad," Ali called, "here."

He charged back and she rewarded him with a treat. "There you go, Wils, clever boy." She hurled the ball along the beach and off he went, chasing it down, skidding across the sand. Ali, heartbeating faster, picked her way up the steep side of the dune, grabbing at clumps of spiky marram grass to steady herself. A few feet from the top, under an overhang, she saw a flash of pink, the thing that had got Wilson excited. Stuffed inside a burrow, concealed by vegetation, something flimsy, bedraggled, pink and green and purple. She knew at once what it was.

A scarf.

Ali would put money on it being one of Melody's.

39

Brian was fussing. He had bought more coffee, he said, a double pack of Lavazza, he just couldn't seem to find it. Pulling at cupboard doors, checking under the sink. Ali asked him to sit down. "Unless." Brian brightened, as if a lightbulb inside his head had suddenly gone on. "Unless I put the shopping down in the hall." Going to look, returning triumphant with a hessian bag from Epicurean. "Knew it!"

"Leave that a minute," Ali said. She glanced at Wilson, who gazed at Brian, his expression doleful. "Come and sit down."

Brian filled the kettle, acting as if it was an ordinary visit, that she had had simply called in to see how he was, let him know there was no news, when she had, moments earlier, told him the body of his missing wife had been discovered in a beach house he knew nothing about miles from home. Brian had not seemed to take it in. She wondered had he heard her. He was whistling, the kettle coming to a boil. His way of coping? Acting as if the words he most dreaded hearing had not in fact been spoken, and that if he ignored them, simply carried on as before, the awful realization facing him, the one where everything good had been taken away, all hope lost, might not be true.

Death in the Countryside

She waited until he had made the coffee and produced a biscuit tin. Waited until he had to stop and sit down.

"Brian," she said, "I'm so sorry." She gave Wilson a nudge and he crept under the table and sat at his side. Brian reached down and patted the spaniel.

"Can you be sure?" Brian said at last.

"I'm sure," she said. He would have to formally identify the body, but Ali was in no doubt. Melody's things were in the house: car keys, driving license, bank cards. The missing passport. Evidence of her affair with Jimmy, comprising love notes "full of soppy drivel," according to Steppenbeck. A real romantic, JC, recklessly wooing Melody the old-fashioned way, not stopping to think that one day it would all come back to haunt him. Then there was the note to Brian, the one Ali had seen on the table: *I've done something stupid.*

"Was it an accident?" Brian was saying. "Her heart?"

"I don't know."

He hadn't touched his coffee. "This place you found her, what was it? What was she doing there?"

Ali told him what little she knew about the seaside property in Northumberland, left to Melody, it seemed, by a woman she had spent a decade working for. "Scottish Borders," Ali said, which was what Jimmy seemed to think. "Her employer was elderly, well-off, no family, apparently. Melody was her live-in companion." Watching Brian closely to see if any of this rang bells. Apparently not.

"Did she ever mention any of this?"

Brian shook his head. "And all this was recent, getting this house?" he queried, baffled.

"Some years ago, as far as I know." Ali treading carefully, conscious that all she knew was what Jimmy Champion had told her. What if he was wrong? What if none of it turned out to be true? She needed to mind what she said to Brian. "It's all a bit sketchy," she said. "We'll need to establish the full facts, which may take time."

"I knew nothing about her inheriting a beach house," Brian said, struggling to make sense of things. "Why would she keep something like that, something . . . *significant*, a secret?"

Ali hadn't the foggiest. Perhaps she wanted somewhere to run to if things went wrong with Brian. A bolt holt, a place of her own, one he knew nothing about. Could she have been going there without his knowledge? No, Brian said, definitely not. Were there other trips she had made alone, aside from the recent ones to Newcastle? He sat shaking his head, deep in thought. An elderly aunt, he said, at last. Scotland, St. Abb's Head area? No longer alive. Sounding unsure. Melody used to visit occasionally, spend a few days. "I knew all about it." A note of defiance in his voice. "If she'd been going to a beach house, *her* beach house, she'd have told me. We didn't keep things from each other."

Ali was quiet. Melody, it seemed, had kept plenty from him. When she was off on those solo trips to see her aunt (*if* there was an aunt, Ali would check) was she really going to *Driftwood*? Why make a secret of it, though? Why not simply tell her husband, take him with her? Had she never properly trusted him? Her head swam. She felt for Brian, still loyal, still determined to think the best of his errant wife, despite all he was now finding out. Perhaps he hadn't known her at all. As Lillian had delighted in pointing out, Melody was unreliable, selfish. *Secretive.* A history of "doing off" without a thought for anyone. Ali had a sudden vision of Lillian, so dismissive of her sister going "missing." Would she shed tears at the news Melody was dead? Or feel vindicated? What would matter more? Ali wondered. Concern for Melody or a sense of triumph for having been right all along? At least Ali wouldn't be the one telling her. Steppenbeck had said he would do it.

"It's a lot to take in," Ali told Brian, feeling inadequate, unable to come up with a form of words that felt appropriate. "You've spent

Death in the Countryside

nearly two weeks worried sick about where she is, and now this, the worst news. I don't think you should be here on your own. Is there someone I can call, get you some company?"

He didn't answer.

Ali reached across the table and put her hand on top of his.

40

When she got home she cried. Tears for Brian rather than for Melody, a woman she hadn't known. She had been reluctant to leave but he insisted he was fine. *Fine.* Given the circumstances, that just wasn't possible. His manner when he'd shown her out, a bit feverish, expressing concern for her having to drive up to Newcastle and then into Northumberland, and back again. All that way, he said. Had she even eaten? His kindness making her well up. He was in shock, of course, still not able to accept what she'd said. His missing wife dead, and in circumstances that made no sense. Not to Brian.

Ali had broached the subject of Jimmy Champion. "You remember I asked if Melody had ever mentioned a Jimmy," she ventured, but Brian didn't seem to recall the conversation. Doing her best to be sensitive as she explained his wife had been meeting a man in secret ("carrying on," as DI Steppenbeck bluntly put it).

On the doorstep, Brian attempting to be upbeat, fussing over Wilson, as if all was normal. "At least we know now," he'd said breezily.

Ali felt awful. "Sure you'll be okay?" He gave a nod, said yes, of course, he could manage perfectly well, Ali thinking it was hardly

Death in the Countryside

five minutes ago he didn't know how to work the cooker, Brian sighing, thinking again.

"Muddle through, any rate," he said.

"Any idea what happened?" Nick asked.

Ali had been shivering when she got home. She had a bath and was now downstairs in her dressing gown. Fleecy pajamas, cozy socks. The fire was going in the living room, Wilson stretched out on the rug in front of it, panting. Too hot but not willing to move. Nick poured wine, handed her a glass. She felt numb, worn out. Seeing Brian had done her in.

She sipped at the wine. "We don't know anything, not yet."

"What about Brian, how's he taken it?"

Ali felt like crying again. She blinked back the tears, drank some more wine. "I don't think any of it sank in." He wouldn't let it. "Acting all chipper, concerned for *me* . . . enough to break your heart."

"Poor bugger."

"She'd been seeing someone," she said. "I tried to prepare him but . . ." Brian stubbornly refusing to acknowledge the unpalatable detail of Melody's other man. "Jimmy Champion, he's a minor celebrity in Newcastle. If it turns out Melody's death wasn't accidental, it'll be all over the press." Even if it turned out she'd passed away of natural causes, someone was bound to get a sniff of her connection to JC and splash it across the papers. Missing woman, high-profile businessman. The chances of it staying under the radar were almost nil. She needed to make sure Brian understood, that he knew how to arm himself against the possibility of reporters on the doorstep, turning up at his business, pumping his workers for information. Then, of course, there was Brian's connection to *The Beat*, which was bound to have the tabloids salivating. She closed her eyes. A storm was coming and there was nothing she could do to protect him. He would simply have to batten down the hatches and ride it out.

Maria Malone

"He had no idea what she was up to?"

"He believed what she'd told him about meeting her sister in Newcastle. It never crossed his mind she was lying." Enjoying lunches with Jimmy, stowing his love notes at the beach house she'd kept secret even from Brian. Had Jimmy really never been there? Was it all as innocent as he made out? Two old flames reigniting a spark from decades earlier, basking in the heat it generated. An ego trip, Ali thought, for both of them, Melody mistaken in the belief it meant more than that. Was that it? Jimmy Champion representing excitement, making her feel special, desired, the way she used to all those years earlier. Carrying on, carried away, Melody daring to dream of a future that was never going to come, not while Jimmy had one eye on his anniversary bash. She groaned. How could they have been so stupid, the pair of them?

"I dread to think what all this will do to Brian," she said. Once the reality dawned and he stopped kidding himself. She would need to be there for him, steer him through whatever horrors lay ahead.

"I'll go round and see him in the morning," Nick said. "See if there's anything I can do. I've got to know him a bit from seeing him on set." Ali nodded, grateful. He topped up her glass. "Is that you done on this now?"

"I suppose so. I mean, I found my missing woman . . ." She shrugged. The discovery of a body was always going to mean handing over the reins to a more experienced senior officer. Steppenbeck, Top Dog, had things under control. Seemed like a decent bloke, a good DI. Not the type who'd need Ali pitching in, although she fully expected him to have further questions for her at some point.

"What's bothering you?" Nick asked.

She turned to face him, upset, her green eyes filling with tears. "I'm not sure I handled this case brilliantly."

"Nonsense. I've never known anyone more thorough, more

Death in the Countryside

dedicated than you. You're churned up, of course you are, a woman's dead. But that's *not* down to you. You're too hard on yourself."

Finding the body had shaken her. What had she been expecting at the beach house? Ideally, Melody, alive and well and licking her wounds after the end of her affair with Jimmy. Feeling foolish, not able to face Brian. With each passing day, less able to go home. Not a happy outcome, exactly—there had been too much heartache for that—but one in which nothing too awful had happened, and where there remained a slender chance of Brian learning the truth from his wife, of them patching things up over time. Ali now felt she knew Brian well enough to think he would have been willing to forgive Melody almost anything. She turned over the events of the last couple of weeks. From the beginning she had suspected that Melody had likely left her husband. Now she questioned whether she had treated her disappearance with sufficient urgency. The missing passport, the note in Brian's desk drawer. It was easy enough to make assumptions. Had Ali been too ready to see what she wanted to see? Had she done her job as well as she could have? It troubled her to think she might have let Brian down in some way, let Melody down. Freeman, too, who'd put his trust in her, based his decisions on what she had told him. He wanted a detailed written report, he said. Chapter and verse. "A thorough review." ASAP. What was he hoping to find? Evidence of impeccable police work? Or the opposite?

41

Brian cleared away the coffee things and did the washing up, wiped down the table. Then he sat down and had a cry. There was wine in the fridge. He poured a glass, a large one, and went into the sitting room with it where he sat in the dark for a bit. He knew what Ali had said, he just didn't want to acknowledge it because, well, once he did, where was there to go other than a deep, dark pit of misery? Melody dead. Quite what she'd been up to he wasn't yet prepared to think in too much detail about, but he understood what Ali was getting at on that subject too. Another man. She could be wrong there, of course. Melody didn't have it in her. Did she? His gaze wandered to the mantelpiece, to the framed photo of his first wife. Wait, wasn't there once a photo of Melody there too, one taken in Funchal on their first holiday? A photo of Brian in a kayak, taken on Windermere, now stood in its place. He gazed at it, remembering Melody taking the ferry that day, walking to Hill Top, while he spent the morning on the water. Had he given the Funchal one to Ali? Surely, he'd have remembered, although . . . so much of what had happened was now a blur. That was what stress does, Evelyn Hooley had said, when he admitted he couldn't quite remember the sequence of events since Melody had gone. Reassuring him it was normal, the brain going into overdrive,

Death in the Countryside

getting things jumbled, filing away details that were distressing, putting them out of sight. Imagine an archive, she said, a kind of storage facility, one that was miles away, with all the things he couldn't quite cope with in a box labeled "sealed" on a shelf too high to reach without a pair of decent stepladders. If that made sense. It did.

Brian was grateful to Evelyn, who had troubles of her own. He gulped down his wine and put the glass on the coffee table, not bothering with a mat, the kind of behavior Melody would have had something to say about. Tears welling up again. There had been photos on the sideboard too, of Melody, of the two of them, but they were no longer there either. He went upstairs to their bedroom, looking for the picture taken on the ferry to Staten Island on their trip to New York. Once on the dressing table, now gone. Every photo missing. How come it hadn't registered until now? Downstairs, he pulled open the top drawer of the sideboard. Napkins, tablemats, coasters and, underneath, the photos, still in their frames, face down. Melody must have put them there, but why? Couldn't she stand looking at them? And what was that supposed to mean? Had she felt she had no place in the house, *their* house, that somehow, for reasons Brian couldn't even guess at, she had no right to occupy pride of place? He couldn't remember if Ali had looked at the contents of the sideboard. If she had, what must she have thought? He turned and cast a look at the photo of Dolores, where it had always been. Melody's pictures removed while Dolores's remained. And he hadn't even noticed. What did that say about him? About Melody? The state of their marriage?

The business with Leslie Masters was a reminder of how easy it was to get things wrong, bark up entirely the wrong tree. He had misjudged the man, he owed him an apology. What about Melody? Had he got things badly wrong there too? His thoughts went to a fraught conversation, one that had come out of nowhere, where Melody said she felt somehow less than Dolores, a poor substitute.

An imposter, she said. He was taken aback, he'd never regarded her as anything other than the woman he loved, thought the world of. Things hadn't been perfect with Dolores; they'd had their ups and downs—didn't everyone? Melody, close to tears, had put him on the spot, just weeks before she disappeared. He knew what he needed to say to put her mind at rest, it was all there inside his head, but somehow, he couldn't get the words out, instead shaking his head, saying *No, it wasn't like that.*

He should have said more, told her everything. Perhaps if he had, she would still be here.

The next morning, she had crept out of bed trying not to wake him, although he was already awake, had been awake all night, they both had. Downstairs he found her making breakfast, crisping streaky bacon, frying eggs, as if the night before had never happened. Whatever Melody thought, his marriage to Dolores had been far from idyllic. She had a way of losing her temper, taking things out on him when her painting wasn't going to plan. He hated that she smoked but she refused to stop. He loved her, of course, as he now loved Melody. He should have explained about Dolores, the flaws, the many failings in their marriage. He didn't, though, he'd have felt as if he was betraying her. He could at least have told Melody that her idea of Dolores, her *ideal*, was way off the mark. He ate his breakfast and said nothing to make her feel better.

At work, he ordered flowers to be sent to the house and agonized over what to put on the card. At times, words defeated him. In the end he wrote *I love you more*. A lyric from his favorite track on *Rubber Soul*. Hoping it was enough.

"Guilt," Evelyn said, when he told her about the photos that were hidden away. "She couldn't stand to look at herself."

"But why?" Brian asked.

"Well, that's something I wouldn't like to speculate on," Evelyn said, although privately she suspected Melody's guilty conscience

Death in the Countryside

was at the root of it, given what Brian had just told her about his wife's illicit meetings with some chap in Newcastle.

She had come straight round when Brian phoned and now sat with him in the kitchen listening, not once interrupting, as he told her what Ali had said.

"Oh God, Brian, I can't tell you how sorry I am." Wrapping him in one of her comforting hugs, insisting she would stay at the house, that he simply could not be left alone. "If you don't mind my saying, love," she said, giving him a long, searching look, "it doesn't seem to me you've taken it in yet. Once the shock wears off, well, you won't know what's hit you."

Was he in shock? Brian wasn't sure how that would manifest itself—bidding a cheery farewell to Ali after she'd broken the terrible news, perhaps. Evelyn had a point. He hadn't properly taken in all that Ali had said, mainly because he had no wish to although, eventually, of course, he would have to. Practicalities would present themselves and he would have no choice but to deal with them. The identification of Melody's body for one. The detective in charge of things up there, a man with a name he hadn't quite got to grips with—Steppenwolf? Something like that–had explained there would be a post mortem, an inquest. Sooner or later, the funeral. As the thoughts crowded in, bringing with them a sense of breathless panic, he swept them aside, despatching them straight to the handy archive folder Evelyn had described, the one marked "sealed," located on the shelf that was out of reach. Safe in the knowledge the only ladders he had weren't long enough to get up there.

42

The morning after breaking the news of Melody's death to Brian, Ali was at home in her office working on the report for her boss, Wilson under the desk, his chin on her foot. Having him there, hearing his doggy snuffles, the occasional sigh, instantly made her feel better. To her surprise, she had slept soundly and woke late, after nine, Nick already gone. A note lay on his pillow: "Ewe's the best. I love ewe." A scrappy drawing of a sheep. She smiled, pulled on saggy tracksuit bottoms, grabbed the Foo Fighters sweatshirt that was hanging on the back of the bedroom door, and took Wilson out. It was a cool morning, cloudy. The chill fresh air, the sight of the spaniel joyfully scampering in the woods, snuffling about among the last of the bluebells, immediately perked her up. The night before, Nick had given her a serious talking to, insisting he knew her well enough to feel certain she had done everything she could to discover what had happened to Melody. Reminding her of other cases, ones where the missing woman had simply chosen to leave, sometimes without explanation, often not wishing to be found. It was what she had needed to hear.

Freeman had told her to work from home, prioritize the report. She decided not to rush it and phoned Lillian, offered her condolences. It was an uncomfortable call, Lillian her usual spiky self,

Death in the Countryside

confirming what Ali suspected, that the "aunt in the Scottish Borders" was fictitious. Cover, most likely, for Melody's secret visits to *Driftwood*. Why she had kept Brian in the dark was a mystery.

For once, there was no need for Ali to put on her uniform as she had no intention of venturing out on police business. She would shower later. "We're having a dress-down day," she said. Wilson liked the sound of that, she could tell.

She taped a notice to the front door to say nobody was home and for police matters to contact the station at Skipden on the number below. Anything urgent, dial 999. She made coffee, spread a thick layer of peanut butter on toast, and carried a tray through to the office, settling in front of the computer. She had barely begun when there was a knock on the door. Under the desk, Wilson stirred. "We're not here," she told him. He sighed and settled back down. Another knock. Surely whoever it was could read the sign she had left. She waited a moment. The knocker went a third time. She got up, Wilson at her side, and went to the door. Chief Superintendent Freeman faced her. Ali, unwashed, in her scruffy clothes, felt herself flush. She had not even put a brush through her hair, hadn't looked in the mirror. She must be a sight. Her boss gave her an appraising look.

"Wren," Freeman said, bending to pat Wilson's head. "Sorry to call unannounced. All right if I come in?"

She led the way to the kitchen (thank goodness it was tidy!) wishing the ground would open up and swallow her. Freeman followed, smelling of sandalwood, immaculate in his uniform.

"Sir, I got going on the report straight away this morning and, well, time must have got away from me." Her face was on fire. "Sorry not to be in uniform."

He waved away her concerns. "Working from home, it makes sense to wear something . . . comfortable."

She cringed, her boss taking in Nick's tatty sweatshirt, the hideous dog-walking trousers. Her slippers had a smiley face on them, for goodness' sake! Was it obvious she'd not yet had a wash? She

233

attempted to smooth her hair, pushing strands off her face, tucking them behind her ears.

Freeman sat at the table while Ali made fresh coffee, grateful to be able to turn her back for a moment, take some deep breaths, compose herself. What was he doing here? It had to be serious, something bad. She was in trouble, she knew it.

Wilson, delighted to see one of his favorite people, positioned himself at Freeman's side. PD Wilson, who always looked well turned out, no matter what, who never experienced a bad hair day, his chestnut and white coat gleaming, a credit to the Force. Freeman ruffled the spaniel's ears. "So, you did a good job in Northumberland yesterday, well done," he told him. The dog's hazel eyes, intelligent, alert, fixed on his superior.

Ali sat down opposite the Chief Superintendent.

"How's the report coming along?" Freeman asked.

"I'm not that far into it." She hesitated. "Sir . . . am I in trouble?"

Freeman's expression gave nothing away. "What makes you say that?"

"A visit from the boss. Makes me think I'm about to be told to stay at home until . . ." she left the sentence hanging. Was he about to say there would be an investigation into her conduct, that she was now suspended pending its outcome?

"This case hasn't been easy," Freeman said. "On you, particularly, working here on your own. If I'd caught a whiff of anything to suggest this was how it would end, I'd have taken a different approach, of course I would. However. Instinct told me our missing woman had simply left. Husband in the clear, surrounded by people. On a TV set of all places"—he raised an eyebrow—"at the crucial time." He was quiet for a moment. "And I was right. She *did* leave. Whether she intended coming back, we don't know. Once we find out what happened, how she died, we might be closer to answering that question."

Death in the Countryside

Ali wanted to ask if it would have made a difference had she found Melody sooner. Might she still be alive. But there was no point. Freeman wouldn't know the answer to that either, not yet.

"You're a bit isolated out here," he went on, frowning. "I know we agreed you'd come into the station one day a week..." He sighed, ran a hand over his bald head.

She was braced for him to say he didn't trust her to be unsupervised, that she was now on desk duties, and had a sudden vision of working shifts on reception, covering for the regular duty sergeant, updating the filing system (long overdue). Stuck in Skipden, no longer a presence in Heft. She felt sick.

"Do you feel adrift here?" Freeman asked, leaning forward in his seat, serious brown eyes on her.

"No, sir. I love it." Squirming at having to face him unwashed, in her scruffs, at a severe disadvantage.

"It doesn't get on top of you, everyone coming to you to deal with their problems?"

She shook her head. "It's why I'm here."

Another sigh. "Let me have that report and I'll think about how best to move forward."

"Does that mean ... ?"

"It means I have some serious thinking to do."

235

43

It was as if the people of Heft had collectively decided to give Ali some breathing space. For a week or so after Melody was found, there were no calls about cans left at the side of the War Memorial or crisp packets on the grass verge next to the school. No reports of alarms going off annoying everyone. Even Roger Felton was uncharacteristically quiet. Driving through town one day, she had spotted him emerging from the paper shop and he had whipped his woolly hat off and bowed his head as the Hilux went past, as if Melody Bright's death was not just Brian's loss but Ali's. Which in a sense it was.

The post mortem revealed Melody was strangled, the scarf found by Wilson hidden away under a clump of marram grass in all likelihood the murder weapon. Degraded, not much on it in the way of DNA, but they were working on it. It was estimated she had died on the day she left home. Dead before she was even reported missing.

Steppenbeck had taken a statement from Brian. "Just tidying up loose ends," he said. They weren't looking at Brian, his presence on the set of *The Beat* when Melody was last captured on CCTV at Piercebridge providing a solid alibi. It was Jimmy Champion they were interested in. They'd found a stash of what Steppenbeck

Death in the Countryside

described as *billets-doux* ("billy-douze") from Melody in his office and a handmade pot covered in her fingerprints. The one she had made and collected from the studio the day she had gone to meet Jimmy at The Fox Hole.

Jimmy's problem was he had no watertight alibi for later that day. The evidence pointed to Melody having died a few hours after he'd seen her when he was where, exactly? At work and then home, he said, alone. Jenny out at a hen do. ("A *hen* do," Steppenbeck, incredulous, told Ali. "She's sixty-odd, you know, you'd think she was beyond the obligatory cowboy hat and Team Bride T-shirt.") CCTV footage from the Quayside, however, showed Jenny looking sensational amid a rowdy group of hens, all strappy heels, mini-skirts, and cut off T-shirts, not a coat between them, confirmation she was very much *not* beyond such things.

Jimmy had gone for a walk, Steppenbeck said. Wandered around Jesmond for a bit, the Dene. Unfortunately for him, there was no CCTV footage to be found confirming this. All Steppenbeck knew for sure was that Jimmy hadn't driven up to *Driftwood*. "Checked the satnav on the Rolls, it went nowhere that night. Course, that doesn't mean he didn't get a taxi . . ." They were looking into that.

Ali tried not to think too much about it. It wasn't her case, she told herself. The fact she struggled to think of Jimmy as a killer didn't mean he was innocent. She knew that people, even those like Jimmy, the ones you might consider unwise but essentially harmless, were sometimes capable of terrible things.

"And it's all above board, this beach house?" Freeman said, frowning. "No fraud? Nothing to say she coerced the old woman into leaving it to her? Because that would explain why she kept quiet about it."

"No, sir, nothing improper," Ali said.

In her forties, Melody had spent the best part of a decade

working for Constance Duff in Seton, in the Scottish Borders. Roxburgh House, the property Constance had once shared with her husband, Stanley, who was something in scrap metal, was too big for her when he died. But Constance didn't want to leave and employed Melody as her live-in companion. Constance provided for her cat, Izzy, and left the remainder of her considerable fortune to an animal shelter on the Greek island of Zakynthos. The beach house, renovated shortly before Stanley's sudden death, went to Melody. Ali had spoken to the Duff family solicitor, who confirmed the will was entirely proper, nothing dubious in the various legacies.

Freeman listened as Ali explained all this. "Why not tell her husband she had a place on the coast?" he asked, baffled. "They could have gone there together, enjoyed it."

Ali had no answer. Clearly, Melody had other plans for *Driftwood*.

44

Ali had the morning off and couldn't think what to do with it. Almost hoping for one of Roger's calls, she realized, more complaints about alarms going off in the dead of night. However, the phone remained stubbornly silent. She picked up a magazine that had come with the Sunday paper and idly leafed through a feature on summer "must-have" skin saviors. When the doorbell went, she was so grateful that someone, anyone, wanted to see her, she practically ran along the hall to let them in. Ever since Freeman had unexpectedly arrived on her doorstep, she had resolved never to be caught out again. Her hair was in an orderly plait, she wore a pristine white T-shirt, olive-green cargo pants, trainers, all items from her recently updated wardrobe. For off-duty wear, she now had at her disposal half a dozen new tops, two pairs of trousers in a slouchy, wide-legged cut, a look she thought of as a smart-casual civilian version of her police uniform, suitable for any eventuality. As for the smiley face slippers Freeman had found her in, they were a thing of the past. To her surprise, Leslie Masters faced her. From his expression he had something important on his mind. Ali thought about Brian stalking him, the file in which he had accused Leslie of everything from murdering his wife in order to be with his (much younger) lover to being the person behind Melody's mysterious disappearance. The prime suspect.

Wilson was pleased too to see Leslie, who sat at the kitchen table, in the seat so frequently occupied of late by Brian. The dog retreated to his bed, pushing the edge of his blanket over the remnants of the cakery-bakery tea towel, ensuring it was properly concealed. A trophy, one he was proud of. Ali made coffee and Leslie Masters placed a folder on the kitchen table, not unlike the one Brian had produced. For a moment Ali had the horrible feeling this folder of Leslie's was somehow connected to Brian's. Perhaps he knew he was being followed and had compiled his own report, logging dates and times, until he had enough to bring a complaint of harassment. If Leslie was on to him, any hope Ali had of dealing with Brian's stalking discreetly would be impossible.

"I know you're busy," Leslie said, "so I'll be brief."

Not like Brian then, who wandered around the houses, up hill, down dale, before getting to the point. Not that she minded. She missed his meandering, she realized. "It's okay, I've got time," she said. All the time in the world, it seemed.

"Tom, my son, went missing," Leslie began, getting right to the point as promised. "Autumn of 2004, twenty years ago. We never found out what happened to him."

"I'm sorry," Ali said.

"We weren't living here then, we were in North Berwick, and Tom was at uni in Edinburgh. He was going to be a vet. I was teaching, French and history, at Stuarts, a private school. My wife was in general practice."

Ali worked hard to stop her face from giving away what she was thinking. Leslie, now working at the tip, had once been a schoolteacher. French and history. The books he had, the paintings, suddenly made sense.

"Tom was in his first year when he met Nora, who was on his course. Lovely girl, from round here." He waited for this to sink in.

Death in the Countryside

"Her mother runs the Bull at Farnley, you might know it." Ali nodded. She and Nick had been there and if she wasn't mistaken, it had been a location for an episode of *The Beat*. "What happened was Tom was here with Nora before they were due back in Edinburgh for the start of their second year. My wife and I were away, on holiday in Cornwall, walking." He took a breath, stared at the table. "Tom went up the Black Stone alone and . . . vanished. His car, the car we'd bought him so he could get home when he needed to, was found there, his gloves on the summit. Otherwise, nothing, not a trace. He was nineteen."

It was coming back to her, the student who had disappeared, apparently into thin air. The boy Violet had mentioned. Ali was in London then, her move to Harrogate not until the following year. Her recollection was patchy, only a few hazy fragments relating to Tom's disappearance. She would have to locate the file, likely in the archive by now, look up the relevant newspaper cuttings. Leslie indicated the folder. "It's all in here," he said.

Ali was thinking about what Brian had said about Leslie's trips to the Black Stone, the flowers he took with him. Flowers for the wife he had "done away with," according to Brian, his own loss sending him toward a place of madness, when, in fact, Leslie was honoring the memory of his missing boy. Something came back to her. The chrysanthemums on the summit the last time she went up the Black Stone with Wilson. The card and its poignant message.

She opened the folder. Newspaper cuttings, photos. Leslie's boy, Tom, laughing, strands of dark hair falling over his eyes.

Of course, there were searches, Leslie told her, a thorough inquiry. He and his wife, Eloise, were contacted at their hotel on the Lizard and returned at once. They had wanted to search too but were asked to go home, to wait. In case Tom showed up there.

"This tragedy you're now dealing with," he said. "Melody. A woman I knew slightly. It's brought so much back into sharp focus, the keen sense of loss, despair, the need to grab on to any possible

241

Maria Malone

explanation, however irrational, in the hope it might lead *somewhere*, provide the answers you're seeking."

Ali had the feeling it was Brian he was talking about. Perhaps he did know Brian was tailing him, his almost unhinged obsession, the unwarranted conviction that Leslie had been pursuing Melody.

"Can I ask, what happened to your wife?" Ali said.

Leslie gave a wry smile. "It wasn't something we could survive, the loss of our only child. I couldn't accept he was gone. As long as we didn't know what had happened to him, there was hope. For me, anyway." He sighed. "Eloise felt differently. She was in despair, and I couldn't offer any comfort because I wouldn't accept that was it, that Tom was never coming back. I wanted us to move here, thought it would help, make us feel closer to him, but she hated the idea. This was the place that stole him from us, she said, the idea of living here turned her stomach. So . . . I moved without her."

"And got a job at the tip."

"And got a job at the tip, which I love."

Ali didn't argue. Nick had already confessed a fondness for the tip, her father too, who called it his happy place. When Violet asked what the attraction was, Gordon would reply "everything, love, everything."

"Is there any reason you're bringing this to me now?" she asked. "Apart from Melody stirring things up again?"

Leslie nodded. "Partly it's Melody, yes, although things have been 'stirred up' as you put it ever since we lost Tom. It never quite *un*stirs itself, if you see what I mean, when a child goes missing." He leaned forward in his seat. "And now there's been an accident, Nora's fiancé, Niall." He closed his eyes briefly. "He's very badly hurt, they're not sure he'll survive."

"I'm so sorry," Ali said. "You're still in touch, then?"

"She's had such a troubled time, dreadful, as you'd expect but, yes, we are—cards at Christmas, that kind of thing. I got a letter

242

Death in the Countryside

recently to say she intends to marry. I sensed she felt guilty for finding happiness when Tom . . ." his voiced tailed off. "Anyway, I went to meet her fiancé, wish them well." He sighed. "Now . . . well, I can only pray there will still be a wedding."

Ali assumed this was the encounter Brian had witnessed, Leslie greeting a woman "half his age," the two of them "all over each other." Not an affair but a bereaved father bestowing his blessing on the former girlfriend of the son he had lost.

They were silent.

"If she loses him, having lost Tom, I wonder"—he sent a look of anguish at Ali—"does a person ever get over such a blow?" He stared at the floor. "And still, where Tom's concerned, we have no answers. I wonder . . . might now be the time to find some?"

It was all in the file, the kind of boy Tom Masters was—bright, gifted, a runner who had completed two half marathons, raising funds for animal charities in the process. Everyone agreed he had a glittering future. And then he vanished.

After Tom's disappearance, Leslie had spoken at length to Nora and made copious, detailed notes. On their last day together, Tom and Nora had been up the Black Stone. Tom was fascinated, she said, with the folklore that surrounded the place, the stories of spirits that inhabited the rocks by day and emerged intent on causing mischief as the sun went down. Folly to be up there in the dark, so legend had it, the spirits would take you.

That night, he and Nora returned from their walk to the pub her mother ran, the Bull. It was busy and Nora helped out in the bar. Tom left her to it, turned in early. Only when she woke in the morning did she see he'd gone out, his car was missing. She tried phoning him, he didn't answer. It was their last night before returning to Edinburgh, to uni, and she wondered if he was cross about her working, leaving him on his own. They'd had words that day, Nora wanting to put things between them on a more casual

243

footing, Tom saying no. Was that it, then? Afraid he was losing Nora he went up the Black Stone alone, despite the darkness, into the clutches of the spirits who waited for him? Everything in Leslie's folder pointed to it: Tom's precious red Ford Escort with its alloy wheels and spot lamps, spoiler on the back, abandoned below, his gloves in a crevice at the foot of the Black Stone.

The only mystery, his body was never found.

Almost twenty years on, Ali wasn't sure what more Leslie Masters thought she could uncover concerning the disappearance of his son. He was looking for answers. So far, no one had been able to tell him anything that gave him peace of mind. His son lost, his marriage broken, his old life abandoned. Alone, consumed by ifs and maybes—if he and his wife hadn't been away, if they'd not bought Tom the car that transported him to the Black Stone and his disappearance. Maybe then he'd still be here, a qualified vet now, approaching forty, working in a rural practice in the Highlands, as he'd wanted to. If. Maybe.

Since losing Tom, Leslie had abruptly changed direction, no longer a well-regarded teacher at a fee-paying school but a lowly worker at the local tip in Heft, his master's gown swapped for a high-vis jacket, the somber work suits Ali pictured him once wearing replaced by faded jeans. Instead of sweeping across the neat lawns of Stuart's, gown flapping, he put on bicycle clips and pedalled to work on a bike he'd saved from being tossed into a skip.

Ali wanted to do her best for him, which meant looking into Nora. Clearly, Leslie was fond of her so she would have to tread carefully. As soon as he left, she put in a call to a colleague in Edinburgh, PC Bridie Keen, new to the Force and as eager to help as her name suggested, who ran through what was in the file regarding Niall Ross's accident. A fall from Arthur's Seat. Pretty banged up, as she put it.

"Anything suspicious?" Ali asked.

Death in the Countryside

"Oh no, nothing," Bridie said, calling Nora, "a lovely lass," who was "in bits," keeping a vigil at the bedside, practically round the clock. "Utterly devoted."

Ali asked if anything about the accident didn't add up. Not a thing, Bridie said. It wasn't the first time there'd been a fall there, nor the first fatality. Not that he was actually dead, she said, hurriedly correcting herself, embarrassed. Not yet, being the implication.

Clearly, no one expected Niall Ross to survive.

45

"Well, this is a nice surprise," Violet said when Ali turned up with Wilson in time for elevenses, something she had foolishly imagined would be part of her daily routine on returning to Heft, and yet had, until now, proved impossible. Just one example of the idyllic version of life she had conjured up bearing little relation to the reality. "I've just made a pot of coffee. Call your dad in, will you?"

"Is he in the garden?"

Violet sighed, her expression one of resignation. "He's in the *gym*, would you believe? My sewing room as was." A hint of indignation. "He's got a *rowing* machine in there and goodness knows what else. I did say I'd make curtains to go in the kitchen at the village hall before the next WI meeting but I can barely get to the Singer to do them. Vital to his training program, so he tells me." The rowing machine, Ali assumed, not the Singer.

"Still set on doing the Great North Run, then?"

"So he says."

Ali found Gordon studying the digital display on the rowing machine. Flushed, as if he'd only recently exerted himself. "Eleven hundred meters in two minutes," he declared when he saw her.

"Is that good?"

Death in the Countryside

"Good? It's brilliant, a new personal best." He was in smart new jogging pants, three stripes on the ankle, the real deal, and trainers, a slim-fitting navy top with the logo of another leading sportswear manufacturer. Every inch a man who took his fitness regime seriously.

"I've joined a running club," he said. "They've given me a personalized program."

Nick, coming home the week before, had spotted him loping along, heading out of Heft on the Earsdale road. Nice stride, Nick said, looking comfortable, fair bit of pace. Was he running on the correct side of the road, Ali had wanted to know. He was, Nick confirmed. And in a neon green top that was hard to miss.

Violet produced carrot cake—"gluten-free, a lot tastier than you might think"—and poured coffee. "How's poor Brian doing?" she said.

Better than Ali expected, on the face of things at least. She was calling in, checking on him every couple of days, and, so far, he seemed to be coping. "Keeping busy," she said.

Gordon nodded. "Best way. Are they going to charge that bloke his wife was seeing?"

As Steppenbeck had predicted, Melody's "affair" had been splashed all over the papers, the same papers that weren't interested in her when she was merely "missing." A suspicious death linked to a wealthy businessman (a captain of industry, according to one report, which was perhaps overstating things) a minor celebrity who starred in his own TV ads and had a catchphrase to boot, manna from heaven for the hacks. Jimmy had been released under investigation, but Ali felt sure Steppenbeck would charge him at some point. "Reeling him in," he'd said. "No hurry."

Ali bit into the cake. Moist and sweet and carroty. Gordon was having cake plus a banana and a handful of almonds, which Ali took to be connected to his fitness regime.

"Should I take a cake round?" Violet asked. "For Brian."

Maria Malone

"I'm sure he'd appreciate it," Ali said. "I don't think it matters if it's gluten-free or not. Brian's a bread man."

"Yes," Violet said. She hesitated. "I did hear Evelyn's taken him under her wing."

"They're friends," Ali said defensively. "I hope there's no tittle-tattle going round town."

"No, no, nothing like that." Violet looked affronted. "I'm just pleased he's got someone looking out for him."

"Works both ways," Gordon chipped in with a broad smile. "He painted Evelyn's kitchen after that fire, you know, just as I was about to offer. Saved me a job there."

"How's work going?" Violet asked Ali. "Have you much on?"

"Something's just come up. An old case I've been asked to look at again." She explained about Leslie Masters, still hopeful of finding out what had become of his missing son, Tom.

"After all this time." Violet frowned. "What more can you do?"

Ali wasn't sure.

Gordon suggested she might find it helpful to retrace Tom's last-known steps. "Get out and have a walk, get some fresh air in your lungs, you and Wilson," he said. "It'll do you both the world of good. And you never know, something might come to you. A lightbulb moment, you know."

The last time Ali had been into the Simonthwaite hills and gone up the Black Stone, was the day, almost four weeks earlier, Brian showed up to say that Melody was missing. Since then she'd had almost no time to herself.

She packed a flask, a water bottle, biscuits for Wilson, and went via town and Hooley's, where she found Brian with a bucket of soapy water sluicing down the shop window and the path at the front of the premises.

"Someone must have thought it would be funny to chuck whitewash at the place last night," he told Ali.

Death in the Countryside

"Any other premises affected?"

"Just Evelyn's." He gazed across the street at the cakery-bakery. "Strange, that, don't you think?"

"You've seen what happened?" Evelyn said when Ali went inside. "Vandalism now. What next, I wonder?"

"You should have called me," Ali said.

"I was planning to but you've enough on and there's no real harm done. Brian was able to come down to clean up while I got the shop open. Here, have a look." She tapped the screen of her phone and showed Ali a series of photos taken earlier, white spatter across the windows and door, the pavement.

"It must have been done through the night," Evelyn said, "because it was dry by the time I got here. Brian used a scraper to take it off." Outside, he was busy sponging off what remained, rubbing at a stubborn spot in the center of the window.

"It has to be them," Evelyn said, nodding at her rivals opposite. "I mean, nothing ever happened here before they came. It was quiet as anything. Boring, almost, I used to think. Now it's a bit too lively for my liking." She fell silent for a moment. "I'm thinking of packing in."

"Really? What about the business?" And what about *you*? Ali was thinking. What would Evelyn do with herself if Hooley's was no more? Come to think of it, what would Heft do if she shut up shop and what it was left with was the cakery-bakery and what her mother called fripperies? Fripperies and sourdough?

"Sell up, I suppose." She managed a thin smile. "Maybe those two over there would want to buy it. Looks like that's what they want, to drive me out."

Ali's heart sank. "Don't do anything rash," she said. "Not while you're upset. Let the dust settle, see how you feel in a day or two."

Evelyn nodded. "When Alan died, I had an offer on the place from Reg Edwards in Skipden. Bakers almost as long as us, the Edwards. Wanted to keep the place as it is, he said, keep what they

249

called its integrity. I'll be honest, I was tempted. They've children already involved in running the shop and it would be a way of keeping the Hooley name going." Another wan smile. "If that matters to anyone other than me." She caught Ali's look. "I won't be here forever, you know, and I've no one to pass it on to."

On the summit of the Black Stone, Ali sheltered from the wind with Wilson. She dropped a handful of Bonios on the ground and took out the flask and the cheese and potato pie she'd bought from Evelyn. Once she and Wilson had eaten, she studied the photos Leslie had given her, the ones taken on the day Nora and Tom had climbed the hill together, hours before he disappeared. Mostly, they were pictures of Tom, taken by Nora. Proper photos she'd had developed. Just one of the two of them together, which must have been taken on a timer or by another walker. No selfies in 2004. Ali had already studied the pictures closely, now she was hoping that being back in the spot where they were taken might provide clues, something she'd not already picked up on. She was looking for reference points, wanting to pinpoint precisely where the photos were taken but they showed little of the landscape. A couple of Tom with what must have been the Black Stone behind him, but that was all. Tom not smiling much, Ali saw, which would tie in with what Nora had said, as good as telling him she wanted to break up. Nora, though, Nora looked happy, which felt off, somehow.

She took the path down the side of the hill, Wilson running ahead. Below, was the Dark Pool, which didn't feature in any of the photos she'd been given. Privately, she wondered if that was where Tom had ended up, although divers had searched at the time. Still, it was vast and deep, choked with vegetation in places, the water murky, uninviting. It made her think of decay, disease. A watery grave where over the years cattle and sheep, wandering down its muddy banks to drink, had lost their footing, slid beneath the surface, and drowned. Ali was also thinking of the woman who'd gone

Death in the Countryside

missing years earlier, now presumed dead, possibly lost in the murk of the Dark Pool. Leslie, aware of the unsolved case, insisting that Tom was a strong swimmer. "He's not in the water," he'd said, "if that's what you think."

How could he be sure, though?

Feeling as if she hadn't achieved much, Ali took the path along the ridge, a chill wind blowing in her face. She pulled her buff up over her mouth and nose while Wilson scampered in front not seeming to notice the cold, the wind. She was out of ideas. All that remained was to tell Leslie that when it came to Tom's disappearance, she was no closer to solving the mystery.

She was on her way back into Heft when she spotted Gordon in his running gear—luminous yellow top, clashing orange tracksuit bottoms—at the Helm crossroads two miles out of town. Impossible to miss. She pulled the Hilux over.

"Don't tell your mother," he said, climbing into the back since Wilson occupied the front passenger seat. "I don't want her thinking I'm incapable of making it home without the local constabulary picking me up."

She told him about the Black Stone, how she had drawn a blank regarding Tom Masters, the photos she had hoped might help turning out to be of little use. "I'm stumped, Dad," she said, annoyed with herself for sounding so defeatist. "I'll just have to tell Leslie I can't help him."

Gordon thought for a moment. "You should speak to Cathy Craven. Lovely lass. Works for the National Park. She gave a talk at the hall a month or two back, the conservation lot booked her. Stories to do with the local area. All sorts I'd never heard. Very interesting. Knows her stuff."

Ali glanced at him in the rear view mirror, not sure how he thought someone from the National Park could help.

"Get her to look at the photos. She's a knowledgeable lass, might just spot something you've missed."

Maria Malone

Perhaps he was right, she had missed something. Something this Cathy, knowledgeable in ways Ali could only imagine, might notice.

At home, she logged onto the National Park website and searched for Cathy Craven. No picture, just a blurb describing her work on conservation projects in Uganda and Tanzania plus a brief stint in Belize prior to settling in her native Yorkshire. She called the main number and left a message asking for Cathy to get back to her.

252

46

Cathy Craven peered at the photos. "Where did you say these were taken?"

"The Black Stone," Ali told her.

"Ah, right." Cathy ferreted in her desk drawer and produced a magnifying glass. "Let's see if this helps." She bent over and studied the pictures methodically, adjusting the magnifier, her face almost touching its thick glass. Wiry steel-gray curls tumbled over her eyes. She took a band from her wrist and gathered her hair into a ponytail. In her fifties, Ali guessed, which still counted as a lass in her father's view.

"Hmm," she said, "interesting."

Ali waited for her to say more. Instead, Cathy's gaze lingered on the photo of Tom in front of the Black Stone, close to where his gloves had been found. "And this one? What do you know about this?"

Ali told her. Cathy smiled. "Interesting," she said again.

"You know," she continued, "there are all kinds of stones and landmarks, each one with its own story. Circle it seven times and you'll ward off evil, that sort of thing. Our Black Stone is reputed to have been a healing stone at one time, a place where people would

253

bring sick children. A wizened crone would appear, all in black, claw-like hands, face obscured by a tattered veil, and promise the child would be well if left in her care overnight. There were stories of miracles." Cathy gave a shake of the head. "Desperate people tend to believe what they want to, you know, even now, when you might think we know better." She fell silent. Ali stayed quiet.

Cathy sighed. "Anyway, word spread, and the stone became something of a place of pilgrimage. Only it wasn't a place of good, as people thought, but of evil and any child left in the care of the old woman died." She gazed past Ali. Unsmiling, eyes like flint. Ali felt a shiver go down her spine. Was this the same "lovely lass" Gordon was so taken with? Ali would bet she hadn't spoken about the evil of the Black Stone with members of the conservation group. Clearly, Cathy knew her audience.

"I rather doubt the woman in black existed," Cathy said, "or, if she did, she was likely a charlatan. As for the children, by the time they reached the stone, they were probably beyond being saved. We're talking sixteenth, seventeenth century. Fever, fits, smallpox, worms . . . sin." She caught Ali's surprised look. "Oh, yes, there was a view that God sent disease to punish transgressions." She bent again and peered through the magnifying glass at the photo. "Fascinating though the legend is," she went on, still poring over the picture, "1 don't actually think this *is* the Black Stone. See this mark in the rock right on the very edge of the photo." She handed the magnifying glass to Ali. "You can see it better with this."

Ali looked. There, as Cathy had said, was a mark, a vertical line running along the stone to the left of Tom's shoulder.

"It's a fissure," Cathy said, "and unless I'm mistaken that means it's more likely to be the Gritstone."

"I've not heard of that."

"And this one." Cathy picked up the only photo that showed

Death in the Countryside

something of the wider landscape. "You'd struggle to pick this view out from the top of the Black Stone."

"I wondered," Ali said. "I couldn't work out where it was taken."

"That's because you've been looking in the wrong place. I'm pretty sure none of these were taken on the Black Stone."

47

Jimmy was being charged with murder. Steppenbeck had called to let Ali know.

"He was there," Steppenbeck said, "at the beach house on the day in question. All this time he's been swearing blind he was nowhere near, telling a pack of lies, it turns out."

Steppenbeck's gut feeling all along was that Jimmy had killed Melody. A crime of passion, he said. It had to have been him. The affair had turned sour, Melody threatening to hurl a grenade that would wreck his homelife, everything he'd worked for, and JC was in a lather, desperate to save his skin. "At any cost, I'd say," according to Steppenbeck. Footage from the car park of The Fox Hole in Piercebridge showed Jimmy and Melody having some sort of domestic, Melody throwing her hands up in frustration, Jimmy grabbing hold of her by the wrist. Letting go and stomping off to the Rolls, "looking pretty shifty," according to Steppenbeck. Melody stalking after him, banging on the window. Another heated exchange before Jimmy roared away leaving her there. "The scarf," he said, "the one you and your Wilson found, she had it on that day. One of the techie guys was able to match the pattern with the CCTV pictures."

Even so, Jimmy was adamant he had gone straight back to

Death in the Countryside

Newcastle and spent the rest of the day at the Scotswood Road shop before returning home to find Jenny had invited her fellow hens round for champagne cocktails ahead of their pub crawl, and heading straight back out for a walk.

That Saturday, after leaving the pub in Piercebridge, Melody kept calling Jimmy, leaving messages, begging him to see her so they could "talk."

"She called every one of his shops that afternoon, multiple times. Some of the calls came in after he'd left, so fair enough." There was a long pause.

"Left to go home?" Ali ventured when it seemed he was waiting for her to prompt him.

"No! That's the thing. He *left,* took one of the sales cars that was parked round the back. And went up the coast . . . to the beach house." Triumphant.

Ali felt as if she had been slapped across the face. When Jimmy insisted the last he'd seen of Melody was at The Fox Hole she had believed him. Looking at her with his brilliant blue eyes. Lying through his perfect teeth.

"You're sure?" she said. Hoping there was still an element of doubt, that she hadn't been completely and utterly taken in.

"Sure as sure can be. One hundred percent. A million percent, as one of my DCs likes to say, even though, as I keep telling him, there's no such thing. A hundred percent is the best it gets, the gold standard of certainty. Beyond all reasonable doubt and all that. Where was I?" He went quiet for a moment. "Right, yes, so one of the lads on the shop floor remembered him going off, leaving the Rolls parked up, which led us to look at the company cars. We checked the various satnavs, and . . . bingo!" Cock-a-hoop. "One of the Mondeos"—a chuckle, as if Steppenbeck was enjoying the thought of Jimmy slumming it in a bog-standard saloon, a sales car!—"told the whole story. He'd put the address in the satnav, since he didn't know where he was going. Bang to rights."

257

Ali was silent, digesting what he'd told her. "And he's admitted it?"

"Can't exactly deny it. Facts are facts."

"I mean . . . has he confessed to killing her?"

"Oh, no, he's had nothing to say about that other than 'no comment' ad nauseam."

"So we're still no clearer on why he did it?"

"To shut her up, I'd say. Let's face it, she was about to blow up his cozy domestic setup. Forty years they've been married, him and Mrs. JC, did he tell you?"

Ali said yes, they were planning a party to celebrate.

"I mean, he stood to lose a lot, everything, you might say, and for what? A fling. Meaningless. Makes you wonder, why do it?"

Why, indeed? Not that it had been meaningless to Melody, not when Jimmy was her one true love, her chance of a happy ever after. She was swept along, seduced by the idea of a grand romance, one last chance of happiness in her twilight years. She can't have given much thought to Brian and what it might do to him when she walked out, which she clearly intended to do sooner or later. Dull, dependable Brian, who had defended her, insisted she would never go behind his back with another man, that she wouldn't just leave without a word. Wrong about almost everything. He really hadn't known her.

"The sad thing is," Steppenbeck was saying, "I like Jimmy." Ali did too. "Poor bastard got himself caught up in something he thought would be a laugh, never suspected it would end up with his girlfriend sprawled on the floor"—the sofa, Ali wanted to point out—"of her secret beach house, her last breath wrung out of her by the man she was crazy about. And"—another chuckle, disbelief at what he was about to reveal—"the murder weapon, the *scarf*, was only one *he* gave her. We found the box in the beach house. Hermes, which don't come cheap, love note tucked inside: *Love you to the moon and back* bollocks. I mean, you couldn't make it up."

48

Cathy Craven was waiting when Ali drove the Hilux into the Forestry Commission car park. She was glowing, as if she'd been for a run already, a warmup for what lay ahead. Her hair was scraped back, kept in check by a stretchy buff. She wore flattering leggings, a short zip-up jacket with the Berghaus logo. Ready for anything. Ali could see her on a summit gazing into the distance, a poster girl for the great outdoors.

"I meant to say to bring walking poles," Cathy said. "It gets quite steep and the terrain's tricky in places."

Ali didn't have poles. Poles were a sign of becoming fearful, old. She wasn't the only one who thought so. The number of people she encountered out walking who felt the need to justify their poles on the grounds of having had recent surgery or an arthritic knee, one woman struggling her way down a difficult descent at Swindale Reservoir claiming the only reason she was using poles was because she "had no hip joint." Poles were for sissies, Ali once told Nick, when he offered to buy her some. Yet here was Cathy, strong, fit, athletic, whose ranger duties involved covering many miles in a single day, yomping over difficult terrain, a woman who took Buckden Pike in her stride, and considered the infamous Horse's Head—a challenge that had left Ali close to tears on the one and

259

Maria Malone

only occasion she took it on—a "decent climb," with Leki poles sticking out of the side netting of her backpack.

"I brought some spares, just in case," she told Ali, opening the boot of her Juke and retrieving them.

They set off along a marked trail at a pace brisker than Ali was used to, Wilson running on ahead, sniffing at the ground, lush vegetation spilling onto the stony path.

"You might want to clip him on the lead," Cathy said. Ali called him to heel, thinking there must be livestock up ahead and they plowed on, reaching a fork in the path, a green marker pointing one way, a red one indicating straight on. They took the red route.

"Watch your step here," Cathy cautioned, pressing on, the path narrowing, ferns brushing against their legs. Now deep into the forest, its canopy creating a sense of gloom.

"Can you feel it?" Cathy asked, stopping abruptly, waiting for Ali to catch up. "Interesting, the atmosphere here always strikes me as . . . peculiar, other worldly. Listen."

They stood in silence, Ali not sure what she was supposed to be hearing.

"Nothing," Cathy said at last. "Not a sound. No birdsong, no rustle of leaves, not a breath of wind. It's as if all around it's devoid of life. You can see why people invested such places with special powers."

Ali suddenly wished she was somewhere else, somewhere with light and sound and . . . people. "Doesn't anyone come up here?" she asked, wondering what had happened to the walkers whose cars were parked below. On the green route, she guessed.

"The nearest village is Copton, three miles down the road," Cathy said, "but what's interesting is how remote it feels up here, as if we're miles from anywhere. It's very unlikely we'll see anyone else. People don't like it, they find it claustrophobic."

Death in the Countryside

Ali could see why.

"We'll proceed with caution on this next bit," Cathy told her, poking at the ground with one of her poles. As far as Ali could tell, the path ahead looked identical to the one that lay behind them.

"What exactly are we watching out for?" Ali asked.

"Look." Cathy took a few paces forward, pushing through the ferns that sprouted on either side, obscuring the path, using her poles to check the terrain. She prodded tentatively at the ground to her right. "There's nothing there," she said. "It's a sheer drop, not that you'd know. The vegetation's hiding it. Keep your dog on your left side."

Ali did as she was told, anxiously edging forward.

"There are a few stretches like this," Cathy said. "You need to know where they are. If you don't . . ." she let her words trail off and gave a slight shrug. "Interesting, a few years back, I was up here on a rescue, a couple who'd come up, the man leading the way, and suddenly he heard his wife shriek. He spun round and she'd gone. I mean *disappeared*. Poor bloke was frantic, calling to her, nothing coming back. He tried to call for help, no phone signal, so he left a water bottle on the path to mark the spot and came back down as fast as he could, dialed 999. What happened was she'd put her foot down on what she *thought* was the path and stepped into thin air, fallen clean through the vegetation, which closed over the top of her and—this was where she got lucky—had her fall broken by a tree sticking out of the hillside. Otherwise"— another shrug—"it was as if she had vanished. Poof! Gone. As if the forest had . . . claimed her. We brought a team up and managed to locate and recover her"—she looked at Wilson and smiled—"at least a rescue dog called Conan did the honors. She was fortunate, not that badly hurt it turned out. She'd lost consciousness and was scared witless when she came to. I doubt she'll ever come up here again."

Ali wanted to turn back. Not just because the forest felt malevolent, able to snatch unsuspecting walkers and send them to what it hoped was a gruesome end. Cathy and her vivid storytelling was getting under her skin. Frankly, she wished she would shut up.

"Not spooking you, am I?" Cathy asked.

"No," Ali lied. "It's . . . *interesting.*" A word Cathy seemed to like.

They went on, taking their time, Ali grateful for the poles she had until recently despised. Next time Nick asked if she would like some she'd say yes. Eventually, they emerged into a small clearing with views across to a range of peaks in the distance.

"You can just about make out the Carlow hills," Cathy informed her. "The photo you showed me, you can see them in the background." She took out her phone and snapped Ali and Wilson. "You'll be able to compare it with the one you've got, but I'd say it was here that picture was taken. And down there"—she indicated the cliff edge beyond which Ali assumed was nothing but a drop of possibly hundreds of feet and certain death—"that's where the Gritstone is. It's not easy to get to but we've come this far, if you're up for it . . ."

Getting to the Gritstone involved a scramble, the trees that sprouted at odd angles down the hillside providing something to grab on to. Ali lost her footing more than once, skidding alarmingly, Cathy catching hold of her. The poles helped. Wilson, who seemed to understand this was not so much a walk as a trek, took his time, staying close to heel, putting tension on the lead whenever she slipped, tugging her back. The stone was a cracked heart, a glowering headstone, and running its length was the fissure Cathy had spotted in the photo of Tom. As if someone had taken a grinder and cut a perfectly straight line into the granite. Again, Cathy took photos so that once Ali got back she could do a comparison with those Leslie had given her.

"So," she said. "I'd say this was where he was, your missing

Death in the Countryside

boy." She gazed out over the crag across the empty valley, turned to Ali. "And for all we know, he's still here, somewhere."

Wilson found him, shrouded by lush ferns. Nothing to say a body lay there. It would have been easy to walk past, miss him entirely. Ali wondered how many had done just that, although where Tom lay beneath his green canopy was not on any marked trail, not part of the landscape walkers would ordinarily venture. Too difficult, too unwieldy, too much of a battle with the vegetation, which reached shoulder height in places.

When Wilson halted abruptly and began to bark, Ali knew they were there, on the brink of solving a mystery that had endured for years. Gingerly, following the direction of his gaze, she prodded at the ferns with one of her borrowed walking poles. Saw a boot, remnants of fabric, the remains of the jeans Tom had been wearing the day he went missing. She stepped back. A specialist team would recover the body and conduct a painstaking examination of the scene. What she needed to do now was ensure it was not disturbed. She had no phone signal and Cathy offered to hike back to the car park to make the necessary call. Watching her head off, confident, surefooted, moving nimbly and swiftly through the undergrowth, Ali felt a surge of gratitude. Cathy, identifying clues in the photos, ones that others had missed, had known where to come. Without her, Tom—and Ali was certain it was Tom—would likely lie undisturbed for another twenty years, forever. Cathy's gray curls bobbed out of view, foliage springing back over the path she had forged, making it invisible once more, impenetrable. This place, Ali thought, shivering.

Above her loomed the Gritstone, precarious from this angle, as if nothing was holding it up and it could topple over, come crashing down and crush her. She was afraid, she realized, afraid to be alone in a landscape that so clearly had the upper hand. "Thank goodness you're here," she told Wilson, his presence a source of comfort. Waiting for Cathy, the recovery team, she understood how stories about such lonely spots gathered weight, becoming part of the being of the place. Stay here long enough and she would believe them too, every word. The atmosphere was peculiar, it emanated from the earth, the rock. All around her the greenery seemed ready to swallow her and she held on to Wilson, gazing after Cathy, not sure she would ever find her way back without her, not without her expert guidance.

Leslie's expression was impossible to read.

Ali had arrived with news no parent wants to hear, and he had been gracious, thanking her for putting herself out, for doing more than anyone else had managed. At least now he knew. Not everything, but some of what had happened to his son, where his life had ended. All those pilgrimages he had made, the laying of flowers over the years, in the wrong place.

"We've not confirmed it's him yet," Ali said. Just in case she was wrong. In her heart, though, she was in no doubt. His driver's license had been recovered. The stout Brasher boots she had glimpsed matched the ones Tom had been wearing. It *was* him. It had to be.

"I don't understand how no one found him before now," Leslie said. Baffled that his boy could lie undiscovered for years, decades.

Ali did her best to describe the spot below the Gritstone, wild, inaccessible. She would speak to Cathy about taking Leslie there so that he could see for himself.

"There must be walkers," he was saying. "How is it possible no one saw him?"

Because no one was looking.

Not there.

"Good work, Wren," Chief Superintendent Freeman told her. "And as for you, boy"—turning his gaze on Wilson, who thumped his tail and sat up straight—"you deserve a medal, clever lad."

Death in the Countryside

"We'd never have managed without Cathy Craven, sir," Ali said.

"A *treat*, that's what's in order here, eh, lad?" Freeman slid open his top drawer and produced a packet of Walkies, offering Wilson a small bone-shaped biscuit. "Banana and peanut butter," Freeman said. "A favorite with Elvis Presley, I believe." He glanced at Ali, then back at Wilson. "The King loved this combination, preferably in a sandwich, deep-fried." Ali smiled. It sounded made up to her, a story. "There used to be a restaurant on Beale Street, *Elvis Presley's Memphis* it was called," Freeman went on, "on the site of what was once the great man's favorite clothing store, where the celebrated deep-fried peanut butter and banana sandwich reigned supreme. I partook and found it surprisingly good." A myth perpetuated by the fast food restaurants of Memphis, keen to cash in on all things Elvis, Ali suspected. "Anyway, extra rations today," Freeman said, shaking a few more of the biscuits out for Wilson, who politely offered his paw before tucking in. "I tell you what, lad," he said, impressed by the spaniel's restraint, I know a few people who could learn a thing or two about manners from you. Some of them in this very building."

Two weeks after Freeman's surprise swoop on Ali at home, he had still not addressed her future. The prospect of reporting for duty at the station in Skipden where she could be supervised more closely hung in the air. Now might be a good time to bring the subject up, while her boss was feeling well disposed toward her.

"I wondered if you'd made a decision, sir," she ventured. "Regarding my . . . position."

He fixed her with a penetrating look. "You're one of my best officers, Wren." Wilson, picking up on the boss's serious tone, sat to attention. Freeman nodded at him. "An exceptional team, the pair of you, doing good work in the community." Ali held her breath. "I still have concerns about you being . . . isolated. However, all things considered, for now we'll keep things as they are and see how we go. All right?"

265

Maria Malone

Relief flooded through her. "Yes, sir, thank you."

After a short silence, he said, "So, what are we looking at with this lad, Tom Masters?" His attention back on the case. "Accident? Foul play? What was he doing there when his car was somewhere else? How did he even *get* there?"

So much didn't add up. "That's it, sir," Ali said, "we don't know."

But she intended to find out.

49

The Bull wasn't open on a Tuesday. Ali and Wilson went round the back and knocked and a plump woman in leggings and a billowing jumper that reached almost to her knees, came to the door. Dangly silver earrings, brown eyes, hair streaked with pink. The landlady, Irene Talbot, Nora's mum.

They sat in the bar, beside the fireplace. Ali went straight to the point. They had found remains the week before, she said, and were in the process of a formal identification.

Irene went pale. "Tom?" she said. "Oh God, Tom? After all this time?"

Ali stayed silent.

Irene had tears in her eyes. "I've prayed they'd find him, so that his parents . . ." she gave Ali a helpless look. "So they could say goodbye. But hearing it now, it's a shock."

"Bound to be," Ali said.

"I mean, we all knew there had to have been an accident, but I suppose I've thought, hoped, really, that as long as he wasn't found he still might be alive."

Much as Leslie had. Ali waited. Sometimes the best thing was simply to let people talk.

"Nora, she'll be devastated." She gazed at Ali despairingly. "I'll have to tell her; how am I going to tell her?"

"I can arrange for a colleague in Edinburgh to speak to her," Ali said, thinking of PC Bridie Keen. "We'll be sensitive, I promise."

"I loved Tom, always hoped they'd make it through uni and end up together."

Did Irene know that Nora had been pulling away from Tom? Ali wondered. That she was finding the relationship a hindrance, Tom cramping her style, perhaps, getting in the way of her enjoying student life in Edinburgh to the full?

"I couldn't think of a better lad for her," Irene was saying. "The opposite of her father. He skipped off when she was a child, went out 'for a paper' one day and never came back. Can you believe it? Devastated, Nora was. She idolized her dad. How losing Tom didn't destroy her I'll never know. She was so young, they both were, nineteen, just about to start their second year." Nora, now an experienced vet, nearing forty. Irene was quiet for a moment. "She still keeps in touch with his father, you know, and when she's home she goes to the Black Stone, lays flowers for Tom."

Ali chose not to say that Tom's body was found nowhere near the Black Stone.

"It's just she's . . ." Irene's voice wobbled. She took a breath, steadied herself. "She's getting married and her fiancé, Niall . . . he's in hospital, really poorly. It's awful, just awful." Tears streamed down her face. "You can't imagine." Ali thought she could. Nora, no stranger to tragedy, the men in her life deserting her one way or another: her father, then Tom, and now her fiancé, who seemed unlikely to survive. "Every minute, she's been at poor Niall's bedside." Another tear spilled out and ran down her face and she wiped at it with the sleeve of her jumper. "They're saying they don't think he'll pull through. Oh, God. Now this. Poor Tom." She searched inside the sleeves of her jumper for a tissue, finding one and dabbing at her face.

Death in the Countryside

"I'm sorry," Ali said, "this must bring so much back for you."

Irene blew her nose and nodded, miserable. "Do you know what happened?" She wiped at her face again.

"Not yet." Ali waited a moment, then said, "I hate to ask, but would you mind telling me what you remember about that night Nora and Tom came back from the Black Stone?"

Irene went to the bar, got a box of tissues and sat with them on her knee. "They were late back, the pub was busy. Nora came down and asked if I needed a hand behind the bar. She helped out for an hour, maybe a bit longer, then went upstairs. They were tired, she said, planning on having an early night. I stayed up late." She gave Ali a sheepish look. "Sometimes, a few of the locals stay on a bit after closing time and we have a drink. Anyway, it was getting on for midnight. I locked up, went up to bed, they'd already turned in. Next morning, Nora came into my room and woke me. Tom was missing, she said."

"Missing?"

Irene nodded. "He'd got up and gone off somewhere. Just like that. It was barely light."

"Did he often go off on his own?"

"No." Irene seemed surprised. "Never. And they were leaving that day, going back to Edinburgh, so it was totally unexpected."

"What did you make of it?"

She was quiet for a moment. "I did wonder . . ." she shrugged. "I was just being stupid." Shaking her head.

"Go on."

"I thought they might have fallen out. Tom seemed a bit preoccupied that weekend, something on his mind, you know? Not his usual cheerful self, a bit distant with Nora." She blew her nose. "If I'm honest . . . I was concerned he might be about to finish things. Me being paranoid, probably."

How had Irene managed to get hold of the wrong end of the stick? Didn't she know what Nora had told the police at the time,

269

that *she* was about to dump Tom? "You didn't think it might be Nora wanting to end things?"

Irene looked bewildered. "No, not Nora, she loved him to bits."

Ali nodded. "When did you report him missing?"

"Nora took my car and went out looking for him. That Escort, his pride and joy it was, she found it at the Black Stone. She went up but he wasn't there." Irene fell silent and stared at the fireplace, logs piled up ready to be lit. "Just his gloves." She gave a tiny smile, remembering. "He used to sit on his gloves when they stopped for their flask, make them into a kind of cushion. It wasn't the first time he'd got up and walked off without them, Nora said. And they were good ones, some expensive make, leather, warm lining. A present from his parents, so they meant something. More than once on walks they'd had to go back and fetch those gloves."

Ali digested this. After a lengthy silence, she said, "When Nora comes home now, does she stay here with you?"

Irene nodded. "I've kept her room, all her stuff from when she was a kid, it's still here."

"Would it be all right if I took a look?" Ali asked.

Irene nodded. "If you think it'll help."

The bed was made up, the one Nora had shared with Tom and, more recently, her fiancé, Niall. A teddy bear sat on the pillow; there was a single bedside chest with a lamp. Narrow wardrobe, the original mahogany wood showing through the chalk paint. A dressing table, a photo of a couple stuck on the mirror. Nora and Niall, Ali guessed. Bookshelves in the alcove next to the window. Ali stood for a moment, taking in the surroundings. Leslie had given her Tom's old gloves, the precious leather ones he was prone to leaving behind on walks. She pulled on a pair of latex gloves and took Tom's from their bag. Barbour. "Here boy," she said, offering them to Wilson. He pushed his snout inside, sneezed. What was Ali hoping to find? Nothing, something, anything that might help explain why Tom

Death in the Countryside

had taken off like that before dawn. Some small scrap to provide answers for Leslie. And for Eloise, who had been unable to stay with her husband once their son was gone. Among Nora's books were *Black Beauty*, the *Famous Five*, *The Cruel Sea*, *Moby Dick*, a few school textbooks. She checked the bedside table drawers: a torch, a copy of *The Corrections* that looked as if it had been dropped in the bath, pocket tissues, a hairbrush. She moved to the dressing table. Nivea cleanser, face cream, a sachet of leave-in hair mask, a tray with earrings, bangles, brooches. She signaled Wilson to check the room. He burrowed under the bed, his bottom sticking up, and reversed out, went to the bookshelves, the dressing table. Ali had opened the wardrobe door. He stuck his head inside and abruptly went still. She looked to see what had caught his interest. A row of shoes, a well-worn pair of sheepskin slippers. He loved shoes, shoes carried all kinds of interesting scents. It wasn't the shoes he was taken with, though, it was a carrier bag, a classy paper one, Browns of York on the side. Ali pulled it out. Photos, some old newspaper clippings about Tom's disappearance, a pair of child's ballet shoes, a sparkly "Happy New Year" headband. Remnants from Nora's past. Ali put the bag on the bed and carefully removed the contents. She felt a brief stab of discomfort at being in the girl's old room, going through her things without her knowledge. Yet Irene had said it was okay. Old birthday cards. Letters from what looked like a school-friend, written in 1998, held together by elastic bands. Ali skimmed through the first one, a series of complaints about the long summer holiday. She had "done nothing," she wrote, been "dragged to Bettys" with her mother (boring!) and "LOVED!" Damon Albarn. Scribbled doodles woven into the text, hearts and kisses, a cake with an arrow and the words "FAT RASCAL." Ali smiled and put it back in its envelope with the others. She found a photo of a girl of about five on a pony on the beach, a man in shorts and a T-shirt next to her, both smiling. Nora and her errant dad, Ali guessed. There was a toiletry bag: eyeshadows, a lipstick, a pot of tinted lip balm, sun

Maria Malone

cream, cotton wool buds. Ali unzipped a pouch and found an old Nokia phone, a sticker on the back, £14.08 written in smudgy blue biro. A leather key fob. Car keys, a Yale, a house key most likely, and clipped to the key ring, a charm, silver by the look of it, a sleek sports car.

Wilson stared hard at the toiletry bag and barked. Ali rewarded him with a Bonio mini.

50

The keys were Tom's. Leslie was in no doubt. "We bought him the Lotus Elite charm for his eighteenth," he said. The phone was now with Spence, the tech guy in Skipden, who seemed able to crack any mobile with ease. It was Tom's. Ali had shown Leslie the sticker on the back. "Yes, that's his. He could never remember his bank pin number—1408—so he put it on the back of the phone, wrote it in pounds and pence, which I thought was risky, but Tom reckoned was safe."

Ali had not told Leslie she had found Tom's things in Nora's bedroom at the Bull and she decided not to correct his assumption they'd been recovered with Tom's body. She knew the find was telling, significant. What Ali wanted to know was what Tom's car keys and his phone were doing in Nora's bedroom. Hidden. She had tried to come up with a logical explanation—that she had been carrying some of his things for him, his phone in her pocket, perhaps, his keys. In which case, how had he managed to slip out of the pub and drive to the Black Stone the day he went missing? Perhaps he had a second set, although not according to Leslie. And even if Leslie was mistaken, why wouldn't Nora have handed over his possessions to the police at the time? Why not say he hadn't taken his phone with him? Surely that would have been relevant.

Maria Malone

Your boyfriend is missing and he doesn't even have his phone on him.

You'd think to tell the police.

Wouldn't you?

Ali had a sense of dread deep in the pit of her stomach.

"Let's hear it, then," Freeman said, and Ali outlined what she had found in Nora's old room, Leslie's positive ID of the keys. The phone had been charged and was working. Ali hoped it would reveal what was going on between Tom and Nora, the state of their relationship, but there was only a single text, the last one Nora had sent him, a couple of days before their trip to Yorkshire. "I love you," she had written. "Forever and ever and ever and ever x x x x x." Its gushing tone at odds with what she had told the police at the time about being on the brink of severing romantic ties.

As for Tom, Tom had not replied.

Ali had spent the night tossing and turning, feeling she was close to learning the truth of what had happened to Tom, some of it at least. Now that she was about to share it with Freeman, she felt anxiety cramping her gut, as if what she had to say was wild, a figment of her fevered imagination. As if Wilson could sense her mood, he stuck close, his body pressing against her leg. For once, Freeman didn't try to lure him with the promise of treats. The atmosphere in the Chief Superintendent's office felt uncharacteristically oppressive. She felt under scrutiny, that it was vital to get her words right, to speak with conviction. She did not want Freeman thinking she had lost the plot.

"Sir," she began, "I think these finds are vital pieces of the puzzle, a means of unlocking what really happened to Tom Masters."

Despite what Nora had told the police at the time, she suspected it was Tom looking to end things, not the other way round, and that Nora, abandoned by the only other man she had loved, her father, had taken this badly. She could not let him leave. On their last day

Death in the Countryside

together, they had gone walking to the Gritstone where the terrain, as Ali now knew, was not for the fainthearted. The Gritstone, a place for lovers, reputed to have supernatural powers. Cathy had told her, place your hands on the stone, whisper the name of your love into its narrow crevice, and they will be yours, forever locked inside. Tom didn't want her, though, and when they returned to Edinburgh, he would walk away. A friend, but no longer a lover. They argued and she pushed him off the crag, sent him to his death.

This was what Ali now believed had happened.

"And you're certain of all this?" Freeman asked.

"I am, sir, yes, it makes sense."

Nora had returned to the Bull alone in Tom's car and parked at the back of the pub. Let herself in and gone upstairs, then reappeared, and helped out behind the bar and in the morning got up early and driven to the Black Stone, leaving Tom's gloves there before walking back. Saying all this to Freeman with certainty, absolute conviction, while at the same time knowing it was speculation, unproven, a theory. She didn't care, it made absolute sense to her, she could feel it in her gut, something Freeman had told her she should always pay attention to. "It's less than two miles from the Black Stone to the pub, sir," she explained. Freeman said nothing.

"She waited until it was getting light and went and woke her mum, said Tom was gone. Went through the charade of searching for him, ringing his phone—which she had switched off—all the rest of it." When Freeman still said nothing, Ali said, "No one saw Tom at the pub that night. People saw his *car* parked at the pub, they saw *Nora* behind the bar and accepted what she said about him being in the flat upstairs, but no one saw *him* and that's because he was *never there*. He was lying at the base of the crag already dead." Or dying. What if he had survived the fall and could have been saved? Nora had simply left him there. If he didn't want her, she wasn't about to wait for him to walk away as her dad had. She would be the one to end things. In her own way.

"How did she happen to have the car keys, his phone?" Freeman asked.

"The photos taken that day showed her carrying a rucksack, while Tom just had his jacket. Maybe he'd given her his things for safekeeping."

"Handy," Freeman said.

"Very," Ali confirmed. "I know I can't produce hard evidence for all of this—"

"For any of it," Freeman pointed out.

"But it makes sense." Nora and Tom were at the Gritstone, the photos confirmed it. Nora had lied about that. And if Tom had fallen accidentally, wouldn't Nora have gone for help?

Freeman sighed. "As it happens, I agree with you," he said. "*But*. If we can't prove it, there's not much we can do."

"And then there's the situation with her fiancé, Niall Ross. Lying in intensive care in Edinburgh after 'accidentally' falling from Arthur's Seat. Doesn't that strike you as suspicious?"

"It does," Freeman agreed. "You know what I think about coincidence, Wren. Two young men involved with the same woman . . . it smacks of foul play to me. *But*." Another sigh. "It's proving it. What about the Edinburgh fella? Can he tell us anything?"

"He's unconscious, sir. Not expected to survive." She felt despair wash over her. It would be impossible to make any of this stick.

"Convenient." A long silence followed. "Right. No one knows we suspect anything, either with regard to Tom, or where Ross is concerned. We're not accusing Nora of anything. Not yet. It wouldn't be out of the way to speak to her, see where you get. Make it look as if you're keeping her informed out of courtesy. See if she trips herself up."

51

The funeral the following Thursday was at St. Michael's. Brian kept things simple. A plain coffin made from ash, a short service conducted by the Rev Lucktaylor, who spoke on Brian's behalf, calling Melody vibrant, good, and decent. Leaving aside the things that could not be spoken of, her lies, her reckless dalliance with Jimmy Champion, her life cut short. Ali was there with Wilson. Nick had taken time off from *The Beat* and was with her parents. Evelyn Hooley had closed the shop. Sandra from the beauty salon sashayed in, spiky stilettoes clacking on the stone floor, a dress that fitted like a second skin, cashmere wrap draped fetchingly across her shoulders, leather gloves, a hat with a veil beneath which her makeup was dramatic, cinematic. Blood red lips. Sultry, dangerous, dressed to kill. As if she'd stepped straight out of a particularly dark episode of *Inspector Montalbano*. In the pew beside her, Roger Felton wore velvet-trimmed dress trousers that might have come from a dinner suit, Phoebe in a skirt of emerald satin that almost reached her ankles. Both, incongruously, in sensible fleece jackets. Carla, the potter, was at the back of the church as well as a few Heft residents with only the most tenuous connection to Melody and Brian. They looked out of place, awkward, as if they sensed they had no business being there.

Brian arrived with the hearse and followed the coffin with its cross of white roses down the nave. He'd had his hair cut and was in a dark gray suit, white shirt, black tie. Behind him, to Ali's utter amazement, were Lillian and Des. When Ali spoke to Lillian to offer condolences she had received a terse response. "I can't say it's any wonder. It was always going to end in tears for that one." *That one.* Her sister. Lillian, now two paces behind Brian, head bowed, in a double-breasted coat with frogging and patent boots that seemed showy, inappropriate. Heavy eye makeup, scarlet lips. Giving Sandra a run for her money. Des in a suit, black tie. Sitting with Brian in the front pew.

Well, well, well.

Afterward, the burial was in the churchyard, Brian one side of the vicar, Lillian clutching a hanky on the other, Des with a hand on his wife's elbow. Evelyn, Nick, Gordon, and Violet standing a little way back. Even further away, Ali and Wilson, mourners, but also on duty.

Ali watched as Brian flung earth onto the coffin. She had worried he might go to pieces, but he appeared composed, in control, turning to shake hands with the vicar once it was over, exchange a few words with Lillian and Des, nod in Ali's direction. She would check on him later. The funeral was one thing, but it was afterward, once the ritual was over, in the quiet, once the mourners had departed and he was alone, that he would feel the true weight of his loss.

She caught up with Lillian as she and Des were on their way out of the churchyard.

"You decided to come," Ali said, stating the obvious. "I'm surprised."

Lillian gave her a hard look. "She's my sister, what did you expect?"

Ali wondered (somewhat uncharitably) if Lillian anticipated that Melody might perhaps have remembered her in her will, that

Death in the Countryside

the beach house, her collection of rather lovely scarves, might end up hers. In the absence of a handy sofa, Des had positioned himself behind his wife.

"In all honesty, I didn't expect to see you here," Ali said, returning her gaze. "Given how resolute you were on the matter of your estrangement from Melody, and, frankly, your lack of concern for her welfare while she was missing." Lillian flushed.

"Who do you think you're talking to?" she demanded, furious.

Ali gave her a long, appraising look, her gaze lingering on the stupid wet-look boots. "No one," she said, "no one at all."

She followed them out and watched as they got into their little white car and drove off.

Later, Ali returned to the churchyard, where Melody now lay under a fresh mound of damp earth. Ali crouched to read the message on the card Brian had left. *For my wife with love and in sorrow*, it read. The gravediggers had left a small wooden stake at the head of the plot, the details of the occupant handwritten on it: M. Bright, and the date. *Single plot.*

Alone in death, exactly as Melody had predicted.

52

Ali had suggested to Nora they meet in the coffee shop on the second floor of the Royal Infirmary. She and Wilson, setting off before it was light, allowed plenty of time for the journey to Edinburgh, arriving ridiculously early. Ali ordered a flat white while they waited, saving a corner of her pastry, and passing it to Wilson under the table. "That's it, mind," she told him. "No more." He licked at the icing sugar on her fingers and settled down at her feet with a sigh. She rubbed sanitizer into her hands and looked around. The café was busy, endless comings and goings, staff with lanyards, visitors, on their own, mostly, scrolling through their phones, the odd newspaper spread out. Outside, it was raining, the June sky a dirty gray. "Dreich," she told Wilson, who thumped his tail on the floor in reply. "That's what the Scots would say about a summer day like this. Dreich."

Ali recognized Nora at once. Still much like her photos from twenty years ago. Same blonde hair, a few lines around her eyes. Ali had thought of her as stuck in that time, a student, nineteen years old, a girl whose boyfriend had vanished in circumstances that were bizarre, inexplicable, but now she was a vet—successful, established, with a life, a future, engaged to a man who came from a family of wealthy farmers. Waiting a long time for her prince to

Death in the Countryside

come, seeing him now unconscious while she kept a vigil at his bedside willing him to wake up. Nora, devoted, not giving up, still hopeful of her happy ever after, although the dreamed-of wedding seemed unlikely to happen. Ali had spoken to one of Niall's doctors, a brief conversation on the phone, during which he said that "between us" Niall would not survive "barring a miracle."

Nora spotted Ali and made her way over, frowning. She looked tired, distracted. All those hours spent at Niall's bedside taking their toll.

"I don't have long," she said, sitting down, refusing the offer of a coffee, pulling her cardigan around her, giving a little shiver.

"I appreciate it's a horrible time for you," Ali said. Under the table, she sensed Wilson on his feet, edging toward Nora, checking her out. "Is there any news, any change with your fiancé?"

Nora looked away, didn't answer.

Ali waited a moment. "It's Tom I wanted to ask you about."

Nora gave her an anguished look, twisted a strand of hair around her fingers. Nails bitten down. "I don't see what more I can say after all this time. And the timing's terrible with all I'm going through here with Niall."

"We found Tom's remains."

"Yes, I know."

"Any idea how he might have got to the Gritstone when his car was parked at the Black Stone?"

She gave a shrug. "Honestly, I couldn't tell you."

"Was he upset that night? I mean, before he went missing?"

"Upset? Why would he have been?"

Ali waited a moment, giving her time to think back, remember what she'd said at the time. When Nora stayed silent, she said, "In your statement, you said you'd told him you wanted to end the relationship. Is that right?"

She dropped her gaze to the table. "We'd talked, that's all, we were fine." Not according to what she'd told the police, they weren't.

Maria Malone

"Your mum thought Tom was about to finish with you."

She looked at Ali. "That's rubbish. I don't know why she'd say that."

Ali held her gaze. "And you're absolutely sure about Tom coming back to the pub with you that evening . . ." Keeping her tone light.

"Of course I am. What are you getting at?" Annoyed. Fury in her dark eyes. "What exactly is this?"

"It's just . . . no one actually saw him."

"*I* saw him! His car was there, loads of people saw it."

"The car, that's right, we have witnesses who saw his car." She gave her a penetrating look. "Do you know about perjury, Nora?"

She pushed her chair back, almost tipping it over and stood. "I have to go. My fiancé is sick." She gave Ali a hard look. "*Dying.* I don't need this." She turned and swept off.

"I think we should get her in," Chief Superintendent Freeman said. "She might be more forthcoming in a police interview room."

Ali didn't think so. She had seen something in Nora, a steel in those coal-dark eyes, a chilly determination to protect herself. Tom belonged in her past now and the discovery of his body didn't alter things, not for her, not when she had so cleverly covered her tracks. Niall was her concern now. Ali wondered what went through her mind as she sat at his bedside, machines keeping him alive. Was she hoping, praying, for the miracle the doctors deemed necessary to bring him back to her? Or was there something altogether darker in her mind, a desire for him to peacefully pass away without ever opening his eyes, without ever being able to tell anyone what he remembered from the day he fell from Arthur's Seat? Was that why Nora was with him day and night? In case he defied all expectation and came round and she needed to ensure his silence once and for all?

Ali had spoken to Leslie, a difficult conversation where she had taken a sledgehammer to some of his most treasured memories

Death in the Countryside

and smashed them to bits. Left him with the unpalatable thought that Nora wasn't Tom's loving girlfriend but his killer, that she had known all along where Tom lay and said nothing, perpetuating the charade of him vanishing after walking up the Black Stone. Returning to lay flowers at the spot where he had supposedly left his gloves.

"I'm not sure I'm taking this in," he said, perplexed. "You think Nora was involved somehow. *Nora*?"

"It looks that way to me, yes."

He was busy making arrangements for Tom's funeral. He had been to see Eloise and they both agreed the service should be at St. Aidan's, in Holt, not far from North Berwick, where Tom's grandparents and his great-aunt Lucy were buried. "They were close," Leslie said. "Thick as thieves, the pair of them."

Ali had found him in good spirits, glad to be doing something at last to honor the memory of his lost boy. Planning the proper goodbye that had until now eluded him and Eloise.

Ali outlined what she believed had happened, choosing her words carefully, explaining it might be difficult, impossible, perhaps, to make what she was saying stick. They might not be able to prosecute. So far, Nora seemed to have an answer for everything. Tom must have left his phone and spare keys in her room without her knowledge, she said. (Not that Tom went anywhere without his phone, according to Leslie, who remained adamant about there being just one set of keys for the Escort). What buoyed Ali was having Freeman on side. If she was expounding some crackpot theory, if there were great, glaring holes in what she was saying, he'd have said so. Freeman was not one to mince his words. She felt sure she had the answers to the unanswered questions about how Tom had ended up where he was, what his phone and keys were doing in an old toiletries bag of Nora's in her room at the Bull.

Proving it was the difficult bit.

The photos taken on Tom and Nora's final walk, photos that were supposed to be at the Black Stone, but which were, in fact,

Maria Malone

taken at the Gritstone, weren't speculation. Cathy Craven's expert testimony was solid. Except, Nora now claimed she must have been mistaken, that she had given police the pictures in error. "I was upset," she said during her formal interview at Skipden police station. "My boyfriend was missing. I was distraught, hardly thinking straight." Defiant. Unafraid. Meeting Ali's gaze, then Freeman's. *Do your worst*, she seemed to be saying.

"Convenient," Freeman said afterward.

Not that Ali was about to let anything go. She had again trawled through the original paperwork and found something filed by PC Neville Hands, tasked at the time with having the film from Nora's camera developed. Ali phoned him, an inspector in Leeds now, the only officer from that era she had been able to track down. He remembered the case well and in some detail. "My first biggie," he said. He had bagged the camera, had the film processed. "Kodak Gold, thirty-six exposures." A chuckle. "Remember, back in the dark ages, when you'd get your photos developed at Boots? Pay extra for the one hour service only to find the prints were mostly out of focus? Not that the ones Nora had taken were, she had a decent camera, the pictures were good." He had logged them, checked the images against what Nora had said, noticed nothing suspicious. A young couple enjoying the countryside of Ravensdale. "I seem to recall the roll wasn't finished," he said. "I think there were still another eight to take."

Ali was impressed. "I'm surprised you can remember in such detail after twenty years."

"Told you, the case was a big deal for me. I wasn't much older than Tom Masters. The lad had everything in front of him, brilliant future and all that, no problems anyone knew about, and he just disappeared. You don't forget something like that. You know there were stories about the spirit of the stone taking him or some such bollocks. They ran a piece in the *News* along those lines, quoting some local nutcase. Anyway, the last pictures on the roll were the

Death in the Countryside

pair of them at the Black Stone, or, as you're now telling me, the Gritstone. Bloody hell, how come no one spotted that?"

"It took an expert to see it," Ali said, "and I don't suppose anyone was looking. I mean, his car was at the Black Stone, his gloves, why would anyone think he was somewhere else?"

"Tell you what, no one suspected the girlfriend. Good luck trying to make it stick after all this time."

She would need more than luck.

Leslie sat stroking Wilson, fussing with the spaniel's ears. Wilson, who loved his ears being played with almost more than anything else tilted his head on one side, jaw slack, his expression one of sheer bliss.

"I'll need to tell Eloise all of this," Leslie said.

They sat silently for a moment, Wilson pushing his nose against Leslie's leg. "Spoiled, aren't you, boy?" he said.

"If there's anything I can do," Ali said.

"I'll let you know."

Another silence ensued.

"I'm still taking it in, what you've said. Wondering about the lad Nora introduced me to, the one she's marrying, Niall. A farmer. Nice young man, I thought."

Now at death's door, the wedding no longer in prospect, the only hope a miracle.

"There's nothing there to suggest what happened was anything other than an accident," Ali said. Not that she thought so, not for a single, solitary second. Yes, falls from Arthur's Seat were not unheard of, the occasional fatality, one recently involving a husband and the wife he was known to be abusing. Unfortunately for him, witnesses had seen the couple arguing shortly before she fell, and she had lived long enough to give a statement which, together with his history of violent behavior, was enough to secure a murder conviction. Sadly, no witnesses to Niall's "fall," which in Ali's view was no accident.

285

Leslie, now faced with something too awful to think about, that his son's girlfriend was somehow instrumental in his death, reminded Ali of Brian. Trying to recalibrate his view of Nora and finding it a struggle, in the same way Brian had been unable to grasp the truth about Melody. If Tom was anything like his father, he must have been a good lad, Ali thought. Kind, keen to inflict as little hurt on Nora as possible. Not one to simply dump her and refuse to take her calls. Ali suspected he had tried to extricate himself without causing a scene and, one way or another, it had got him killed.

"We don't yet know everything," Ali said. The truth was, despite what she thought she knew, they had almost nothing in the way of hard, practical evidence. "But we're still investigating. I wanted you to know where we're at."

He looked at her with sad eyes. "I thought when you found him, we'd finally got an answer, uncovered the truth, some of it at least. But all it's done is throw up more questions."

53

"**W**hy the long face? As the barman said to the racehorse when it popped in for a pint." Gordon chuckled at his own joke.

Ali rolled her eyes. "Dad."

"Dad, what? The old ones are the best, you know, which is why they still get wheeled out. *I haven't spoken to the mother-in-law for ten years—I don't like to interrupt her!* Les Dawson, that." He grinned. "*Last night I slept like a log—I woke up in the fireplace.* That's one of Doddy's."

"Boom, boom."

"Doctor, doctor, I feel like a pack of cards . . . I'll *deal* with you later!"

Ali groaned. Les Dawson to the Beano via Ken Dodd in the space of a few seconds.

It was Sunday and they were in her mother's old sewing room, now officially Gordon's gym. A poster was tacked to the wall, a series of exercises using a resistance band. He had got one for Ali, which so far remained in its packet. His expression became suddenly serious. "I'm just trying to cheer you up, love. You look like you need it."

"Sorry, thanks."

The night before, Nick had been on a similar mission, cooking what he called a blowout meal of cherry tomatoes and burrata on garlicky toasted bread, carbonara with crispy pancetta. Uncorking a bottle of pricey Chianti "because you're worth it." A feast, he had promised. Something to take her mind off things. The food was delicious, but with every mouthful she found herself thinking about Leslie, at home alone, grieving all over again for his son. He had seemed at a loss earlier, utterly confused, no idea how to start to unravel all that Ali had told him. Her thoughts were on Niall Ross too. Half dead. Tom and Niall, one a teenager, the other still in his thirties, two falls, Nora the link between the two. Ali ate her carbonara wondering if investigating when there was no guarantee of ever getting to the truth was helpful. Was her digging making it all worse?

"Calling Ali, come in," Nick had said. "Can I have my wife back, please?"

She had been neglecting him, putting everything she had into work. Even when they were together she was elsewhere, her mind on Nora, on Leslie, Brian, Evelyn, complaints about house alarms, and now a story doing the rounds that Troy Conrado intended to rename Heft Hall—"Disneyfy it," according to Miss Shaw. "Angel Heights, apparently," she had said, disgusted. *Sacre bleu*. Ali would bring the matter up when she embarked on her peace mission to Conrado, find out what she could, not that it was a police matter. His house, he could call it what he liked. Meanwhile, she would make more effort with Nick, let him know she loved him and appreciated his support. Must try harder, she told herself.

"Doctor, doctor." Gordon chuckled, bringing her back to the present. "I feel invisible. Sorry, I can't 'see you' now!"

Ali laughed. "I remember you telling me that one when I was about six."

Violet popped her head round the door of what was once her domain, the Singer now in a corner, huddled under its cover.

Death in the Countryside

"Someone else had to run up those curtains," she said, sending an accusing look in Gordon's direction. "For the WI."

"You can still squeeze in," he said. "You could be sewing while I'm rowing."

Violet made a face. "I can't be sewing with your father puffing and panting, rowing the length of the Skir, or wherever he thinks he's going," she said to Ali, ignoring Gordon. She had made what she called "energy bites," peanut butter and coconut, raisins, oats, and something else Ali didn't catch. "For your dad, his *regime*." Surprisingly tasty, they were.

"Any news from town?" Ali asked.

"You heard Evelyn's talking of selling up?" Violet said.

"I didn't think she was serious," Ali replied. She hoped not, anyway. It really would be a crime if the cakery-bakery women drove her out. Perhaps she needed to pay Ruth and Terri another visit.

"She told me she's been looking at a shop at the other end of town, the old sweet shop. Empty for years, looks like it's falling down, but it's far enough away from the patisserie to mean she wouldn't have to stare down the opposition every day."

"I can't see her moving premises," Gordon said.

"She sounded half-hearted, said she could always just sell up, retire."

"And do what?" Ali was alarmed. She couldn't imagine Evelyn giving up work, not yet. What on earth would she do with herself?

"Retiring was the best thing I ever did," Gordon said. "I've never been so busy, only now I'm busy doing the things I want to do."

"Same here," Violet said. "Work's not everything, you know."

"You two have each other," Ali said, "Evelyn's on her own, it's different."

Violet looked away, busied herself rearranging the energy bites on their plate. When she looked up, Gordon caught her eye. Ali looked from one to the other. "Am I missing something?"

Evelyn and Brian were spending a good deal of time in each other's company, Ali was pleased to learn. Two people who'd otherwise be alone, not forgetting Evelyn's cat, Trevor, who had taken to Brian surprisingly well, according to Violet. "He's tricky, Trevor, a one-woman cat, won't entertain anyone else, but then Brian was round at Evelyn's the other day, the boiler playing up so he had a look at it, and afterward, Brian and Evelyn were having a cuppa at the kitchen table and Trevor only went and jumped on his knee!"

"If that's not an endorsement I don't know what is," Gordon said, impressed. "Brian's having a look at the Beetle for me too when he gets a minute."

"That's good," Ali said. She felt put out. Why hadn't Trevor warmed to her instead of making himself scarce when she called on Evelyn? Ali, who considered herself a cat lover, felt snubbed. It had to be Wilson he objected to. "Well, I've never set eyes on this Trevor," she said coolly. "All the times I've been in Evelyn's house there's been no sign of him. Not even a stray hair." She thought of Evelyn's kitchen chairs, upholstered in some sort of velvety fabric, the type that would definitely attract cat hairs and yet were pristine. "Are we even sure Trevor exists?"

Gordon looked amused. "We are, aye. Don't take it personally, love."

54

A new week and Ali was on her way out of Skipden police station with Wilson after another briefing with Freeman, another reminder she had yet to make peace with Troy Conrado, when Jean on the front desk stopped her.

"Just taken a call for you," she said, handing Ali a piece of paper. Dr. Fraser Murdoch. Mobile number and direct work line (Royal Edinburgh Hospital) To do with Niall Ross, Ali guessed, fearing the worst. "Lovely accent," Jean said. "Proper *och aye the noo* and all that." Ali doubted anyone in Edinburgh, or indeed the whole of Scotland, ever actually said och aye the noo. It was probably considered an insult.

She called Murdoch's mobile number from the Hilux, braced for bad news. "This is Sergeant Ali Wren, from Heft," she said.

"Ah, right, thanks for getting back to me. You're very efficient, I only called half an hour ago."

"No problem. Is this about Niall?"

"It is, yes." Silence, then, "I wonder if we could meet, talk properly."

"Has there been a change in his condition?"

"That's not why I'm calling, no." She felt a rush of relief. "I should explain, I'm not treating Niall. I'm a doctor at the Royal but he's not my patient. He's my best friend and I've been keeping an eye on how he's doing. It's just . . . well, I think it's better if we speak face to face."

She was about to start up the Hilux when something Gordon had said came back to her. *Don't take it personally.* It got her thinking about how often crime *was* personal, often deeply so. Melody and Jimmy. Tom and Nora. She thought of Evelyn and the rival bakers opposite. Strangers who had arrived in Heft and turned Evelyn's settled existence on its head. It gnawed away at Ali why two talented young women who, in theory, could have settled anywhere, would choose to put roots down directly opposite one of the most long-established and best-known bakers in the entire Yorkshire Dales. Why?

She cut the engine and went back into the station. The tech guy, Spence, who knew his way round the Internet like nobody else and was expert at delving deep, recovering information others might simply never find, could surely help her out. She had noticed that no one at the station called him by his proper name, Spencer Cavendish, which sounded vaguely aristocratic. To Ali's bemusement, everybody referred to him as Alf. "So why is he called Alf?" she'd asked the duty sergeant. "Alien Life Form," he had replied.

She found him in his office, the windows covered with blackout blinds, white boards covered in scribblings—numbers, inspirational quotes, the odd equation—laptops, desktops, tablets, phones, boxes filled with cables and chargers and batteries. Never had he been given a device he wasn't able to access, he said. "What about when they're password protected?" Ali had asked. He had aimed a laser-like look at her as if she had just said something ludicrous, the first time he had really looked at her, since usually his focus was on a screen. One blue eye, one green, she noticed. Like David Bowie. People thought he was an alien too. "I can always work out a password," he said. "You'd be surprised how many people use the same

Death in the Countryside

ones, pick the same numbers. Or even"—he gave her a look of utter disbelief—"write them down somewhere obvious."

As Tom had, on the sticker on his phone.

"Can you get into social media accounts?" she asked.

"Sure."

"Would you be able to look at something for me?"

She told him what she knew about the cakery-bakery women. "They had a shop in London called something like"—she thought for a moment—"Peckham Rye, maybe."

He frowned. "That's a place. Could be a bakery, I suppose."

Or their idea of a joke, Ali thought.

"Anyway, leave it with me." Already hunched over his screen typing away, a curtain of shiny brown hair obscuring half his face.

Ali wasn't sure how Spence had ended up in Skipden, he could probably have gone anywhere—GCHQ, if he wanted. It was rumored he'd excelled at Massachusetts Institute of Technology, but no one seemed sure. In fact, no one seemed to know a thing about him, his background, where he was from.

"That's because he's not from here," one of the PCs told her when she asked.

"Yorkshire, you mean?"

"*Here*," the PC said. "As in Planet Earth."

55

Ali left Wilson in the Hilux and went to the door bearing a peace offering, a tin of biscuits. She had ordered them online from a company with the catchy name Biscuiteers. A vegan selection with the appearance of a bunch of gingerbread flowers, iced by hand. Gift wrapped at additional expense. All in all, she had spent a small fortune.

Troy Conrado's assistant let her in and whipped the biscuits off her. "He's a germophobe, I'll have to give them a spray before he gets them," she said, with a roll of the eyes that let Ali know exactly what she thought of that.

She was shown into the library where Conrado had introduced an array of ultra-modern furniture at odds with the oak shelves that lined the walls with their ancient leather-bound volumes. She balanced on the edge of a sleek swivel recliner upholstered in bright orange leather. A curved sofa, white leather, wholly impractical, occupied the center of the room. On a vast coffee table were copies of *Time* magazine and *Closer*. *TV Quick* lay open on an arm of the sofa.

Conrado burst in, phone in hand, embroidered shirt tucked into white drainpipe jeans. Tan puffer boots, Canada Goose logo visible.

Death in the Countryside

"Hey, how are you," he bellowed, not waiting for her to answer, flinging himself onto the sofa and stretching out, puffer boots on the snowy white leather. "You warm enough? Can we get some heating in here? Ellie! Can I get my wrap please? Mercy me, I hate the cold, don't you?"

Ali had always assumed no one actually said mercy me, that it belonged in the same category as och aye the noo.

"Thermals," she said. "That's what you'll need to get you through a Yorkshire winter." If he was suffering in June, he would never cope once it got cold. "Vests, long johns. A heated gilet, maybe. You can get all sorts these days."

Conrado gave her a curious look, as if she was speaking in a language unfamiliar to him. Ellie arrived with a wrap the size of a horse blanket and draped it round his shoulders.

"Thermals," he told her. "Make a note."

She aimed another eye roll Ali's way as she exited the room.

"I'm sorry we got off to a bad start," Ali said, keen to mend fences swiftly and get out of there. "I hope you'll accept my apology. I brought you some biscuits, Ellie has them."

"Aw, forget it," he said. "You know, *biscuit* isn't a word in my vocabulary. Literally. I've not eaten a cookie since"—he thought for a moment, deep in concentration, not the smallest change in his expression, which was remarkable—"Thanksgiving, 1999, when I wolfed down a whole packet, messy break-up, don't ask"—she hadn't been going to—"and had to make myself sick afterward." He ran a hand over his flat stomach, which Ali suspected would be as taut as his face. "Got to take care of the bodywork."

"Right."

He waved a hand at her. "Friends, then. I'll be having a little gathering here for Christmas, nothing excessive, just enough to fill the ballroom, five hundred max. I hope you'll join us." Five hundred. "I'm just about to have invitations printed. *Angel Heights requests the pleasure of your company.* Angel Heights, like it?"

295

She nodded. "It's certainly different."

"That's right. Different is as different does."

Ali blinked. What was that supposed to mean? "I wonder, did you choose the name for its . . . associations?"

Conrado attempted a frown. Nothing moved. "What would those be?"

"Oh, Angel Heights was an asylum not far from here. There was a terrible fire, around seventeen-hundred and something, started deliberately it seemed, all the lunatics burned alive. Screams heard echoing all over the valley. So legend has it." Conrado sat up, panic in his eyes. "The locals think of Angel Heights as a . . . hex, a harbinger of doom." His jaw dropped. "Whereas the name *Heft Hall* is immortalized in a famous poem. Ted Hughes or Simon Armitage, one of the big ones. 'What heft this hall/stolid and true/ the place of love/the place of light/my home, my heart, my steer this night/the Heft, the Hall, it calls me/my peace, my rest, Heft Hall.' I'm sure you must have heard it."

Conrado's mouth hung open, a look that did nothing for him. There was probably something his surgeon could do about that, Ali thought. "So, no more Heft Hall in future," she said sweetly.

Conrado came to, gathered himself. His mouth clamped shut and then flapped open again. "You know, I guess it doesn't pay to be too hasty. I mean history counts for something, doesn't it?"

Ali excused herself and returned to Wilson feeling as if she had just scored a memorable win. The equivalent of a League One side knocking Man U out of the FA Cup, which Leeds United had managed in 2010, as Nick was so fond of telling her. She smiled.

It was amazing what you could find online these days. The blog she and Spence had cobbled together, for instance—"Facts versus Fiction, Tall Tales of rural North Yorkshire"—in which the story of Angel Heights took pride of place. "Angel Heights." When Conrado checked, which Ali felt sure he would, now that she had whetted his appetite, he would find, just as she had described, details of

Death in the Countryside

the inferno at the once-notorious mental hospital, (which fell within the "tall tales" category of the blog and was therefore a figment of an overactive imagination, not that this vital detail was obvious) and other fanciful myths and legends, some with a grain of truth to them. As for the Heft Hall poem, something similar to the lines she had quoted at Troy also featured on the bogus website. Unattributed, no mention of the poet laureate, past or present. Apologies to Ted Hughes and Simon Armitage, Ali had made the whole thing up.

56

"There's a Rolls Royce Phantom parked outside," Nick said.

Ali went to take a look. It was early, just gone eight in the morning, the bin men due any time, and there, taking up half the road was a luxury saloon. At its side stood a driver in a suit and tie, flat cap, gloves, deadpan expression. As Ali approached, the privacy glass on the window at the back slid down to reveal pillowy leather upholstery, walnut veneer trim, a headliner that looked like a night sky studded with stars. And in its midst Jenny Champion, Mrs. JC herself, visor-like shades covering most of her face. Ali caught a waft of jasmine.

"Sergeant Wren," Jenny said, pushing the glasses onto the top of her head. "I wonder if I might have a word?"

"Not if it's about Jimmy," Ali told her.

"Too early? I can come back."

"Jenny, you can't be here. I might be called as a witness, *you* might."

Jenny gave her a pleading look. "I don't know who else to talk to. Jimmy's innocent, you've got to help me prove it."

"I can't, I'm sorry."

She sat at the kitchen table, in the chair previously occupied by Brian, then Leslie. Somehow, it had become the place for lost souls

Death in the Countryside

to wash up and pour out their hearts. Now it was Jenny's turn, Jenny with her glorious hair ("it's all extensions") and French manicure, her flawless no-makeup makeup. Also, in essence, lost. Lost without Jimmy, now facing a charge of murder and on remand in Stafford Court prison.

"Stafford Court," she said. "Terrible place. It's debatable he'll last long enough to go on trial. Absolute hell hole, full of roughnecks. Food fit to poison you."

Stafford Court was a new facility, more like a budget hotel than a prison, from what Ali had heard. As for the food, a well-known TV chef had been drafted in to ensure it was balanced, nutritionally sound. "Five star grub," according to a critic who appeared occasionally on *MasterChef* and wrote a column for one of the Sunday papers.

Nick made a pot of coffee and sat facing Jenny. "It must be very hard," he said.

"You've no idea."

On the other side of the kitchen, Ali leaned against the counter, arms folded, watching Jenny, who seemed completely at home, complimenting Nick on the coffee, the mugs, the vase on the dresser with its display of roses from the garden. She had her back to Ali. Wilson, unsure how to read the visit—work? A personal call? Something in between?—retreated to his bed. The air was filled with the pleasing scent of freshly ground coffee beans and Jenny's heady perfume. It had proved impossible to make her leave. She was too used to getting her own way, employing charm and persuasion and tearful desperation to break through Ali's resolve. Finally, Ali ushered her in on the understanding she could speak to Nick. Ali would have no part in whatever they discussed. "Is that clear?" Jenny had smiled sweetly. "Perfect, thank you, Sergeant."

Ali had called Brian who said of course, send the Phantom round to his place for an hour or so, and the driver was dispatched with directions to Glebe Farm. The car would attract little attention at Brian's, where exotic motors were part and parcel of everyday life. At least now the bin men would be able to get through.

"I always know when Jimmy's lying," Jenny was saying. Nick nodded. "He can't get anything past me."

Ali could believe it.

"Like when he said he was happy for me to book the Copthorne for our anniversary do next year." She took a drink of her coffee. "That was definitely a lie. See, I knew for a fact he'd already booked Shearer's"—Ali caught Nick's slightly baffled look—"which he'd said nothing to me about, mind. So, obviously, he was never going to be happy about the venue *I* wanted. It was written all over his face, I could see right through him." Ali imagined Jenny aiming a laser-like stare at Jimmy until he crumbled. "But. Anyway. He told me he didn't kill that poor woman and I believe him. I could see it in his eyes. He'd never lie about something that big." Ali saw her reach over and place a hand on Nick's wrist, old friends the two of them already. "Believe you me, Nick, if I had even the *slightest* doubt, I'd be telling him to do the right thing, cough up, face the music." She drank some more coffee. "You'll have to tell me what these beans are, they're the business." Nick smiled, bashful, flattered, falling under Jenny's spell. Ali wanted to give him a shake. Jenny tapped his wrist. "You know when you just *know*?" she said. Nick nodded, captivated. "Well, *I* know he's innocent."

Silence stretched between them, Jenny's hand still on Nick's wrist. He glanced at Ali for guidance.

"Just thinking out loud here," Ali mused, "wondering why Jimmy would have lied about having gone to the beach house on the day he tried to break things off with Melody."

Jenny leaned closer to Nick. "Can I let you in on a little secret?" Nick nodded. "My Jimmy, he can be . . . stupid. I mean, he's a man." Her grip now firm on his wrist. "Of course, not *all* men are as daft as Jimmy."

Death in the Countryside

Ali gazed at Jenny's back, picturing her brilliant, winning smile now aimed at Nick.

"What happened, if you ask me, he panicked," Jenny said. "Thought if he admitted to being at the beach house, they'd find a way of blaming him for her death. He was scared." Her shoulders went up and down, a tiny gesture that managed to say her husband was a prize idiot at times. "I mean that's exactly it. If *I'd* had anything to do with it, he'd have been straight from the off. The truth will set you free and all that. Don't you agree?" Nick was nodding. "The detective handling the case, he's clever, not the sort you want to mess about. Sharp enough to cut himself, that one. So Jimmy did himself no favors lying and, if you ask me, his brief hasn't helped either. It's all 'no comment,' don't admit to anything. Which just puts everyone's backs up and makes you look guilty as sin."

Nick topped up her coffee and started talking about a storyline on *The Beat*, a farm manager for the big estate, who'd been having an affair and panicked when he woke up to find his mistress dead in bed beside him. "Accidental, a natural death," Nick said. "All he had to do was come clean, but he went and complicated things by trying to cover it up."

"You work on *The Beat*?" Jenny was saying. "I love that show."

Ali rolled her eyes, not that Nick, spellbound by the phenomenon that was Jenny Champion, noticed.

"It wouldn't hurt to give it another look," Nick said. "*You* told *me* you didn't think Jimmy was the killer."

"That was before I knew he'd been to the beach house! And *lied* about it."

Jenny had left. Only just. When she phoned for her driver, Brian had the bonnet up on the Phantom and was inspecting the engine, so Jenny said to take his time, no rush. Ali gritted her teeth, Nick made more coffee, and they gossiped about Lee Elliot,

301

Inspector Connor Sinclair on *The Beat*. Gruff bachelor, unlucky in love. Gene Hunt meets Jimmy Perez. "My absolute favorite, I *love* him," Jenny cooed. "And you *know* him. Wow and *wow*."

"I can't interfere," Ali now told Nick. "It's Steppenbeck's case and he won't see the funny side if I start poking my nose in. If he finds out Jenny was here . . ." She made a helpless gesture. "If *Freeman* finds out, I'm in deep trouble."

"Maybe you could just have another teeny look at the paperwork, then you can tell Jenny you've given it your absolute best shot."

"I can't believe how easily she got you wrapped round her finger."

"I feel sorry for her. She's in a horrible position. And she knows Jimmy better than anyone. If she believes him, well . . ." he sighed. "She's standing by her man. After everything. Seeking truth and justice. Isn't that to be admired?" He gazed at Ali.

She gave him an exasperated look. "All right. If it makes you happy, I'll look through the file again. But I can tell you now, nothing I say or do is going to get Jimmy off the hook."

57

The following Wednesday, Ali had arranged to meet Fraser Murdoch at the station in Skipden. "I can come to Heft if that's easier for you," he'd said, but Ali told him no. For the time being, she'd had enough of police business taking over her kitchen.

He was waiting in the station's cramped reception area when Ali arrived with Wilson, studying a poster Jean had put up of British garden birds. It covered the spot where someone had scratched an obscenity into the plaster. Ali showed him into a bare interview room, offered him a coffee.

"I won't, thanks," he said. "I just had one in town and that's my limit. Another cup and I'll be jangling." Dr. Fraser Murdoch had blond curly hair, pale blue eyes, a soft Scottish accent. He wore denims, trainers, a white shirt.

"Any news on Niall?" Ali asked.

"No change," he said. "I went in this morning, early, before I drove down. Hoping for something but he was just the same. I told him to get himself better, that I was coming to see you."

Ali wondered what he had to tell her that merited a drive from Edinburgh. And what he thought she might be able to offer that would make him feel his journey south had been worthwhile.

303

"I was at school with Niall, we've been friends forever," Fraser said. "We still play rugby together." He sighed. "Or rather, we did. In the past we'd go on hikes—Ben Nevis, the Black Cuillin. Challenging stuff, some of it." He gave Ali a long look. "The thing is I find it hard to believe Niall would take a fall from Arthur's Seat."

Ali agreed. She wondered how much Fraser knew about Nora, about Tom and his fall. The discovery of his remains had attracted a good deal of coverage, with some of the newspapers—the local *News* among them—suggesting police incompetence for having concentrated their search efforts in the wrong place when Tom first went missing. Ali had let that one pass; as long as the press were having a go at the police, no one was looking at Nora, which was how Ali preferred things. For now, at least.

"So, what do you think happened to make him fall?" she asked.

Fraser sighed. "Well, for a start, I don't believe there was a fall."

Ali waited for him to go on.

"You met Nora?" he said.

"I did, yes. Did she tell you?"

He gave a thin smile. "Oh, Nora wouldn't tell me anything, we're not exactly on good terms. One of Niall's doctors said you'd been up to the hospital, spoken to him, had a chat with her."

"It wasn't to do with Niall," Ali said. "Not directly."

He nodded. "I'm up to date on her ex. Tom Masters. Another unfortunate 'fall,' I understand."

"There's nothing to suggest Tom's death wasn't an accident." Nothing to prove it, at any rate. "Lucky for us, we had a breakthrough, or we might still not have found him."

"Was that it, then—luck? Or good police work?" When Ali didn't answer, he said, "And Nora. Don't you think two 'accidents' like this involving a girl like her is too much of a coincidence?"

"What do you mean, 'a girl like her'?"

He frowned. "She always wanted Niall all to herself. The last

Death in the Countryside

of her neck felt clammy. Wilson, sensing her sudden change in mood, pushed at her hand. She stroked his ear, the fur soft and silky. Spence was tapping at a keyboard. On another screen, images of Lillian and Des appeared, in case Ali was still in any doubt who was of interest.

"So Melody made a call to the number at this address at 3.53 p.m. on the day she died. A call that lasted eight minutes."

Ali was thinking frantically. No one was home that day. She had asked. A weekend spa break at Matford Hall, Lillian said, the hotel confirming the booking. "They weren't home," she told Spence.

"Of course, just because she was on the line for eight minutes isn't conclusive proof of her having a conversation with anyone," he said entirely reasonably. "She might have got through to a message service. Might even have just hung on the line, not knowing what to do."

"For eight minutes?"

He shrugged. "There's very little activity on this line. Last call they made was"—he tapped several keys, scrolled through a screen filled with numbers—"August 2020. They might never check for messages. Lots of people have landlines that are more or less redundant now."

Ali wondered how Spence knew so much about Lillian and Des's home phone usage. She decided not to ask. "They couldn't have diverted calls from that number to one of their mobiles?"

He looked at her. "They could, let's just see," More tapping, more numbers and symbols filling up his screen. Gobbledegook, it seemed to her, like some kind of advanced, unreadable computer code. "No, they didn't put the calls on divert."

How did he know this stuff?

She phoned Steppenbeck. "My fault, I missed it, I'm sorry."

"If you missed it, so did we. I had someone here go over that log, check the numbers against Jimmy's shops. Although I don't see what difference it makes now, now we've charged him."

Ali wasn't so sure. It felt like the kind of loose end that might unravel and prove to be a severe trip hazard unless it was properly secured.

58

Des was outside washing the car, soapy water running off the roof and over the windscreen, when Ali and Wilson showed up. The day after discovering her blunder with the phone records, Ali had felt compelled to pay the Firths another visit, letting Steppenbeck know what she was doing. Tidying up a loose end that would otherwise drive her mad.

"Is Lillian here? I need a word."

"I already told you, I've not spoken to Melody for years," Lillian said. She was in the living room, arms folded, an upright vacuum cleaner at her side. She didn't ask if Ali wanted to sit down, no offer of tea.

"She phoned the house." Ali shifted her weight so that she was uncomfortably close to Lillian, Wilson straining to sniff her bare ankle. She tutted and took a step back. "The day she went missing," Ali said. "She called you, was on the line for eight minutes."

"What time was this?"

"A few minutes to four in the afternoon," Ali said. Melody at the beach house. Distraught. Jimmy refusing to speak to her, her dreams in pieces. It was a sure measure of how desperate she must have been to have turned to Lillian.

"As you know, I was at Matford Hall. I had a treatment booked at four, a hot stone massage, you can check with the spa. I was changed, relaxing in my robe, sipping a collagen boost, by, oh, 3.45." She aimed a vicious smile at Ali. "By all means check, I'm sure they'll confirm it. Tell her, Des."

Ali glanced at him, confident, positioned behind the sofa. He gave Ali a nod.

"So, just to be absolutely clear, you didn't speak to Melody on that Saturday?"

Lillian gave her a defiant look. "We've been helpful, invited you into our home," she said, her breath hot on Ali's cheek. "You come here, no warning, asking questions, practically *accusing* me."

"No one's accusing you of anything," Ali said mildly.

"As for the funeral, the way you spoke to me was a disgrace, I've a good mind to put a complaint in."

"As you wish. If you can simply state that you didn't speak to Melody when she called here that day, I'll be off." She gave Lillian a penetrating look. "Yes or no?"

"No. I did not," Lillian said in a voice that was too loud for the room, which felt cramped, what with the three of them crowded in, plus Wilson and the vacuum cleaner.

Ali looked at Des. He gave an apologetic shrug. "Sorry, no."

Des showed her out. The suds had started to dry on the car, leaving streaks all over the white paintwork. He'd have to start again. Back in the Hilux, Ali made a note of what Lillian had said. Something was niggling her, what she wasn't sure. Possibly nothing more than Lillian's tone, defensive, and at the same time combative. That attitude of hers, pretending to be helpful when she was anything but. Des slopped water over the roof of the car while Ali flicked back through her notes, finding the ones she had made after her first visit, when she and Wilson had carried out their impromptu search of the house and car, and there it was, the thing that was bothering her.

310

Death in the Countryside

The car in the garage was a Skoda Fabia, but the one Des was washing, the one she'd seen them drive away from the funeral in, was a Nissan. Electric. She had registered something that day that didn't quite fit but hadn't worked out what. Two white cars that at first glance looked alike. She got back out of the Hilux and wandered over to Des.

"You've changed your car," she said. "What happened to the Fabia?"

"In the garage," he said. "We park this one on the road. Tend to use it a bit more these days. Lillian, doing her bit for the planet."

A phone call made to their landline. A car Ali didn't know they had. Back in the Hilux, she phoned Skipden and asked Jean to put her through to Spence. "Could you check some details for me?" she asked.

"This is becoming a habit," he said, sounding as if he didn't mind at all. "Shoot."

She gave him the registration plate of the Nissan. Moments later, he confirmed it had been registered for more than a year to Lillian "at the address you're parked up at right now." Ali smiled. Probably guessed she was there. Or he really was an alien with special powers. Likely, he had eyes on her.

She made one more call, to Matford Hall, where she spoke to the assistant manager (reservations) Kelly. Booking in the name of Firth, she said. It took Kelly a moment to locate the spa bookings, Lillian's hot stone massage on the Saturday at 4 p.m. "With Yasmin. We ask clients to be in the spa area at least fifteen minutes early to get changed and be in the right frame of mind for their treatment." Ali wondered what that might be—relaxed, serene, zen-like? What if you turned up stressed and angry and tearful? Would they turn you away?

"One last thing," Ali said, "do you have any spa appointments on the system for Mr. Firth?"

"They had lunch in the granary on Sunday," Kelly said, "before they left." She hesitated. "I don't know if it's important, but he wasn't actually staying with us. Just Mrs. Firth. Single room occupancy, which tends to be the case with spa breaks. Unless the gentleman plays golf, of course." She laughed. "We have two courses, and there's a driving range a couple of miles down the road. Is Mr. Firth a golfer?" Ali didn't think so.

"So," Kelly said, "there's a reservation for them for afternoon tea on the Friday . . . then it looks like he must have left his wife in our capable hands and returned in time for lunch on Sunday."

59

"The beauty of the electric car, Wren, is that it has what you might call a very vocal app," Steppenbeck said. "One that can't wait to blab about what it's been up to, where it's been. It practically tells you what the driver had for breakfast." He grinned. "I'm exaggerating, but not much."

Steppenbeck had turned up within twenty minutes of Ali's call and arrested Des. Ali had watched from the Hilux, Des soaping the Nissan, two marked police cars arriving, lights flashing, no sirens. Des stopped to watch them cruise along the street and park, block the road outside number 39. He had a bucket in one hand, a sponge in the other, when Steppenbeck approached and read him his rights. By the time Lillian became aware of the lights flashing through the hedge and came out to see what was going on, Des was on his way to Tanner Bank police station for questioning.

Steppenbeck steered Lillian seamlessly toward the second car and eased her inside. A third patrol car pulled up and took the place of the others. One or two neighbors emerged to see what was going on. A uniformed officer now stood at the semi's open front door, another at the side of the half-washed Nissan. The forensics team would be there soon, a recovery vehicle for the Nissan.

Steppenbeck made his way over to the Hilux. Ali got out, rolled

313

the window down on the passenger side so Steppenbeck could greet Wilson.

"Nice little car, the Nissan," he said, leaning through the open window, ruffling Wilson's fur. Wilson responded by licking the side of his face.

"All right, canny lad," Steppenbeck laughed, pushing the spaniel off. "Take it easy." He nodded at Ali. "Good work, Wren."

Des found himself in an interview room, no suitable piece of furniture for him to take refuge behind. He sat at a desk facing Steppenbeck who asked what had "really" happened on the afternoon in question, starting with the phone call he had taken from Melody. Des insisted he hadn't spoken to her, that Steppenbeck had got it all wrong, and if he wasn't released *immediately* he would sue for false imprisonment. He stood up, attempting to leave.

"Not talking," Steppenbeck told Ali when he phoned later. "Funny how many of them think if they just keep quiet it'll all go away. They've seen all the 'no comment' bollocks on TV and think that's the way to go. So, I said, no bother, we'll talk to your car, then. Nothing on the satnav, he'd wiped that—although we were able to recover it in about two seconds flat. Your spaceman—Spence, is it?—helped there. But what really told the story was the app. Miles covered, energy consumption, routes taken. Where you've parked, how long for . . . you name it, it's all there, every last detail. Smashing motor, the Leaf, there's a poem about it, you know, an ode." Ali didn't. He recited a few lines, something about taking a corner too fast and coming to grief, turning over a new leaf. "Roger McGough."

Full of surprises, Steppenbeck.

What the Nissan's stats showed was that within ten minutes of Melody's call to the landline, Des was in his car and heading out of Newcastle on his way to the beach house. "Thirty-four miles, took him forty-two minutes, must have put his foot down a bit. Slightly higher energy consumption than you might expect. There's

Death in the Countryside

a map that shows the precise route taken and where the car ends up. In Des's case, in a parking bay belonging to one of the caravans just further along from *Driftwood*. He was there for just under an hour. In fact, might as well be precise since we've got all the info—fifty-seven minutes after parking up, he was driving away again, heading back home, by a slightly different route. Took a bit longer on the way back." Called at the Co-op on Grange Road where he spent six minutes and purchased some Walkers Sensations (Thai sweet chilli) and a bottle of Verdicchio, which he paid for with a debit card. Seven minutes forty seconds later, he started up the Leaf and continued his journey home, arriving just under nine minutes later.

Steppenbeck was right, the detail obtained via the app was impressive.

Des denied hurting Melody. She had given him "the wrong idea," made him think she'd invited him there for . . . you know. No, Steppenbeck had countered, he didn't. Things had got "out of hand" according to Des, Melody acting like a "mad bitch." Lashing out at him. He'd been forced to defend himself. He "might" have pushed her, that was all.

"Since we know exactly how she was killed, throttled with her own scarf, that was never going to hold up. All this crap about fending off her advances when the truth is he strangled her and tried to get rid of her scarf on the beach. We had another look at that, by the way, and there are traces of DNA that match his, so, basically, bang to rights." Steppenbeck was quiet for a moment. "And who found the murder weapon? Officer Wilson. Put the phone on speaker, Wren." He waited a moment. "Bonny lad, Wilson, sterling work there, make sure you get a decent treat." Wilson, hearing the DI's voice and always tuned in for the word "treat," perked up. Ali fished in her bag for the tin of Beautiful Joe's she always had on her and gave it a shake.

"Good boy," she said, feeding him a handful of dried liver pieces.

"What about the man they'd already charged?" Brian asked. "The one Melody was . . . involved with."

"They released him. He had nothing to do with her death," Ali said. Her murder. Whatever JC was—naïve, daft, a fool, stupid, conceited (just some of the words Jenny Champion had applied to her husband)—he was not a killer. Jimmy, already miles away, on his way back to Newcastle in the borrowed sales car, before Melody's call to Des.

Brian was quiet, digesting what she'd told him. It was a warm evening, the sound of a cockerel calling somewhere, and he was in the garden at the back of the house, a bottle of wine in an ice bucket on the patio table, juicy green olives in a bowl. Looking well, his blue shirt expertly pressed—"I've found someone in Heft to do the ironing"—dark blue jeans, tan deck shoes. Bare ankles. Evelyn was due, arriving as Ali was talking him through what the police now knew about Des. Seeing Brian's face, she went straight into the house, allowing them the space to finish their conversation uninterrupted.

"They came to the funeral," Brian said. "Made a mockery of her."

Ali said nothing. Wilson shuffled nearer to Brian and sat on his foot.

Brian patted his head absentmindedly. "Did she know—the wife, Lillian?" His expression was pained. "Melody's sister."

"We don't think so, no."

Even Lillian wasn't that bad. Ali hoped not, anyway.

They sat quietly for a minute or so. "I did my best," he said at last. "Tried to make her happy. I'm not sure she ever was."

Ali left him in the garden and went into the house where Evelyn waited in the kitchen.

"Not more bad news?" she asked, anxious.

"I'll leave it to Brian to tell you." She gave her arm a squeeze. "He's going to need his friends now."

60

The cakery-bakery was closed. Ceased trading without notice and no one, not even Roger Felton, who seemed to know everything about all matters Heft, knew why. Predictably, complaints about the sudden closure were directed at Ali, among them one from a disgruntled customer who had come "all the way from Skipden" to collect a "special" birthday cake. Had she paid in advance? Ali asked. That was hardly the point, the woman said, it was a question of trust, good faith. Ali took her details and promised to look into it. Sometimes it was easier to tell people what they wanted to hear, even though an unfulfilled cake order, even a "special" one, was hardly a crime.

The Maid in Yorkshire people finally got back to Ali about the alarm on the house behind the vicarage which kept going off and causing a nuisance. They had arrived to get the place ready for the owners—a big birthday weekend, apparently, a "special" visit (special being the word of the moment, Ali decided)—only to find the alarm disconnected, its wires cut, the box removed and left on the step at the kitchen door. No burglary, no sign of anyone trying to get in, simply the alarm disabled. Who would do such a thing? An irate neighbor, pushed to the limit by the alarm sounding at unsociable hours, and taking matters into their own hands? Ali speculated. Roger Felton knew nothing about that either.

Barely a cloud in the sky, a perfect June day. They set off early with a picnic: a flask, Hooley Hefts, Beautiful Joe's for Wilson.

"How long since we moved here? Nick asked.

Ali took a moment to think. "Almost six months."

"Six months. And this is the first time we've got out for a jaunt, a decent walk," Nick said. Ali frowned. "A *proper* walk, I mean. Out in *t'wilds*." Adopting the local dialect.

She gave him a look. "What was that meant to be?"

"I'm working on my Yorkshire accent," he said, pleased with himself. "Ee bah gum."

"I wouldn't try that in Heft, if I were you, they'll run you out of town."

"Nowt so queer as folk."

Ali shook her head. "We'll call at the surgery on the way back, make an appointment with Dr. Mitra."

"Why?" Frowning. "What's up?"

"You, you're 'up.' You've got a severe case of what's known as YDS—'Yorkshire Dialect Syndrome.'" She gave him a look. "Slipping into an accent that's not your own is a recognized medical condition, a kind of imposter syndrome." She thought for a moment. "In these parts, it might even be considered a crime."

"Aye, 'appen," Nick said cheerfully. "You daft 'apeth."

"You sound like that PC from *The Beat*, the broad Yorkshire one."

He looked chuffed. "Thanks."

He was right, though, about this being their first proper outing. Too focused on work, too little time left for each other. Ali, on her mission impossible to be all things to all people.

"From now on," she said, determined, "I'm taking at least one day off a week, having a life, one that's not all work."

Nick laughed. "Right."

Death in the Countryside

"We've a couple of dos to look forward to, anyway," she said. An invitation had arrived, an elegant card, gold-edged, inviting them to celebrate with Jimmy and Jenny their forty years of marriage. The venue: Shearer's Bar. Dress code: black & white. The Champions' way of letting the world know they were very much United.

And Troy Conrado had been in touch about his housewarming—Hoedown at Heft Hall. "Cowboy boots and plaid," he told Ali.

Several of the locals who'd been thorns in the American's side— Roger and Phoebe Felton, Miss Shaw, among them—were on the guest list. A truce of sorts. And Freeman. Ali looking forward to seeing him in a barn dance get-up. To her relief, talk of renaming the hall "Angel Heights" seemed to have quietly gone away. And Heft Hall was due to appear in a forthcoming episode of *The Beat,* the artificial turf now gone, the lawns restored to their full natural glory, ready for their small screen debut.

They made their way along the bottom of the crag, Wilson snuffling in the undergrowth, emerging grinning, ears flapping. When they reached the spot, he would let them know.

"Are you going to tell me what happened with the Battle of the Bakers?" Nick called to her as they negotiated the narrow path, forging their way through bracken that was waist high, Ali, in front, her new walking poles getting their first outing. Enjoying the feel of them, the way they drove her forward and gave her arms, her upper body, a workout.

Inspired by Cathy Craven, she had invested in some quality outdoor gear, splashing a small fortune on a pair of high-waisted leggings, immaculately cut, in eye-catching turquoise, and the recommended lightweight shirt ("breathable" fabric, lots of useful pockets) that went with them. A jazzy bandana kept her copper hair in order. She stopped and turned, waited for Nick to catch up. She had been wrong about the poles, they weren't for sissies, they were for serious walkers.

"You need to get some of these," she told him, holding one up.

"You've changed your tune."

Ali smiled and pressed on.

"Well?" Nick prompted. "What went on with the bun fight?"

Spence had done a search on the cakery-bakery women, as Ali requested, and presented her with a document that finally explained what had brought them to Heft, their motive for setting up shop right opposite Evelyn. As Ali had suspected, it was indeed personal.

"They were trying to put Evelyn out of business," she now told Nick.

What Spence discovered when he started digging was that Ruth Carlisle was not simply a stranger who had come to Heft and by coincidence set up a rival bakery close to Hooley's. Her mother was, in fact, the sister of Evelyn's late husband, Alan. She had married an ornithologist and moved away, ended up living on a nature reserve in Norfolk. Lost touch with her brother, had barely known Evelyn. A drifting apart. Rita Hooley, as she was before she married, had never had any interest in inheriting the family business. Made to help out in the shop when she was younger, she couldn't get away from Heft fast enough. All the same, baking was part of her DNA, something she passed on to her daughter, a talented patissière, who came to feel it was an injustice that her mother had got nothing from a business that was, surely, half hers, and was now owned and run by a woman who was not even a Hooley by blood. Ruth had set out to destroy Evelyn.

Ali stood with Nick admiring the view across to the Carlow hills. "Nearly there," she said.

"Why?" Nick persisted, keen to get to the bottom of the demise of the cakery-bakery. "I mean, why shut up shop like that when they were doing so well? What happened?" The sudden departure of the women was the talk of the town.

Death in the Countryside

Ali shook her head. "I doubt we'll ever find out." She wasn't going to tell. It was Evelyn's decision who else could know. When Ali had explained to Evelyn that a niece, a woman she had never met, was responsible for the vendetta against her business, she was staggered. "Why didn't she just come and talk to me? Surely, if we'd talked, if she'd told me how she felt, we could have sorted something out."

Ali hoped she was right, although, in her experience, talking was not necessarily a guarantee of bringing about peace. Sometimes, it inflamed matters further, resulting in even more misunderstanding, greater distress. Rifts became deeper, vitriol intensified. She was thinking of Lillian. Talking was one thing, listening another. Sometimes the sense of moral outrage, of righteous indignation, on one side or the other, made a peaceful resolution impossible. There were people (Ali had come across plenty) who perceived themselves as victims, no matter what, and Evelyn's niece was one. A chunk of the Hooley business was hers, she asserted. It was her *right*, she said, her *birthright*. What had happened wasn't fair. Ali had simply shrugged. Life wasn't fair. It was short too, too short for such bitterness, for blaming Evelyn, the aunt who had no idea her niece even existed. What would people think, Ali asked Ruth, once they knew what had really brought her to Heft?

"I've no children of my own," Evelyn told Ali, clearly struggling to make sense of what she now knew. "I'd have liked the chance to know her, that's what's so silly, so unnecessary. The daft thing is, I've no one to leave the business to. There's only Trevor, and I don't suppose he'd be much use." Trevor. Ali still hadn't met him, hadn't even seen him. She had a sudden image of Trevor in white overalls overseeing the bakery, keeping the production of Hooley Hefts going. Once the picture was in her mind, she found she couldn't shake it.

Thanks to Spence, only Ali and Evelyn knew who the rival bakers really were, what they'd been up to. Their secret. Ali wouldn't breathe a word, not even to Nick. Case closed.

They continued along the overgrown path, Ali employing the poles to ensure the ground she was about to step onto was solid. Once they were beyond the treacherous stretch, she unclipped Wilson and he trotted ahead. "Good boy," she said, as he came to a sudden halt at the place where Tom had lain in the shadow of the Gritstone above. Ali had brought forget-me-nots and placed them on the ground. For a moment, she stood, Wilson at her heel, Nick with his arm around her shoulder.

Nick broke the silence. "What about his parents?"

Leslie was in North Berwick with Eloise, arranging the long overdue memorial service for Tom. Ali dared to hope they might find a way of reconciling now they'd got their boy back.

"And the girl?" Nick asked. "Nora—what's happening with her?"

Nothing. They hadn't enough to charge her. She had got away with it.

"We'd never be able to prove it was her," Ali said. "Unless . . ."

"What?"

She shook her head. "Unless something else came to light." Unlikely after so many years. Nora, the one that got away. Meanwhile, Niall Ross lay in a coma from which he was unlikely to wake.

They stood a while longer taking in the view, Ali reminded of why she had wanted to come back, her need to return to Heft, her anchor. Where past, present, and future merged into one.

A breeze caught at the ferns and around them leaves whispered. Across the valley, low in the sky, a fighter jet roared past. The sun slipped away behind a cloud. She felt at peace, in the right place. Where she belonged.

"Let's go home," she said.

Two Months Later

n Edinburgh, Dr. Fraser Murdoch was at the bedside of his friend, Niall, who was not getting any worse, nor showing signs of recovering either. No change, the doctors treating him said. The clock on the far side of the room showed it was after two in the morning. Fraser had got into the habit of coming to see Niall at odd hours. When he could be sure Nora wouldn't be there. He sensed she wasn't keen on him visiting. *He* wasn't keen on *her* sitting with Niall either, given his suspicions, but there was nothing he could do about it.

Of late, she had begun acting as if it was on her say-so who saw Niall. Making Fraser feel he was somehow overstepping the mark by spending quite so much time with his friend. They'd almost had words the week before when Nora arrived and found Fraser dozing in the hard upright armchair at the side of the bed. She woke him, reprimanded him. It wasn't his place to be there so much, she said pointedly, Niall was her fiancé, her responsibility.

"Am I caring too much, is that it?" he had asked mildly.

"That's not what I'm saying," she snapped.

"We're all stressed, overtired," he said, attempting to soothe her frayed feelings.

"If you find it so stressful don't come."

Maria Malone

"I can't not come. Niall's my buddy, my oldest friend."

And she was his wife-to-be, she pointed out. *Was*, Fraser thought. Not anymore. Still, staking her claim, establishing a pecking order. *Fiancée trumps friend*, she seemed to say. Dismissing Fraser, making him unwelcome. Not that she could stop him visiting, nor could she be there all the time, policing who came and went and how long they stayed.

As it happened, the wee small hours suited him. At the end of a shift, before he went home, he'd make his way to the third floor, pull up a chair next to his pal and sit in the dimly lit room, talk about whatever came into his head. He looked at his watch. Two twenty-two. Ever since he was a boy, Fraser had held various (irrational) superstitions to do with numbers. Two was his favorite.

"Look at that," he told Niall. "Two twenty-two, man, it's a beautiful thing."

Niall's eyelids fluttered and Fraser leaned in closer, took hold of his hand. "Pal, if you feel like waking up, now would be a very good time."

He watched, hardly daring to breathe, found himself silently praying, the words a jumble . . . *the Lord is with Thee . . . pray for us*. He'd not been to Mass for years. *Please God. I'll do anything, anything. if You just bring him back.*

"Niall, come on, pal, I was just about to tell you the never-ending saga of my boiler troubles, so if I were you, I'd wake up right now, spare yourself the ins and outs of a dodgy pressure valve." Squeezing his hand. Another prayer. Niall's eyes firmly shut. An involuntary spasm, perhaps. Nothing to get excited about.

"So," he began. The eyelids moved again, he felt sure of it. "Are you having me on?" He clasped his friend's hand. Abruptly, Niall's eyes opened, looked right at him.

"Is that you?" Fraser said, his own eyes filling with tears. "You back with us?"

Death in the Countryside

Niall gazed up at him.

"You know where you are?" Eyeing the red Call button on the wall just out of reach. To get to it he might have to let go of his pal's hand and he couldn't, not just yet. He laughed. "You gave us all a proper fright."

"Nora," Niall said.

Fraser felt his heart sink. His first thought, Nora. Of course. She should have been with him when he came round. She would never forgive Fraser. "Aye," he said, "I'll let her know, get her in, she'll be so chuffed."

Niall said something, his voice cracking with the strain, barely managing a whisper. Fraser gave him water to sip through a straw. "Take your time," he said. He leaned in close, Niall's warm breath on his cheek, not able to make out what his friend was trying to tell him, his voice small, rasping. Exhausted from the effort, Niall's eyes closed again, his hand limp in Fraser's.

Desperate to keep him there, conscious, Fraser said, "All those hills the pair of us went up, and you go and take a fall from Arthur's Seat." No response. "Wait till Nora hears you've woken up."

. Niall opened his eyes. His voice was barely there. "No," he said. "No."

Fraser craned to hear. Had he forgotten who she was?

"She . . . Nora." Seconds ticked by. "She . . . pushed me."

Fraser felt something break, his insides dissolve, the air inside the room like ice. He could barely breathe, his heart thumping against his ribs. Niall's eyes on him, intense, afraid, pleading, confirmation of what he had suspected all along. The reason for him going to see Ali Wren, seeking out an ally, someone who understood.

Nora.

He swallowed the bitter taste at the back of his throat. *Nora.* Nora had tried to kill Niall. Fraser thought he might be sick. "I've got you," he told him. Tears ran down his face onto the hand that

325

gripped Niall's, and he gave a squeeze, a gesture to say he was there, going nowhere. Not now, never.

Without letting go, without taking his eyes off his friend, he leaned across the bed, the tips of his fingers grazing the red button, and summoned help. [ends]

Acknowledgments

With thanks to my agent, Joanna Kaliszewska at the bks Agency, my editor Carolyn Mays, Swati Gamble, and the team at Bedford Square. Also, my thanks to the team at Crooked Lane in the US.

My love and thanks to Kathleen Malone for the adventures in Yorkshire and so much more.

June Taylor, Beverley Morgan, Geraldine Cassidy, Edward Harland, I am eternally grateful.

Dawn Allen, Andrea Arnold, Helen Barbour, Angie Bentley, Ingrid Connell, Frank DeAngelis, Sarah Doole, John Fairley, Jenny 'Kitty' Harding, Andy Harries, Anne Hollis, Douglas Hosdale, Steve Lidgerwood, Maggie Marfitt-Smith, Emma Peak, Keith Richardson, Ashley Roller Inciong, Vicki Stowe, Jo Turnbull, Joyce 'Mrs Joon' Taylor, Michael Waldman and Gordon Wise. You all did your bit, thank you.

All the remarkable service dogs everywhere and those who work with them.

With love and gratitude to my family in Penzance, in Drymen, and in the North-East.

Peggy, John, Peter, Joe, I miss you.

Finally, with love to Mick Miller, there is no better guide to the Dales than you. I can't thank you enough. For everything.

Author's Note

This is a work of fiction, the town of Heft wholly imagined. My apologies to anyone hoping to find Hooley's and its famous pies (other excellent bakeries do exist). Actual places, including Harrogate and Bradford, have been handily situated within easy reach of fictional Ravensdale. St James' Park, home of Newcastle United, has also somehow sneaked its way in. Well, it had to.